GHOSTS
OF WAR

GHOSTS OF WAR

BENNETT R. COLES

TITAN BOOKS

Ghosts of War
Print edition ISBN: 9781783294244
Electronic edition ISBN: 9781783294251

Published by Titan Books
A division of Titan Publishing Group Ltd
144 Southwark Street, London SE1 0UP

First Titan Books edition: August 2016
2 4 6 8 10 9 7 5 3 1

Visit our website: www.titanbooks.com

A CIP catalogue record for this title is available from the British Library.

Printed and bound in the United States.

Did you enjoy this book? We love to hear from our readers.
Please email us at readerfeedback@titanemail.com or write to us at
Reader Feedback at the above address.

To receive advance information, news, competitions, and exclusive offers
online, please sign up for the Titan newsletter on our website:
www.titanbooks.com

TO EMMA, MY BELOVED

DRAMATIS PERSONAE

MAIN CHARACTERS

Lieutenant Katja Emmes (Terran strike officer)
Commander Charity Brisebois (Terran intelligence officer, known as "Breeze")
Lieutenant Commander Thomas Kane (Terran line officer)
Sublieutenant Jack Mallory (Terran pilot officer)

Kete Obadele (Centauri agent)

NEIL ARMSTRONG CREW MEMBERS

Captain Andy Lincoln (commanding officer)
Lieutenant Helena Grey (science officer)
Sublieutenant Amanda Smith (junior research officer)

OTHER TERRAN MILITARY PERSONNEL

Admiral Eric Chandler (Director of the Dark Bomb project)
Brigadier Alexander Korolev (commander of the Levantine Regiment)
Admiral Randall Bush (commander of the Research Squadron)

THE EMMES FAMILY

Storm Banner Leader Günther Emmes
Miriam Emmes
Merje Emmes (a lawyer)
Michael Emmes (a teacher)
Stormtrooper Soren Emmes

GLOSSARY

AAR	anti-armor robot
AAW	anti-attack warfare
AF	Astral Force
AG	artificial gravity
APR	anti-personnel robot
CO	commanding officer (or captain)
FAC	fast-attack craft
XO	executive officer

OFFICER TRADES

Line officer in charge of the general operations of the Astral Force warships, this trade is exclusive to the Fleet

Strike officer commanding AF ground operations, this trade is exclusive to the Corps

Pilot officer operators of the Astral Force small craft, this trade exists in both Fleet and Corps depending on the craft being piloted

Support officer divided into three distinct sub-trades—Supply, Engineering, and Intelligence—this trade fulfills the Astral Force non-combat roles for both Fleet and Corps

EXTRA-DIMENSIONAL

Brane	a region of spacetime which consists of three spatial dimensions and one time dimension; humans exist in one of several known branes
Bulk	an area of spacetime which consists of four spatial dimensions and one time dimension
Ctholian Deep	a region of the Bulk more than 16 peets away from the brane in which humans exist
Peet	the unit of measurement to describe how far away into the fourth dimension something is, from the brane in which humans exist
Weakbrane	another three-dimensional region of spacetime displaced from humans within the Bulk

SHIPBOARD

Aft	toward the back of the ship
Bow	front of the ship
Bridge	the command center of the ship
Bulkhead	wall
Deck	floor
Deckhead	ceiling
Forward	toward the front of the ship
Flats	corridor
Frame	an air-tight bulkhead which divides one section of the ship from another
Galley	kitchen
Hatch	a permanent access point built into a deck (as opposed to a door which is built into a bulkhead)
Hardpoint	a small mounting on the outer hull which holds a weapon until the weapon is launched
Heads	toilet
Ladder	a steep stairway leading from one deck to another
Main cave	main cafeteria
Passageway	corridor
Port	left
Rack	bed; also a verb meaning to sleep
Starboard	right
Stern	back of the ship
Washplace	sink, shower

1

After months of being androgynous, it was nice to be a woman again.

Katja Emmes hardly recognized herself in the reflection of the tram's broad window—but she did recognize the admiring glances from male passengers, noticing eyes on her from several angles.

There was the young man to her left by the door. Quick, but awkward, his own legs would trip him up under fire. Then there was the man seated at eleven o'clock. Overweight but powerful, more aware of his surroundings than his slouched posture suggested. Two men wearing suits stood to her right. Poor at hiding their intentions and little strength, they would just stand in shock once the shooting began.

Target priority was the seated man, Double-tap.

Awkward youth, single with chaser.

Pair of suits, hold and question if possible.

Katja blinked, and loosened her grip on the pole. No one needed to be taken down. She was home, on Earth.

She looked again at her reflection. Her slender frame was heavily reinforced with well-used muscle, shoulders and arms highlighted by the sleeveless dress that clung to her figure. The girl in Katja bemoaned the fact that her hips were a bit wider than her chest, but the professional knew it was a result of being in shape. Months of rehab had softened her, but the regime of the last few weeks was starting to show results.

Her face was what she recognized the least. The mop of long, curly blonde hair was a world away from the cropped halo of this morning, and every time she moved her head she felt the tickling across her neck and shoulders. She didn't usually indulge in a hair lengthener, but today was different.

It wasn't every day she came home from her first war.

The tram slowed to a stop, the pleasant voice announcing arrival at the Santa Fe Law Courts. Katja grabbed her small hover-case and stepped down through the door into the unfiltered heat. She caught the faint fusion haze of the tram as she took her first deep breath of pure air. Her nostrils burned with the dryness and her eyes began to water. She blinked quickly to clear them, and took short, shallow breaths. She'd forgotten how dry North America was. A breeze gusted between the buildings as she strolled toward the broad, imposing front of the courts.

The building was more than two hundred years old, and a beautiful example of the Gaian style of architecture. The facade had been worked to appear as one solid slab of the local red stone, with windows recessed tastefully behind ledges of long grass and flowers. The walls and roof curved as if they had been formed by thousands of years of wind. The only break in the smooth face was a steady stream of water that flowed down a crevice to form a pool to the left of the main entrance.

Just outside was a large crowd of what could only be reporters. Katja had seen the news, announcing that a big military trial was scheduled to conclude today.

Insubordinate bastard.

Her lips tightened as she started up the wide steps from the street. Some officer in the Corps had disobeyed orders and caused an embarrassing defeat in one of the minor theatres. This had stolen the spotlight from the great victory they had achieved in Centauria, where Katja had served, robbing the Astral Force of a very public triumph.

It was lucky for the accused that the name of any military defendant remained secret until a guilty verdict was pronounced. She could think of a few things she'd like to do to him, if she could hunt him down.

One of the reporters spotted her and detached himself from the crowd, cameraman in tow. She recognized him from one of the major networks, but couldn't remember his name. He was tall and broad-shouldered, outweighing her by at least forty kilos. He had greater reach, but probably not speed.

"Excuse me, miss." He gave her a disarming smile. He was quite good-looking, with a shock of brown hair and boyish features. "I'm Chuck Merriman, ANL. Can I take a moment of your time?"

She was tempted to brush past him with a brusque "no comment," as was proper in her position, but today she was just plain Katja, and all the rules were changed.

"Of course."

She held his eyes for an extra moment.

Merriman stepped slightly aside to give his cameraman the chance to adjust his optic visor. The fellow winked with slow deliberation to activate the visor's camera, then gave Merriman the thumbs-up.

The reporter adopted an easy tone. "I'm collecting public opinions on the ongoing military case," he said. "Are you familiar with it?"

"Who isn't?"

"Do you think the officer is guilty as charged?"

"Hard to say without all the details," she replied, "but the fact is, he disobeyed orders, which is inexcusable. The fact that he got his entire platoon killed just makes it worse."

"Some reports have said that the rebels in the colonies were better trained and more extensively equipped than anyone expected. What do you think of the theory that he was improvising, because the rebels had compromised the Corps' tactics?"

"Corps doctrine is designed to retain flexibility in a wide variety of situations." She shrugged. "He had options—*and* he had explicit orders."

Merriman's eyebrows rose. "Strong opinion," he noted. "Sounds like you know a thing or two about taking orders. Do you serve?"

Katja's stomach tightened. This wasn't a good place to be, an officer speaking unofficially to the press. Time for a half-truth.

"My fath—my daddy's in the Army. He never shuts up about this sort of thing." She opened her eyes a little wider, trying for a dumb-blonde look.

Merriman's own eyes narrowed slightly, but his tone didn't change.

"Do you support the death penalty against the Astral officer on trial?"

Yes. "Well, umm, that's pretty serious, but I think what he did was pretty serious, too."

Merriman nodded. "I believe 'inexcusable' was the word you used a second ago."

"Umm… yeah."

There was a pause, as Merriman and his cameraman—who was staring at her in that unnervingly intent way unique to optically augmented people—waited for more. She glanced down at her shoes.

"Umm, can I go?"

Merriman eyed her with what she suspected was amused curiosity, but his smile never wavered.

"Of course, Miss…"

"Katja." She extended her hand.

He shook it. "Miss Katja."

She hurried away, keeping her eyes on the cave-like opening of the courts and away from the flurry of reporters. At least the State had the sense to keep the media out.

The security sensors were discreet but not invisible, and Katja slowed her pace as she passed through the building's main doors. As a serving combat veteran there were few places out-of-bounds to her, she knew, but caution was prudent in a politically charged atmosphere. No alarms sounded and no guards emerged, which meant the tiny personal implant in her chest had been accepted.

Inside the air was cool and moist, the courts bustling with late-afternoon activity. She noted immediately the armed guards by the gates that led to the secure zone, sized up the group of youths milling about to her left, the scruffy-looking couple chatting by the fountain ahead, and a custodial robot beginning its rounds in the far right corner.

Then she saw Merje. Her sister wore a deep green pantsuit,

the expensive cut accentuating the very subtle curves of her slim body. Long, straight, blonde hair hung halfway down her back, and her delicate features lit up as she spotted Katja. She rushed over and embraced her. Katja's heart soared, suddenly realizing just how much she needed a hug. She wrapped her arms around Merje's bird-like ribcage, so tightly she heard her gasp.

She released instantly, pulling back to rest her hands on Merje's bony shoulders.

"Hey, nerd."

"Hey, scary." Merje cast her hand out to take in the vast lobby. "Welcome to my world. Sorry about the paparazzi."

Katja glanced back. "Yeah, I had to run the gauntlet."

"Nothing like a high-profile military case to bring them out in swarms."

A sudden, unpleasant thought struck her. "You're not defending this traitor, are you?"

"Not personally, no—thank goodness, but it's taken up a lot of the firm's resources. Your arrival actually got me out of some pretty dreary research."

Her sister's firm was defending that bastard?

"Did you have a good trip?" Merje took her arm and began walking toward a side exit.

She shook her arm loose. "It's called a deployment—not a trip—and there was this little thing called a war."

"Yeah, yeah," her sister responded. "Welcome home. Are you staying long?"

"I don't know." They exited the courts, stepped onto a side street, and Merje flagged down an automated cab.

"I'm not sure whether to thank you or slap you for the invitation to the military gala," Merje said as Katja climbed into the cab and stowed her case.

"I thought you'd like a fancy ball—isn't that your thing?"

Merje flopped down across from her, not bothering to buckle up. "Oh, I enjoy getting drunk and being charmed out of my cocktail dress as much as the next girl, but another evening with the family? Come on, Katty."

Katja shrugged in sympathy as she watched the once-familiar streets of Santa Fe rush past. The worst thing about spending the evening with their father was the knowledge that they'd have to do it again in just a week, at the gala military ball in Longreach. There the Emmes family members were to be touted as heroes of Terra, for their collective service to the State. The full eye of the worlds' media would be on them.

What a joke.

The drive to the secure residential zone was quick. Katja had barely begun to form what she wanted to say to her father before the cab glided to a stop outside a beautiful, Federation-era house on a tree-lined street—the Emmes family home.

They paused on the sidewalk. Merje uplinked a request to have a cab available on short notice.

"Here we go," Katja sighed. "You ready?"

Merje gave her a sidelong glance. "No. But that's never stopped me before."

The security system identified them immediately and opened the gate. It informed them that they were expected in the courtyard, and they passed under the arched walkway that gave access to the inner sanctum. Even before they were through a delicate figure appeared at the far end, watching expectantly.

Miriam Emmes looked paler than last time, but her smile was warm.

"Welcome home, Katja." The hug was gentle, as everything with her had to be.

"Hi, Mom."

"Darling, I love your hair like that. Why don't you always keep it long?"

"Three reasons. It gets in the way, it's no good in zero-g, and it doesn't make me look mean."

"You shouldn't have to look mean."

"When fifty troopers are expected to obey my every word, it helps."

Her brother Michael appeared in the archway as their mother greeted Merje.

"Hi, Katty." He gave her a hug. "Fifty troopers to boss around, eh? I bet when that hair's gone, you're pretty butch."

Katja's jaw clenched. Was he baiting her?

"Don't fuck with me today."

Michael raised his hands. "Whoa, whoa, Katty. Shift target left." He glanced back toward the courtyard. "Save it for Father and Soren."

"Sorry." She took a deep breath. "Where are our comrades-in-arms, anyway?"

"Father's out back with Rachel and the kids," he said. "Soren and the Tart haven't arrived yet."

"Michael!" Their mother frowned disapprovingly. "She'll be family soon."

"She'll be a perfect addition," he replied.

Led by their mother, they emerged into the sprawling, lush courtyard. Sunshine beat down on well-groomed grass, and Katja's eye was drawn immediately to the sudden movement of two little kids—her niece and nephew, she presumed—racing frantically across the lawn into the waiting arms of a crouched figure.

Storm Banner Leader Günther Freidrich Emmes didn't look up as his wife and children emerged. Instead, he let his grandchildren tackle him, tipping backward onto the grass. His powerful words mixed with their excited shrieks, echoing across the yard.

Katja frowned. He'd lost none of his quickness or power. His thick, white hair was closely cropped, and stood in stark contrast to the tanned, weathered face that turned toward her. He rose and strolled across the grass, sizing her up with what seemed more curiosity than affection.

"Katja, you look healthy." His words were flattened by the tones of their native Finnish, but carried with alarming ease. She forced herself to stand her ground, arms firmly at her side. Maybe this time he would give her a hug, but there was no way she was going to initiate it.

"Thank you, Father," she replied, also in Finnish. "You're looking well."

He gave a sidelong glance to her sister. "Merje, you're thin. Are you eating enough? Or spending it all on clothes?"

"Drugs, mostly," came the acid reply.

He just nodded, then turned his attention back to Katja.

"What's this I hear about you going Fleet?"

"Fast-attack," she said quickly. "I was the strike officer aboard a small ship that did boardings and covert strikes planetside." His expression didn't convince Katja that he was impressed. "It's considered elite."

"Hm," he grunted. "I just thought, what with the colonies rebelling and all, you might want to stay with your regiment and fight. This 'fast-attack' sounds pretty cushy during a war."

Katja felt her cheeks flushing. His words were so damn unfair, but she refused to crow about her combat experiences like some juvenile braggart.

"You have no idea how much time I spent planetside."

"Well, when we all get out there, I'll be sure to look for you." He turned away and with a childish bellow charged playfully at his grandchildren. They screamed and took off down the garden, laughing.

Katja pursed her lips and looked away.

Merje had hypothesized years ago that the reason the Emmes household was alcohol-free was to stop their mother from drinking herself to death. After all, she elaborated, what other possible outcome lay for a woman who had to spend her life with their father?

As she sat down to dinner, Katja looked across the table and wondered idly if the Tart had given any thought to this matter, considering her fiancé was the spitting image of his father. Stormtrooper Soren Emmes was Merje's fraternal twin, but Katja couldn't conceive of a human being more unlike her stylish, willowy sister. Soren was thick and powerful, his dark hair buzzed down in a typical high-and-tight.

The Tart herself—Hong, if Katja remembered correctly— was a plastic representation of what might have been a pretty girl once, with a pneumatic body squeezed into a colorful dress that, while reaching her neck, elbows, and knees, left little to the imagination. Katja had seen that color of pink in hair before, but never on a woman attending the birthday dinner of her future father-in-law.

Her mother didn't seem to notice as she served up the main course to her guests. Soren and his fiancée sat across from the sisters at their mother's end of the table, with Michael and his family occupying the places of honor near the patriarch. Hearty chatter about the Army and the teaching profession dominated the first course of dinner, in English for Hong's sake, while precious little was mentioned of the Astral Force or the legal profession.

"So, Hong," the Voice said from the other end of the table, "has my boy taken you to any formal events yet?"

"Oh yeah," Soren responded. "We were at the Valentine's Ball just a month ago. It was great! We had the newbies puking in their caps by the time the sun came up."

"Soren!" Their mother fussed with the napkin in her lap. "You can save your drinking stories until after dinner, I think."

"Oh come on, Mom," he said. "I bet you were out there with the boys when you were young."

She glanced sternly at her son. "No, darling, I wasn't." She smiled at everyone. "Please, it'll get cold."

Katja obediently dug into her meal.

"Katja," a small voice said, "you were in the Army, weren't you? What was it like as a woman?"

She glanced up, unsure at first who had spoken. Then she noticed Hong staring at her expectantly.

"No, she was never in the Army!" Soren said, mouth full of food. Katja would have happily let the subject drop at that, but Hong still stared at her, more confused than curious. So she put down her utensils.

"I'm not in the Army," she explained. "I'm in the Astral Force. Basically, the Army fights on the surface of planets, and the Astral Force fights in space. We also help the Army by making a bridgehead for them."

"You build bridges?"

It's like talking to a child, she reminded herself.

"No," she said aloud. "We attack the planet first, and create a safe place for the Army to land."

Soren nudged his fiancée. "In other words, they get us there, and then we do all the fighting."

"You're welcome to join us on a drop sometime, Meathead," Katja offered.

He sneered at her. "How much time have you actually spent on the ground?"

"How many theatres of operation have you seen?"

"Enough to bag me some jee-hads."

"Do you even know what planet you were on?"

"Doesn't matter," he insisted. "If I'm there, I'm there to fight."

"Soren," the Voice said from the end of the table, "that's enough. Our colleagues in the Astral Force do good work for us."

Silence fell at that. Soren shrugged and continued eating, while Katja exchanged a look with Merje. Had their father just complimented the Astral Force?

"Of course," he continued, "that doesn't mean we live in a perfect world. Hong, remind me, what do you do for a living?"

"Oh, well, I'm hoping to be an actress, but right now it's mostly been modeling, and dancing."

"So if you were starring in a movie, you know that the director is important?"

"Oh, yeah!" Her eyes widened. "He's totally important."

"So imagine you had the choice of two directors. One used to be an actor himself, has learned from the best directors before him, and has finally pulled together all his experience to start making his own films." He let that sink in, then continued. "The other one went to directors' school, made a couple of films in school, and has now just started working. Which one would you want?"

She glanced at Soren, then whispered to him. He nodded.

"The first one," she said. "The one with all the experience."

"Good answer."

Michael leaned forward wearily. "Father, please..."

"So naturally, if having an experienced director is important for a film, I'd say that it's important to have an experienced leader when you're sending soldiers in to die."

Katja could hear her own heartbeat in her ears, and she stared intently at her food. She should have seen this coming.

"You see, Hong, the Army trains its leaders from the bottom. I started out as a stormtrooper, just like Soren, and through years of experience I worked my way up to a position of authority— and there are soldiers who are even higher than me. Every one of them deserves their rank. The United Army was founded forty-seven years ago on principles developed over six thousand years of warfare. We are the pinnacle of military thought, unmatched in history.

"But the Astral Force hung on to the old ways," he continued. "They retained the class system that crippled our planet's armies for millennia. Most of the Astral Force are good, hard-working troopers and sailors, but they're held enslaved to an aristocracy who call themselves officers. Fresh out of school, having never seen blood, these officers are supposed to lead their battle-hardened troops into combat. Does that make sense to you?"

Hong was speechless, frozen in her chair.

Soren nodded eagerly. "I'm so glad we got rid of officers," he agreed. "Bunch of idiots."

"This Astral Force trial all over the news is just another example of how inexperienced officers get people killed. He should receive the death penalty—but thanks to the lawyers, justice is perverted once again."

"Ohh-kay." Merje pushed back her chair and stood. "That's enough for one year. Mom, thanks for dinner as always. Sorry I can't stay."

"Merje." The Voice deepened dangerously. "Do not disrespect your mother by leaving again."

"I'm not the one showing disrespect here, you arrogant prick."

Deathly silence fell over the table.

Merje turned to Hong. "Tart, you better enjoy your pretty little soldier while you can, because if we go to war he'll be the first one blown to pieces. Just make sure you marry him and get knocked up before he goes. It's better, legally."

Soren leapt to his feet, his arm lashing out across the table. Finally.

Katja exploded from her chair. She grabbed the narrowest part of his wrist and redirected his blow past Merje. She rolled his arm and smashed down her free hand on his exposed elbow. Her palm bounced off the cracked joint and snapped back into his jaw.

Soren stepped back, more stunned than injured. Michael and Rachel grabbed the children and fled to the courtyard. Their mother rose from her chair and left. Hong sat motionless, mouth hanging open. Merje stepped behind Katja.

Storm Banner Leader Emmes stood.

"Stop fighting in my house, you pair of apes," he roared. "Soren, you get distracted too easily. Don't lose sight of where the real threat lies. Merje's annoying, but she can't hurt you. Katja can kill you." His voice lowered even further. "If you want to survive in combat, learn that lesson.

"Katja," he said, "you're too instinctive—you don't think. You broadened the conflict and put yourself at risk for no good reason. God help you if you ever have to lead troops in real combat.

"Merje," he continued, "get out of my house."

Katja felt Merje's hand squeeze her arm as she started to leave. "See you at the funeral." Then she listened to her sister's deliberately leisurely stride. To the high heels clicking on the stone floor of the foyer. To the door shutting.

She sighed.

Her father had already returned to his meal, and wasn't looking up. Soren's smirk was fast returning as he wrapped an arm around Hong. Michael and his family were outside, and their mother had disappeared to the kitchen.

Just your average family get-together.

Her sister wouldn't wait for long, she knew, so she hurried into the kitchen.

"Mom, I'm sorry about that," she said quickly. "I'll go and get Merje."

Her mother stood very still, both hands leaning against the counter. She stared off into the distance.

"Please stay away from me."

Katja's heart tore in half. "I'm sorry."

"I'm so afraid of that gala."

Katja nodded. "Everything will be fine," she said. "I'll make sure of it."

"Goodbye, darling."

And that was that, she knew. Katja turned and left.

The auto cab had already pulled up by the time she dashed out to the street. Merje glanced over her shoulder as she climbed in, leaving the door open. Katja jumped in and shut the door. She stared at her sister for a long moment, searching for her mood as the cab started to move.

Merje gave her a dangerous smile. "You still have a place in Longreach?"

Katja thought back to the transient officers' quarters, just inside the gates of the complex that housed the space elevator.

"Not permanent," she replied cautiously, "but I can get a place. Why?"

Merje pulled a wafer-thin device out of her purse. "The next flight to Longreach is in forty minutes." She studied the screen. "Let's go."

"You want to go to Australia... *tonight*?"

"You have something better to do here?"

"Right now I'd like to just hide away and sleep for a few months." Katja looked out at the dark Santa Fe streets rushing past. She pulled off her shoes one at a time and rubbed the sore spots on her heels.

"Oh, stop feeling sorry for yourself." Merje uplinked and confirmed their tickets.

The cab delivered them to the skyport within minutes, and Merje climbed out with renewed energy. "Now come on. I want to get good and drunk on the flight. We can sleep when we get to your place. Then I have to buy an outfit—Longreach shopping is awesome."

Katja felt a smile tug at her lips.

She followed her sister onto the skyjet and straight to the on-board lounge. Merje ordered them some fancy cocktails and Katja leaned back to watch the lights of North America fall away as the skyjet soared upward. It was more than two hours to Australia.

She drank every cocktail Merje gave her, and soon was giggling almost non-stop at her sister's steady banter about daily life in the big city.

Then, with the blinking lights of the Australian space elevators just peeking over the horizon ahead, there was a sudden, long silence at the table. She looked away from the window, wondering if Merje had drunk herself into a stupor.

Her sister was watching her carefully. "Enough about me, Katty," she said, and her eyes were surprisingly clear. "How are you?"

"Me? Uhh, fine." She was taken aback by the sudden shift in tone. The liquor dulled any ready response.

Merje took a sip of her drink, but kept watch over the wide rim of the glass.

"The media hasn't told us much, but I get the feeling things were pretty hairy out there. Were you in Sirius, or Centauria?"

Hearing the names of the two rebellious colonies drew forth images of smoke and fire, shattered buildings, burning spaceships, bullets flying overhead... and the dead. Sirians, Centauris, her own troops, everywhere the dead. Her spine and ribs began to burn. Centauri slugs struck her torso. Her head hit the deck in front of Sirian rapists. Orbital bombardment blinded her. The utter blackness of the abyss froze her.

"Katty?"

She blinked, and focused. "What?"

Merje reached over the table and took her hand. "Do you want to talk about it?"

What was she supposed to say? Her lip quivered. She shut her eyes tight to hold in the tears. Lowering her chin, she squeezed Merje's hand as tightly as she could. What in the worlds could she say?

She pressed her fist against her forehead, tears trickling down her cheeks. What could she say that anyone would understand?

2

The weapon was clear plastic, difficult for any sensor to detect, but hard enough to shatter human bone. It was easy to conceal, but in this part of Longreach most people knew how to spot unusual bulges.

Kete Obadele had never been to Earth before, and even years of training hadn't prepared him for the squalor of a Terran working-class city. Tired pedestrians made their silent ways along the chipped sidewalk, hardly noticing their fellow citizens under the hoods held tight against the dust of the latest sandstorm. The red buildings towered on either side of the street, hemming in what had once been part of the endless expanse known as the Outback, creating a narrow valley of artificial, wind-blasted walls, stray trash swirling in the eddies, and public busses hissing by with little regard for pedestrian safety.

Power was mostly reliable, but so many lights had been broken that as evening settled over Longreach, the street drifted into dusty shadows. Perfect for a murder.

The target alighted from the next bus, stopping by the corner where Kete stood idly with the waiting commuters. In the shuffle of off-loading and loading passengers, Kete merged into the crowd of people moving away from the vehicle, slipping easily into the wake of his target.

The object of his attention was thin and frail under his coat, Kete knew, but moved with considerable vigor in his step. No doubt his mood was buoyed by a day working for the rich and famous, and by dreams of one day leaving behind this ragged community in favor of the opulence of one of the protected wards. He was surprisingly young, meaning he was either very lucky or—more likely—very talented and hard working.

Inspired by hope and dreams. It was a good way for an ambitious young man to die, Kete told himself.

The target strode two blocks along the main thoroughfare before turning onto one of the side streets. Residential blocks towered up on both sides, but the dark forms of sleeping bums suggested that even these massive apartment complexes were insufficient for all the poor souls seeking a home in one of Earth's greatest cities. Kete increased his pace, closing the distance. The shadows deepened as they left the bus route farther behind, but still there were too many witnesses out here in the open. Kete had studied the target's routine, and knew that his window of opportunity would be small.

The doors to the apartment block were hanging slightly ajar, the security system long in need of repair. The target pushed one door aside, holding it open as Kete hurried to slip in behind him. That morning the lobby had been lit by a single overhead light, but Kete had smashed it around noon, and now only the knee-high emergency lights cast their dim, red glow. The target made straight for the glowing lights of the elevator controls.

There was no one else in the lobby.

Kete pulled a dagger free from his sleeve. In three long strides he reached the target, grabbed his shoulder, and spun him around, the open front of the coat flying free and revealing the unprotected, skinny torso. The dagger punched through the thin fabric of the shirt, through the ribs and into the target's beating heart. Kete slapped his free hand over the target's mouth to silence any noise, twisting the dagger sharply to ensure a clean kill.

Within seconds the target slumped forward. Kete took the weight and, dagger still embedded, dragged the body over to the maintenance closet he knew was on the left side of the lobby. Pushing open the door, he lay the body down among the dusty equipment and pulled out a powerful headlamp to wrap around his own head. The door slid shut again with only a few rusted squeaks, cocooning Kete for the last phase of his task.

The target's shirt tore away easily enough, but his young ribs were strong. Trying to crack them by leverage from within proved impossible. Kete pulled the dagger free, wiped the blood off his hand on the target's coat and steadied his grip for a hard strike. He slammed the blade down against the center of the chest, feeling the breastbone crack. Two more strikes and the central portion had broken free from the ribcage. Some precision cutting of flesh, and the lump of bone came loose in his hand.

Digging through the marrow was delicate work, but Kete's enhanced eyesight let him guide the tip of the dagger at a micro level. He could glean the presence of the identification chip inside the bone, and used his extra sensors to guide his eyes and hands as he searched for the tiny device.

Finally, his blade emerged with the prize. Perhaps a tenth the size of a small fingernail, it was primitive to Kete's eyes, but it represented one of the most advanced elements of Terran security. It was Kete's ticket into the rarefied central realm of the enemy.

Slipping the identification chip into a stealth bag and then deep into one of his hidden pockets, Kete replaced the broken breastbone in the gouged chest cavity and laid the shredded shirt across it. With no identity chip to check, the local law enforcement would have great difficulty learning the identity of this victim. Certainly they wouldn't expect anyone in this neighborhood to have had top-level security clearance.

It was a well-known, brutal fact that Terran citizens did occasionally "disappear" if they displeased their political masters, and not even local law enforcement would have an appetite to investigate too far into a dead-end death like this. The truth would very likely be lost.

Just as Kete had planned.

Less than an hour later, he emerged from the shower in his luxury apartment, any last trace of his mission scrubbed clean. Donning a set of comfortable lounge wear he settled down at his dining table—made of real wood—and pulled the stolen identity chip from its stealth bag.

Blending seamlessly into the Terran State net was neither a quick nor easy thing to do. Terran citizens were tracked from cradle to grave, and inserting an entire, full-blown life into the net without raising any alarms was akin to balancing a very large series of pins while moving via tightrope between spinning tops.

Choosing a profession with exceptional independence had been essential, as was an origin shrouded in mystery. Thus Kete Obadele had become Kit Moro, raised in the ashes of a West African shantytown, with an unknown father and a mother who was one of thousands who had withered away during one of the later MAS outbreaks. According to the records he had attended several charity schools, where few graduates could be easily traced, and then received a degree from a massive State institution where tens of thousands were processed in anonymity each year.

He had earned a quiet living these past two decades, as a freelance journalist with extensive experience off-world. As an augmented cameraman, he wasn't expected to be an on-screen presence, instead bringing back stunning visuals that were often sold to networks and private journalists on the condition that no credit was given to the source. The story had been plausible enough to get him work with no less than ANL, and the great inquisitor Chuck Merriman seemed to have accepted it without question.

Although he would never let himself relax while on a mission, Kete allowed himself a small twinge of satisfaction that he had succeeded so far. He was inside Terran society and, as the last few weeks had shown, he was well-placed to move about unnoticed—because no one ever noticed the cameraman.

Next he needed to become a cancer.

Getting clearance to become a cameraman inside the high-security zones was another matter altogether, and Kete knew his fabricated life as Kit Moro left way too many unanswered questions. He could never have applied for top-level security and maintained his cover.

No, the only option had been to get his hands on a legitimate Terran ID that had already been cleared. Terran cyber-security was in most ways laughably simple, but when it came to military encryptions, it was surprisingly robust. Kete had even taken the precaution of capturing a chip from a person who held the same profession as his alter-ego. Thus, his target had been an unfortunate young cameraman doing contract work for ANL.

As he lifted up the stolen chip, Kete's mind had already begun to analyze it. Several days, perhaps even weeks, would be needed to track down every nuance of the security protocols contained within, and then replicate them in his own, Centauri-designed chip. This operation required patience, he knew, and great care at every step.

At least he wasn't alone. All across Earth other Centauri agents were quietly slipping themselves into the fabric of Terran life. Although they would never meet on their foreign world, they shared a singular vision and worked together toward a simple goal.

War was coming to Terra. War and vengeance.

3

The true soldier scorned the media, nosy parasites who did nothing but make trouble. If given the chance, said soldier would quite happily muzzle every last reporter in Terra, or at least banish them to reporting local bake-offs and school track meets.

Yet, as Thomas Kane approached the entrance to the military gala, he saw the crowd of reporters jostling for position behind the velvet ropes, and forced a smile to his lips. After twenty years of working to improve his station in life, he knew that the media were tools like any other. If neglected, they could become a blunt object that swung wildly in all directions, but if handled well they could be sharpened to cut with surgical precision.

Anything to do with the military was a hot news item right now, with the recent rebellion in the colonies still sending repercussions through politics and the economy. Rumors of a colonial terrorist threat here at home had been ruthlessly quashed, but journalists had an annoying way of ignoring what the military told them. The recent trial of that Corps officer had stolen the spotlight and tonight's gala was, in Thomas's opinion, an obvious attempt to draw the public's attention away from the negative aspects of the conflict.

Still, who was he to disobey explicit orders to treat his new wife to a black tie event?

Soma Kane craned her neck. "Do you see any of the major networks?"

"A couple, I think." He offered his arm. "This gala's bigger than I thought."

She wrapped her delicate, jeweled hand around his forearm and smoothed her gown. Most of her day had been spent getting ready for this evening, and it showed. Barely as tall as his shoulder even in her heels, she carried herself with the regal assurance of the Jovian elite. The rich colors of her dress brought out the deep lustre of her dark skin and complemented the beads worked into her long black hair.

It was a short walk up to the imposing entrance of the Astral Force Headquarters, ambient lights creating the illusion of daytime over the deep-blue carpet that flowed like a waterfall down the center of the broad, marble steps. Fully armored soldiers stood in the shadows just beyond the light, but otherwise it was a scene of glamour and style. Thomas instinctively glanced down to check his dress uniform.

His high-collar blacks sported shoulder boards with twin silver bars plus star—indicating his rank and appointment—and his breast gleamed with the accomplishments of two decades in the service of Terra. Qualification badges for Fleet warfare director, Corps infantry commander and Joint fast-attack spoke to his breadth of training, and five medals heralded his experience and dedication to duty. His eyes lingered on one particular decoration, the Distinguished Service Medal, which he had earned during the... recent troubles.

A few cameras focused on Thomas and Soma as they ascended the steps, even if no reporters spoke to them. He stole another look at his wife and appreciated anew how beautiful she was. A colder part of his brain assessed that together they were quite a media target, and he wondered if they might merit one of the supporting photos on a "society montage" in one of the tabloids—a tall, decorated veteran and a beautiful, wealthy socialite. Mixed-race marriages were all the vogue right now, so that alone would probably earn them a place on a media spread.

They passed through subtle security at the entrance to the building and were politely directed into the vast open room that could serve as a parade ground, a sports arena, or even an execution site, but tonight had been beautified into a ballroom.

Banners of every major military command hung between the pillars, the bright lights at floor level fading upward into the clever illusion of a starry sky overhead.

Hundreds of guests already mingled on the polished floor, and at the far end of the room an entire array of machines from both the Army and the Astral Force were on display. His eyes automatically sought out the dark, sleek, and familiar shape of a fast-attack craft, but after only a moment's longing gaze, his attention focused again on his social responsibilities.

Tonight's receiving line was high-powered indeed. And electronic security, while invisible to the casual observer, was omnipresent. A discreet scan of their personal, embedded identity chips—the thought of which naturally brought to Thomas the image of Soma's perfect breasts, and the complete absence of an implant scar between them—had already identified them to the senior officer at the head of the receiving line, and they were announced.

"Lieutenant Commander Thomas Kane and Mrs. Soma Kane."

Thomas kept his face neutral. Although his actual rank was lieutenant, as the skipper of a fast-attack craft he'd enjoyed the appointment to lieutenant commander. But since his ship was now little more than a cloud of shattered parts on a thousand-year orbit falling in toward the sun, he knew that his appointment was only a bureaucrat's whim away from being removed. The less attention brought to this fact, the better.

Sure enough, the Fleet Marshall glanced at Thomas's shoulder-boards. He kissed Soma's hand, introduced his wife, then looked again at Thomas.

"How are you settling into your command, Mr. Kane?"

This wasn't the way an ambitious young officer was supposed to meet his supreme commander—returned from battle having lost the first vessel entrusted to him—but media training had taught him to turn difficult questions to his advantage.

"She was a fine ship, sir," he replied confidently, "but she was lost in the breakout from Centauria."

"What ship?" Exactly the right follow-up.

"*Rapier*, sir." It was too easy.

The Fleet Marshall's predatory glare softened. Down the

receiving line, other very senior officers looked over with sudden interest. Apparently the entire Astral Force and even the Army had heard the name of the little ship that had unleashed Terra's newest weapon.

As Thomas introduced his wife along the line to a virtual galaxy of military brass, he forced an expression of humility to lock down the smile that fought hard to split his features. No matter what else had happened during the troubles, his final mission had at least earned him some fame.

The air was cool and fragrant inside the ballroom, despite the hundreds of people and several teams of newsmen circulating, capturing the moment. Soma pointed at one media team that was focused on a particular Astral Force officer.

"Oh look! There's Uncle Eric."

There indeed was Soma's godfather, Captain—no, *Admiral*—Eric Chandler. Resplendent in the gold-trimmed, high-collar blacks of a flag officer, he had his listeners enthralled. Above-average height, sharp featured with just enough gray to add distinction, Chandler was exactly the sort of hero the Astral Force needed right now.

An inspiration to Thomas since the days when they'd both been junior officers in the old destroyer *Victoria*, Chandler had kept a subtle eye on his young colleague for years—even arranging for Thomas to meet the lovely daughter of the richest man on Ganymede. Yet Chandler had sent his regrets to Thomas and Soma's wedding. That spoke volumes of how much the relationship between mentor and protégé had deteriorated.

Thomas's *Rapier* had been under the overall command of Chandler's expeditionary force, providing an ideal opportunity for an ambitious junior officer to shine. In the long months of combat, however, there had been both good and bad times, and even now Thomas wasn't sure where the balance lay.

Nevertheless, for better or worse, Chandler still provided his best hope for continued success in the Astral Force. Now that Chandler was an admiral, Thomas had dug around to discover the responsibilities of his mentor's new position as an admiral. This was his chance to make the pitch. He followed in Soma's wake as she glided across the floor.

Chandler noticed them and broke off his discussion with the reporters. He met Soma, kissing her on both cheeks, asking about the wedding and apologizing profusely for not attending. Soma laughed off his efforts and congratulated him on his recent successes. The entire exchange was captured by the hovering reporters. Finally, Chandler turned his gaze to Thomas.

His bright eyes were inscrutable.

"Good to see you again, Thomas," he said warmly. "Congratulations on your marriage to this lovely girl."

"I'm a very lucky man, sir." Thomas shook his hand. "Congratulations to you as well, Admiral."

Chandler nodded slightly and returned his attention to the reporters. Cameras clicked when he introduced Soma as the heiress of the Mehta family of Ganymede, and Thomas felt himself melt into the background. Hardly surprising, really, when he was up against a newly minted war hero and a Jovian heiress.

Looking around the room, he noticed another media grouping of sudden, intense interest to him. An entire family was being interviewed—two men in Army uniforms, one man in the dress suit of a retired Army veteran, two civilian women, and one woman from the Astral Force.

Katja.

His heart leapt. Her high-collar blacks sparkled with badges and medals, including the Astral Star for valor in combat, but her face was carefully neutral as she listened to another family member speaking to the reporter. Her small body was firm and smooth under that uniform, he knew, but he immediately shook off those memories. It was just good to see her.

Keeping half an ear on Chandler and his wife, he watched the Emmes family interview. It was fascinating to see the interaction, matching faces to the rare but colorful comments Katja had made about her family. And there was no mistaking the powerful Army man with the Cross of Valor on a ribbon around his neck. That was Katja's father. Whoever happened to be speaking fell silent if Papa Emmes opened his mouth, and all eyes darted toward the patriarch at regular intervals.

All except Katja's sister, he noted curiously, who instead seemed rather bored by the entire affair. She listened politely when Katja or their mother spoke, but otherwise was surreptitiously looking around the room. Her eyes met his for a moment, with the flash of a smile before she looked away.

Soma squeezed up to his arm again. "I'm going to get us some drinks," she murmured. "I think Uncle Eric has something very exciting to discuss with you."

In a gust of sweet scent his wife disappeared, and Thomas turned his eyes to his mentor. Chandler's easy rapport, reserved for the media, was gone, and Thomas recognized the grim set of his jaw only too well.

"Thomas," he said without preamble, "I've got a situation. The Fleet Marshall is launching a formal investigation into the way the Astral Force conducted the war."

Instinctively Thomas glanced back toward the receiving line, and the man whose hand he had just recently shaken. A Fleet Marshall Investigation, he knew, was a rare and frightening thing.

"What's being investigated, sir?"

"Basically, Parliament's decided that somebody in the military has to pay for this war," Chandler growled, his voice low. "As far as they're concerned, the whole thing was a disaster for the State, and they've decided it cost us too much, both in terms of resources and prestige."

Thomas nodded thoughtfully, mind racing even as he swallowed the bitter taste of betrayal by their political masters.

"I suppose the recent Astral trial was part of that?"

Chandler glanced around, further lowering his voice.

"From what I heard through the command channel, that officer was just a hard-working ape who did his best in a bad situation. I'm not surprised the lawyers got him off. The fact that he walked is even more embarrassing for the State, and the Fleet Marshall's been ordered to ensure that the next trial doesn't end the same way." He looked as if he'd tasted something bad. "Parliament wants to know why it took so long to win, and why we took so many losses.

"They want someone to blame. And that person is going to die."

Chandler's blunt words seemed to chill the air between them. Thomas had only ever seen the result of one Fleet Marshall Investigation before, while still a cadet at the Astral College.

He'd stood silently in his rank while an admiral was led out to the dais at the front of the parade ground and, in front of several thousand cadets, summarily shot. It had been a very effective lesson in obedience.

"Yes, sir."

"We've convinced the Parliamentary defense committee to use one of our own to lead the investigation," Chandler continued, "since civilians don't have the expertise to know where to look. They wouldn't allow a combatant—too close to the decision-making—but they accepted my suggestion of a senior support officer."

Thomas listened carefully. He wasn't a support officer—unless Chandler intended to bury him in the rear echelon. He wasn't a senior officer either—again, unless Chandler had plans...

"The careers of a lot of people can be made or broken by this war," Chandler concluded. "The last thing we need is for the politicians to start blaming my expeditionary force. I need this problem to go away. Fast."

"I understand, sir," Thomas said slowly, trying very hard not to look at Chandler's new admiral's rank. Thinking quickly, he lined up his pitch. "I think I might be able to help."

"Oh?"

"As I understand it, there's been a program established to conduct in-depth research on the Dark Bomb, and I've also heard that the research isn't going very well." At that Chandler stiffened almost imperceptibly, but his voice remained neutral.

"Of course there's research underway," he said cautiously. "We need to develop that big stick to keep the Centauris in line, in case they decide to get ambitious again. As to how it's going, that's a problem for some fat admiral in the Research Squadron."

Chandler had already maneuvered himself to be assigned the head of the project, Thomas knew. Aside from combat, it would be the most effective career-builder in years.

"No doubt," Thomas agreed, "and I'm sure, sir, that the Research admiral is supervising it to the best of his ability." Chandler shot him an appreciative smile. "But I've heard from the inside that things aren't going well, and I think I might have a solution."

"I'd expect little else." Chandler's smile faded, but his bemused expression did not. "I always taught you to come, not with problems, but with solutions."

Thomas nodded. "The problem, sir, is the ship in question." He lowered his voice conspiratorially. "The *Neil Armstrong* is missing a key element of her command team—the XO. They have a captain who's been Research his whole career, a science officer who's just recently been promoted from the ranks, and a cox'n close to retirement. They need a strong, capable XO to go in there, motivate the team, and get the research back on track." He paused, then went in for the kill.

"They have enough scientists on board already. In my opinion, this officer should be from Fleet, so he can instill some discipline. Ideally he'd have experience in their field of research, so he can effectively guide them despite his lack of scientific qualifications."

"And where, Thomas, would we find such an officer?" Chandler clasped his hands behind his back.

"I respectfully submit my name, sir. I'm qualified, currently idle, and I have a personal interest in this. It was my technical submission to your staff back in Centauria that prompted the Dark Bomb mission—one which I personally commanded."

Chandler looked him over for a moment, his expression intensifying but still glinting with good humor.

"You realize that the XO of an explorer-class Research ship usually holds the rank of commander?" he responded. "I doubt I could conjure up a promotion without causing some serious political ripples."

Thomas had anticipated this response. "Perhaps it could just be a temporary assignment, from *Rapier*. I'd keep my appointment to Lieutenant Commander, which would give me all the authority I need to take charge. When the research is moving well again, Astral HQ can decide whether to post me there permanently or assign a more qualified officer. Either way, we'll have achieved our primary mission of getting the Dark Bomb research back on track."

Chandler glanced around again. "I'm impressed, Thomas, and you're right. The program's not off to a good start. The fat bastard who's in charge of those eggheads has already started bragging about how Research is going to develop Terra's newest weapon. He's already calling it 'the Peacemaker.'" He practically spat the word. "He's trying to take control of the project, or at least take credit for it."

Thomas quickly searched his memory. The head of the Research Squadron was an Admiral Bush, and he was indeed somewhat overweight.

"I've been able to secure the project director position for one of our people," Chandler continued, "reporting directly to me, and I think I've been able to get at least one other member of your crew posted to *Armstrong*."

Katja? Thomas's heart tightened in his chest. "As XO, sir, I'd be able to ensure that Expeditionary Force 15 is fully recognized for our part in developing and deploying that weapon."

Chandler nodded. "I'll get you out there. Don't let those Research monkeys claim our discovery as their own. The Dark Bomb is our best defense against that Fleet Marshall Investigation."

Message received, Thomas thought to himself. He was being used as a pawn for now, but Chandler had the power to make great things happen in the future. "Thank you, sir. I'm looking forward to it."

"Good." Chandler nodded. "You'll get your orders in the next day or two. Until then, go find that beautiful wife of yours." With a hearty slap on the arm, he strode off.

Thomas glanced around. Soma was nowhere to be seen, and there was no one nearby worth speaking to.

Unconsciously at first—or so he convinced himself—he moved toward Katja. Sidling up to a respectful distance, he watched as a reporter asked her father what appeared to be a concluding question. All eyes were on the patriarch, except for Katja's sister who gave Thomas another, longer glance. She was pretty, he had to admit, and more high-fashion than Katja's blunt, no-nonsense style.

He broke her gaze, reminding himself that he was a married man, and focused instead on the reporter, Chuck Merriman, one of the major war correspondents for ANL. He was impressed that the Emmes family rated so significant a media resource—just a further reminder of the efforts the military was undertaking to bolster its image.

The interview concluded, and Merriman's cameraman gave the all-clear. As one, the members of the Emmes family relaxed and shifted apart, shattering the cozy family image. Katja muttered something to her sister and craned her neck to look through the crowd. Her eyes froze when they reached Thomas.

He smiled and gave her a little wave. Despite his desire to speak to her, he felt his confidence suddenly waver.

She hesitated, eyes locked on him. Her face was stoic, and he felt himself growing tense. Their farewell had been friendly and professional, but that didn't mean everything had been resolved.

Finally she stalked over and reached out.

"Lieutenant Commander Kane—good evening."

"Hi, Katja," he said as he took her tiny hand in his, trying to put as much affection into the shake as he could. "It's nice to see you." She held his grip for a long time, the depths of her dark eyes unreadable. Her lips were pursed tight.

As the silence became awkward, Chuck Merriman approached. Thomas released her hand and smiled automatically for the newsman. Merriman's attention, however, was on Katja.

"Lieutenant Emmes, a moment?" A wry grin lit up his features. "Or, if you prefer, *Miss* Katja? I don't often get surprises like that." It seemed a very strange thing to say, but she relaxed visibly, and looked up at the reporter with the best coy expression Thomas had ever seen from her.

"A woman needs to be able to surprise, Mr. Merriman," she responded. "How else can the news be interesting?"

Merriman's casual amusement expertly covered his searching gaze, Thomas noticed. He doubted anything was ever truly "off the record" with this reporter.

"It's kind of fun to be surprised, actually," Merriman said, and he shrugged. "I thought there was something different about you that day, but I didn't make the connection. I guess your beautiful hair led me astray."

Katja brushed her hair out of her face, the awkward motion revealing how unused she was to doing so. Thomas had only ever known her with a cropped halo, and this new look was fascinating.

"If that's all it takes, Mr. Merriman, you must get distracted often."

The reporter laughed again. "If it's all right, I'd like to do some follow-up interviews with you. The public love human interest stories, and I think a series of pieces following the lives of three serving family members would really be inspiring."

She hesitated, but only for a moment.

"All right," she said, "but I'm not sure where I'm posted next."

"That's fine. My network will liaise with the Astral Force, and I'll find you."

"Well, if I stumble across you again, then I'll know that it's permissible to speak to you—and I'll even use my full name."

He thanked her with a winning smile then nodded to Thomas. "Sorry for interrupting, Lieutenant Commander."

Thomas watched Merriman retreat and turned back to Katja.

"He's right. You do look beautiful."

Her expression immediately hardened.

"Don't start with me, Kane."

He paused. "Sorry," he responded. "I just meant that I like your new hairstyle. Are you going to keep it?"

Her tone lightened. "I doubt it."

"Not too useful under a helmet, I guess."

"I guess." She seemed to sag a bit. This wasn't the Katja he knew. He began watching her carefully.

"You said to Merriman that you don't know where you're posted yet. I figured your regiment would get some down time, after the last year."

"They're being reinforced, and are getting ready to deploy as peacekeepers to another colony."

"Wow. No rest for the wicked."

"I'm not going."

He blinked. Katja turning down an operational tour? A grim suspicion began to form in his mind. "Have you been posted to another unit?"

She glanced over her shoulder, toward her family. None were within earshot, but she stepped in very close to him, barely lifting her eyes.

"I've been deemed unfit for a combat unit. I've been buried in an admin backwater until I sort myself out." Her eyes suddenly shone with moisture and she dropped her gaze. "But how can I sort myself out, sitting around here on Earth when every day I get closer to killing one of these damn civilians?"

Her words solidified his growing suspicion, and suddenly he saw her with new clarity. The deep fatigue in her shoulders propped up by sheer will, the haunted fog in her eyes, the terrible emotion so close to the surface. This was not a healthy Katja Emmes standing in front of him.

He remembered his own state of mind when he'd returned from his first combat tour. The Astral Force worked hard to take care of its troopers, but only if they were willing to be helped.

"It's a tough adjustment to make," he said, "coming home the first time. Did you get any treatment from the docs?"

"I'm drugged right now, Thomas."

And that couldn't continue indefinitely, he knew. She needed to stay busy, in uniform. "Think of your admin posting as a break. With the way things are going, they'll have plenty of work for you on the front line, soon enough."

She considered in silence, then nodded. "Maybe you're right."

"Right about what?" another voice asked, approaching rapidly from behind.

Thomas turned, and nearly stumbled as Soma stepped up and threw an arm around his waist. Her large eyes bore into Katja. He slipped his arm over her shoulders and held her close, taking a champagne flute from the server who had been carrying a tray in Soma's wake. He handed it to her and smiled.

"Just talking shop," he said. "Nothing interesting. This is one of my officers I was telling you about. Lieutenant Katja Emmes. Lieutenant, please allow me to introduce my wife, Soma."

Katja's face shifted into a smiling mask, a single tremble marring her bottom lip. Soma disengaged from him and gently pressed her hand against Katja's shoulder, kissing the air just next to her cheeks.

"Thomas has told me so much about you, Lieutenant Emmes, but he never mentioned how beautiful you are." Her smile was broad, but her eyes were carefully level.

Katja's smile didn't shift. "He spoke often of your beauty, Mrs. Kane, but I see now how inadequate his words were." She dropped her eyes quickly. "I don't mean to intrude, and I should probably get back to my family."

Soma returned to her position against Thomas. "How nice to meet you."

Katja gave him a curt nod. "A pleasure, sir."

Thomas took the second drink from the waiting server and clinked his wife's glass.

"To a happy day."

She smiled and drank, but her gaze surveyed the crowd.

"Oh, there's Chuck!" she said. "We have to say hello." She took his hand and led him toward where Chuck Merriman was chatting with his cameraman. The reporter looked up immediately at their approach. His broad smile returned, and he stepped forward to kiss Soma's cheeks.

"Well, hello, gorgeous," he said. "Who let you onto the planet?" Soma smacked him lightly on the chest and nestled in against Thomas again.

"I married my way on," she replied. "That's how everyone's doing it these days."

Merriman's eyes focused on Thomas, and shifted momentarily toward Katja's departing form before returning. He extended his hand.

"We haven't formally met... Chuck Merriman."

"Thomas Kane. I didn't know my wife was so newsworthy." He gave her a playful squeeze. "Do you have a past I should know about, dear?"

She laughed. "Chuck and I go way back. Where did we first meet—Mars, somewhere?"

He shrugged. "Who knows? I'd say it was a long time ago, but that's impossible because you're so young." She laughed again, then toasted him with her champagne flute before downing it.

"Chuck, you should do a piece on Thomas," she said. "He's a hero from the war."

"I'd be happy to." He gave Thomas an appraising look. "What was your role?" The suddenness of it took him off-guard, but Thomas easily summoned his best look of heroic humility.

"I commanded one of our fast-attack craft. It—" Suddenly Soma interrupted him.

"I think we should make our way toward the displays," she said. "Most of the VIPs are trying for the dramatic backdrop."

Chuck smiled at Thomas as she pushed off into the crowd, headed for the dark, looming shape of the black fast-attack craft.

"Looks like you have your hands full, Thomas," he commented. They started after her through the clumps of chatting people, his cameraman following obediently behind. Thomas tried to keep sight of his tiny wife, ignoring the urge to look out for a tiny blonde in an Astral uniform.

"You have no idea, Chuck."

4

It was late when his rented apartment finally came into sight, and Kete Obadele rubbed his hands across his eyes. The movement didn't go unnoticed.

"The camera implant must really take its toll, Kit," Chuck Merriman said from the driver's seat. "Is your head ready to explode?"

Kete didn't feel the slightest discomfort from the "camera implant"—as a minor subroutine in his overall sensor suite, the visual recorder was almost an afterthought.

The bulk of his mental energy was currently devoted to sorting for later analysis the terabytes of data he'd recorded throughout the gala, accessed via the Terran security sensors. The sheer numbers were giving him ample opportunity to start building a framework theory on how they interacted with one another. It was a tiny first step.

"You get used to it," he replied with a tired smile, "but sometimes I'm so beat I forget to shut it down. That can make for some embarrassing footage."

Chuck laughed and shook his head. "You'll never see me putting computers inside my brain. That's what I have a network for."

The car drifted silently to a stop outside Kete's building. Shops at ground level supported two stories of apartments above. Glass and plastic, the exterior was modern but unremarkable.

Little traffic disturbed the quiet street at this hour, and the only thing Kete heard as he stepped out into the warm, dry air was the distant pulse of a sky shuttle. He looked around casually, scanning for anything unusual, then tucked his head back down through the open car door.

"Thanks for the ride, Chuck," he said. "I'll get the visuals uploaded before morning."

"No worries. I'm just glad the network actually assigned me a dedicated cameraman. I really appreciate you helping me out with this project. I figure it's pretty dull compared to your usual assignments."

Kete gave a friendly laugh. "Sometimes dull is good, my friend—and how can I say no to your boss?"

"If you ever figure it out, let me know." The reporter grinned and gently closed the door. Kete waved and turned toward his building as the silent car moved off down the street.

The paved street. He took a moment to stare at such a Terran artifact. These people had given up wheels on private vehicles more than a hundred years ago. Why they insisted on still blackening their cities with ribbons of crushed rock and poison was just one of the many mysteries to him. An ubiquitous feature few Earthlings ever noticed, to Kete the paved street was one of the most obvious symbols of this culture's ignorant worship of tradition over reality, of pride over prudence.

The common Centauri opinion was that there were Terrans actively trying to destroy the Earth, but he'd spent enough time on this world now to know that most Terrans didn't give it much thought beyond what the State told them to think.

He ascended the outside stairs to the second floor and palm-swiped his lock. His landlord had been surprised when Kete didn't want the usual optical security system, but Kete quickly explained that he was an optically augmented journalist. That had satisfied any objections. Terrans, he knew, generally didn't ask too many questions if you could make your first answer both plausible and slightly exotic.

His apartment was furnished with all the style expected of a man of Kit Moro's wealth, though there was nothing on display that could be called a personal item. As Kete sat down and unlocked the shielded case kept snug underneath the opaque desk table, he felt a moment of pity for Terrans and their requirement to store their memories on external devices.

Still, as a home base this apartment was more than adequate, and it was an excellent place to hide in plain sight. He hoped the other agents were comfortable as well. Eventually, though, he would need to find a more suitable location for the endgame. He had enough respect for the Terran counter-intelligence services, and particularly their ultra-secret Astral Special Forces, to know that complacency on this mission would mean a quick death.

He checked for messages, and only one waited for him, a cryptic verse from his colleague, Valeria Moretti. He smiled, immediately understanding the hidden meaning of her poem. The portable jump gate had been delivered to the drop point. He marveled at her ability to add her own form of low-grade code, in rhyming couplets no less, to the already impenetrable Centauri security systems.

He wasn't sure how he felt about the mission that portable jump gate would support, though. Jump gates were massive, deep-space constructs funded by major government projects— and now Centauria expected him to just create a new one? That mission was thankfully still weeks away. He needed to get some clarity on it.

As he started the upload of this evening's espionage to the Centauri datalink, he summoned images of Rupa and their daughters from the mountain vacation they had taken last year. The girls' shining faces as they played in snow for the first time was a sight that would forever bring a smile to his face. Rupa had been more content to stand on the path, bundled in her long coat and heavy boots, but even she had joined in the inevitable snowball fight. What an arm she'd had! Kete could still almost feel the icy meltwater trickling down the back of his coat.

A sudden mental silence alerted him to the fact that the upload was complete. He resealed the case and purged his own storage net. If he was ever discovered, it was wise not to give the Terrans any idea of what he'd been accumulating. For all their society's backwardness regarding implants, Terran intelligence forces were remarkably adept at deconstructing even a well-defended Centauri mind.

He leaned back in the only comfortable chair in the apartment, and sighed. It had been an exhausting day capping a string of exhausting days. When he'd been called to become Chuck Merriman's cameraman, it had hardly been a surprise. It seemed the previous cameraman had "stopped returning calls," and was nowhere to be found.

Tonight's gala had been the first big test of his synthetically augmented identity chip, and the fact that Kete was still free and alive spoke to the effectiveness of his efforts.

Images of Rupa and the girls still played through his mind, and he indulged for just a moment as his eyes slid closed. Those were happy times, but as he flipped through the recorded pictures, he sensed other images seeping into his mind, like tendrils of smoke. Just wisps at first, hints that grew to envelop his carefully controlled memory access.

Flashes outshone his pictures, and the heavy coat on Rupa faded to that simple, comfortable outfit she'd been wearing that hellish night. The smiles on the girls' faces began to stretch, morphing into screams as memory gave way to nightmare.

"No!"

He opened his eyes and stared around the room, grounding himself in reality. Memory access channels began shutting down automatically, following his pre-set responses alert to dangerous infiltration. Still he was tired, and it was hard to seal all the gaps. The smoke of memory seeped in, and despite all his training, all his discipline as an agent of the Centauri government, he felt his mind slowly, inexorably slipping back...

"Daddy, Daddy! The stars are falling from heaven!"

Kete kept his eyes on the v-ware screen projected at his work station, irritated that his train of thought had been interrupted. He'd promised the girls that he'd come and play as soon as he was finished. Didn't they understand that these interruptions only slowed him down?

"That's great, honey," he called. "Try and catch some for me."

Olivia—at least, he thought it was Olivia—shouted something

back in her usual, excited manner. He was vaguely aware of the thumping of little feet headed out to the deck, but his attention remained on the analysis in front of him.

Reports from the front lines indicated that at least half the Terran fleet was still in port, with perhaps two star forces worth of ships being readied for departure. The combined Centauri-Procyoni squadrons had repelled the latest Terran assault on the jump gates, and the mighty Astral Base Five was effectively out of the fight. Most of the Terran forces scattered through the colonies had been destroyed, but some forces were still unaccounted for, most notably the remains of the expeditionary force in Sirius.

Finding the missing Terran warships wasn't the highest priority, as long as the jump gate accesses were held by friendly forces. Yet it was still Kete's job to find them, and he was determined to help his government tie up that particular loose end while the generals and admirals planned the main assault into Terran space.

Letting his thoughts soar free, he looked and listened for hints that might point the way to the rogue Terran ships. Errant radio signals, unusual bends in spacetime, even subtle shifts in temperature within the Sirian solar system might be enough. He loosed general queries, listened to what drifted back. It was work that required patience, and stillness of mind.

"Daddy! Come and look!"

Kete sighed in frustration. Checking the time, he realized that the girls were already up past their bedtime. Perhaps the war effort could take second place to his family, at least for a short while. He withdrew from the Cloud, locked his secure terminal, and rose from his chair.

It was a short walk through the dining room to the open doors leading out to the deck, and he saw both girls in pajamas, leaning against the railing and staring upward. Rupa was next to them and was looking out toward the night sky with equal rapture. She heard him coming and motioned with interest for him to join them.

The night air was cool. It had lost the crispness of winter, but Kete still shivered slightly in his t-shirt and jeans. He put his arm around Rupa's shoulders and gently pulled her against him, resting his other hand on Olivia's head.

"What's going on?" he asked.

"Look, Daddy!" little Jess cried, pointing all across the southern sky. "Look at the stars!"

At first all he saw were the familiar, twinkling points in the sky, some obscured by the scattered clouds common at this time of year. Then slowly he began to notice motion, like low-orbit ships, but moving very fast. Bolts of light lashed out from these moving stars, occasionally resulting in a sudden flare as bolts met new stars. It was a silent dance of light far above them, and he stood as riveted as his family.

Then, as his gaze drifted down toward the horizon, he saw that some of the stars were moving together. He blinked, wondering if he'd been staring into the electronic ether for too long. No, a large group of tiny stars were moving slowly in the sky, their lengthening tails very low against the dark surface of the world. He held Rupa just a little closer, quickly counting perhaps fifty shooting stars in the tight cluster.

Then a flash tore his eyes away from the distant sight. An orange meteor streaked down from the southern sky, smashing into the valley that stretched away from their ridge-top home. It came so fast and with such silence that Kete for a moment doubted it was real, and then the first explosion ripped upward from the ground. It occurred in a major industrial park, he realized—and then, seconds later, the thunderous fury of sound swept over them like a tidal wave.

Kete instinctively ducked and pulled Rupa down with him. The girls screamed and cowered against the deck. Meteors began to rain from the sky, streaking silently ahead of their colossal sound waves as they burned through the atmosphere to pound down on the industrial park and its surrounding blocks. New bolts of energy began to fire upward from the landscape, but even Kete could tell that they were firing in a blind panic. The relentless bombardment of the industrial park, by contrast, revealed a deadly precision that made Kete's heart go cold.

The bombardment stopped suddenly, but he had already guessed that no reprieve would be coming. The large formation of shooting stars he'd seen on the horizon had faded from view, but in the chaotic light of the burning industrial park he saw the glints of flight and movement. He activated his visual recorder and strained to maximum zoom. Even from his distance of nearly ten kilometers he recognized the dark, boxy forms of Terran drop ships.

"Oh, no, no, no…"

Rupa rose to her knees and clung to his shoulder.

"What is it? What's happening?"

Kete slowly tore his eyes away from the horror he could see on the dark plain below, shutting down his visual augments to look at his wife with his natural eyes. The worry in her gaze turned to raw fear as she saw in him the emotion he was unable to suppress. He'd been an agent of the government for twenty years, had seen the worst of humanity across the star systems, but he'd never imagined that it would come to this.

He'd never imagined it would come here.

"Take the girls," he said, rising to his feet and pulling her up with him. "Get down in the basement and stay there. Don't open the door for anyone except me."

Rupa didn't move. Her mouth hung open in shock. Kete looked again at the valley, saw new flashes of light in and around the industrial park as the Terran troopers fought their way outward onto his home soil. Centauri home soil.

He looked in desperation at his wife. At his precious, innocent daughters. He knew what Terran troops were capable of doing. Olivia and Jess stared up at him in shock, tears trickling down their cheeks. Rupa touched his arm.

"Kete, what's happening?"

He leaned in to her, pointing down toward what he now realized was the Terran landing zone.

"Terra is here," he said, trying to keep his voice calm. "I don't know how, but they're here. Their troops are on the ground, and probably headed this way." He scooped up Jess, handed her to Rupa and then hefted Olivia into his own arms. "Get to the basement and stay down there. Things are going to get very dangerous up at street level."

He strode inside, Olivia unresisting in his arms. The stairs to the basement were only seconds away and he pounded down them into the relative safety of the dug-out, foundation-reinforced space. Rupa was close behind him, depositing Jess in the soft, teddy bear chair before wiping tears from her cheeks.

"Where are you going?"

He kissed Olivia and placed her in a chair next to her favorite doll-house table.

"I have to get to the local militia barracks."

"No! God, no!" Rupa's tears flowed freely. "Stay with us."

There wasn't time for sentiment. The Terrans were coming.

"I have to, you know that," he said. "But the robotic army already will be deploying, so I'll just be guarding the command posts. The machines will take them down."

Rupa cringed visibly at the mention of Centauri's own war machines, those nightmare robotic beasts that supposedly made war more "humane." Before his wife could recover her wits, Kete crouched down and gave Olivia a hug and a kiss.

"Daddy has to go and see what's happening, but you stay down here with Mummy. Okay?" The girl was too stunned to reply. Kete immediately moved to embrace the younger Jess. "It's too noisy upstairs right now, so you stay here with Mummy and Olivia, okay?"

Jess nodded dumbly, automatically throwing her arms around him in a hug. He held her tight for a long, sweet moment, then rose to kiss his wife. There were no more words either of them could say. She tried to smile. He kissed her again and, with one last look at his entire world, raced back up the stairs.

He blinked in the darkness of his Terran apartment, fighting down the nightmare. The room was flooded with shadow.

Pulling himself up from the chair, he stumbled through to the kitchen for some water. He hated losing control of his mind, hated the need of his grief to relive that terrifying, terrible night back in Centauria. He clung to the images of Rupa, Olivia, and Jess. It was for them he had come here. For them he would happily risk everything he had left to bring down the Terran State.

As he gratefully sipped at a glass of cool water, he refocused his mind on the mission. This was a war of civilizations, a war Centauria was determined to wage for the sake of all humankind. The first part of this war had foolishly been fought on Terra's terms. The next part would be on Centauria's and—

The glass slipped from his hand, clunking against the counter and spilling forth its contents. The Astral Force officer Chuck had interviewed this evening. Kete hadn't recognized her through the long hair and different clothes, but he had seen her before.

The angel of death had a name.

Lieutenant Katja Emmes.

5

The concussion knocked Katja to her knees. Ears ringing, she frantically grabbed for her assault rifle. Through blurred vision she assessed the jumble of movements to her left as a crowd of charging civilians.

"Get back!" she screamed, blindly pointing her rifle at them.

The mob surged forward. She struggled to her feet, firing warning shots into the group. Single bodies burst open as the exploding rounds impacted, but the mass of rebellious colonists closed relentlessly. Her vision cleared, and she saw the hatred in their eyes. But she felt no fear—only pity. She knew what was coming next.

Like orange meteors, the orbital bombardment shells struck down, obliterating the street and vaporizing the crowd. Katja tried to run, but her legs were leaden. The bombardment continued, blasts raining ever closer. She forced her legs to move, and with agonizing slowness she backed away from the onslaught, but not fast enough.

Never fast enough.

The last orbital blast struck the ground in front of her. A wall of super-heated air slammed her backward into the darkness. She didn't know if her scream was out loud or not. There was no echo off the walls.

* * *

She paused, feeling soft, cushioned fabric against her cheek. The dazzling light hadn't faded, but was suddenly more yellow, more real. She winced against the brightness, and exhaled deeply at the pounding in her head.

Slowly, slowly, the nightmare images faded from her mind. Dead civilians. Smashed machinery. Orbital bombardment.

With effort, she pushed herself to a sitting position on the couch, holding up a hand to block the glare from the broad window across from her. Eyes down, she saw that she was still wearing her polished black shoes and dress pants from the gala. Her tunic lay heaped on the floor by the armchair. At first glance nothing looked ruined, she assessed with relief.

Her gaze rose further, taking in the room. Comfortable but less-than-stylish furniture formed a seating area.

Adjacent kitchen with breakfast bar.

Two closed doors leading to bedroom and bathroom.

A beautiful view of Longreach through the giant window. Private officer quarters at the surface component of Astral Base One.

She sighed.

The bedroom door opened to reveal Merje tying the belt of the standard-issue bathrobe that had no doubt been supplied with the suite. Her long, blonde hair was twisted grotesquely by a combination of product and restless sleep, but her eyes were bright with concern.

"You okay?"

Katja nodded slightly. Apparently her scream hadn't been just part of the dream. She blinked again to shake off the last of the images, not wanting to think of how many times she'd seen them in the night. She pulled free the hair that was sticking to her cheek and rose with a long, deep breath.

Merje crossed to the window and gazed outward.

"Beautiful city you have here," she said. "Wish I could stay."

Katja shuffled over to join her. The sun was already overhead in the cloudless sky, pouring its heat and glare down on the curving skyline of Earth's first spaceport. The vast, artificial reservoir—rather unimaginatively named by the State as Lake Sapphire—was a deep-blue centerpiece among the red architecture, with lines of green marking the pedestrian thoroughfares in the central core. In the distance, the city gave way to the stark beauty of the Australian Outback, but here in the well-to-do Astral quarter, residents could enjoy all the comforts of a modern metropolis.

Most of the local State buildings were here, and to Katja's right the scene was dominated by the six, perfectly straight military elevator lines that stretched upward two thousand kilometers to the orbiting behemoth known as Astral Base One. Their presence helped make Longreach the planet's center of commerce, and most of the Earth's corporations and banking entities maintained their headquarters within the city complex. Behind her rested the sweeping grounds of the Astral College. It was her alma mater, and had been home for four years.

Her eyes protested against the sunlight and she dragged herself over to one of the raised chairs at the breakfast bar.

"What time is it?"

"About lunchtime," Merje said, passing her on the way to the fridge. "Does the Fleet stock your room with food too?"

An open, empty fridge offered a silent reply, and Katja looked to the appliances on the counter.

"There's coffee," she said. "Make me some too."

She rubbed her eyes slowly, listening to the quiet clicks and whirrs as Merje operated the coffee machine. Moments later she breathed in the deep, comforting aroma of a fresh cup and smiled as Merje handed it to her.

"You know," Merje said, partly hiding her wry expression behind her mug as she sipped her own coffee, "I think we would have done better last night if you hadn't knocked that guy on his ass."

Katja frowned, then recalled the pair of teachers—at least, that was their story—who had been very generous with drinks at the club to which Merje had dragged her. They'd been fairly cute, she recalled, and not particularly boorish, and she remembered appreciating the flattering attention of a man. Why *had* she straight-armed him right off his chair?

"At least now I can tell all the folks back at the firm that I've had a gun pointed at me." Merje leaned up against the counter across from her, wry smile still in place. "But for next time, I'm happy to stay the nerd. You're the scary one, remember?"

Katja was still puzzling over why she'd hit the man. "They were just stun guns," she said absently, "every bouncer has one."

"I know what they are. I've just never had one pointed at me before."

"Did those two guys get kicked out as well?"

"Nope. Just us, honey. We are so bad-ass."

Katja chewed her lip in thought. "So the guy didn't provoke me?"

"Not that I saw. I was hoping you'd tell me."

Her mind was a complete blank. "I don't know."

Merje straightened and rounded the counter, heading for the armchair and activating the TV wall. Katja turned in her seat, trying to guess her sister's mood as the familiar chatter of the 24-hour news network softly filled the room, but her hung-over brain still struggled.

Why had she hit a complete stranger?

"Up until then," Merje said, "it was quite a pleasant evening. I even liked the gala. The Fleet sure puts on a good spread."

Annoyance flickered through her. Everyone was calling the Astral Force "the Fleet" these days, as if the vacuum-heads were the only thing that mattered. It was the Corps that had invaded the Centauri homeworld, troopers like her who had carved the name Expeditionary Force 15 into the history books. But as she watched the images drift by on the TV screen, shot after shot highlighted Fleet warships patrolling majestically in low orbit.

Apparently the newly minted Admiral Chandler was giving yet another interview, no doubt drinking in the honors showered upon him as a hero of the war. Katja had yet to see a single mention of those who had been at the bloody end of the business in the attack on Abeona. If anything, the Corps had done more than the Fleet to safeguard Terran interests, but the media loved those big, shiny ships…

"And there was plenty of talent, too," Merje was saying. "Your boys scrub up nice in their uniforms." She reached over and grabbed Katja's abandoned tunic, tossing it up onto the couch. "Especially that yummy biscuit you were talking to so intimately. Who was that guy, the one you dashed off with right after our interview?"

Katja's cheeks flushed, and blood pounded in her ears. Suddenly everything fell into place. That guy at the club had made a comment about returning war veterans, and how they were getting all kinds of extra privileges for not having done much.

"Thomas Kane," she muttered. "He was my CO, and he's doing pretty well for himself." Like getting married into the plutocracy, and getting some cushy job on his rise to the top. And getting *married*. *Damn you, you bastard.*

Merje sipped her coffee. "Hmm." Katja glanced up. Her sister was watching her with a carefully neutral expression, soft eyes probing.

"What?"

"Nothing." Merje shook her head and smiled. "Good for him."

Katja dropped her gaze, annoyed that her cheeks still burned. Merje was too perceptive sometimes. She flicked the hair out of her face again and downed her coffee.

"I'm going to have a shower."

Merje nodded absently, eyes on the news. "How much longer can I crash here?"

"I'm on leave for five more days." She wondered how much more "fun" she could endure before donning her uniform once again. "They'll kick you out of here when I head back to my post."

"Maybe I'll just find myself a cute Fleet boy, and stay longer."

Katja wondered who would be more at risk—Merje or the Astral Force.

Toothpaste, soap, and extended hot water combined to liberate Katja from most of her headache and general crappiness. When she re-emerged into the sunshine of the living room, wearing the brightly patterned sundress she'd bought on a whim yesterday, she almost felt ready to smile.

Merje was still watching the news, but her upright position, forward in the chair, indicated more than a passing interest.

"They were just talking about the Astral trial we were handling," she said without taking her eyes off the screen. "The firm is getting some amazing publicity over this."

Any thoughts of smiling disappeared. Katja fought down new anger.

"So what part did you play in that, exactly?"

"I did a lot of the research, and I helped prep the defendant for being on the stand."

Merje hadn't personally defended that mutineer, Katja reminded herself. She supposed that made it *somewhat* better.

"But there's still all this chatter on the networks about the violence coming to Terra one day," Merje muttered. "Why can't people just accept that there was no actual war, and that it's over?"

"What do you mean there was no war?"

"It was a police action, right? Some colonists rebelled and you brave servants of Terra sorted them out."

Katja felt the sudden need to put some space between herself and her sister.

"I'm heading down to the cafeteria," she said abruptly. "You want anything?"

"Just bring me back some fruit or something." Suddenly Merje turned. "Oh, and can you bring me back yesterday evening where I *don't* get a gun pointed at me?" Her smile had that slight edge to it Katja had learned to back away from.

The corridor outside was open to the dry, warm air, and offered a spectacular view across the irrigated playing fields toward the Astral College buildings. A mixture of dark, solar-glass and local red stone, the main buildings sat at the top of a gentle rise looking every bit the elite scholastic institution. Smaller buildings on the far side of the playing fields housed the shooting ranges, and down near the shores of Lake Sapphire were the stubby boat sheds.

Katja took a moment to drink it in, the dusty smell of the Outback conjuring memories of the simpler, happier times of her cadet years. Then she dismissed the notion and walked with purpose toward the elevator. Her college years had been neither simple nor happy—they just seemed so in comparison to life today.

A swift ride down and she found herself strolling into the large, economically furnished dining hall made available to all residents in her building. The lunchtime rush was waning, but most of the tables were still occupied by junior officers from both Fleet and Corps. Many were in uniform, and Katja wondered for a moment if she was breaking some new regulation by dining in her bright, summery outfit. A few patrons were clustered in amiable groups, but most dined alone, hardly glancing up at those forced to share their table. Most were transients like her, she knew, but some poor sods found themselves living here for months while on a course or while waiting for their ship to return.

None of the food options particularly excited her, but she knew she had to start eating properly if she was going to get back into fighting shape. She piled her plate with proteins and vitamins and found a spare seat at a nearby table. Those already seated barely took notice. One Fleet lieutenant did smile at her, but she noticed that his eyes spent more time on her figure than her face, and she ignored his overture. The steak and chicken on her plate was the only sort of meat she was interested in right now.

She was just shoveling the last awkward lettuce leaf into her mouth when laughter from a nearby table caught her ear. It wasn't the first outburst she'd heard over the general din of the cafeteria, but something familiar about it caused her eyes to snap up.

Two tables away, a group of very young officers was just breaking apart as their meal drew to a close. Little more than children, she reckoned they were less than a year out of the College and probably still in training. One in particular drew her gaze as he rose to his feet, his laughter just fading.

He was stocky in his blue Fleet coveralls, and not overly tall. His brown hair was shaggy by regulation standards, but she wasn't too surprised as she noticed the single bar on each shoulder and wings on his chest that declared him a sublieutenant pilot. The other subbies at the table were all watching him, hanging on the words he said just too quietly for her to hear. A roar of laughter followed, and he waved in farewell as he turned to leave.

Katja suddenly recognized him—could hardly believe his transformation—and launched herself from her chair to follow him toward the exit. Her movement caught his eye, and his glance lingered upon her slightly longer than it might have. When he noticed her gaze back at him he averted his eyes shyly, and continued to walk.

"Excuse me, are you a pilot?" She strode up, feeling a smile burst across her features, and touched his arm. He turned in surprise, unconsciously looking her up and down.

"Uhh, yeah. I'm Jack Mallory. I'm a pilot." There was no recognition in his eyes, but he tried to return her smile. "Why would a pretty lady like you want to know?"

She took a step back and put her hands on her hips.

"I'm Katja Emmes. I'm a Strike officer, and I *still* might shoot you if you give me a reason."

Dawning comprehension broke awkwardly over his features, and his cheeks paled perceptibly.

"Oh... I'm so sorry, ma'am! I didn't recognize you with..." His voice trailed off as he gestured broadly at her appearance. "Where did you get that hair?"

There was something unique, she suddenly realized, about the bonds formed in combat. Jack was still the punk kid who spent more time thinking about tits than tactics, but damn, it was good to see him.

She reached out and gently touched his cheek.

"I barely recognized *you*, Subbie," she said. "The plastic surgeons did a great job."

He moved his head to break physical contact with her, his own hand brushing quickly over his face.

"Yeah... It's good to be me again."

Not the carefree response she'd expected. She nodded back toward his table.

"Were those friends of yours from the College?"

"Not friends so much, just some guys a year behind me. They're in the middle of flight training now, and wanted to hear the war stories."

"That must be fun, impressing the boys from back home."

Jack shrugged. "It's easy to impress folks who weren't there." His eyes suddenly searched hers, and she nodded. Trying to tell an outsider what real combat was like...

"It can be hard to talk about."

"I guess it gets easier?"

This was a thought pattern she had lived in fear of since the day she returned, and she shoved it down quickly. Change of subject.

"Are you just passing through Longreach?"

He frowned. "No, I'm posted to some stupid Research ship.

They sent me there because of my operational experience with the Dark Bomb, but as usual nobody's listening to me."

"Which ship?"

"*Neil Armstrong*. We've been in and out half a dozen times since I joined, but I don't think we've actually done any real data collection—and they just don't run things like we did."

Katja listened as Jack described what sounded like a fairly dysfunctional command structure, from the distracted CO to the power-hungry science officer. He lost her pretty quickly when he started to explain the purpose of their core research assignment, which was to investigate the depths of the Bulk and how dark energy could be manipulated in a semi-controlled fashion.... blah blah blah. But Jack's ship, it seemed, was the Astral Force's vanguard for Dark Bomb research.

At least he was doing something important.

As she watched him, she began to notice something very strange. His face had been rebuilt by Astral surgeons, no doubt to match his appearance before his capture and torture, and while his features possessed perfect symmetry and form, she realized that there was something lifeless about them. His eyes still shone as always, and every part of his face moved as it should, but without vitality. It was like looking at a particularly clever simulation.

It was hard to watch without remembering the violence that had caused it. This kid had been forced to bear the psychological scars of war for the rest of his life. Apparently he would bear the physical scars as well.

The nightmare started to seep into her conscious mind again, and she angrily fought it down. Maybe hanging out with her wartime colleagues wasn't the best thing for her right now. She clasped him in a quick hug.

"Listen, I gotta go," she said abruptly. "Take care of yourself, Subbie." Barely feeling his hands brush against her, she turned and fled. His face, the memories, the dreams.

She suddenly hated her new dress and comfy shoes. She hated the smell of product in her hair. She hated her entire existence. As soon as she got back to her room she was canceling the rest of her leave and heading back to that administrative backwater to which she'd been posted.

6

Understanding five-dimensional spacetime wasn't easy. Sublieutenant Jack Mallory knew this well enough. He also knew that a single combat tour and a bachelor's degree in Physics & Philosophy didn't make him an expert. Nevertheless, he wasn't used to feeling quite this useless.

He scanned the flight controls of his Hawk, glanced at the inactive monitors for his extra-dimensional sensors and, with a sigh, stared out again through the cockpit polyglass at the starry abyss. He'd always imagined that he'd learn to recognize the different colonies by their starscapes, but after training in Terra, deployments to Sirius and Centauria, and now back on home turf, he'd come to the sad conclusion that stars looked the same no matter where you went. Even this far south of the Solar System's ecliptic, billions of kilometers from the usual shipping lanes, he might as well have been sitting on a rooftop on Earth.

Behind him, in the main cabin of the Hawk, the scientists were starting to raise their voices at each other. Jack guessed the package still wasn't ready for deployment. They'd launched from the *Neil Armstrong* more than three hours ago, made a quick sprint to clear from the ship's gravimetric signature, and then set up to launch a series of probes. But apparently there was still disagreement over the settings for the receivers. Still, after three hours.

There wasn't even anything for him to keep busy with as the

pilot. The engines were idling, the ship drifting on inertia so as not to hinder the experiment with any accelerations. His usual flight sensors were set to their lowest power setting, capable of little more than telling him when the Hawk was about to crash into something. The hunt sensors, his primary warfare suite, were completely powered down.

The day's experiment was designed to test some ivory tower hypothesis about massive interactions in the Bulk—that hidden, fourth spatial dimension invisible to the regular human experience—and the scientists didn't want any military sensors "mucking things up." Jack had learned to trust his hunt controls with his life, and he doubted anything the scientists had was any better.

At least they were finally doing an experiment that actually involved the Bulk. It had been pretty exciting to learn that he'd been assigned to a Research ship charged with uncovering the underlying warped-geometric laws that had been revealed by his little idea during the breakout from Centauria. He'd expected to join a team of extra-dimensional specialists keen on hearing about his real-world experience, but so far, after three weeks on board, all he'd seen was a bunch of people who argued a lot and seemed to spend most of their time working on research for improving power generation.

Listening to their discussion now, he wondered whether he should dust off one of his first year Physics & Philosophy texts, and start providing some education.

The waiting was getting painful, and it suddenly occurred to him how even he, a humble pilot, could help move things along. He did another routine sweep of his controls, then unstrapped from his seat. It wasn't like there was much traffic way out here to worry about. He swung himself around, and peered back into the main compartment.

He had three passengers today—the best and brightest of *Armstrong*'s science staff—all moving with the awkwardness of those used to the comfort of a ship with artificial gravity. Chief Lopez was floating near one of the control panels, typing instructions. He had a tight, red face. Lieutenant Helena Grey hovered over him, watching the screen very carefully. She was the ship's science officer, which apparently made her the most brilliant scientist too. At least, it seemed as if every academic discussion eventually went her way.

Jack stole a glance at his third passenger, Sublieutenant Amanda Smith. She caught his eye and smiled, her bright eyes revealing a mixture of apology and sad humor. He smiled quickly and looked away. A subbie like him, she was about his age and was one of the only people who actually chatted with him when off-duty.

"Hey, guys." He drifted slowly aft into the main cabin. "I had an idea about how I could help out."

Helena looked up in irritation. "I'll tell you when we're ready."

Jack gestured back toward the cockpit. "We've only got so much fuel. I was just thinking that maybe I could start sowing the probes now, while you get set up."

Helena rolled her eyes. "No," she said. "When you set up an experiment you don't mess with the environment. You don't start it with fluid parameters and you wait... Until. Everything's. Ready."

Jack fought down his frustration and glided back to his seat. If he'd waited until he was "ready" before launching gravitorpedoes on the Centauri stealth ships...

He checked the flight controls, hunt controls, and the visual. Then he noticed Amanda floating into his peripheral. She still wore a pretty smile, even though her face was heavy with fatigue. Between work, standing watch, and studying, Jack doubted she had any time to sleep.

"Don't worry." She placed her hand on his shoulder. "They don't listen to me either."

He tried to laugh. "Maybe when you finally get your PhD you'll be taken seriously."

Her smile vanished. "Point taken." Looking more tired than ever, she pushed off and retreated into the main compartment.

He sighed, amazed anew at his ability for obtuseness, and nervous habit drew his hand across his face. Even six weeks after the surgery, he still expected to feel the unnatural bumps of re-knitted bone. No scars, the doctors had said. No one would ever know.

He saw his reflection in one of the blank screens on his hunt controls. His unruly brown hair was the same, his eyes were still his, and the muscles in his reconstructed face all moved appropriately… but it *wasn't* him. It never would be again.

The scream of the collision alarm jolted him from his thoughts. A small craft was bearing down on the Hawk at high speed.

How long had it been there?

There was no time to assess.

He grabbed the stick, yanked hard to starboard and pushed the throttles forward. G-forces tried to wrench him from his seat and he vaguely heard crashes and shouts behind him. The incoming craft flashed past. He reversed his turn and hauled around to port, straining to get a visual. He saw a single, obscuring shadow moving right to left against the backdrop of stars, and he tightened his turn to intercept, flipping his external communications circuit.

"Unknown vessel, this is Terran Warship Eagle-One," he said tersely. "State your intentions, over."

No response filtered through the faint crackle of deep space, but he saw sunlight flicker off an edge of the shadow, indicating an aspect shift. A new alarm flashed on his console. He was being radiated.

He flicked open the countermeasures switch and pressed the button. The Hawk's hull shuddered three times as chaff and flares roared from their launchers. Somebody behind him screamed.

"Unknown vessel," he repeated, "this is Terran Warship Eagle-One. Break off your approach or I will fire upon you."

A tiny voice at the back of his mind reminded him that a Hawk didn't really rate being called a warship, and more importantly this research bird didn't carry any weapons. Jack ignored it, activated his hunt controls, and swept into a diving attack vector, calculating when to release flares so he could hit the target as he passed. A hand grabbed the back of his seat. Helena pulled herself, wide-eyed and sweating, into Jack's view.

"What the hell are you doing?"

Jack didn't take his eyes off the target. "Unknown vessel came at us on a collision course, no response to hails, lit us up with possible fire-control radar. I'm warning him off."

Helena sputtered something incoherent. Jack looked at his flight controls and refined his timing for the flare launch. The enemy craft broke away suddenly and increased speed. Jack confirmed that it was heading away from *Neil Armstrong* and pulled back from his attack. It seemed like his bluff had worked, and since he didn't actually have any weapons, there was no sense in pushing his luck.

Helena was staring at him with something that looked almost like fear. It took her a long moment to find her voice.

"What did you just do?"

Jack didn't bother repeating his previous tactical report. He sensed that Helena's question was of a much larger nature.

"Uhh, I defended the ship."

"Against what? That was a civilian craft you just buzzed."

This wasn't the reaction he'd expected. "Actually, they buzzed us."

"Did they? Or were we just two ships crossing in the same area of space?"

Jack considered, and realized with a sinking heart that he'd been too busy lamenting his reconstructed face to pay attention.

"I don't know," he admitted, "but they shone a fire-control radar at us."

Helena's face went blank for a moment. "How can you tell?"

He pointed at the EM alarm. Helena's eyes followed but she clearly didn't understand. Amanda appeared on Jack's other side, holding a bandage to her blood-matted hair.

"The equipment's zeroized from all the shaking," she said. "It's going to take a few hours to reset."

Helena smacked a hand against Jack's seat. "*Dammit.*" She rubbed her eyes and exhaled slowly. "Okay, hot-shot, you've ruined the day's work, caused injuries, and probably scared the hell out of some local. Take us back to the ship."

Jack obliged with a sinking heart, locking in on *Armstrong*'s beacon. He looked back to see if Amanda was all right, but she'd retreated to the very after end of the cabin. His flight controls, now at full power, showed the unknown craft still racing away at high speed, and as the adrenaline rush began to ease, he wondered just how badly he'd screwed up.

* * *

"I think you did exactly the right thing."

Jack looked up from his glass of water, surprised. Thomas Kane had listened silently during his entire recounting of the incident, moving from his seat only moments ago to collect some of the fresh dessert that had just been laid out by the cooks. He spoke over his shoulder.

He took a sip, glancing around the wardroom to ensure Thomas was speaking to him.

"Really?"

"Absolutely." His calm baritone voice was as reassuring as ever.

"I figured I just flashed back to war-mode, and overreacted."

"Maybe."

"But that's not so good when we're in our home system, on a peaceful science mission."

Thomas strolled back from the duff table, a plate of dessert in each hand. "You did absolutely the right thing, Jack. Just in absolutely the wrong place." His easy smile robbed the words of malice. "Terra's been cleared of the last of the rebels, and the Fleet is camped out at the remaining jump gates, but things are still pretty raw, and I'd rather have a stranger in my sights than wind up in his."

Jack laughed. "No worries about my causing too much damage. *Armstrong*'s Hawks are about as well-armed as my mom's new fridge."

Thomas nodded wryly. "Just be glad you didn't have Katja in the Hawk with you. She'd have suited up and boarded the bastard."

He laughed again, still trying to reconcile his memories of that scary trooper with the beautiful woman he'd met in the cafeteria Earthside. Her tender hug was a long way from their first embrace, when she'd hauled his broken body off the ground in Sirius and carried him to safety. Even so, he couldn't help but think it was kind of the same sentiment.

"Have you seen her since we got back?" he asked.

Thomas took a bite of his cake and chewed, glancing away. He nodded, swallowing.

"She was at the big military gala with her family."

"She looks great out of her uniform."

A sharp look. "What?"

"In civvies. She's grown her hair too."

Thomas nodded strangely. "Yeah, it looks nice."

Jack appreciated having Thomas on board. If not exactly a friend—their relative seniorities were more than fifteen years apart—he was at least a familiar face. And with Thomas as the acting-XO of this Research ship, Jack had at least some confidence that the mission would make sense.

The door from the passageway slid open, admitting two members of the science department. Amanda glanced at Jack briefly then took a seat at the far end of the room. Petty Officer Li approached and starting pushing one of the couches up against the bulkhead.

Thomas looked over his shoulder. "Do you need us to move?"

Li nodded. "Sorry, sir. I need to set up for a science department meeting."

Jack searched his memory for any staff meetings today as Thomas rose and pushed his chair back against the bulkhead. Jack knew he still wasn't that great at figuring out this ship's routine, but he could have sworn that staff meetings were always just after breakfast. He glanced at his watch. Mid-afternoon.

Thomas seemed to be reading his mind. He leaned in and spoke quietly.

"Good luck with the meeting, Jack. Remember: you did the right thing." Clearing his duff plate to the galley window, Thomas left the wardroom. Not technically part of the science department, his casual presence as the second-in-command wouldn't be appreciated by the science officer.

Li finished arranging the furniture into a hollow square and sat down. He glanced over at Jack with an odd expression.

"Playing fighter-jock this morning, sir?"

Jack shrugged. "He came right at me in a classic attack maneuver."

The petty officer just shook his head and looked away. "Whatever," he said. "No civvy would touch an AF ship."

The wardroom filled quickly, and before long Jack counted fifteen crew members present, including himself, Amanda, Chief Lopez, all three petty officers, and the rest of the department. He noticed that they seemed to cluster at the other end of the room, and he suddenly sensed a distinct separation between himself and everyone else.

Helena burst in, not even sitting down.

"Well, this morning was wasted. Not only did Lopez put in the wrong settings, but then Mallory over there screwed up all our equipment with his idiot stunt. We're going to have to amend the entire schedule." She threw down a display pad on the central coffee table. "I've just spent an hour going over the next few days, and I don't know when we're going to find the time."

All eyes lingered on the pad where it lay. Helena's gaze moved angrily across the room.

"Well?" she said. "Any brilliant suggestions?"

Jack mentally reviewed the flying schedule for the next few days. There was some routine maintenance on the Hawk that could wait until after he'd ferried some of the crew to Astral Base Three.

"Ma'am, I can squeeze in an extra flying window the day after tomorrow, just before I transfer our passengers at Ganymede," he offered. "That would give us about four hours—"

"Great," she said. "So we could try and conduct our Bulk experiments in the biggest planetary gravity well in Terra. Why don't we just fly right into the sun and be done with it?"

Jack frowned—he hadn't thought of that. "Right. Sorry. It has to be done in minimum curvature, no more than..." He searched his memory. "Two percent radial."

Amanda began to speak, but Helena rolled right over her.

"You know what, Jack?" she snapped. "I am sick of your sarcasm, and I am sick of your cowboy attitude as to what this ship does."

Jack felt like he'd been physically struck. Where did that come from? He tried his best to smile.

"Sorry, ma'am. I'm just trying to understand."

Helena's face went a dangerous shade of red.

"Wipe that smirk off your face, and don't try and suck up to me. I get enough of that from Smith." She jerked a dismissive hand at the junior science officer.

Amanda's jaw dropped, tired eyes blinking in shock.

Helena threw up her hands. "Honestly, with Lopez and his pet theories, Smith and her stupid questions, and a pilot who can't even fly straight—"

"Ma'am," Lopez raised a cautioning hand. "Please."

Helena paused, clearly reining in her anger. "Well, I'm frustrated." She tapped the pad on the table. "You people need to sort out the program and get our schedule back on line. I have a meeting with Admiral Bush at the end of this week, and I'd better have something good to tell him." She gave a last menacing glare, and departed.

Silence descended again. Li eventually swore to himself and the crew members started muttering to each other. No one made any move to look at the pad. In Jack's experience, the chief petty officer usually took charge at moments like this, but Lopez just sat frowning with his head resting on his fists. Jack looked carefully at Amanda, hoping to see some life, but her frame sagged back against the couch.

With Helena gone and Thomas not involved, there were no lieutenants present, but someone had to take charge.

Jack waited.

Finally, Li hauled himself to his feet—but all he did was head for the door.

"Well, I got shit to do."

His movement broke the spell, and the crew started to lift themselves from their seats. Jack stood quickly.

"Hey, hey—hang on, guys!" he said loudly. "We still gotta solve this problem. That experiment has to get done." He knew it was his actions that had ruined the morning, and the last thing he needed was this problem to stick around and give Helena even more reason to hate him.

Everyone more or less paused, and some even looked at him expectantly. Lopez finally roused himself and reached for the pad. Amanda looked up with the first glimmer of interest.

Lopez held the pad up. "You got any ideas, sir?"

He took the display and quickly scanned the operations schedule. Most of it was meaningless milspeak, but he knew enough to recognize when one event ended and another started.

"Uhhh..."

The petty officers who had momentarily paused turned again for the door. Lopez watched Jack for a moment, then started to gather up his gear.

Jack took a wild stab at it.

"Umm, who's the... C.E.R.A.?"

One of the petty officers stopped. Jack thought his name was Singh. The man just gave him a withering stare.

"Are you kidding me?"

"No, why?"

"The Chief Engine Room Artificer," Singh replied, condescension thick in his voice. "Have you even been on a ship before?"

Jack brushed off the disdain in the hope of making progress.

"Yeah, a couple," he replied, "but I fly a lot. Anyway, what's this serial the Chief has scheduled tomorrow afternoon—delaying drills?"

Singh shared a smug scoff with the other petty officers. "It's when they do drills in the engine room. That's the big room where they keep the thing that makes us move."

"So can we fly at the same time?"

"You can do whatever the hell you want. Just don't ask for sudden bursts of power."

With cautious excitement he looked to Amanda.

"Can you have your experiment ready to go for then?"

She sighed. "Yeah, but there's a rule about launching a Hawk during delaying drills. It's a sensitive maneuver when power's unreliable. We never do it."

He looked back at Singh. "I'll only need two or three minutes to get through the airlock. Can you talk to the Chief, and ask him to guarantee me stable power for that long?"

Crossed arms. "No."

"Yes." Lopez stood. "Just get your bird launched on time at the start of the serial, sir. We'll coordinate with Engineering." A glare quelled the imminent protest from Singh.

Jack handed the schedule to Amanda. "Does our experiment conflict with this serial that happens right before it?"

She shook her head. "They're unrelated... but let me check with the captain." Glances passed between all assembled, then the department members filed out with body language Jack recognized as, if not actually agreement, at least not disagreement. He risked another glance at Amanda, trying to guess her mood.

"Sorry about your head."

She shrugged, eyes focused on the deck. "It's not bad... but I think you overreacted a bit."

He swallowed back sudden frustration. Why did everyone here think it was such a big deal? Didn't they realize the Astral Force had just been in a war? He decided maybe a quick lesson in tactics would help.

"I'm not so sure about that," he said. "It was pretty strange that he wasn't broadcasting his beacon, and if he'd had regular flight sensors active, he'd never have gotten that close to us. His whole flight pattern was suspicious."

"Like deep-space pilots always obey the rules." Amanda shrugged dismissively. "He was probably trying to conserve power."

He discarded his retort, suddenly recognizing her disinterest in continuing the conversation.

"Maybe," he allowed. "Either way I screwed up your experiment, and I'd like to help."

She finally looked up. "Thanks. I don't hear that too often these days."

As a fellow subbie, he felt for her. "This isn't a very happy ship, is it?"

"I don't know. It's my first."

"But have people always been like this on board?"

"Yeah, pretty much."

He smiled. "Well, for the record, I've never heard you ask a stupid question, and I ask them all the time." He gestured toward where Singh had stood. "But if I ask enough of them, I usually find my way."

She smiled back, and Jack saw a slight sparkle in her eyes again.

"Well, let's get this experiment re-scheduled."

As he followed her out the door, suddenly he didn't feel quite so useless.

7

Kete really wondered how Terrans accomplished as much as they did. Having chosen as a society to remain "unplugged," they were forced as individuals to focus on little more than one thing at a time, and as a group had only linear communication methods with which to collaborate.

Throw enough money, resources, and sheer, raw power into the mix, and he supposed just about any problem could be fixed, but with such inefficiency. He only had to look past the lush, irrigated parks around Lake Sapphire to see the dead and deserted Outback, and get a sense of how much damage Terrans had done to humanity's homeworld in their quest for dominance and control.

It was satisfyingly ironic, then, that he could use their inefficiencies—and indeed their raw power—to search effortlessly through their society. His mission remained the priority, and it was complex enough, but his task had taken on yet another element, now that he knew the identity of his family's murderer.

Katja Emmes wasn't going to be a distraction though. She was just another element of the overall plan Kete drew together, another subject for consideration as he hijacked the badly secured, omnidimensional government communications channels that burned so hot through the Terran proto-Cloud, a Centauri child could have tapped into them.

He had spent several weeks sifting through these channels,

studying the Terran mood as the war faded quickly from the collective consciousness, searching through those details of Astral Force personnel records that were free to the public. He pieced together hypotheses about the behavior of critical State offices and individuals, and ran scenarios to try and predict the various outcomes.

This stage now complete, he found himself strolling toward a deli located just off one of the main pedestrian boulevards in downtown Longreach. Sunlight sparkled off the waves on Lake Sapphire, the reservoir disturbed by dozens of pleasure craft. He noted the straight, utilitarian State bureaucracy buildings, located just beyond the bustling boardwalk, and wondered if they might serve well for the first strike.

The ultimate goal was easy to see.

His clothes were new that morning from one of the most exclusive men's stores in the district. Subtle, even unremarkable to the casual observer, they spoke of easy confidence and extremely deep pockets to those in the know—and his target was in the know.

The deli was popular with the well-paid professionals of the downtown core, but it also attracted its share of Astral Force personnel. As Kete stepped into the cool interior of the restaurant, he cast a slow, casual gaze right-to-left across the room, immediately spotting the person who was innocently enjoying lunch in the same corner of the deli as usual, at the same time as usual. He bought a drink at the counter and leisurely wove his way through the tables, taking a moment to observe his target in the flesh for the first time.

In official images she was attractive, but in person even Kete had to admit that she was quite striking. She had the soft, smooth features so characteristic of her native France, with long, dark-brown hair that had been cut shorter and made straighter than recent photos suggested. Her small movements were confident and graceful, with a practiced ease that came from a lifetime of knowing that she was watched.

Kete doubted that she even noticed his gaze on her, so accustomed was she to enjoying the attention of men. In her stylish civilian clothes she gave no hint that she was anything other than one of the many successful women in their prime who graced the elite districts of Longreach.

In fact, she was a senior officer in Astral Intelligence, astonishingly successful in her career even after coming to it late from a series of interesting adventures in her youth. She was a veteran of the recent invasion of Kete's homeworld, the current project director of top-secret research into a new killer weapon, and a former cabin mate of Katja Emmes. Thirty-four years old as of last Wednesday, unmarried, well-educated, well-connected: Commander Charity Brittany Delaine Marie Brisebois.

He sat down at the table in front of her, not looking at her but instead casting his gaze out through the windows to the boulevard, before retrieving a brand-new personal media device from his satchel and making a subtle show of manipulating its screen with apparent difficulty. The entire device was laughably simple—and mildly disturbing for being so completely external— but he continued his illusion of struggle.

Finally he frowned, then sighed softly, and laid the device down on the table. He took a sip of his drink and looked out the window again, then glanced in mock frustration at the device.

Then he pretended to notice that Commander Brisebois was watching him. He flicked his eyes toward her, but instead of averting her gaze like most people might have, she held his eyes with an easy confidence that, even though he expected it, impressed him.

"Having trouble with your Baryon?" Her tone was neutral, her eyes still assessing whether he was worth her attention. He gave a slight self-deprecating laugh.

"No, no trouble at all," he said. "I've learned to expect that each time I come home, Quantum will have launched a new device that yet again 'redefines society.'" He hefted the razor-thin screen and rolled it into a cylinder. "The flexibility I figured out pretty quick, but the brains I'm still working on."

She arched an eyebrow, but otherwise gave no acknowledgement beyond taking a sip of her drink while she seemed to tap her fingers randomly on the table.

A moment later, his Baryon pulsated with three gentle, green glows to indicate that he had a message. He unrolled it and looked at the screen. It was from her—a standard message showing him where to find the Help Menu, followed by a smile.

He chuckled and shook his head before tossing her an amused glance. She said nothing, but was smiling behind her glass as she raised her own Baryon, which had been lying flat on the table.

Establishing contact with the target was always the hardest part of an op. Being a spy gave new meaning to the expression, "one chance to make a first impression." While Kete had faith in his ability to roll with any encounter, no matter how many bad turns it took, succeeding on the first attempt was very satisfying.

In this case he'd used the fact that Brisebois had just received a new Baryon for her birthday. Waves of data had been streaming to and from the device, indicating that she loved her new toy.

His expensive clothes had helped him catch her eye, and she would have been intrigued by the fact that he had completely ignored her upon sitting down at his table. Still, it was the Baryon that had given her the excuse to speak.

Textbook procedure. It was as if they'd been reading from a script. Now he needed to move things along just a little bit faster.

"So if I wanted to send a message on this thing..." He flicked at the Baryon. "...other than line of sight to the table next to mine, how would I find the right address?"

Her eyes danced. "You'd just look in the directory, and locate the name of the person you wanted to message. It's in the Help File."

He smiled slightly. "And what if my device is new, and my directory is empty?"

"Completely empty?"

"Completely."

The intensity of her stare as she rushed to a decision was actually quite intoxicating. Her blue eyes became, if possible, even more vivid, and while he didn't fear that she could read him any more clearly, he felt as if her soul was illuminated to him.

"Charity Brisebois," she said suddenly. "But call me Breeze."

"Kit Moro," he answered. "I get called all kinds of things. Your choice."

"Kitten?"

"Maybe not."

She laughed—truly, letting her guard down.

He was in.

It was certainly easy to get sucked into the appeal of Terran society, Kete admitted to himself. In order to ensure access to the right people, he'd had to create his identity as one of the privileged. A government or military background would have held the highest status, but it would have been too difficult to fake, and he would have been exposed to potential run-ins with "former" workmates.

"Teacher" would have offered a very high position, but that was a closely watched, well-regulated profession that didn't serve anonymity.

While Kete had created a privileged identity, and easily enough, he had no illusions about where the real power lay. Wealth. His journalist alter-ego operated outside the regular economic channels, so Kit Moro's lifestyle was lavish enough that he was placed above the realm where potentially embarrassing questions might be asked.

He'd made himself so rich that he was above reproach.

There was nothing like this sort of divide in Centauria, but as he slipped on the jacket of his designer suit and strolled down through the warm, desert evening to the waiting cab, Kete understood the lure of Terran wealth and the power that came with it. He uploaded Breeze's directions to the cab's automatic pilot, then sat back in comfort as the smooth, silent vehicle cut across traffic to the VIP lane. It flashed through the checkpoints without even slowing down, his identity transmitted and cleared by security in the blink of an eye.

Longreach was a prosperous city by Terran standards, its size and culture comparing even to the oldest cities on Mars. While it certainly didn't have the thousands of years of history some of Earth's cities possessed, it had weathered the Gray Death better than most, and due to its central role as a spaceport it had recovered faster than the rest.

Even so, it had its secure wards. Kete had rented his apartment in the Astral ward in order to stay close to his military targets, but he'd learned that the very exclusive actually preferred the Highland ward, which was on the western outskirts of the metropolis. Breeze lived in the Astral ward, he knew, but her invitation to dinner was at a bistro in Highland. She hadn't actually revealed her address to him—he wondered if she was hoping he'd think that she lived out here.

Once through the final checkpoint, the cab increased speed and rose up to follow the transit lane through one of the dim residential wards. High-rise buildings flashed by on either side too fast for him to focus on them, but as he looked out toward the horizon he saw kilometer after kilometer of apartments, interspersed regularly with shopping and mass entertainment districts. He shook his head, marveling again at the human ability to ignore the lessons of the past.

By the most recent census, more than five million people were crammed into Longreach, all sucking up the same water, polluting the same air, and draining the weak Australian soil of any life. With energy as cheap and plentiful as it was, and planetary transport as easy and extensive as it was, there was no reason why these inhabitants couldn't live spread over an area radiating a thousand kilometers in every direction. Less congestion, less crowding, and less impact on the still-delicate environment.

Less risk of another outbreak.

The high-rises eventually gave way to dark greenhouses, and Kete watched with curiosity as the bright lights on the low hill ahead grew distinctly into a central core of streets surrounded by individual houses, all nestled spaciously among the dark woodlands. The retreat of the rich. His cab slowed and lowered into the traffic lane, slipping into the light stream of private cars moving into the core.

The exclusive district was bathed in a diffuse, ambient light as bright as a cloudy day, and Kete almost had to shield his eyes after the darkness of his plebian transit. All along the broad sidewalks, the well-to-do strolled past the boutiques and restaurants.

The cab slid to a stop outside one particular establishment. It was a highly rated Ethiopian, and Kete wondered if Breeze was trying to appeal to his African heritage. Supposedly his ancestors were West African, but had lived on Abeona for so many generations that any connection to Earth was purely of academic interest. Still, as he climbed out of the cab, he reminded himself that he was playing a role that required him to *be* African, which apparently in Terra meant a jealous affinity for any cultural aspect of the Continent of Light.

The face of the restaurant was made of real wood, he noticed, and the rich smell of nature was a welcome reprieve from the city. The transparent polyglass doors slid open silently at his approach, and as he entered the smell of wood was surpassed by the rich scents of fine cuisine. The gentle murmur of conversations mixed with background music through the softly lit space, and Kete barely had time to scan the tables before he was greeted by a handsome, smiling young man in traditional Ethiopian dress.

"Good evening, Mr. Moro. Commander Brisebois has just arrived—may I show you to your table?"

Kete nodded without deigning to speak, as was appropriate for a man of his wealth, and followed the young man past tables hemmed by beautifully decorated, low screens that provided privacy for those seated while maintaining the feel of airy openness overall. He was led to a table in the middle of the floor, where no doubt any passer-by would be able to see the fact that Breeze was dining with an African.

She was good, he admitted, and very subtle.

"Good evening, Kit." Breeze stood as he approached, offering a welcoming smile and reaching out to clasp his elbows. They exchanged kisses on both cheeks, then Kete gestured for her to take her seat again.

"You look beautiful, Charity."

As he took his seat and let the napkin be placed in his lap, he took a moment to reflect on just how true his statement was. Her form-fitting black dress was enticing while not revealing, with matching sapphire necklace and earrings bringing out the vivid blue of her eyes. It was hard to believe that this was a military officer sitting across from him, but from what he'd learned from her past, Breeze was never one to do things the regular way.

Their conversation over drinks was little more than light banter, and Kete could tell he was being probed. He made no effort to tease hidden information out of her, however, focusing instead on a delicate game of revealing enough about "Kit Moro" to ease her curiosity, but being wittily evasive enough to keep her intrigued.

A selection of shared entrées shifted their chatter toward food, wine, and travel, and as he poured Breeze her third glass of chianti, Kete made his first real foray of the evening.

"At least travel here on Earth is never more dangerous than an overdue booster shot," he commented. "Things certainly got hairy in the colonies a while back."

Breeze casually mopped up the last of the sauce on her plate with some flatbread, but he saw her expression flicker for a moment. She lifted wide eyes to him, her face the perfect imitation of awe.

"Did you do filming during the troubles?"

He shrugged modestly. "It was hard to get close to the real action, but I captured a few images."

"Which colony were you in?"

"Centauria." Real images of the horror threatened to seep into his conscious mind, and he locked them down. "Our troops really did a number on Abeona."

She took a sip of wine, suddenly examining him with real interest.

"You were on the Centauri homeworld?"

He nodded. "You must have friends who served in one of the colonial strike forces. I'll bet they have stories to tell."

"Oh, I'm sure they'd be too modest to brag."

Kete adopted his most earnest expression. "I don't think it's bragging. It was what had to be done after that sneak attack by colonial forces. Taking the fight to the enemy was the right thing to do."

She watched him, the intensity of her stare hinting at her internal debate. Kete helped her along.

"I'd love the chance to meet one of them," he said. "Not as a journalist, just as a grateful citizen."

Her gaze softened into a coy smile, and she leaned forward to speak quietly.

"Well, Kit, today is your lucky day."

He feigned a blank expression for a moment, watched her raise her eyebrows suggestively, then let the realization dawn across his features. He leaned in as well, lowering his voice.

"You're kidding."

"A woman can be full of surprises."

"What was your role?"

"Classified, good sir."

He narrowed his eyes playfully. "Now, Breeze, we're off the record this evening."

She considered for a second. "I had a few roles, but I think the most interesting was being aboard one of our fast-attack craft."

He made sure he looked impressed. "That's pretty hard core," he said. "You've certainly surprised me."

She leaned back and took another sip of wine. "I'm sure you have a few surprises as well, Mr. Moro." He ignored the bait, and pressed forward as if he'd just thought of something.

"You know, Chuck Merriman and I did a piece a few weeks ago on a military family. I think the daughter was fast-attack—what was her name? Katja Emmes. Do you know her?"

Breeze's face hardened behind a smile that momentarily turned to ice.

Interesting, he thought.

"Yes," she said. "As a matter of fact I do. She's very brave, but a little crazy I think, too."

"So you worked together?"

"On occasion." She took another, longer sip of wine. "The State doesn't always pick the most deserving veterans for media attention. I think your assignment would have been more for her father's sake than hers."

The naked animosity burning through her carefully controlled features wasn't what Kete had expected. Yet another strand of the story he needed to incorporate into his plan.

"So you don't think she deserves to be singled out?"

"Oh she was singled out all right. Singled right out of her regiment and buried in a dead-end job." Her expression turned dangerous for just a moment. "I have connections."

He backed off. "You don't have to say anything more to impress me, Breeze. I don't even compare my time in the field to what soldiers like you went through. I really mean it—from a grateful citizen, thanks."

With effort she relaxed in her seat and glanced casually around the restaurant.

"There are some things I can't talk about," she said, striving to regain her composure, "but you know what was really interesting about my time in the colonies?"

"What?"

Her seductive smile returned. "I'm sure you've heard about how invasion forces always send in a reconnaissance team beforehand, to scope out the enemy defenses?"

"Sure. I understand it's one of the most elite roles in the Corps."

"Is it?" She gave him a studiously casual expression. "Hmm."

He doubted very much that she was being completely accurate with him, but the mission required him to see the war on her terms. So he sat back in impressed silence. Breeze delicately dabbed her lips with her napkin, eyes on him the entire time. Suddenly she was enjoying the conversation again, now that it was all about her, but she offered no further embellishment, and he didn't probe further.

Still, he'd scored another success. She'd revealed details about her recent past, and the door was now open for him to explore further. If things continued this well, it was only a matter of time before she became an active asset.

8

The hot, bitter liquid was a welcome antidote to the heavy fatigue Thomas felt as he settled into his favorite chair, holding a cup of coffee. There was a lot of vacation time to use up after a deployment, but some mornings he honestly wished he was in space so that he could have a break.

He took another long sip and rested his head against the high, cushioned chair back. Enjoying the warm, filtered sunlight streaming over him through the floor-to-ceiling windows, he stretched and felt his muscles protest at even so slight a movement.

Soma was still asleep, of course. He wished he could stay in bed as long as his younger wife, but two decades of military life had trained his mind to reach full alertness after a maximum of eight hours down, no matter what his body said. He'd left her in their imperial-sized bed, sprawled among the scattered sheets as she'd been some time before dawn.

Judging from the angle of the sun, Thomas guessed it was almost noon.

Another sip of the coffee and he activated his Baryon. Soma usually preferred the passive input of the video wall this early in the morning, but he preferred the control—and, most of all, the silence—of his personal device. It was the latest gadget, he knew, and a must-have for anyone who wanted to stay connected.

He scanned his messages, noting with satisfaction that his efforts to get into Soma's elite circle were paying off. There was a funny photo from Tiffany, a golf invitation from Quinton, and a promising message from Chuck Merriman.

The reporter had made some subtle inquiries, and there was definitely media interest in an exclusive on the Dark Bomb, but it had to be something substantial.

Thomas frowned. His involvement with the project had been announced three weeks ago, and wasn't news anymore, so he needed to conjure up an angle to give the story some *oomph*. He took a thoughtful sip of coffee as he considered how he might link his high-profile marriage to his professional success, but realized that bringing in Soma was getting off message.

This story had to be about *him*.

What he really needed was to get media exposure out of his role in *Neil Armstrong*'s research, but as neither the science officer nor the commanding officer, his role would be pretty peripheral.

He skimmed his messages again as the caffeine started to dull the throbbing in his skull. Jack Mallory had called during the night, he noticed with surprise. Nice kid, Jack. Dumb as a post, but at the same time smart as hell. He'd been instrumental in creating the proto-bomb in the first place, although he was certainly wreaking havoc aboard the *Armstrong* these days. He'd been a good source of information concerning activities aboard the *Armstrong*, though, more so even than what Thomas had been able to observe first-hand.

On an impulse he hit the reply button.

The Baryon screen indicated that the call was going through, and eventually lit up with Jack's youthful features. Thomas was still surprised to see him without a broken, deformed face, but he was getting used to it.

"Good morning, Jack."

The newly crafted face beamed in recognition. "Hi, sir. Thanks for calling me back."

"Your first call was at three in the morning."

A typically stunned expression replaced the smile. "What? But I… ohh. Time zones. Umm, well, thanks for calling me back first thing."

Suddenly Thomas realized he was still in his bathrobe, and that his hair was probably a mess, so he didn't bother correcting Jack's assumption.

"Well, I figured you wouldn't disturb me unless it was important."

"Oh, I thought you'd want to know this, sir," Jack replied. "Guess who came by the ship for a visit yesterday?"

"Who?"

"Breeze!" the young man said quickly. "She just swooped in with a couple of goons, and had a long meeting with the captain. She didn't look too pleased when she left, and neither did he. What's she got to do with Research, anyway?"

Nothing, Thomas mused, but she knew how to place herself at the center of the action even faster than he did.

"Thanks for letting me know, Jack," he said. "I'll look into it." Disconnecting, he drained the rest of his coffee.

So Charity Brisebois was getting in the way again. Chandler said that he had one of his own staff appointed as project director. With a sinking heart, Thomas guessed who that might be.

Vacation be damned, he needed to act.

Leaving Soma to her restless slumber, Thomas scrubbed himself, donned an expertly pressed garrison uniform, and caught the first skycraft to Longreach. Then he boarded a cab to Astral Headquarters. He marched swiftly down the corridors he knew well enough, and into the receiving room of the Fleet's newest flag officer.

The admiral's flag lieutenant sat industriously at her desk in that outer room, turning curious eyes up to greet Thomas as he entered.

"Good afternoon," he declared. "I need to see the admiral."

Her cool expression indicated that she wasn't going to be easily intimidated. No doubt a dozen people stormed into the office each day with the same demand, and no doubt Thomas was far from the most senior of them.

"The admiral's very busy," she replied. "May I take your name?"

"Lieutenant Commander Thomas Kane."

"Please take a seat," she said. "I'll see what his schedule looks like."

Thomas remained standing, watching as she manipulated her console in what was no doubt a discreet message to her boss. He enjoyed a satisfied smile when her narrow eyebrows arched slightly. She consciously eased her severe expression and actually smiled at him as she rose to her feet.

"Admiral Chandler will see you, sir."

"Thank you." He moved toward the door and strode through into Chandler's inner office.

The room was easily the size of an average family home, half of it centered around the desk and its court of chairs, the other around a receiving area for high-ranking guests. Three-dimensional star maps mounted on modern pedestals mixed with more ancient trophies from centuries of space flight.

The admiral was seated behind his desk, silhouetted against a floor-to-ceiling window that was tinted against the afternoon heat. Thomas moved immediately toward one of the chairs nearest the desk, if nothing else to get the sun out of his eyes and better assess his old mentor's mood. Chandler didn't rise, but his expression was relaxed as he leaned his elbows on the desk and watched Thomas approach.

"Sir, I'm sorry to disturb you," Thomas said, "but I felt I had to make an unusual report to you."

Chandler indicated for him to sit. "The last time you popped in unannounced you'd just single-handedly saved your ship, but not before you'd saved mine. I wouldn't expect you to waste my time with bullshit."

That was a warning...

"The research aboard *Armstrong* isn't going well, sir. The science officer appears to have been promoted past her level of competence, the captain is a fool, and for some strange reason Admiral Bush keeps directly interfering with our program. However, I think I have a solution."

The admiral's face hardened. "I hadn't heard of any problems," he said. "Do tell."

"From what I can figure out, Bush is way more interested in his ships winning civilian science awards than in conducting Astral Force core research. Over the past two months the *Armstrong* has been focusing seventy-five percent of its field time on power generation." He paused, then continued. "I've checked the journals, and power generation is the hot topic for all the leading institutes and prize committees.

"Captain Lincoln, our CO, has only been in command for three months, having been promoted out of one of the smaller Research ships, where he managed to win nearly a dozen awards over the past decade. It turns out that Bush himself used to command *Armstrong*, and now that he's an admiral, I think he wants to turn some of Lincoln's magic into fame for his old ship. The dutiful captain is only too happy to comply."

Chandler shook his head. "Doesn't surprise me," he responded. "The Fleet should take back that entire squadron and make it military again."

"Until then, sir, I have a quick solution. The way *Armstrong*'s been doing her power generation experiments is very time-intensive, and I've come up with a way to automate most of it." Actually, it had been Sublieutenant Amanda Smith who'd been bitching to Jack about easier ways to do the experiments, but Thomas didn't mind taking credit for things he'd overheard. He'd fact-checked it on his own, after all.

"That would keep the admiral and our CO happy," he continued, "but it would free up resources to get back onto the Dark Bomb research program."

"So why don't you just do it?"

It was Thomas's turn to shake his head. "The science officer, Helena Grey, is a wily old witch who guards her department jealously. She's not smart enough to see the best processes, and she doesn't take criticism well."

Chandler began to show impatience. "You're the XO—make it happen!"

Thomas dared to laugh slightly. "I would, sir, except Lieutenant Grey seems to have a... special relationship with Admiral Bush. I've seen it a couple of times, where she'll complain about something—or someone—and if it doesn't get fixed to her satisfaction, two or three days later a rocket will come down from the admiral, ordering us to do exactly what Grey would have wanted." He paused to let that sink in. "Sir, this is petty, shipboard stuff no admiral would ever bother himself with—unless he had a special relationship with one of the crew."

Chandler sighed in disgust. "And your captain?"

"Spineless, sir. He's basically admitted to me that he knows exactly what's going on, but he's too concerned with his own career to risk defying Admiral Bush."

"If you're asking me to try to tell another admiral how to run his squadron…"

"No, sir," Thomas insisted. "But if you can casually mention to Admiral Bush about these self-directed power monitors—the best are made by a company called Piccolo—I'm sure he'll jump at getting them on board *Armstrong*. He can win his prizes, and we can get back to doing our job."

"Are these monitors expensive?"

"Hell, yes—and very prestigious for any lab to have."

Chandler smiled, and reached for his comms panel. "It's a good idea, Thomas. Let me make a call." He gestured. "Coffee's in the outer office."

Thomas knew the sound of a dismissal. He rose with a polite nod and exited to the outer office. The pretty flag lieutenant was busy at her desk, barely glancing up as he emerged. A year ago he might have made the effort to strike up a conversation, but the still-new pressure of the ring on his left hand reminded him that those days were over. He was married to Soma now, and he knew what trouble a misplaced dalliance could create.

He spotted the coffee machine against the wall and focused his full attention on making himself a nice cappuccino. If the young hottie at the desk wanted to surreptitiously check out his butt while he did so, he was okay with that.

Just as the last froth of the hot drink poured into his cup he heard the sound of a door opening. He glanced toward Chandler's office but realized that in fact it was the door from the hallway outside. A new visitor had arrived, and Thomas turned back to collect his coffee as his heart suddenly beat faster. The reaction irritated him, and he purposefully kept his back turned as he took a slow sip and listened.

"Good morning, ma'am."

"Commander Brisebois, here to see the admiral."

"Yes, ma'am, I'll let him know you're here." A moment later she added, "He's on the phone but you're welcome to take a seat for a minute."

Talk about misplaced dalliances.

In the reflection of the dark glass of the coffee maker, he could just make out Breeze's uniformed figure. He'd really hoped their paths would have parted forever, but he realized now how in vain that hope had been. She'd discovered a powerful patron in Eric Chandler, just like he had, and she'd accomplished more in six months than Thomas had managed in fifteen years.

He wouldn't have been so worried except for the fact that Breeze knew how close Chandler and Soma were. She also knew something else that had to stay forever hidden from both of them.

Still, if his current plan worked, he might just have the leverage he needed to keep her beautiful mouth shut.

"Thomas, is that you?"

He turned slowly, cup and saucer in hand. "Why, hello, ma'am. How nice to see you."

She smirked. "Yes, how nice," she responded. "What brings you to visit the admiral?"

"Oh, just minor housekeeping. Some of *Rapier*'s crew are only now being reassigned, and he and I were finalizing a few details."

She processed his answer carefully. "Well, that's good," she said. "I've been so busy since we got back, it's hard to remember that some of our shipmates are still sitting around idle."

"Yes, I hear you've been busy," he responded. "Young Jack Mallory said he saw you on one of the Research ships, just yesterday. Don't tell me you're going into space again."

Her smile came quickly, but not with perfect ease. "Oh, no. I'm the project director here at headquarters. It's quite an honor, actually. This project is considered vital to Astral interests."

Apparently she hadn't checked *Armstrong*'s officer list.

"How interesting," he said. "And how's the project going?"

"Fine."

"Really? My understanding is that it's behind schedule."

The smile faded. "Don't cause trouble, Thomas," she said, lowering her voice. "I have an awful lot on my mind these days." Her expression was light, but he'd learned to recognize when she was moving to the attack.

"What else is occupying your time?"

"Oh, just the little matter of a Fleet Marshall Investigation. Honestly, I'm flattered that Admiral Chandler feels he can trust me with so much. Then again, I was one of his *senior* staff officers during the campaign." Her field promotion still made the bile rise in Thomas's throat.

"You're leading the investigation?"

Her eyes danced dangerously. "I'm the perfect candidate. So close to the cause of the trouble, but removed enough to be objective." She shook her head in a great show of regret. "So many Terran lives lost, colonists attacking our own solar system... Parliament sees it as a great embarrassment. How could one little fast-attack craft cause so much suffering? The common people need to be reassured that those to blame will be held accountable."

Thomas could hear the thrill behind her words. He began to feel very afraid.

"And who's to blame?" he asked. "Why is *Rapier* being drawn into this?"

"Not the ship, nor her valiant crew," Breeze said, "and *certainly* not her strike team." She pouted slightly. "Just the commanders."

Thomas felt the anger rise. "So Katja and me?"

"No, I don't think so," she replied. "Just one of you."

"Which one of us?"

Breeze's cruel smile finally showed through.

"I just can't decide," she said. "Maybe I'll let you do it."

"What?"

She leaned in close enough that he could smell her sweet perfume. "One of you is going down, Thomas. Either you or your precious little pet—I can spin the evidence either way." She eyed him up and down. "So I'm curious to see what kind of man you really are. Do you protect yourself, or your loyal subordinate?"

Thomas bit down his anger, reminding himself that he still had a trump card.

"Bring it on, Breeze."

"Good."

Silence descended. Thomas stepped back and sipped at his cappuccino, and Breeze glanced casually at her tablet. The door to Chandler's office snapped open. The admiral looked out, noting both officers who were standing before him.

"Oh, Breeze, good," he said. "Perfect timing. I want to talk about your research report, especially after my last conversation. Thomas, I just got off the phone with Admiral Bush, and he agrees. You can start shipping up that extra equipment to *Armstrong* tomorrow morning."

"Thank you, sir." Thomas took considerable satisfaction in watching Breeze's shocked gaze snap over to him.

Chandler retreated into his office. "Let's go, Breeze—that report."

Thomas smiled at her. "Oh, yes, I didn't have time to tell you. I've taken over as XO of *Armstrong*, to get the research back on track. Apparently it's way behind, and Admiral Chandler wants a trusted man on the inside to ensure success."

Breeze's lips parted, but she couldn't quite produce a response. Thomas gave her arm a squeeze and leaned in.

"Looks like your career is in my hands, Project Director. I hope your report didn't say that things are going well. The admiral doesn't like being lied to."

Her cheeks flushed momentarily, but she regained her outward calm remarkably quickly.

"You think this will protect you?"

"Yes, unless you plan on learning five-dimensional warped geometry in your spare time. You're the project director of this research, Breeze, and I'm the only person on that ship of fools who can deliver the results to you."

"Then I guess it's Katja for the chair."

"Just try and hurt her, Breeze. I dare you."

She gave him a look that was almost respect, before turning and walking into Chandler's office.

9

Katja dropped the fork onto her half-eaten stew and sat back. The rain was still pelting against the window of her office, the heavy dampness of the air seeping through the thin fabric of her garrison uniform.

The beef stew had appealed at the time, a good, thick meal to ward off the chill, but now she couldn't bear another bite. She sighed and rubbed a hand across her face as she tossed the remainder of her lunch into the trash.

She stared at the screen for a moment longer. The curt, mil-speak message was only two paragraphs long, but it was the first genuine direction she'd received in weeks. It summed up what her career had been reduced to. She'd been assigned to this tiny airlift station on the eastern edge of the Malayan archipelago, to take formal command of the three drop ships and their maintenance crews, and provide local lift services as requested by military forces.

Damn.

Why was the Corps making such a big deal about her psychological test results? Of *course* she was affected by her time in combat—who wouldn't be? Hadn't she proved her worth in combat several times over? It hardly seemed fair for a recipient of the Astral Star to be banished to some backwater, while young pups like Jack Mallory got sent right back into space.

Jack had already sent her a few messages, describing his

new ship and the strange command structure of a Research vessel. Katja smiled slightly as she imagined the young man set loose like a happy bull in a china shop full of petrie dishes, and wondered how his bubbling enthusiasm would mesh with stringent experimental protocols.

Apparently Thomas Kane had joined him on the ship, and that was interesting news. She'd have bet Thomas would have aimed higher in his post-war career, but at least he'd be able to keep Jack on target. She didn't envy either of them their new lives in lab coats, but at least they were still contributing to Terra's well-being.

The three screens built into her desk stared up expectantly, their insatiable demand for administrative oversight crying out to her. She stared back at them, taking a moment to curse the doctors and their "compassion."

She'd done all the usual post-traumatic training—it was part of the fourth-year curriculum at the Astral College—and she knew they'd done right by posting her here. A nice, slow-paced administrative posting kept her connected to operations, as the three drop ships under her command were theoretically available to reinforce local troops in case of invasion or insurrection. It also kept her out of stressful situations, a textbook example of where to post a struggling combat veteran.

It was hell.

Cradling her chin, she looked out again at the dark gray evening visible through her window. Northern Oceania had sounded so exotic, with its green mountains and glistening beaches. No one had mentioned the monsoon, and despite the State Terraform Department's best efforts, the rains still lasted for nearly half the year. She'd been here over a month and had yet to see a day without a downpour.

She leaned back, closing her eyes.

The tears were suddenly close, much closer than they ever got during the day. Her vision blurred like the rain-pelted window. It was only a matter of time before her family found out where she was, laying out her shame for all to see. Decorated veteran Katja Emmes, cracked after her first combat tour and buried in a washed-out backwater.

Sadness turned to the anger that was becoming her friend these days, as it pushed aside more vulnerable feelings and she wrapped herself in it like an old blanket as she began typing up her weekly logistic requirements message. A gentle buzz in her ear distracted her. It was the military line. She accepted the call.

"Lieutenant Emmes."

"*Good afternoon, Miss Katja.*" The voice was slightly garbled and the length of delay suggested a transmission from beyond orbit. "*This is Chuck Merriman, ANL.*"

Her hands clenched into fists, but she forced them to relax.

"Hello, Mr. Merriman."

"*I'm sorry to disturb you on duty, but you haven't been returning my calls to your civilian number.*"

She leaned back in her chair, vaguely remembering deleting all of her messages over the past few days.

"I've been very busy. How did you reach me on this military circuit?"

Even through the clutter she heard his wry amusement.

"*It's a public number, Lieutenant. I just spoke to your base operator, and asked to be patched through.*"

She took a long, final deep breath, and made a note to speak to the idiot trooper who'd obligingly given access to the media.

"Well, you just caught me between meetings, so make it fast."

"*I'm going to be in your region next week, and I was hoping to do a follow-up interview like we discussed back at Longreach. Would there be a good time for me to drop in for an hour or so?*"

There was no way her father was going to see her rotting in this backwater—not on the system-wide news.

"I'm afraid I'll be very busy with operations for the next while," she said, keeping her voice level. "Perhaps you'd have better luck catching up with my father—I think he's still here on Earth."

"*Mars, actually—low-g combat training. I'm definitely going to meet up with him, but since I was in the area I wanted to take advantage of my proximity to you.*"

Merriman knew with greater accuracy the whereabouts of her own family. That spoke volumes, and it wasn't the only thing that didn't sit right.

"What do you mean you're in the area?" she asked pointedly. "What else is going on?"

A gentle laugh. *"Although it may surprise you, Miss Katja, you're not the only important thing in my life. I've been covering the strikes in Papua New Guinea for the last two weeks."*

Katja stood bolt upright. Strikes in Papua New Guinea? Where were her orders? Then she recalled watching the news—they were labor strikes, not combat strikes. It had to do with munitions workers trying to organize a union, or some nonsense like that. As if the State would ever let such a critical industry start calling the shots. Where the hell were Terran citizens getting these ideas?

Now she felt stupid. "Mr. Merriman, thanks for your call," she said. "I have your contact information, so I'll get back to you." She broke the connection before he could respond, and sat down again, sighing. He was just a reporter doing his job, and she supposed it should be an honor, but she was going to decide how the worlds saw her.

This was not it.

She was a combat veteran of the most elite fighting force in Terra, and there was nothing her father, Chuck Merriman, or even those fucking doctors could do to take that away from her.

She heard a knock on the open door. Sergeant Huebner filled the door frame.

"Lieutenant Emmes, ma'am?"

"Yes, Sergeant?"

"Ma'am, the Army's outside. They say they want our drop ships to lift them to Goa."

She called up the day's operational schedule. Of her three drop ships, one was in maintenance, one was being used for training, and one was on standby. No lift had been scheduled.

"We've got nothing planned," she said. "Did they give you a movement order?"

"Uhh, no, ma'am."

"Did you ask for one?"

His dull silence was answer enough. She'd already been wondering how she could put a positive spin on Huebner's annual assessment.

He's not very bright, but can lift heavy things.

"Tell them I'll be right there." She pushed back her chair and rounded the desk. Obligingly, he withdrew.

A glance at the rain on her window prompted her to reach for her combat jacket. Her hand froze in mid-motion, however, as her eyes fell upon her tunic hanging against the wall. She brushed her fingers on the qualification badges, one for Strike Officer and a second, smaller one for Fast Attack, and she reminded herself that most Terrans would never—*could* never— earn such qualifications.

She was part of an elite, and even if living within that elite made it seem routine, she reminded herself that it was exceptional. Below the badges were the newest additions to her uniform, to her career, to her life. Two medals. On the outside was the campaign medal for the recent troubles—known officially as the Colonial Uprising—with bars for Sirius and Centauria. Next to it, in the place of honor over her heart, was the Astral Star. The third-highest award for valor in the Terran military, it set her apart from her peers, declared her truly exceptional, even among the elite.

Yet it had earned her little more than a glance from her father, and it hadn't prevented her being shipped off to an Astral backwater to rot while the doctors wrung their hands over her precious mental state.

Maybe those doctors should view the recordings from her helmet-cam. As she reached to pull the tunic from its hanger, she remembered the severed limbs of Centauri crew members floating in zero-g around her, of blood floating in ever-growing spherical globs around the smoky interior of the enemy battle cruiser as she and her three troopers blasted it apart from the inside.

The smoke began to move, sucked by the ominous wind that spoke of an uncontained breech in the hull. The hatch ahead opened for a moment. Bullets pinged off her armored spacesuit as Hernandez pushed her aside and returned fire. She burst through into the darkened space, firing her explosive rounds at the hidden Centauri crew. A bullet cracked off her faceplate. She tucked into a ball as she floated helplessly upward, more shots pinging her helmet.

Maybe those doctors should watch her helmet-cam as the deck exploded downward and revealed an APR robot staring back up at her. As she felt herself flung aside and watched as rockets smashed up into Hernandez, blowing his powerful body apart like scraps of meat. She scrambled along the top of the corridor in zero-g.

"APRs! APRs!" she screamed to Assad and Jackson, still trapped one deck below. "Get out of there!"

Maybe those fucking doctors should watch as Assad and Jackson were blasted to pieces by the Centauri war machines. Listen to the radio chatter as Sergeant Chang reported his own team's casualties in the engine room. The smoke moved faster, riding the precious air out into the vacuum of space. Katja was cut off and alone. Ignoring Chang's attempts to fight his way to her, she ordered him and his team to escape even while she followed the river of smoke through a buckled door and into a darkened, outer compartment.

The air pressure dropped outside her spacesuit. On her external audio she heard the frantic calls of enemy troops approaching. Only one way out. She pointed her rifle at the crack in the bulkhead and fired twice. The hull exploded outward and she felt the tidal wave of escaping air carry her forward. She crashed through the opening. Spinning stars, and then darkness.

Silence and darkness.

Silence and darkness.

"Ma'am?"

She opened her eyes, gaze darting around the dim, gray walls of her office. Rain pelted against the window. The air was still. The walls were stable. The tunic hung from her balled fist, soft fabric clutched between her fingers. She shook off the nightmare and took several deep, calming breaths.

"Ma'am?"

Huebner had reappeared.

Forcing her fingers to relax, she slipped the tunic on in a swift motion.

"Let's deal with these Army idiots."

The rain bounced high off the paved surface of the courtyard, breaking down into mud the long tracks of dirt that had fallen off the three dark-green armored vehicles that loomed in front of her. She stepped to the edge of the building's canopy, just out of the rain but in clear sight of the dozen or so Army soldiers who stared down at her from their machines.

"Which one of you requested the lift?" she asked.

"That'd be me." It was a man in the second vehicle. "I just need your drop ships for a couple of hours."

"And you are?"

"Storm Banner Leader Ciotti." He glared down at her.

Her stomach twisted in a knot. The same rank as her father, and a senior enlisted rank—but still enlisted. She was an officer, whether the Army recognized it or not.

"Well, Storm Banner Leader Ciotti, your command hasn't sent any requests for Astral Force assistance. Do you have an urgent operational requirement?"

His glare took on a shade of contempt. He glanced at his watching soldiers, then climbed down from the vehicle. He was at least as tall as Huebner, and with his full combat gear could have blocked out the sun. He loomed over her, bare inches away. She fought the urge to step back and tilted her face up to meet his eye. Rain pelted her cheeks.

"You're new here, Lieutenant." He spat the rank. "And you don't know how it works. We have a standing agreement with this station, upheld by your predecessor, where we can use the drop ships when we need them, without having to do all the paperwork. Now I suggest you start issuing orders to make that happen."

She felt her face flushing, the rage suddenly welling up within her.

"The only order I'm issuing," she forced herself to say, "is for you to take your vehicles and get out of my compound. If you're still here in sixty seconds, I'm arresting you."

Ciotti sneered. "You don't have the stones, Princess."

The cheap insult shouldn't have phased her, but the next thing she knew her pistol was out and aimed at Ciotti's face. Her hand was steady, finger on the trigger. Ciotti's sneer vanished.

"Get back in your vehicle." With vicious anticipation she

willed him to disobey. It would be so sweet, and so justified under military law. "Get out of my compound. If you say any words other than 'yes, ma'am,' I will pull this trigger. Do you understand?"

He stared at her for a long moment, jaw clenched. There was clear comprehension in his gaze, but no fear that she could see. This probably wasn't the first time he'd stared down the barrel of a gun—but it wasn't the first time she'd aimed one either.

Finally he looked away and forced the words from his mouth. "Yes, ma'am."

He stepped back cautiously, turned and climbed slowly up his vehicle. A few quick orders and the Army machines whined to life and rolled away. Only then did Katja lower the pistol and holster it.

She kept her grip on the holster to stop her hand from shaking, fighting down sudden fear. Not of any loudmouth soldier, but of herself.

10

That an entire civilization could forget one of its greatest achievements seemed inconceivable. That the rulers of a civilization would purposefully hide such an achievement from their people, and *make* them forget, was horrifying.

As Kete slipped into his spacesuit, he thought about the explorers who reached this same area of space, more than six decades ago, in a craft that had been state-of-the-art for the time.

His sloop was fitted with all the luxury conveniences expected of a playboy. However, as a civilian craft it was woefully lacking in extra-dimensional technology. While many rich yacht owners demanded the most expensive gear and the navigation system was top-notch, he'd had to delve into the historical records to locate his target—the first jump gate.

It had always intrigued him that the jump gate—the greatest triumph of science over nature—was one of the most unimpressive sights to behold. Invisible save for a slight ripple of the background stars, it was like a tear in spacetime that folded over itself. Kete could understand anew the trepidation that those first explorers must have felt as they activated this first such miracle.

The first gate hadn't even reached a tenth of the distance to Centauria, and before it could be employed, Terran adventurers had traveled at sublight speed for months in order to set up the opposite gate, sent the ready signal, then waited for months, on station in the deep blackness.

Where Kete sat now, a second ship had then entered the gate, hoping not to be obliterated. Both ships returned moments later, and the concept of the jump gate was proven viable. Subsequent missions had set up a line of jump gates, each four light-months apart, as new explorers pushed further and further into deep space, and finally crossed the vast gulf that lay between humankind's first and second homes.

Years later, when the modern jump gates to all the "colonies" had been built, Terra had placed them far to the north of Sol, lined up together in order that all traffic could be monitored from the gargantuan Astral Base Five. The old jump-gate-lines had officially been deactivated due to their unstable nature. Yet here they were, forgotten, unmonitored but still very much active.

Kete had used them to make his secret entries and exits to Terran space—although the last time had been hairy, with that Astral Force Hawk pouncing on him as soon as he'd emerged into Terran space. Why "Eagle-One" had been in this corner of space he had no idea, but as he maneuvered his sloop on ultra-low power toward his designated coordinates, Kete couldn't help but glance nervously at the starry backdrop for evidence of movement. He couldn't afford to be picked off by a Terran sentry ship.

He couldn't fail. *Not this close.*

Floating across the spacious bridge of the sloop, Kete unlocked the dark-energy sensor he'd used for his past jumps. It was small enough to hold with one hand, and it connected easily to the power supply. He activated it, and within minutes it detected the faint but unmistakable signature of the old jump gate, the spacetime tunnel held open by tiny amounts of dark energy corralled by artificial initons.

Now came the hard part. He could operate safely to within two kilometers of the gate, but Kete had enough self-preservation instinct to keep a bit more distance between the old tear and the one he was about to cut open.

Not that he didn't trust Centauri technology, but one didn't just create a new jump gate every day. In fact, no one did.

Those early explorers may have been nervous before they

jumped, but at least they'd had dozens of safety vessels standing by, and knew there was a sister ship waiting on the other end. Kete was on his own here, and he was going to jump more than ten times as far. Worse, he would be jumping into a gravity well. Abeona wasn't that big a planet, but every schoolkid knew that jump gates were only stable in very flat spacetime. Not that he didn't trust Centauri technology, he reminded himself, but this was insane.

My world is depending on me, he reminded himself as he sealed his helmet and strapped into his seat. This test jump was only the first phase of getting gates closer to a planet's surface. If it didn't work then the whole plan was dead.

Locking his position at twenty kilometers from the old gate he launched the device that had been delivered to him after Valeria's message. The U-shaped object was no bigger than his chair, and reflected the light of the distant sun as it drifted away from him. At first it remained inert, like a reddish horseshoe sailing in slow motion toward eternity.

Then, as he watched, it flickered with white light.

The stars beyond it began to wobble, shifting violently—just once—before returning to their original positions.

He looked down at his dark-energy sensor. Where before there had been one jump gate, now there were two. To his untrained eye the dark-energy signatures looked identical, except that the new one was larger and more clearly defined than the old. That, at least, was reassuring. And more important tactically, any normal sensor sweep wouldn't distinguish that there were actually two gates now. The new gate was effectively hiding in the shadow of the old one.

Taking manual control of the sloop's thrusters he pushed forward, aiming his sleek nose upward so that the horseshoe would pass just beneath him.

Nothing changed in the starscape, and only the gentle push of the chair against his suit hinted that he was moving at all.

The stars directly ahead suddenly rippled.

His entire body suddenly *stretched*, then he gasped at the smack of compression.

Abruptly the starscape was replaced by the massive, beautiful, green-blue orb of Abeona. Dozens of tiny dark shapes moved across the global backdrop, navigation lights blinking as they passed. The civilian radio squawked to life with a buzz of traffic.

Kete started breathing again. Then fought down the urge to vomit as relief flooded through him.

The jump gate had worked, and he was home.

Yet this wasn't so much the home he'd always known. Even from this distance he could see the ugly black scars on the surface, left by concentrated Terran bombardment, and to the south his eyes were drawn to the sparkling dance of millions of broken fragments spreading out from three separate clouds into a thin, artificial ring around the planet. The wreckage of the mighty orbital stations that had so dramatically failed to stop the Terran attack.

Quickly he activated the sloop's standard flight controls and scanned for any closing contacts. Before the system could even finish its first sweep, however, a familiar voice sounded through the secure radio routed to his helmet.

"*Romeo, Romeo, wherefore art thou, Romeo?*"

He smiled as he opened the channel.

"Romeo's a bit dazed, but he sure knows a pretty planet when he sees one. I suppose now I have to call you Juliet?" His sensors easily tracked the vessel inbound lazily off his starboard bow, and he could hear Valeria Moretti's grin behind her words.

"Negative, Romeo. Just stay the strong, silent type while I hook up with you."

He unlocked his helmet and removed it, letting it float freely as he ensured his sloop maintained a steady velocity. Valeria's ship was closing his, and a Navy battlecruiser loitered nearby, no doubt in silent-running mode and carrying a few extra passengers from Centauri intelligence.

Valeria maneuvered her craft smoothly alongside, and within a few minutes he heard the clicks and hisses of her airlock coupling to his. He unstrapped from his seat and pushed back through the cabin.

He was as prepared as he could be, but he still had to steel his expression as the airlock hatch opened. Wrapped in a custom spacesuit, Valeria's legless body seemed almost comically bulbous, but her eyes were as bright as ever as a smile burst through the scarring in her face.

She floated forward, set down a bag of equipment, and gripped his shoulders, planting a firm kiss on each of his cheeks. He returned the gesture and pulled her into a heartfelt hug. It was good to see her.

Then he realized that she was hugging him back. He looked down in surprise.

"You have your whole arm back!"

"Where have you been?" She pushed back and held the right limb up proudly, rolling her new fingers. "This baby finished regenerating weeks ago. Next week we start on one of the legs."

He purposefully didn't look at the suited stump of her torso. "They took away your robotics?"

She shook her head. "No use in zero-g; I left them on Abeona. I intend to leave them behind permanently by the time you're set up for the next phase."

Kete knew that limb regeneration was a slow, often painful process, where care had to be taken to ensure the proper stem cell development and nerve connectivity growth.

"Why push yourself?" he asked. "You don't want to grow a lame leg."

She folded her arms—*both her arms!*—and gave him a firm stare. "Because I can't really sneak around on Earth with a robotic one." He tried to protest, but she spoke quickly. "I'm coming as part of the strike team, Kete. Don't even try and stop me."

He saw anew the faint burn scars on her face, thought of the two and a half limbs she'd lost during the invasion. She'd endured even more than he had, and underneath her flamboyant style he recognized a much darker energy than that which held open the jump gates. His soul had been crushed by the Terran attack, but hers had been inflamed.

"Stop you?" he replied. "I'll just be trying to get out of your way."

He invited her to hover in the sloop's opulent lounge and opened bulbs of sparkling water for them. He could have activated the artificial gravity, but her incomplete body would be more comfortable in a weightless environment.

"So the new jump gate worked," he stated with as much casual indifference as he could muster.

"Yeah, the brainiacs watching in our friendly Navy escort will be delighted. Looks like we can jump into a gravity well after all."

"They weren't sure?"

She gave him a rueful glance. "They've done a few non-living tests before now. But you were the first sentient biological to do it. Congratulations."

"Well, I'm glad I can make the brainiacs happy. Let me get the data from the jump transmitted over to them."

They chatted for a long time while the sloop transmitted extra-dimensional telemetry to the battlecruiser, at first exchanging tactical and mission-specific information, moving to the latest politics in both Centauria and Terra, and eventually descending into casual gossip.

It was good to hear the news from home, and Kete wished that his orders required a return to the surface of Abeona. Sadly, this trip was only to prove that the portable jump gate could emerge safely in a gravity well, and take new equipment back with him—their leisurely chat was probably already in violation of the mission timelines.

"They've decided not to rebuild the houses on our street," Valeria said suddenly.

Kete took a sip of his water. "Why?"

Her stare took on new intensity. "They want to build a war memorial."

His chest tightened. "Do you know the details?"

"Not specifically. The Cloud's been whispering for months about recognizing the sacrifices of all those who died, but lately I've heard more specific announcements about what they're calling 'The Battle of Southridge.'"

The Battle of Southridge. He'd never expected his quiet suburban neighborhood to give its name to military history. The very thought caused him to flush with anger.

"I'll want to see that."

Valeria indicated the bag of equipment. "I'll make sure the gate's other end is set up so you can."

Kete glanced at the bag. The next jump would be between the surfaces of two planets—not a method of travel he'd ever have wanted to pick, even if it meant the successful completion of his mission. Although he trusted Centauri technology, and he knew that his government would never throw his life away on unproven science, he knew that his chances of surviving such a gravimetrically affected jump were fair to poor.

But the risks were worth it. And if any of the Centauri agents now on Terra had to be risked, he was happy to volunteer. Unlike the others, his life on Abeona was over.

As he looked out at the beautiful, glowing orb of his homeworld, his mind slowly, inexorably, drifted back to that terrible night.

The distant crackle of combat was audible far below, and he risked a glance from the deck of his house. The fighting still seemed to be contained close to the industrial park far below, but flying elements had clearly added new chaos to the battlefield. Even as he watched he saw something explode in the air over the low, dark buildings and spiral downward to a fiery impact.

He tore himself from the scene and went into his office. The Cloud was thundering with millions of panicked inputs from all over Abeona. It was impossible to make sense of anything, but he guessed that his town wasn't the only target being hit. Where the hell had the Terrans come from?

Any inquiries he might have tried were drowned out by a sudden, overwhelming message from the government, rippling through his internal circuits.

<All militia report to station. All civilians seek shelter.>

The order was so powerful, so desperate, Kete doubted a single Centauri citizen could resist it. He withdrew immediately and cast out a local call to any militia who might be augmented as he was.

Valeria, his neighbor three doors down, was just activating her car and agreed to pick Kete up. He ran to the bedroom for his emergency militia pack. She already had the car door open when he ran down to the grass street.

They greeted each other with equal amounts of wordless shock. Valeria swung the car around and sailed up the dark street to pause at the main intersection. She made to turn left and head into town, but froze at her controls.

Kete followed her gaze.

Coming up to the ridgeline from town, moving in perfect, ruthless unity, a group of silver war machines churned up the road under their tracks. Vaguely humanoid as each rose more than two meters above its armored chassis, the anti-personnel robots—APRs—mounted a devastating array of weapons across their silver bodies. Missile launchers, rotary cannons, hyperbaric pulse guns—these machines had been specifically designed to combat Terran troopers, maintaining both fear and firepower as their arsenals. The lead APR seemed to glance momentarily at Kete and Valeria in the car, but otherwise the column of war machines rolled past indifferently.

Even after they'd disappeared below the ridge heading south, Valeria didn't get the car moving again. Kete looked over at his neighbor, at the white knuckles and wide eyes.

"Trade places," he said, throwing open his door. "Let me drive."

Only when Kete had rounded the car and opened Valeria's door did she finally react, sliding across to the passenger seat. He strapped in and gunned the car forward, racing down the dark road toward the lights of town.

They passed two more columns of APRs heading into battle, and Kete thought he spotted several flying machines streaking past overhead, as well. In the continual flashes of surface fire and Terran strike fighter attacks, however, it was hard to be sure what was where. He just kept the car headed away from the battlefield, and hoped that no Terran considered him a threat.

Dozens of cars were strewn about the militia depot, abandoned by their drivers in their haste to report for duty. Kete and Valeria ran through the impromptu barricades and, their neural IDs verified by the guards, crowded into the main room of the depot. The wall of noise inside was enough to rival the thunder of the Terran bombardment.

Kete gave Valeria's arm a squeeze then waded alone into the crowd, struggling to locate his unit. Dozens of men and women jostled for space as they scrambled into combat fatigues, fought with unfamiliar webbing, and gathered their various items of weaponry. Kete had donned his webbing at the house, and didn't bother with fatigues, heading instead straight for the rifle lock-up. Harried quartermasters had long since given up trying to record which weapon was signed out to which soldier, and were practically throwing rifles over the counter at whoever pushed up to receive one.

Kete caught his firearm, grabbing an armful of loaded magazines that were being pushed out onto the counter by a pair of army cadets. Struggling to cradle everything as he moved back out of the crowd, he scanned the room for any of the officers or senior NCOs from his unit.

He caught the eye of Major Mullaly, whom he usually knew as Ted the investment banker. Mullaly motioned him over even as he gathered a group of soldiers around him. Just as Kete struggled up he saw the major's eyes go vacant for a moment as he conferred via Cloud to military command, and he took the opportunity to stuff magazines into his webbing and load the final one into the rifle itself.

"You got grenades?" someone asked him, holding up a crate.

He shook his head, taking several of the weapons.

He was the only one not in uniform, but the only comment anyone made was to hand him a sticky patch for his shoulder, noting his rank of sergeant. It adhered instantly to his t-shirt and provided all the formality this night seemed to need. The other soldiers around him, he realized, were his fellow NCOs and a couple of officers.

Major Mullaly suddenly returned in mind, and spoke.

"Here's the deal," he barked. "Terran Astral troops have landed here in Riverport, as well as in Starfall and Firsthome. It looks like brigade strength at each landing, with limited orbital bombardment support. Their ships are under-strength in orbit and our littoral defenses are hoping to cut off their supply lines to isolate the troops on the ground."

He went on to explain the tactical situation relevant to them in Riverport, confirming Kete's observation that the main landing zone had been at the industrial park south of his home, shielded from the town's main defenses by the very ridge that his house sat upon. Robotic forces were engaging the invaders and containment was the main objective while the Centauri orbital guard fought to cut off any resupply or escape.

"Our mission," he concluded, projecting a map for all to see, "is to secure the ridgeline and hold it against the Terran advance. The army is moving artillery spotters into place right now, up on the ridge, and that should help a lot in slowing the enemy down."

Kete examined the map. The ridgeline. Southridge, actually—the neighborhood where he lived. He felt a mixture of relief and fear knowing that his street might become the best-defended part of the city. Yet it also would become a critical battleground.

"Form up your units," Mullaly said, "and load them into the transports that are arriving. When we get to the top of the ridge keep your men close to the transports, as they'll be the best cover we—"

Explosions rocked the crowded room.

Kete fell to his knees and struggled against the mass of sweating bodies tumbling around him. Through the smoke he saw militiamen struggling to stand and raise their weapons. Their bodies were hurled backward as slugs exploded out through their torsos. Screams pierced through the din of rifle fire. Kete slipped and fell to all fours as soldiers around him struggled to move.

He caught a glimpse of something metallic that emerged through the smoke, and thought it was an APR, but this was no silver machine. It was a dark-green, mechanical monster that ripped apart the wall of the depot like paper, and strode into the fray on mighty legs. Huge cannons mounted on the beast's wrists fired exploding rounds indiscriminately into the mass of uniforms, splattering the best and brightest of Riverport across wall, ceiling, and floor.

Kete dove flat to the ground, gritting his teeth in horror as he heard the rapid-fire slugs punch through his fellow soldiers, felt their smashed body parts rain down on him. The whirr and thump of the Terran shock trooper's mechanical feet stomping through the room was nothing that could be called human, yet inside that armored figure, behind those non-stop automatic cannons, was an actual human being driving his three-meter tall, powered exoskeleton.

It was a human who consciously slaughtered the hundreds of people trapped there.

He stayed down, half-buried in gore, until the last echo of the shock trooper had faded. In the awful silence that followed, he slowly raised his head and looked around. The sight that greeted his eyes was unspeakable, and he vomited before he could even rise to his knees.

Two or three other militiamen were stirring in the carnage. Forcing himself to move, he clambered over the bodies to help them to their feet. Those few survivors wordlessly made their way through the broken wall and gaggled together outside.

Three military transports had arrived, but they had been smashed by the shock trooper attack. Splattered remains of human bodies were littered around in the shadows, but as the minutes passed more and more survivors emerged from the darkness into which they had fled.

Shocked, pale faces peered around, looking for someone who was in charge. He saw no one above the rank of corporal, and eventually came to the sick conclusion that all the senior leaders had been inside the depot getting their orders when the attack came. The command structure of the entire local militia had been wiped out in a single assault.

That told him immediately where he could turn. Moving quietly into the shadow of a smoking transport, he uplinked to the Cloud. What he found there was confused, but some semblance of sanity seemed to be returning to the Centauri communal dimension.

The Terrans were not yet contained, but Riverport local defenses were moving into place. Artillery rained down on the invaders, and their armor had been successfully lured away from their main infantry group, thus exposing the latter to direct fire. The skies were heavily contested, but the defenders would be able to move across open ground, though it would be dangerous.

Kete zeroed in on a command channel, and reported the situation at his depot. His ID was validated, and he was accepted into the circle.

<What's your strength?> came the query through the Cloud.

He surveyed the militiamen milling around him.

<About fifty. Armed with personal weapons and with no protective transport.>

A quick consensus emerged, instructing him to take his force and join up with another militia unit six kilometers to the west. That unit was being re-tasked to secure the ridgeline and the artillery spotters.

<We'll meet them on the ridge,> he sent. <Where are the spotters?>

The exact location was slow to emerge. The spotters had detected an open Cloud conduit on the ridge, and had taken up a position where it was located. A vague impression appeared, of a house on the ridge, along with a sense of relief that such a secure circuit had been found.

Kete's heart turned to ice.

There was only one direct Cloud conduit on his street, and he hadn't shut it down in his rush to meet Valeria. The artillery spotters were in *his* house. The top priority for the Terrans would be to destroy those spotters, and neutralize the artillery.

"On me, on me!"

Kete was already running toward the mass of civilian cars, many of which were undamaged by the shock trooper attack. The militia around him seemed to awake from their collective stupor, and they obeyed as he ordered them to pile into every available vehicle and follow him back to the ridge.

Oh, dear God.

Leading the impromptu armada, Kete pushed to maximum the throttle of the strange car he drove. He instructed his passenger—a corporal—to relay his plan back over the voice circuit to the other soldiers.

"Friendly artillery is using a house on the ridge as a spotter site. We need to get up there and protect that house, and make sure any civilians in the area are evacuated before Terran troops attack."

Oh, dear God.

Rupa, Olivia, Jess.

* * *

The jump back to Terran space was uneventful, the shock of extra-dimensional travel banishing any last grip the nightmare had on him.

Once Kete had assured himself that the new jump gate was virtually invisible to casual spacetime probes, and that if it was detected it would likely be associated with the old, less stable Terran gate, he cleared the area, rejoined the space lanes and reactivated his beacon. Just another civilian out for a cruise.

As he made his way back through Terran space, he knew his death became more likely with each passing moment. That didn't matter, however—not on this mission.

Still, there were matters he had to resolve back on Earth.

11

Within twelve hours of returning to Earth, Kete had slithered into the military personnel records and discovered the location of the person whose name would never appear on a monument to the Battle of Southridge, but who deserved to have her name painted with blood across it.

Katja Andreia Emmes.

He crossed one leg casually over the other as he sat back in the plush leather chair. Ignoring the attendant who silently placed the glass of scotch on his side table, he mentally probed the check-in counter of the skyport executive lounge, hidden behind the false wall at his ten o'clock.

The lounge itself was comfortably full, with angular, minimalist chairs and couches arranged in a variety of patterns to cater to both the grouped travelers who wanted to chat and the solo travelers who wanted to be left alone. Like the rest of the Hanoi skyport, it was an airy, open space with sunlight flooding in through tinted, sloped ceiling panels.

About a third of the seats were occupied, mostly by business travelers and a handful of military personnel, most of them staring dully at the individual holo-viewers available at each seat. One woman was a senior State technocrat, but the electronic chatter radiating from her small team of assistants wasn't of immediate interest to him. He recorded the data nonetheless, just in case there was some tidbit of value.

An auto-alert drew his attention fully to the hidden check-in counter. His contact of interest had just been cleared to enter. Dragging the weightless image of his holo-viewer up to eye level in order to hide his face, he looked through the projected images toward the doorway.

Moments later, Katja Emmes strode into view. Dressed like the other military transients in her dark-blue duty uniform, she carried only a small black bag in her left hand. With her neat wedge-shape cap worn over shoulder-length blonde hair, knee-length skirt, and modest high heels revealing shapely calves, Kete might have easily taken her for any pretty, young staff officer. Her appearance was a world away from Kete's eternal image of the blackened, torn face visible under shorn, bloody hair and full Terran battle armor.

Emmes glanced his way, her face darkening to a frown. Instantly he refocused his gaze on the holo-viewer, desperately fighting down a swell of emotions. As she found a seat on the far side of the lounge, he locked on to the omnidirectional, encoded flicker of her military ID chip. Best to keep his distance.

It had taken longer than expected to locate her posting at the airlift station. None of her personal transmissions had revealed where she'd gone, and he'd been forced to dig directly into the Astral Force records. Risky, but now that he was in, he could check her personnel file at will.

No sooner had he located her posting than it had been changed—and abruptly, sending her back to Longreach on medical leave. Nothing in her file indicated why, but a message from one of the nearby Army units mentioned her by name. It had been most revealing.

Apparently the sender, one Storm Banner Leader Ciotti, had been threatened by an Astral officer. He didn't take kindly to it—a fact he'd been sure to communicate to the local Astral Force commander. The report didn't detail the circumstances, but it tied in with his growing opinion of Emmes's nature.

His Baryon pulsed blue, indicating an incoming call. He waved aside the holo-viewer and accepted the call. Chuck Merriman's face appeared.

Bait taken.

"Hey Kit," the reporter said. "You called?"

"Hi, Chuck," Kete replied. "Yeah, I was just following up on that Emmes family piece we worked on."

"Oh, yeah. I just got back from Mars, where I was shooting a follow-up with the father."

"Did he loosen up at all?"

"Not really, but his unit was doing low-g maneuvers, so at least I was able to snag some interesting stock footage." He smiled wryly. "I really could have used your expertise, buddy."

Kete smiled back. "Any time the network's willing to pay, I'm yours."

Chuck laughed. "They don't like paying for two of us to go off-planet. No, I just need to keep the Emmes family all on Earth somehow."

Kete glanced up at Emmes, seated with her back to him.

"Well, that's actually why I called you. I happen to be in the same skyport lounge as the daughter right now." He'd dipped the bait, and now he started tugging the line. "We're on the same flight to Longreach—where are you?"

Chuck's eyes lit up. "I'll be in Longreach by the time you land." New excitement entered his voice. "I've been trying to nail her down for weeks for a follow-on. Is she in uniform?"

"Undress blues."

"Perfect!" Merriman exclaimed. "What time does your flight land?"

Kete glanced at his itinerary. "Five-fifteen."

Chuck checked his watch. "Crap. Okay, I'll be there. If you don't see me in Arrivals, just stall her for a few minutes until I arrive."

Hooked.

"Stall her?"

"You know, use that equatorial charm of yours…" The room behind Chuck erupted into motion as the reporter gathered his things. "I've got the budget for a quick interview, and we can piece some standard visuals together afterward, based on what she's been up to."

"You got it, buddy." Kete forced an easy smile. "I'll see you in Longreach, with the subject suitably stalled."

Chuck signed off.

Kete dropped the Baryon to his lap and took a slow, thoughtful breath. Everything was coming together with the mission, but he hadn't planned on getting so close to his family's murderer. A most unusual sensation settled over him. Uncertainty.

He rubbed a hand over his face and chastised himself. There was nothing particularly challenging about Katja Emmes. Charity Brisebois was by far the more complex subject. He was a professional, and he just had to put his personal feelings aside.

Their flight was called, and Kete held back to ensure that Emmes remained where he could see her. She didn't disappoint, marching swiftly toward the skycraft entrance at the head of the executive class gaggle. He moved along within the crowd, noting idly the swell of regular citizens behind the gates, waiting for their turn to board. Crossing the threshold into the craft, he was directed past a few rows of crammed seats, and then up the broad stairs.

The bulkheads of the executive deck were almost completely transparent, with a dome overhead, and avant-garde furniture was scattered cleverly around a central bar. Passengers chose seats here and there, but Kete wandered up to the bar, tracking Emmes's ID beacon to see where she sat. Loitering with a drink was an unremarkable way to delay choosing his own seat.

The fresh-faced young barman moved efficiently to produce a scotch, while Emmes settled into a port-side seat, crossed one knee over the other, and stared out the window. A male sublieutenant approached her with forced casualness and said something Kete couldn't hear. Emmes turned in surprise. The sublieutenant said something else, to which Emmes nodded toward the qualification badges on her tunic, then replied with an expression of abyssal darkness.

The younger officer retreated immediately. Kete just caught his gesture of shivering as he rejoined some friends.

Okay, Kete concluded, making friendly conversation is out. Just how exactly Chuck expected him to stall Katja at the airport remained a mystery.

* * *

The flight was reasonably quick, but during that time Kete probed the skycraft's systems to determine how much luggage Emmes was bringing home with her. Three large bags, apparently. This reinforced the idea that her posting had been canceled.

From his seat on one of the centerline couches, he risked a quick glance at her. She wore a morose expression, staring blankly out at the upper atmosphere. He wished he could get into her thoughts directly, but the complete lack of Terran implants rendered his kind of probing useless. Whatever thoughts tormented Emmes, they were her own.

Kete did another sweep of the cabin, collecting a few more signals from the technocrat's staff, as the skycraft whistled in to land at Longreach. This time he moved quickly to the head of the line, actually bumping into Emmes as she strode for the stairs.

"Excuse me." She glanced up at him vaguely.

Actual physical contact. He had once again touched the killer of his family. Ignoring the icy shiver that rippled through him, he hurried to keep pace past the still-seated common passengers and out into the skyport arrivals area.

Executive luggage was off-loaded first, he knew. As he followed Emmes toward the pickup station, he dropped back slightly and called Chuck.

"We've landed. Where are you?"

"I'm just in the cab—five minutes away. Can you stall her?"

"I'll try my best."

She'd taken position at the luggage pickup, hover-cart ready beside her. Kete had no bags to collect, but an idea suddenly struck him. He grabbed a cart of his own and guided it to the far right-hand side of the station, where he knew the bags would first appear. Other passengers began to crowd in next to him, obscuring him from Katja further down the line.

Moments later the platform began to move, and the first bags began to appear. Several kit bags passed by, no doubt belonging to the other military passengers on the flight. He watched carefully, spied a bag with the tag "EMMES, K.A. 886," and hauled it up onto his cart. More bags continued to flow past including, eventually, two more with Emmes's name stenciled across them. Passengers began to drift away with their collected luggage, and soon he could see her again, standing with her two bags and staring impatiently at the trickle of cases still emerging.

His Baryon flashed green. Chuck had arrived.

He made a subtle show of checking the name on "his" bag, then sighed, placed it back onto the platform and leaned over to look through the hatch where the luggage was emerging. He then pushed aside the cart and followed behind Emmes toward the exit.

The arrivals hall was a towering, sun-filled chamber with marble floors and imitation-sandstone walls that rose in majestic solemnity for more than ten meters, before splitting into massive, diamond-shaped windows. Their upper halves were parted by expanding columns of stone that reached up to form a magnificent, fan-vaulted ceiling more than thirty meters above the polished floor. All along the sandstone walls between the exits and rendezvous points were temperature-controlled, mini-biomes representing diverse climates of Earth.

The arrivals hall was outfitted for both skycraft and the space elevators, and this vast chamber was the largest single entry point to planet Earth. All around him he saw newcomers stopping and staring at their surroundings, awed by the beauty of this gateway to humanity's home—and by extension awed also by the power of the State that could support such a monument.

He felt a distinct satisfaction knowing that its fate was in his hands.

Emmes didn't slow her pace to stare, and it was only the fact that she was weighed down by a luggage cart that Kete could easily catch up to her. No less than three porters hurried over to assist her, and she was increasingly caustic in her response to each of them.

She was more than halfway across the cathedral-like hall before Chuck Merriman intercepted her.

"Miss Katja," Chuck was saying as Kete approached. "A moment of your time, please."

She tried to ignore him, but he subtly stopped the forward motion of her cart and smiled as he towered over her. Kete caught up, but she didn't even glance his way.

"Mr. Merriman," she said, "you are a persistent man."

"In this case I think I'm just lucky," he said smoothly. "I had no idea you were passing through the skyport, and I realize you probably just want to get home, but could we arrange for that follow-on interview we've discussed?"

She glanced around furtively. The crowds slowly moved past them like molasses, and with her laden cart she had limited options. Then, to Kete's surprise, she smiled.

"Why don't you ask me your questions right now?" she suggested. "I'm going on leave, and I won't want to think about the Astral Force once I get home."

Chuck nodded. "It would be my pleasure, thank you." He glanced around the hall. "Kit, do you think that arctic biome would be a good backdrop?"

It took a moment for Kete to realize Chuck was speaking to him. Recovering quickly, he surveyed the sparkling ice and pale rocks pressing against their retaining wall.

"Yes, I'd say so."

Emmes seemed to notice him for the first time. "You remember my cameraman, Kit Moro?" Chuck gestured to him with one hand, and took her cart with the other.

She stared at him strangely with her dark eyes, then turned away. Chuck tried his best to engage her in disarming conversation as they all made their way toward the frigid backdrop, and Kete had to admit he was vaguely successful. At least she stopped frowning.

Chuck got her positioned with expert ease, her dark-blue uniform and blonde hair standing out brilliantly against the pale, dramatic background. Kete donned his "camera" visor and stood so he could capture her in quarter profile, then Chuck took station next to him to give her a focal point just off-camera.

On Chuck's command, they began.

Emmes was wooden at first, but slowly began to relax under Chuck's friendly, encouraging barrage. Kete kept his stare focused on her, but subtly shifted his attention to probing her military ID. It was rare to be this close to a member of the military for an extended period of time, and if he could break down at least some of the encryption of her device, it might prove invaluable later on.

The coding was complex, but there were ultimately only so

many different ways to mask a signal, and his previous work on Breeze's ID had already eliminated certain alternatives. He allowed his semiconscious to compare the two, and four groupings emerged quickly, as well as a few outliers that he noted but set aside for later. The first group was—

"Stop filming."

Kete broke off his thought-web and realized that Emmes was staring at him. He glanced at Chuck, whose eyebrows were raised in mild surprise.

"I'm sorry?" Chuck queried.

Emmes looked back and forth between them.

"Stop filming," she said firmly. "It's making me uncomfortable. That will have to be enough."

Chuck tossed Kete a quick glance, and he shrugged. Then the reporter frowned.

"I think we have enough visuals of you, Miss Katja," he said, "but I really need a bit more substance." She made to protest, but he raised placating hands. "We won't film, I promise—I'll just record it with my Baryon. I can drop the audio over some stock footage. If I can just ask a few more questions, then I won't have to bother you again."

She stared at him for a moment, and Kete was sure she was going to say no. To his surprise, she nodded.

He made a show of lowering his eyes to the floor so that it was obvious he wasn't filming, and Chuck picked up the interview where they had left off. Emmes needed a few moments to regain her composure, but she carried on quickly enough.

Kete kept his eyes down and re-engaged his thought-web, focusing on gathering as much data as he could from her ID beacon, and saving it for later analysis. Much of what he recorded would prove irrelevant, but he knew time was short, and he didn't have the luxury of identifying the information he needed to break the encryption.

He saw her foot move toward him. His arm swung up instinctively and slammed into her wrist, barely knocking aside the fist that was aimed at his face. She crouched into a combat stance, dark eyes wide in a mixture of shock and aggression.

Kete realized he'd dropped into a defensive stance of his

own, and he quickly stepped back, hands raised in a purposeful display of amateurish defense.

"Whoa! What the hell's going on?" Chuck stepped back and held up his arm.

"I said no filming," she hissed. Emmes's stare burned into Kete. He gestured in confusion, keeping silent to minimize his presence.

"Lieutenant, no one was filming." Chuck stepped partly between them. "I was just recording the audio on my Baryon. I can assure you, we're respecting your wishes."

Confusion mixed into her glare, diluting her anger with doubt. She relaxed her stance, took a deep, heavy breath and stared at the floor.

"I'm sorry," she said. "I'm very tired and I have to go home. I assume you have enough material that you won't bother me again?"

Chuck nodded. "Yes. Thank you very much, Miss Katja."

She again took control of her luggage cart and started for the exit. Her tiny form was quickly lost in the crowds.

Kete straightened his shirt as Chuck sidled up to him.

"You okay?" the reporter asked.

"Yeah."

"I assume she hit you first?"

"What?"

Chuck eyed him curiously. "Honestly, it happened so fast, I don't know what you guys just did. One second she's answering my question, the next limbs are flying, and you two squared off."

Kete gave his best look of ignorance. "I have no idea," he said. "She just took a shot at me, and I blocked it, thank goodness."

"That was a pretty nifty move."

He shrugged. "I travel a lot."

Chuck snorted derisively. "You hang out in hellholes a lot, you mean. Remind me to bring you along the next time I have to interview a drug lord."

He forced himself to laugh. "No thanks."

Chuck's gaze wandered to where Emmes had disappeared into the crowd. "She's an interesting lady, that's for sure."

Kete nodded. "She certainly is."

You have no idea, you poor, ignorant Terran, he added silently. *She is very interesting indeed.*

12

Thomas knelt down, pressing his hand into the soft, warm grass, and smiled. It was still moist at the roots—the irrigation system worked with remarkable efficiency—and so green. Not like the yellow scrub in the playgrounds in his parents' neighborhood. He reckoned this was even nicer than the playing fields at the Astral College.

But then, this was the first grass he could truly call his own, so no doubt he was biased.

The sound of rustling footsteps caught his ear, and a pair of small feet moved into his view, jeweled toes scrunching into the lawn. He glanced up at his wife, resplendent in her light, summer wrap and dazzling jewelry. Soma's eyes shone with excitement as she crouched down beside him.

"The grass is perfect, darling," she said, mocking him playfully. "Everyone's going to be very impressed."

Thomas smiled. "I thought the pond was meant to impress."

"Oh, yes, but people don't stand in the pond." She laughed. "At least, not until some drunken fool starts splashing in it."

"I can't imagine who that might be, dear."

She gave him a mischievous smile. "That was weeks ago! Besides, I wouldn't want to ruin my wrap."

"You could always take it off, first."

"Why, Lieutenant Commander…" She tried to look shocked, but was smirking too much. "What would the guests say?"

"That you are the most beautiful woman on Earth."

She leaned in to kiss him, sliding onto her back and pulling him down. The passion grew, and Thomas willingly lost himself to her embrace. She tasted of vodka and mint, making the kiss that much sweeter.

A quiet voice in his earpiece disturbed the moment.

"Sir, madam, the first of your guests have arrived. Mr. Errol Meads and Ms. Jade Kennedy." Thomas sat up with a start, looking toward the back of the house. Soma's fingers caressed the short hair at the back of his head.

"Darling, really, you shouldn't be so jumpy," she said. "We're married, after all."

He climbed to his feet and offered her a hand, effortlessly pulling her up. With a sly smile she straightened her wrap and moved to greet their guests. Thomas hung back, knowing that these were her friends, and that he was part of the grand tour she wanted to take them on.

Members of the Jovian elite, she wanted to impress them with her garden of real grass and real surface water under an open, blue sky. Her bona fide war hero husband was the centerpiece of the display. He strolled over to the pond and absently busied himself with tossing a few grains of food into the water for the golden koi.

He heard laughter behind him, and light-hearted voices approaching.

"Darling," Soma called, "our guests are arriving." Thomas turned, affecting his best expression of polite interest and the hint of a smile. These were rich, influential people, but he was an Astral Force officer born on Earth, and he intended to greet them as equals.

Errol and Jade were both perfectly groomed in the latest summer fashion, arms bare to the shoulders and legs bare to the knees. They were surprisingly pale, and Thomas thought he could detect the beginnings of an artificial tan working to tint Jade's skin. Both visitors eyed him with great interest.

"This is my husband," Soma said, taking his arm, "Lieutenant Commander Thomas Kane."

Errol extended his hand. "A pleasure, Commander. Good

work out there in the colonies."

Thomas shook his hand firmly, and kissed Jade's offered fingers. "The pleasure's mine. It's good to be home," he said. "How long have you been on Earth?"

"Barely a week. The damned visa process is still a nuisance."

"I understand they've stepped up security these past few months."

"Like the colonists would ever try anything here in Terra," Errol scoffed.

"But at least we had some extra days on Mars," Jade added. "Have you been to Mars?"

Thomas had, and he slipped easily into the conversation about this resort versus that, and the best viewpoints along the Valles Maneris. Soma excused herself as more guests arrived, each one announced discreetly in the earpieces both he and his wife wore, and by the time drinks had been passed around there was quite a crowd around him.

The reporter Chuck Merriman was among them, although at the sight of Thomas's expression he promised that everything was "off the record." That resulted in a gale of disbelieving laughter.

It didn't take long before one of the women delicately dipped a toe into the pond's cool water, and Thomas found confidence in the fascination exhibited by these residents of Jupiter's moons, in what he considered the simplest things.

Talk inevitably came around to recent troubles in the colonies. One of the guests, a Mr. Quinton Speirs, claimed to have been aboard a starliner not far from the Terran jump gates when the Centauri fleet had attacked. He gave what he obviously considered a riveting account of the liner's diversion away from the trouble. He hadn't actually seen the fighting, but had heard the reports almost in real-time.

Another guest, a Ms. Maxine Zhou, was good friends with a senior officer on the Astral Base near Ganymede. She reported breathlessly that the military had actually been more concerned about the incursion than the media let on. This drew a flurry of opinions from the assembled guests, each apparently formed by exclusive information they had from the inside.

Thomas listened with interest, eager to break in but not

wanting it to show. He kept his face carefully neutral at some of the more absurd suggestions, and waited for his opportunity. Chuck Merriman, he noticed, was also listening more than speaking, and Thomas occasionally made eye contact with him as if to communicate some private amusement. Chuck kept his expression one of polite interest for a while, but eventually he began to respond to Thomas with eye rolls and smirks.

"Any credible reporter," Chuck announced suddenly, cutting into the chatter, "will try to find the most reliable source. If we really want to know what happened out there, maybe we should ask a military veteran."

Conversation drifted off as all eyes turned to Thomas. He adopted an expression of thoughtful humility.

"Maxine was right when she said that the military was concerned about the uprising," he confirmed. "Although we've been containing the situation in Sirius for years, no one expected Centauria and the other, more civilized colonies to harbor such extremists. We had to move quickly, and in force, in order to respond."

"Were you at the battle at the jump gates?" someone asked.

"No, I was already deployed to Sirius, in command of a fast-attack craft," he replied. "We were sneak-attacked by the Centauri fleet, but we managed to scatter them." That was a gross misrepresentation of the truth, Thomas knew, but he'd been briefed on what the official story was to be. "Some Sirian warlords tried to use the confusion to spread terror, but a quick strike on Cerberus put that to rest."

The rest of the story was punctuated by frequent questions, but within a few minutes Thomas had laid out a version of the real battle in both Sirius and Centauria. He used a carefully measured tone that played down his role, while at the same time hinting at his unsung heroism. He'd been practicing the story in his mind for weeks, waiting for exactly this sort of social opportunity.

His guests held their expressions in various degrees of cool interest, but he could tell that each one was riveted. No doubt they'd all go home bragging of their personal friendship with a hero from the front lines, and re-tell his story many times over.

"Sir, madam." It was a servant. "Admiral Randall Bush and the officers of the *Neil Armstrong* have arrived."

Perfect timing. He'd purposefully told his new Research colleagues that the party started an hour later than it did, to give him enough solo time with the wealthy guests to establish his position as a veteran. Not that he expected these bumbling eggheads to upstage him, but every opportunity had to be played properly.

"Excuse me, ladies and gentlemen," he said. "Some of my Astral Force colleagues have just arrived." Leaving Soma to lead the gossip about the war, he started toward the house to receive his new guests.

"Commander Brisebois," she stated simply as the neural scan flashed over her. It was still fun to say, though her rank really wasn't new anymore.

What was even more fun, she realized, was to watch the subtle but unmistakable surprise whenever some flunky realized that she was someone important. The surprise was usually greater when she was in civilian clothes which, due to her position in Intelligence, was most days.

The servant stiffened slightly, and quickly turned his attention to her companion.

"Kit Moro," he said, keeping his head steady for the neural scan. The servant studied his readout with sudden interest. He glanced up at Kit.

"You have an optical implant."

Kit smiled and produced his media card. "I'm a freelance cameraman—it's registered." He cast a sidelong glance of resigned amusement at Breeze as the servant conducted a quick verification. It was common, at security checks not manned by the State itself, to have to resort to more old-school proof. Private citizens and organizations didn't have the same level of access to the universal ID chip implants.

"You'll have to keep it deactivated while inside the residence," the servant said firmly.

"With pleasure."

His easy confidence was probably what Breeze liked most about him. There were plenty of men who could match him with good looks and style, but most of them were trying very hard to impress. Rarely did she meet someone who seemed so at ease with the world. As they passed through the gate and into the residence, he reached out smoothly to drape her arm in his—a move that could either be the courtesy of a gentleman or the advance of a suitor.

It intrigued Breeze that she couldn't tell which.

"Thank you for coming," she said suddenly. She realized that her words might sound too eager, and when he glanced over she rolled her eyes slightly. "I never know who's going to be at this sort of thing, and it's good to know I'll have at least one interesting companion."

"The Astral Force's best and brightest?" he protested. "How could they not be interesting?" His wry expression matched exactly what she was thinking.

The reception hall of Thomas's house was flooded with sunlight, but comfortably cool. Marble floors sparkled under whitewashed walls, and open arches led to a lush, green lawn beyond. Guests were already mingling in small pockets, and with no uniforms to guide her Breeze had to look sharp to spot the most interesting targets. Admiral Chandler was supposed to be here, she knew, and hopefully a few more flag officers would deign to attend. In particular she needed to find that slime ball Bush. She wanted to talk to him...

She needn't have worried, though, for Admiral Bush noticed her almost immediately, abandoning the hors d'oeuvres and descending like a plump pigeon. His tubby figure wasn't complemented by his choice of outfit, and Breeze really wished he'd pay for the surgery and get a full head of hair. Their professional relationship to date had been cordial, and she'd let him play the role of magnanimous admiral, but his lascivious glances were becoming a bit too much even for her.

"How nice to see you, Breeze, welcome." His soft face was all smiles as he reached to kiss her hand. "And I don't believe I've met your husband."

She laughed easily, squeezing the hand that still held hers, and brushing Kit's shoulder.

"Oh, Admiral, you underestimate me!" she replied. "I'm not

ready to settle down just yet." She freed her hand from his grasp and placed it in the small of Kit's back. "But I agree that this gentleman is worth a second look."

"Kit Moro. It's a pleasure to meet you, Admiral."

Bush shook Kit's hand and beamed. "The pleasure's mine, sir."

She pressed her hand against his back just a bit more firmly. "Kit, I'm sorry but I need to discuss business with the admiral for just a moment. Could you get us some drinks? I promise we'll be done by the time you get back."

He feigned a tiny sigh. "The trouble with being a civilian among the military." He flashed her an easy smile and stepped back. "I'll take my time." With a graceful turn he strolled away toward the elaborate bar on the far side of the garden. She couldn't help but watch him go for a moment, but quickly turned back to business.

"Sir, thank you for a few moments," she began. "As the head of Intelligence's Dark Bomb project, I'm very keen to meet the research team involved."

Pride beamed from his dark eyes. "I've given it top priority, and assigned my flagship to the task. They have orders to cooperate with your office, as required."

"Thank you, sir. My team has sent over some initial questions regarding dark matter concentrations at depth, but we haven't received anything back."

Bush frowned slightly. "How long ago did you send the request?"

"Three weeks, and I know that the *Armstrong* has deployed during that time."

His frown deepened. "I'll speak to Captain Lincoln. Whatever you need, Breeze, you just tell me."

"Thank you, sir," she said with a smile. "I'm sure there's a reasonable explanation."

"In fact, I'll introduce you to the senior staff, and you can ask them yourself." He gestured, and Breeze saw Thomas Kane, standing in the small cluster of officers just outside on the grass. It was annoying to have him so closely involved in her first important project, but at least now she was the senior officer. He looked relaxed in his civilian clothes, drink in one hand and gorgeous wife in the other. Despite her distaste for him, she had to acknowledge that he'd done rather well in the months since they'd returned.

Somehow his career was still on track, and his marriage had gone ahead, thanks to the devil's bargain he'd been forced to strike with her. She'd never met Soma before, but seeing the two of them together now—mixed race, decent difference in height, good genes all around—she felt an uncharacteristic pang of envy. He was at the age when to remain single would seem odd, and with his wife's wealth to match his own experience as a veteran, he had taken an important step toward securing a profitable future.

Unwittingly, she glanced back through the arches toward the bar, where Kit was chatting casually with the server, killing time to give her a few minutes for business. He was self-made, so no pedigree, but she had plenty of that, and the balance might be beneficial.

His dark, handsome features would certainly be telegenic, and his exotic career would add a touch of dash uncommon in a civilian. He was from Earth, which wasn't as good as interworldly, but their mixed African-European genes would produce beautiful children. Her military service would be up in a year, and it was time to start thinking about options. She could do worse.

She and Bush moved toward the group that included Thomas, and he was the first to notice her approach, his eyes flashing with surprise, almost fear. She adopted her most engaging smile and stepped ahead of the admiral to greet him like a long-lost friend. She grasped his shoulders and kissed him fully on both cheeks, knowing that this was just a *bit* too familiar.

"Oh, Thomas, how wonderful to see you!"

He held his ground, smiling politely as his wife's grip tightened around him.

"As much a pleasure as always, Breeze."

Quick introductions saw Breeze acquainted with the new Mrs. Kane and Lieutenant Helena Grey of the *Armstrong*. Captain Andy Lincoln she'd already met on her only visit to the ship, and she was eager to grill him again on the lack of response to her inquiries about the Dark Bomb research, but Soma's presence made such classified talk impossible.

Kit rejoined her with drinks.

Having regained his composure quickly, Thomas took the conversational lead. His wife made what Breeze considered a very obvious show of hanging on his every word, but so, strangely, did Lieutenant Grey. For an old nag, Helena certainly poured on the feminine charm, directing it equally toward Thomas, Andy, Admiral Bush, and even Kit.

Bush seemed strangely fond of her—*he hadn't, had he?*—and Thomas navigated her charms with ease. Andy Lincoln, Breeze determined quickly, was clueless in a conversation that wasn't about his job, and Kit sailed along with the flow of chatter as if he'd known these people for years.

"So you and Breeze served on the same ship in the recent troubles?" he asked at one point.

"Careful with your military terms," Breeze chided Kit. "Even I winced at that. We serve 'in' ships, not 'on' them."

"My apologies," he offered with a slight bow towards Thomas, "to all those who served *in* a ship."

Thomas kept his expression carefully neutral, she noted with quiet amusement. And his discomfort had nothing to do with Kit's misuse of sacred jargon, she knew.

"Yes, we were both in the fast-attack craft *Rapier*."

"And we both did time on Admiral Chandler's staff," she added, "when *Rapier* was out of commission."

"So you both must know Katja Emmes?" Kit asked.

Breeze was startled into silence. Why did Kit keep coming back to that bitch? She glanced at Thomas just in time to see the red fading quickly from his cheeks. Amused, she decided to let him answer the question.

"She was also in *Rapier*," he finally replied. "Except for when she was part of the planetary strike force."

"You mean Abeona?" Kit said smoothly. "When your force attacked the Centauri homeworld?"

"That's right," Thomas acknowledged. "Katja was on the surface, and Breeze and I were in orbit."

Kit's face displayed admiration. "She sounds like one brave lady."

Annoyance got the better of her, and Breeze tried to deflect the conversation.

"Crazy lady is more like it," she replied. "Nearly got herself killed, standing too close to her own bombardment order. If it hadn't been for Thomas coordinating the battle overhead, she might have got her entire platoon killed."

Thomas's face creased in the most open display of real emotion she'd seen yet.

"Hardly, Breeze," he said, and he turned. "You're right, Kit— she's very brave."

"Why do you ask?" Soma interjected. "Do you know her?"

Kit shrugged. "I did the filming for her interview with Chuck—a piece he's been doing on that family of veterans. I'm almost surprised to not see her here." He laughed. "With Breeze and Thomas working together again, why not Emmes?"

"I'm not sure how useful a strike officer would be on a Research mission," Bush joked, to automatic laughter. Breeze forced herself to laugh, then assumed a serious look.

"Actually, I understand she's been removed from duty."

"Breeze…" Thomas warned.

She nodded, looking at everyone in the group to ensure she had their full attention.

"Apparently she pulled a weapon on a senior Army member, in her own barracks." The disapproving clucks and murmurs she heard made her feel a little better.

"Sounds serious," Kit commented. "What happens to troopers who do that sort of thing?"

Anger flashed up again, but she suppressed it in a moment, through long practice. She forced a sweet smile to her face and she rubbed her hand against Kit's arm.

"They get treated," she responded. "The Astral Force takes care of its own. I'm sure she'll be fine."

Thomas and Soma suddenly looked at each other and nodded. He tapped his ear.

"We've just been told that Admiral Chandler has arrived," he announced. "Admiral Bush, would you care to join us as we greet him?" The fat flag officer squeaked some affirmative response and waddled off in the wake of Kane's flowing movements toward the house.

Kit didn't miss a beat in what could have become an

awkward silence, and he politely inquired into the duties of a Research ship. Lincoln, suddenly back in his element, began gushing about all the scientific awards his last command had won, and of his big plans for *Neil Armstrong*. Breeze listened with growing irritation, not only because the conversation was boring, but because she was beginning to get a sense of why her inquiries weren't being answered. Kit, on the other hand, seemed engrossed, and she couldn't gauge his sincerity at all.

He was smooth, no question.

Helena suddenly declared that she was going to freshen up, and invited Breeze to join her. It was the classic escape plan for any woman, and Breeze took it gratefully.

"I'm sorry about the captain," Helena said quietly as they crossed the wide lawn together. "He loves his special experiments and the chance to win awards."

"I don't want to take away from his success," Breeze replied, "but I need that Dark Bomb information."

"I know, dear," Helena responded. "Trust me, no one is more frustrated than me—and I'm the one who has to try and produce viable scientific results from the mish-mash of data this team produces."

Breeze doubted the sincerity of this cunning old bat, but at least she could speak her mind to someone with the power to help her.

"We all know how to keep our bosses happy while still getting the job done," she offered. "Get Thomas on your side, and let *him* fight with the captain."

Helena rolled her eyes. "Oh, please. Kane is no better. He doesn't know the first thing about science, or leadership. He just hides away with Andy and plans the latest ridiculous assignment to drop on us."

Breeze found that hard to believe, but it was gratifying nonetheless to imagine Thomas as an incompetent.

"Well, it wouldn't be the first time he's messed up."

Helena nodded sympathetically, her face turning very earnest. "Science is a different world from warfare, and now I have two combat idiots who think they're special forces or something, coming in and ruining what was once a happy ship."

"Two?" Breeze responded. "Is Captain Lincoln from the Fleet?"

"Lincoln?" Helena scoffed. "He doesn't have a fighting bone in his body—I think he'd wet himself if we had to go through a jump gate." She shook her head and pointed to a nearby young couple laughing over drinks. "No, Kane brought a little friend along with him to *Armstrong*—that giggling idiot Jack Mallory."

Breeze sighed in frustration. Hadn't anyone euthanized that puppy yet?

"He's on your ship?"

"Yes, and ruining half the experiments we set out to perform," Helena said. "He keeps flirting with my doctoral candidate, too—like he is right now."

Breeze wasn't sure what to believe. Jack was a moron in some ways, but a scary genius in others. He probably knew more about dark matter and the Bulk than this embittered old crow. More likely he was too busy chasing tail to realize it. A pretty clear picture began to emerge of what was going on aboard that damn research ship.

Excusing herself from Helena, she figured it was time to go and rescue Kit from Andy's ravings. She strolled back slowly, though, curious now that she knew Jack Mallory was in the picture.

He was indeed talking and laughing with a young woman, whom Breeze recognized from the *Armstrong* records as Sublieutenant Amanda Smith. She was plain and plump, not the sort she'd expect Jack to chase. Indeed, as she watched more closely, she decided pretty quickly that the opposite was the case. Jack looked upon Amanda with little more than innocent friendship, but she looked back at him with something that was quite a bit more.

Breeze's mood had darkened just enough that she decided to get this little floozy's mind back on her job. She put a slink in her walk and glided right up to them, interrupting Amanda in mid-sentence.

"Hey, Jack."

He jumped at her touch, eyes widening as he realized who was standing before him. That stupid grin split his features.

"Wow. Hi, Breeze." He responded clumsily to her cheek

kisses, automatically putting his hands on her waist. "What are you doing here?"

She didn't shake off his hands, and even placed hers on his arms. "Wouldn't you like to know?" she replied. "A girl has to be mysterious though." It was the perfect line to accompany the deep smolder with which she bore down on him.

He didn't stand a chance. The poor boy tried to speak but couldn't form words over his grin.

"Are you in town for a while?" she asked. "We should get together... like old times."

"Uhh, yeah," he said. "That'd be great. My ship is in and out a lot, but—"

"I'll call you."

"Yeah. Yeah, thanks."

She released him and stepped away, casting a contemptuous glance at Amanda. The little scientist's face was stony and her eyes blazed. Not at Breeze—she wouldn't dare—but at Jack.

Sometimes it just felt good to hurt somebody.

13

As Soma introduced the newly arrived Admiral Chandler to the admiring Jovian masses, Thomas excused himself and made a beeline for his most unwelcome guest. He spotted Breeze walking away from Jack and Amanda, predatory eyes scanning the garden party.

She was stunning. There was just no other word for it. Her dark brown hair was shorter than he remembered and ironed straight, the tips just brushing against her bare shoulders. Her blue eyes were highlighted by her form-fitting, strapless summer dress, and her long legs were revealed through high slits with every step. She wore only minor jewelry, instead highlighting her natural assets to draw the eye.

She treated him to her most dazzling smile.

"Thomas, thanks for letting us crash your party."

He stepped in her path, stopping her with hands on her elbows. To disguise the gesture he smiled and leaned in to whisper in her ear.

"What are you doing here?"

"I heard you were having a little get-together." In her heels she was nearly his height, and she gave him a sly look. "Since we work together, I assumed it was an accident that I wasn't invited."

"It's a private party."

"No doubt." She looked over his shoulder toward the pond and Soma's cluster of friends. Then she ran a hand across the thin fabric of his shirt. "Maybe I should steal you away for a private party of our own." The subtle scent of her perfume and the warm proximity of her body was intoxicating, but he forced himself to take a step back.

"I don't think my wife would appreciate that."

Breeze's smile turned to ice. "I don't think your wife would appreciate knowing that you enjoyed a few 'private parties' during the war," she said. "You *were* engaged at the time, weren't you?"

He crossed his arms. "What do you want, Breeze?"

"I need to know how to proceed with my Fleet Marshall Investigation," she said, dropping the pretenses. "I need to be sure who's going to take the fall. You, or your sweet Katja?"

"Why does anyone have to take the fall?"

"Because certain members of the government have been embarrassed by this war, and they want villains to sacrifice," she replied. "No one too senior, of course, but not some lowly trooper." She gestured smoothly with her hand. "It has to be someone just right—network ratings matter."

"Then come after me, Breeze."

She considered for a moment, studying him.

"I hope you understand what this means."

"I do."

"Are you really ready to widow dear Soma?"

"She'll be at my side when I deliver the folded flag to your family."

Her smile turned sincere. "I must admit, I'm a little surprised. I really didn't think you had that kind of nobility in you."

"Katja's war is done," he said. "This one is ours."

"Well said, Thomas."

He glanced over to where Kit Moro was still trapped in a conversation with Andy Lincoln. "You seem to be making friends since our return."

Breeze maintained a nonchalant expression. "I needed a date."

Moro excused himself from Lincoln, who looked disappointed at having lost his audience, before moving to speak to a cute blonde who had just emerged from the house.

Thomas's mood lightened instantly. "Uh-oh." He looked back at Breeze, sudden amusement growing as he saw her cheeks redden almost imperceptibly. "You might be losing your date."

She laughed lightly. "I don't own him. He can talk to whoever he wants." Her habitual charm returned as she stroked his back. "Mrs. Kane might get jealous, but I don't."

"No? Well that's good," he said. "Because your date is chatting up Katja."

The hand dropped away like a stone, and Breeze took an involuntary step forward. Thomas couldn't keep the smirk off his face.

"Hardly recognize her with that long hair, hmm?" he noted. "And she's certainly stayed fit, hasn't she?"

But he, too, had lost his audience. Breeze was already stalking off, leaving a wake of sweet perfume.

Breeze moved with purpose. What was so fascinating about that little blonde psychopath?

Katja noticed her approach and took a single step backward, bare feet flexing on the grass. Breeze forced herself to slow down, chastising herself for overreacting. Kit followed Katja's gaze and glanced casually over his shoulder, greeting Breeze with a warm smile.

"Ah, here she is." He extended his arm and gently pulled her close. "I was just talking to Lieutenant Emmes about how you and I met. Apparently the good lieutenant is still trying to figure out her new Baryon. Maybe you should show her a few tricks."

"I doubt the lieutenant would be interested in my little tricks," Breeze said as lightly as she could muster.

"You've got that right," Katja said. The long hair and simple dress were a remarkable transformation, but that cold, butchy voice was as hard as ever. It made Breeze want to shift the target of her investigation, just out of spite—but she and Thomas had reached an understanding, and he'd prove more satisfying prey anyway.

Katja was good at killing things, but she had all the social subtlety of a mother walrus. There was still a pretty good chance, in Breeze's estimation, that she'd do herself in before too long. She didn't need any help.

"I'm *so* glad you're feeling better, Katja," she said, starting to pull Kit away. "You should probably say hello to Thomas, before his guests steal him again."

Katja didn't reply. She gave Kit a strange glance, and then marched off at a brisk pace.

Maybe, Breeze thought, *I'm being too hard on mother walruses.*

Katja didn't have far to go. Thomas was hovering nearby, although with the overall noise of the party, his words of greeting were lost. He gave her elbow a quick squeeze, then stepped distinctly back. They exchanged a few comments, then Thomas pointed over toward Jack, who'd been abandoned by his hapless admirer.

Katja brightened visibly, and she walked across the grass to greet the young pilot. Kit nodded in Jack's direction.

"Another friend of yours?"

She felt a moment of envy at the easy rapport between Thomas, Katja, and Jack, but brushed it off with a laugh.

"Just a kid I used to know, like a little brother."

He raised a single eyebrow, but laughed as well.

"I see that Admiral Chandler is holding court," he observed. "Do you want to sidle our way in?"

Sure enough, Chandler was in the middle of a large group of guests. Normally she wouldn't miss a chance to further ingratiate herself to the man who was fast becoming her patron, but she suddenly found herself weary of the games. What she really wanted, she decided, was to have a nice, non-political evening with a man she found fascinating.

"No thanks," she said. "I just can't help feeling bad for you."

Surprise creased his handsome features. "Why?"

"Because you've been in Longreach a month, and you still haven't tasted the best Italian food on the planet."

Comprehension dawned. "Ahh, yes: the fabulous Emilio's. I thought you were all talk."

"Oh you'll find I'm much more than that." She took his arm and together they headed for the security gate.

Thomas watched Breeze disappear into the house with her date, and felt a wave of relief. It was impossible to tell what damage she'd caused, but he was pretty sure he'd minimized her impact.

Katja's laughter suddenly brought him back to his immediate surroundings. Jack was just finishing a story, much to her obvious delight.

"That sounds normal," she said. "I usually got hurt flying with you, too."

Thus encouraged, Jack launched into another story. Katja seemed comfortable in her surroundings, and he felt it safe to excuse himself. Nothing like a pilot, apparently, to soothe a nervous female. He made sure to compliment Katja on her dress. Her lack of jewelry and bare feet made her look a bit rustic next to the Jovians, but she'd clearly made an effort to appear civilian.

He left her in Jack's care. Finally making his way back to Soma's crowd, he saw that canapés were being circulated. Accepting a glass of wine, he scanned the crowd for Chuck Merriman, a potential ally. The reporter and those in his conversation cluster regarded Thomas with curiosity as he approached.

"We thought we'd lost you," Chuck commented.

"Oh, just saying hi to a few old friends."

"You're just too much in demand."

Thomas laughed and raised his glass. "Here's to the freedom we fought for—the freedom to drink away my entire day."

Polite laughter rippled through the group as they clinked glasses and drank. Thomas made a point of catching Chuck's eye and subtly motioning toward the pond, then excused himself and wandered over to the buffet. He absently selected a few morsels, watching until he saw Chuck separate himself from the group and wander nonchalantly away.

Thomas quickly approached, before anyone else could get in the way. Despite the outward serenity in his conversation with Breeze, he knew that they were now playing the game for keeps. He needed powerful allies, and fast.

"Chuck, Soma tells me that your star is rising in the media business."

The reporter shrugged with easy modesty. "I've been lucky enough to break a few good stories."

"There's been a lot of coverage of the recent troubles, but most of it has been superficial," Thomas said. "I was hoping we could get something a bit more... substantial... offered to the public."

"Well, you know how it is with the military," Merriman said, looking around. "All the best news gets hushed up." He looked vaguely interested, though. "We have to toe the line most of the time, or the State feels the need to get involved."

"I hear you." Thomas glanced over at Chandler, still surrounded by admirers, and Bush, who was eagerly trying to join the limelight. "But if I could get official sanction, would you be interested to get the inside track on some high-profile weapons research?"

There was nothing vague about his interest now as Chuck turned toward Thomas.

"It would certainly make for a good story," he agreed. "What do you have in mind?"

"Have you heard anything about the Dark Bomb?"

14

The glass door to her balcony thumped under the buffeting wind, then hissed with the brush of fine dust grains skimming off the city streets.

Katja winced at the sound, but forced herself not to back away. The sun in the sky was golden yellow, not the hot white of Sirius nor the deep orange of Centauria. Even through the glass she could feel the heat on her face, and she reveled in the enveloping warmth of home.

Home. This was her new home. She cast her eyes across the busy urban street. Scores of people moved under the partial relief of the awnings jutting from each building, cars and buses passing efficiently along the black road toward the broken, white-capped surface of Lake Sapphire. The boardwalk was busy despite the rising winds, although some of the cafes were starting to gather in their deck furniture.

She tried to pick out individual details, tried to guess at pedestrians' destinations or purposes, but once she'd assessed their gaits and builds—and their threat levels—her imagination failed her. All these people, just living their lives and caring their cares, oblivious to her presence...

Katja couldn't imagine it.

She stepped out of the direct sunlight, back into the cool relief of her apartment. Her eyes adjusted quickly as she shuffled around the room, running her hand along the backs of the furniture that had just been delivered that day. It was new, and of a style Merje said was very much the fashion. It had the name of some place in Italy, which she'd already forgotten, but she admired the clean, simple lines and elegant construction. Perhaps guests would complement her on it when she threw a party.

The very thought elicited a snort.

The entire apartment was built in a similar style. She'd rented it mainly because of its location—if she was going to get back into society she figured she had to be in the thick of things. There was something very appealing, almost military, in the straight lines and unadorned walls. She paused at the end of the couch and took in the entire room.

Home. This was her new home.

She'd slept late again, but couldn't muster the energy to care. Not that anyone was expecting her any time soon. One of the beauties of being placed on medical leave—no obligations. The other was an increase in her drug dosage, which kept everything nice and quiet in her mind. She considered lying down for a nap, but then remembered that if she wanted to eat later, she needed to go shopping.

With a slow turn of her head she spotted the grocery bag. The drugs were good at keeping the nightmares at bay, but they made her feel like a simpleton. She had to focus on getting the bag onto her shoulder, and she held it tight as she carefully collected her Baryon and confirmed that the shopping list had been saved.

Out in the hallway, one other person was waiting for the elevator. Male, graying, extra weight in the midsection. He smiled at her. She smiled back, reminding herself that she wasn't on duty. To him, she was just Katja, the pretty girl from down the hall. The elevator door opened and he motioned politely for her to enter.

"Nice weather today," she said, attempting a casual conversation.

His face creased in a puzzled expression. "The wind storm's expected to get worse."

As the elevator descended, her mind jumbled with how to respond as a civilian would, and she pushed down the considerations of poor visibility and restricted tactical movement.

The door opened to the first floor before she could form her response. The man smiled at her again and exited. She followed.

The sound of his shoes clicking on the marble floor of the lobby faded rapidly, and Katja listened absently to the soft brush of her own sandals as she walked slowly to the doors. They opened automatically as she approached, and the wall of heat from the unfiltered air crashed over her like a tidal wave. The blast surprised her, even scared her, and she gritted her teeth as nightmare images fought upward in her mind.

The dark, residential street on Abeona.

The house with the Centauri spotters. The explosion as the orbital bombardment obliterated it, and nearly killed her with the concussion.

She felt the drugs respond, and her anxiety began to fade. The images lingered for a moment longer, though, and with new clarity she remembered a dark form bending over her as she lay in the aftermath. Probably one of the medics, she guessed, reaching for her neck to check her pulse. Strange she'd never remembered him before.

With a deep breath she started down the sidewalk, blending into the pedestrian crowd. With her light dress and blonde bob she was just another girl out doing her shopping, she reminded herself. She was safe on Earth, safe at home.

The welcome cool of the market helped to lift her spirits, and she took her time selecting the various vegetables she intended to whip into a stir-fry. In this part of Longreach it was hard to find a bad piece of food, but she still indulged in the search for the perfect pepper. The sheer banality of her quest was soothing, and she was vaguely aware that she was even smiling as she finally made her selections.

At the bakery she took a different tack and randomly grabbed a baguette without inspecting it, trusting fate and whim to make the choice for her. The fact that she did this suddenly struck her as rather funny. She smiled as she headed for her final stop—the butcher's counter.

A cleaver slammed down on the chopping block as one of the

butchers expertly prepared a side of beef. The blade sliced cleanly through the hunk of meat, tearing muscle and sinew. Slabs of flesh lay on the red-stained wood. Not strewn and splattered, like the effects of her explosive rounds, but piled almost neatly. No blood seeped from the dead flesh. Unlike the living bodies that exploded with a pull of her trigger. Blood spraying across walls. Human beings, splattered like so much livestock.

The woman in front of her pointed out which of the steaks she wanted, and the server expertly picked it out, weighed it, and began wrapping it up. No blood spurting as she frantically pressed a bandage against a neck wound. Holding it tight even as she struggled to get another sealant-gel pack from her medic-kit. Hot, thick blood seeping through her fingers, pouring out the life of the young trooper in her platoon whose name she'd never even learned.

She'd only been in command for a few hours. How could she possibly know all fifty of them?

Katja leaned her hand against the clear glass of the butchery counter, vaguely aware as her shopping bag fell to the floor. She clenched her stomach muscles, unable to stop the dry heaves that spasmed upward. The drugs dulled the images of the boy's eyes, staring up at her in shock and terror, those eyes above the last pulses of his blood oozing down her hand.

Firm hands gripped her shoulders.

"Miss, are you all right?"

She opened her eyes, turning her gaze away from the rows of flesh piled behind the glass. A uniformed security guard had a hand on her shoulder, and was observing her with concern. She stared back at him, begging him to understand.

"I didn't even know his name," she said, the words catching in her throat. "There wasn't time. Wei was dead, and we had to move."

The guard's expression turned wary.

"Miss, I think I'd like you to leave the store."

Katja stepped back, forcing him to release his grip on her shoulder. Her foot nudged into the dropped shopping bag, causing her to stumble. He reached out sharply for her. She knocked his hand away with a single swipe of her arm. She shuffled her feet clear, crouching into a combat stance. Her eyes flicked left and right.

Other shoppers stood at a very respectful distance, staring in shock. Behind her, the butchers backed away from their tools. She realized her arms were up for defense, and she slowly lowered them. The normally bustling market had descended into an eerie silence.

And all those fucking civilians, just staring at her.

Another guard joined the first, hand resting uneasily on his holstered stun gun.

Target priority, far guard with hand on gun, double-tap.

Near guard, multiple center-mass and back away.

Butchers, cover and keep them clear of their blades.

Her fingers went numb as the drugs surged to life within her, deadening her resolve. A wave of fatigue washed over her and she slumped in her stance. The first guard inched closer.

"Miss, I need you to leave. Now."

She nodded, stooping to collect her shopping bag. The guards took station at her sides, each holding an elbow and steering her subtly but firmly toward the exit. She was allowed to pay for her groceries, then escorted well away from the premises.

Outside, the heat blasted her again. She kept her eyes down and moved through the crowds of faceless civilians under the glare of the sun. She felt like there were eyes on her, not from the people she passed, but from *somewhere*. Twice she glanced over her shoulder, thinking someone was following her, but then chided herself for her paranoia.

She was a decorated veteran. Terran security forces didn't follow veterans. At least, not usually. She'd heard rumours that Astral Special Forces were occasionally called in to quietly clean up embarrassing messes made by veterans. But surely some spilled groceries wouldn't count. She glanced over her shoulder again, quickening her pace.

No one spoke to her, not even in the elevator as she rode back up to her apartment. These people had their own petty concerns, she realized. Nobody cared about her. She was just getting paranoid.

The sun had moved while she was gone, and the apartment

was no longer flooded with light. She dropped her shopping bag on the floor and crawled onto the couch, reaching for the new Baryon she'd bought on a whim. It was the newest social gadget, promising unlimited ease in staying connected with friends.

It had seemed like an exciting idea at the time—all those friends she was going to communicate with on the Baryon, just like all those friends she was going to invite to that big bash at her new apartment. She sighed shakily as she activated the device. What friends? Anyone she could think of from her old life—before the war—seemed hollow and irrelevant. What could she possibly talk about with any of them?

Why would she want to?

To her surprise, there were three messages waiting for her. The first was from Jack Mallory—how had he found her so quickly? He wrote about his new ship in the Research Squadron, and how it was a lot of work but nothing like getting shot at. Katja was touched at his efforts to keep in contact, but his cheerful message only reminded her of the sad truth. She was unfit for duty. This kid pilot was home from his first war and already back out into space. She was incapable even of manning a surface garrison without causing an incident between the Astral Force and the Army.

She deleted his message.

The next one was from Breeze. It was a sickly sweet note saying how she'd heard that Katja had been put on medical leave, and how much she hoped for a speedy recovery. Katja deleted it with a stabbing motion.

Bitch.

Although it did make Katja think for a moment. What was up with that guy? Chuck Merriman's cameraman, and now Breeze's date to the party? Kit Moro—that was his name. He'd made a point of speaking to her at Thomas's place. It had been a weird conversation. She'd have to search the network for more info on him.

The final message was from Merje. It was written in her sister's usual acid wit, with a link to a news story that had aired two days ago. It was the first of Chuck Merriman's follow-up stories on the glorious Emmes family, and naturally it focused on their father.

Katja watched the minute-long piece with idle interest, curious to see her father's public face. The story followed his leadership over one of the Army's mid-sized formations, a storm banner, in a simulated peacekeeping operation on Mars. Cutting back and forth between interesting military movements and an interview with the stern-faced veteran, Katja had to admit that it was a very flattering piece. Storm Banner Leader Emmes cut a striking figure, ardent in his support for Terran policy, and modest in his own heroic achievements throughout a forty-year career. It was the image of her father she remembered from childhood.

It was the image she'd always wanted to emulate.

Sitting up, she pondered the Baryon controls, eventually figuring out how to search for a contact. Fairly quickly she found the coordinates for SBL Günther Emmes, and, taking a deep breath, pressed to call.

The hand-held screen lit up moments later with her father's face.

"Hello?"

No doubt he'd seen her name when his device rang, and his neutral expression sapped her confidence. But what had she expected from the man, laughter and joy?

"Hi, Father," she said. "I saw you on the news. Very nice story." He stared back at her, expression unchanging as he slipped into speaking Finnish.

"Populist propaganda, but necessary to help rebuild the military's reputation," he said curtly. "I was honored to do it."

She paused, trying to collect her thoughts, and to switch her brain over to communicating effectively in her second language. At least the language part came easily.

"Father," she said. "I... I wanted to ask you a question."

"Go ahead."

How to summarize what she was trying to say? She couldn't even make sense of it herself. He continued to stare at her expectantly over the screen, and she decided to go for the direct approach.

"Father, did you have trouble coming home, after your first real mission?"

She braced for the scornful retort. She was surprised by his face suddenly softening into a thoughtful expression.

"Are you having trouble?"

She didn't really want to tell him about the incident in the market.

"I don't know," she replied, "but I think so."

She had his full attention now, she could tell.

"Have you caused any trouble?"

"No," she said quickly. "Well, except I think I'm a vegetarian now."

He nodded. "Have you spoken to your own medical corps?"

"Yes, and they're trying to help me."

"That's good, but Katja Andreia, ultimately you have to help yourself. War is a nasty, brutal business, and it's not for the weak." She hated how his simple words could carry so much damnation in them.

"I'm not weak," she replied. "I'm trying, but I don't know what to do." His face was hardening again, she could see. "What did you do?"

He thought for a moment. "I separated the two worlds. What happened in one world didn't affect what happened in the other, and I understood that the rules were different in each one. That's how I could be an effective soldier, and an effective father."

Katja pondered his words. She suddenly wondered just how well her father had really coped—though at least he hadn't made a scene in a public place.

"I can't tell you what to do," he said firmly. "Each soldier has to find his or her own way to deal with it. In the end it comes down to personal strength. Those who have it, survive."

She could feel the tears coming very close to the surface and she furiously fought them down. She wasn't going to cry in front of her father.

"I am strong," she said. "You have no idea."

He was unimpressed. "I just hope the Astral Force hasn't wasted ten years of training and resources on an opera singer."

She pressed her lips tightly, letting the drugs mellow out the old bitterness.

"I am not an opera singer," she hissed. "I am an officer in the Astral Corps."

"Then act like it, and pull yourself together."

This was pointless. She sniffed and brushed away a single irritating tear.

"Good-bye, Father."

She broke the connection, threw the Baryon down on the coffee table, then sat in silence for a long time, listening idly to the muffled buffeting of the wind against her windows.

No one was going to help her. She'd have to find the solution herself. It was hard to access military memories, now that the drugs were acting in full force, but she strained to recall non-combat events, times in barracks when her peers had talked about their past experiences. How had *they* dealt with it? She recalled a lot of laughter, a lot of off-color jokes.

Katja sagged where she sat. She really didn't feel like laughing.

There was something else that had seemed to help, though, and she made her way into the kitchen. Sure enough, in the fridge she found the six-pack of beer that she'd bought yesterday, thinking it would be useful to offer guests. She popped open a bottle and took a long swig, savoring the cool, bitter taste. Beers after an exercise had always been the tradition in the Levantine Regiment, and beers after a battle had been the recipe for release during the recent troubles. Why not beers after a war?

It made sense to her.

The first bottle empty, she reached for the second.

15

"**D**o you think alcohol would help?"

Jack turned in his seat as Amanda slowly looked up from the blackened pieces of the inter-dimensional probe they'd recovered into the Hawk. In each hand she held a significant chunk of the main data storage unit, with couplings and broken sensor casings scattered on the deck behind her. Other damaged probes lay nearby.

"I think it would put me to sleep," she said, "but thanks."

He couldn't stop a snicker from bursting past his lips, then he turned back to his board and did a quick sweep of the visual, flight controls, and hunt controls. Flight rules demanded that he get eight hours of uninterrupted sleep before any mission. Those rules had been thrown out the airlock in wartime, and apparently they'd never even existed in the Research Squadron.

"I meant cleaning alcohol," he said. "To get the carbon off. It cleans well, but evaporates before it can drain into any cracks. We've got some in the Hawk's maintenance kit."

She considered his suggestion. "Oh. Sure, it couldn't hurt."

Neil Armstrong was looming closer on the port bow, and Jack quickly checked the Hawk's landing systems.

"Okay, just let me get this bird in the nest, and we'll get into the lab for a good rubdown."

He established comms with the *Armstrong* bridge and requested automatic recovery. Word came back that it would be at least fifteen minutes before the system was brought on line and proper personnel were in place. Jack frowned. The Hawk certainly had the fuel to loiter, but he didn't think he had the patience. Why had the bridge not planned ahead, and pre-set the automatic landing system? It's not like his return to the ship was unexpected.

He glanced back at his passenger. Amanda held one of the broken pieces in her hands, and was staring blankly at it. She didn't have the endurance for a long wait either. Maybe it was concern for his fellow subbie, or maybe it was just the end of his tolerance for Research incompetence...

He keyed his radio.

"Apollo, this is Eagle-One. I have time-sensitive data on board, and cannot wait for the auto-recovery. I am inbound on final approach and request you open the outer airlock door, over."

There was a long silence, which Jack firmly ignored as he pressed the Hawk forward to close his mothership. The *Armstrong*'s vast arrowhead shape was illuminated by floodlights, and he easily picked out the quartet of flashing red beacons that indicated the airlock leading to the hangar.

The door, he noted, was still closed.

"Apollo, this is Eagle-One," he repeated. "I am inbound on final approach and request you open the airlock door immediately. Over."

The charcoal-colored door finally began to slide open. There was still no helpful information forthcoming on the radio— small stuff like the ship's course and speed—but Jack had done this sort of thing more than once, and he glided toward the lumbering *Armstrong* with a mixture of flight controls and pilot's eye to guide him.

Amanda appeared beside him.

"What are you doing?"

"Landing. I suggest you strap in."

She vanished from his peripheral and he heard the frantic clicking of her restraints.

"Is something wrong?" she asked. "Why aren't we being auto-recovered?"

He didn't take his eyes off the gaping hangar door, judging

the slight movements of the red beacon lights on all corners to assess his bearing movement.

"System wasn't ready, but *Armstrong*'s got a pretty big hangar door."

"Did the captain clear this?"

"I don't know, but they opened the door."

She made some sound that seemed less than supportive of his plan, but thankfully stopped distracting him. The airlock opening was looming large, making visual reckoning less reliable. All four beacons were drawing away from him, which was good. He nudged the Hawk down, guessing at the overhead clearance this research bird would need.

The opening grew to encompass his entire view. He tracked one of the blinking red lights for any bearing shift.

Steady... steady...

Artificial gravity caught a hold of the Hawk and gently lowered it to the deck. Jack nudged forward to the standard marker and waited as the outer door began to close astern of him. He released the controls and sat back with a smile of satisfaction.

"Not bad, eh?" He glanced back at Amanda.

She stared blankly at him. "What?"

"The landing!" he said, and he chortled. "Dropped her in light as a feather *and* saved us fifteen minutes of floating out there."

She shook her head and smiled. "Very heroic, but next time can you just follow the procedures? I'd rather be late than splattered along the side of the ship."

The inner doors began to open, and Jack monitored the deck clamps as they took hold of his Hawk and drew it into the hangar. Sometimes he really didn't understand these people.

The probes were easy enough to pile onto a cargo cart, and within minutes Jack was pushing their experimental data load through the corridors of *Armstrong*, the Hawk's cleaning bottles rattling on the top. Soon they were seated on opposite sides of one of the worktables, a long pile of sensor probes laid out in front of them.

He unsealed the bottle and moistened two cloths. Handing Amanda one of them, he grasped the nearest chunk of the damaged probe's storage units and started to rub vigorously at the accumulation of black dust.

They'd sown the line of sensors three days ago, launching as soon as *Armstrong* had cleared far enough from Earth's gravity well to allow Bulk observations to be collected without an excess of gravimetric distortion. It was the first dedicated Dark Bomb data research they'd conducted in weeks, but he'd been barely given an hour to place the sensors before Captain Lincoln himself was on the radio telling him to hurry back. There was a once-a-century near-miss of two asteroids scheduled to occur within hours, and the captain wanted *Armstrong* to be front and center for this highly publicized event.

"At least some of them survived," he commented, pleased that alcohol was starting to clear off some of the carbon. "I didn't really care for the other probes, anyway."

She glanced up slightly. "Not your style?"

"They were weak." He held up the piece in his hand. "Now this little guy—still ticking even after being cracked in half. That's dedication. He's earned my respect."

Amanda laughed. "I didn't know it was so personal with you."

"You wanna play in deep, dark space, you better be tough."

Her expression twisted between a smile and a scoff. He put the piece down to flex his arms in front of his chest in a classic manly pose.

"You better be mean!" he growled.

She tried to hide her grin. He pulled another pose, growling.

"Just... clean," she said, and she laughed.

He took up his cloth and broken sensor again, and growled as he hunkered over his work, polishing with new vigor.

"I think that one's clean enough," she said, reaching over to still his fingers. Her hands were warm on his, and he felt a rush up his arms. Her round face still sagged with fatigue, but her vivacious eyes made him smile.

He pulled his hands away and placed the newly cleaned probe between them. He didn't like people staring at him for long, for fear they might notice the artificial nature of his face.

"Okay, this one passes muster," he allowed. "Let's see if the recorder can come out." He fiddled with the minute controls, working the casing open despite the surface imperfections caused by thousands of microscopic impacts.

More than half of the probes he'd sown were contaminated by dust. Some were merely grubby from the exposure while others, like this one, had suffered significant damage. Still more had been completely smashed, their data lost. Already hindered by its proximity to gravity wells, this experiment was suffering from potential contamination by an errant cloud of gas.

He eventually worked the data card free and presented it triumphantly to Amanda. She took it with a raised eyebrow and inserted it into the computer.

A few manipulations of the screen and she nodded.

"It looks intact, although I'll have to analyze the gravimetric effect of the gas cloud." She frowned, then rubbed her temples and swore quietly. "They don't make my job easy."

Jack grabbed the data storage from another damaged probe and started cleaning it with a freshly moistened cloth. While he did so, he rounded the table to watch her work.

"Whatcha doing?"

She indicated the separate windows displayed on her screen. "This on the right is the raw data from the probes, showing the intensity of the graviton waves as they propagate through the Bulk. The red patches here show the reflection back from the weakbrane, but in among them we should, theoretically, see reflections from the Deep."

Jack nodded. Perched as they were in the three-dimensional brane that comprised the usual human experience, it was only with gravity that they could investigate the fourth spatial dimension, the Bulk. The weakbrane was another brane farther into the Bulk that could distort and even reflect gravitational effects.

Far beyond that, sixteen peets into the Bulk, lay the Chtholian Deep, that mysterious region of unknown extra-dimensional space where dark matter finally surrendered all power to dark energy. Stealth ships operated routinely in the Bulk, and Jack had learned how to hunt them down wherever they might hide, but no stealth ship had ever ventured sixteen peets into the bulk. The only man-made object to ever successfully interact with the Deep was *Rapier*'s specially modified torpedo—the prototype Dark Bomb.

"And this," Amanda said, pointing at the left-hand screen, "is the Fleet cosmographic survey which shows how strong and how far in we find the weakbrane in this area of space. As we feed in the data from the probes, I'm going to have the computer start correcting for known weakbrane interferences, to give us a clear picture of what really happened to our gravitons. I just hope the gas cloud didn't dislocate our probes, otherwise there's no way I can trust the results."

"Can't you just estimate?"

"Not if I want to be taken seriously by the scientific community."

"I don't mean just random guessing," he said. "I mean an informed, educated guess. It's not like we can ever really know exactly where subatomic particles are, anyway."

She turned in her seat. Her expression was clouded between curiosity and disdain. "I'm too tired to know if you're joking or not." He wasn't sure if that was a statement or a question. She stared dully at him for a moment longer, then clarified. "Are you joking?"

He thought back to the guesswork he'd used to hunt Centauri stealth ships.

"No, not really," he asserted. "In my experience, you never have all the information, so you go with your best guess based on experience and training."

"That would explain why you weren't selected for post-grad work."

There was no need for cheap shots. "Hey, Doctor-to-Be, I think I did some pretty decent science out there with my little Dark Bomb experiment."

"Sure, except it wasn't actually science. It was a half-baked, practical application of a scientific hypothesis. If anything it was engineering, and risky."

He heard his own voice rising. "Well sometimes we don't have the luxury of labs and grants and—"

"Jack, please." She held up a silencing hand, which drooped to rest against his flight suit. "What you did was amazing, yes, as a wartime maneuver, but did it work out like you predicted it would?"

"Yes." He caught himself and considered. "Well, okay, no.

The singularity was a lot stronger than I expected."

She nodded. "About a thousand times stronger, if I read the reports right. And did you intend to collapse the jump gate?"

"No."

Her hand fell back to her side. "So you threw together an experiment based on a partial theory and some guesswork. The results were three orders of magnitude away from prediction, and had a catastrophic impact on the surrounding environment. Forgive me if I'd like my predictions to be a little more reliable."

She turned back to the terminal.

"You've been saying since you came on board that real combat isn't like our carefully controlled lab. Well, what I'm saying is that real science isn't like your chaotic rodeo, where gravitons are thrown around like confetti. I need to figure out what's really happening when we manipulate the Bulk, because the consequences of getting it wrong could be a lot more serious next time."

He nodded, knowing she was right, but too tired to voice his agreement. Instead, he grabbed another probe fragment and started to clean, watching idly as she slowly compared data between her two screens.

He frowned. "Is that a black or a red terminal?" Black terminals aboard the ship were restricted to lower classifications of data, while red terminals—specially encrypted and shielded—were the portals used to view the Astral Force's most militarily sensitive information.

She didn't look up. "Black, why?"

He pointed at the cosmographic survey data. "Has that been de-classified? On my last deployment that was top secret, need-to-know stuff. How did you get it on a black terminal?"

"Jack, relax. Research ships don't worry about that sort of thing. We have to be able to access the best information to ensure the validity of our data. I don't want to be slogging through classification fields every time I want to check a static parameter. If you think I'm going slow now, imagine if I had to play by your combat rules."

"Uhh, yeah..." he said doubtfully. "But there's this little thing called Terran security. You know, that thing we all defend?"

Amanda started to roll her eyes, but as she looked up directly at Jack she changed her mind, and grinned.

"Mr. Mallory," she hissed in her best impression of Helena, "I've had just about enough of your cheek."

He grinned back and stuck his belly out as far as he could.

"Oh, Helena, good," he warbled with a high squeak. "I was just thinking I'd like to see a bit of cheek."

She pulled her skin back taut over her features.

"Oh, Admiral Bush, you can see my cheek any time."

A low, dangerous voice interrupted them. "What is going on here?"

He looked over to the door, and felt his heart sink as Lieutenant Helena Grey crossed her arms sternly. Her deep-set eyes bore into him, then into Amanda.

"Hi, ma'am," he said with forced cheer. "We're retrieving the data from the broken probes."

"By making stupid faces at each other?"

He couldn't help but laugh, although he knew it wouldn't improve the situation.

"No, sorry," he said. "We're really tired."

"You think you're tired?" Helena stormed through the lab to stab a finger in Jack's face. "I was up for hours last night proofreading Amanda's sorry attempt at a solar wind article, then I had to ensure that our regular weekly reports were submitted." She lowered the finger, but continued. "Now I've just spent three hours in Admiral Bush's quarters, explaining why we're so far behind on our core research—and when I come down here, I find you two acting like school children!"

Amanda pointed at the screen. "Ma'am, look," she said. "We have sixty-eight percent of the data recovered, and I'm already working on filtering for the weakbrane influence."

Helena glared at the screen, her eyes flicking between the patterns of dots and colored patches. Jack had often seen Thomas or Katja conduct rapid info assessments, but in Helena's stare he saw none of the same piercing awareness. Her furious expression remained frozen on her wrinkled face.

Eventually, she simply humphed.

Jack had long ago realized he was never going to be in

Helena's good favor, but he also knew that she was required to sign off on Amanda's field time, prior to her thesis defense. So he was happy to draw the fire.

"Ma'am, we'll be able to work faster if we can get a red terminal set up in the lab," he suggested. "We may need to refer to top-secret info, in order to ensure that accurate baselines are established."

She silenced him with a sharp wave of her hand.

"Don't feed me that!" she snapped. "Just because you did a combat deployment doesn't make you some kind of scientist. Red terminals are slower, they require authentication codes, it takes forever to transfer data from one system to the other… and they just aren't needed. Weapons ranges and intelligence reports aren't important to our work."

"No, but hyper-accurate astro spatial data like this is." Jack pointed at the cosmographic survey info on Amanda's screen. "And we shouldn't be able to access it on a black terminal."

Her face seemed to crinkle like thin plastic as it screwed up in confusion. Jack wondered idly if his own face looked like that when he frowned.

"It's right there," she said. "So what's the problem?"

It took him a moment. "The problem," he said slowly, "is that a non-secret terminal is displaying secret information. That's a security breach."

"That's not your concern."

"Yes it is," he blurted before he could stop himself. "It's everybody's concern."

"Not mine… and *not* yours."

"I'd bet it will be a concern to Lieutenant Commander Kane." He regretted the words as soon as they escaped his mouth. Thomas's recent inquiries hadn't sat well with Helena—a fact that quickly became evident.

Her face reddened with anger, but her voice remained very quiet.

"Don't waste my time with that nonsense," she said grimly. "Are you a Centauri spy?" She tossed her chin at Amanda. "Are you? We disabled those security protocols years ago, because they just got in the way. I don't need any more interference from outsiders who don't understand Research—and don't think you can go crying to our new acting-XO just because you're both from the combat Fleet. Keep your cloak-and-dagger for the bridge, Sublieutenant Mallory, and stop wasting my time and that of my team."

Jack made to reply, but she held up a finger for silence. Then she tapped Amanda so hard on the shoulder Jack heard the impact.

"Admiral Bush wants to know how many other science teams were at the asteroid rendezvous," she said, "and he wants a preliminary report on this Dark Bomb experiment by the evening brief."

Amanda didn't even glance up. "Yes, ma'am."

Helena shot Jack another glare, then stalked out of the lab.

He suddenly remembered the probe in his hand. He struggled to open the casing as he rounded the table again and took his earlier seat across from Amanda. Data card removed, he handed it to her.

"So how many science teams *were* there at the asteroid ballet?"

Amanda shrugged. "There were seven vessels, weren't there?" She focused dully on her console.

"Yeah, but I wonder if some of the planet-based institutes shared observation ships. It's not cheap to RV with an asteroid, let alone two."

"You did it pretty well."

"I've had practice."

"Oh yeah?" She glanced up at him, a flicker of interest in her eyes.

"Stealth ships are harder to find in the Bulk than asteroids. They're smaller, they change course, and they're actually trying to hide."

"How do you track them?"

Jack scrubbed at the dust on another probe for a moment, wondering just how much Amanda really wanted to hear about anti-stealth warfare. He thought it was pretty cool, but he was beginning to realize that sometimes he blabbered on a bit too much about things. He looked at her tired eyes, and decided she was just being polite.

"There's a reason ASW is called Awfully Slow Warfare," he replied. "I'll tell you sometime, when you're not already almost asleep."

"I'd like that." The corners of her lips curled up appreciatively. She looked at him for a moment longer, then went back to her work.

"How did your asteroid report come together in the end?"

She sighed. "Well, apparently we were the first to submit to the Martian Academy, so that made the captain happy."

"Are you pleased with the results?"

"No, they're garbage." She scoffed. "Just like everything we're slinging out of here these days."

"Why's that?"

A yawn blanked out her answer momentarily, and she hunched her shoulders in a suppressed stretch.

"Because we don't have time to do anything properly. It's just one damn special experiment after another. As soon as I finish analyzing one set of data, I have to switch gears and take on another." She gave a frustrated sigh. "It's not like they're even in my field! Sure, the gravimetric interaction of two asteroids passing near each other is sort of close to Bulk research, but while you were laying these sensors I was writing up that stupid report on fluctuations in solar wind."

"Why are we studying solar wind?"

"Because apparently it's a hot topic in some scientific circles, and Captain Lincoln wants us to get in on the action."

"But it's got nothing to do with the Dark Bomb."

"Doesn't seem to matter."

"So why are we doing it?"

"Because the fucking captain *wants* it!"

Jack leaned back in his chair, startled by her rudeness. Then an idea struck him. He placed the broken piece on the table and rose.

"I have something that might help us get this experiment done—and done right. I'll be back in a minute."

Trudging out into the clean, well-lit passageway, he couldn't help but compare it to the frigid, dim, reinforced honeycomb that had been the central route through the *Rapier*. He rubbed his hand across his rebuilt cheekbone, blinking away the memories of piloting the ship in zero-g and zero-atmo, toward a collapsing jump gate, fighting the pull of the singularity with every ounce of power he could wrench from the fast-attack craft.

And these scientists think they know stress. With sudden violence, he punched the control to his cabin. *They don't know shit.*

At the back of his locker, in a small, black medicine bag, was a bottle of amphetamines. He'd been issued them during the deployment, when he'd been hunting stealth ships sixteen of every twenty-four hours. He hadn't finished the bottle before combat ceased, and no one had ever asked for them back. They weren't pretty, but Amanda was burning out fast. If he was going to help her, he thought he might pop one himself.

He made a quick side trip to the wardroom galley to bring her some water. *And maybe a snack*, he thought suddenly. It was mid-afternoon, and the galley was empty, so Jack quietly helped himself to a pair of drinking pods before glancing through the fridge to choose a snack.

Over the ever-present hum of machinery, he heard a pair of voices coming from the wardroom, but it wasn't until he closed the fridge that he recognized them to be Helena and Thomas. He delicately placed his forage on the counter, and inched toward the narrow servery door.

Thomas was sitting forward in one of the armchairs, listening and nodding as Helena spoke. Jack was too late to hear what she had said, but he clearly heard Thomas's reply.

"I'm glad I'm not the only one who sees this," he said. "These special experiments are wasting all of our resources. I'm not sure I get why we're chasing these civilian issues. What's the captain's thinking?"

"Prestige," Helena replied with an exaggerated sigh. "Lincoln has always wanted to be a famous scientist, but he's not very good at research himself. Instead, he focused on promotion so he could direct a team of good scientists. Being the leader of a team can bring just as much fame as being the person who does the discovering."

"Okay, I get that," Thomas said, leaning back thoughtfully. "But why so many? Can't he see that by trying to tackle every topic that comes along, we're doing a half-ass job on each one?"

"I spoke to his previous ship, the *Katherine E. Page*," she responded. "He was in command for fifteen years there, and they say it was constant chaos. He was always chasing the hot topics, always counting how many times *Page* papers were cited, always trying to get media exposure."

"Well, he must have done a good job," Thomas said. "He told me that *Page* won Research Institute of the Year last year."

"He tells everyone that. He's very proud of it, and no doubt he wants to do the same with *Armstrong*."

"I'd think if we can conduct strategically vital research to develop the Dark Bomb, *that* would be worth some notoriety," he suggested.

Helena reached out to place a hand on Thomas's knee.

That's interesting, Jack mused.

"Not if the research remains top secret," she said. "Lincoln doesn't want Astral praise—he wants to win a Nobel prize."

Thomas smiled. "So it's up to you and me to get the core research done, and still keep Captain Lincoln happy."

She squeezed his knee. "I'm so glad you're here, Thomas. It's refreshing to see some common sense again."

Jack was stunned. Who was this charming, agreeable woman? If he hadn't recognized the dyed-blonde hair and bony hands, he might have thought Thomas was talking to a complete stranger.

"How long have you been on board?" Thomas asked.

"Thirty years. I joined as an admin assistant," she said. "The early years were hard work, but then we got a new captain—a very young Randall Bush—and he gave me the chance I'd always wanted when he transferred me to the science department as a junior analyst."

"So you worked all the way up?" he asked. "No formal training?"

"I don't even have a degree, but sometimes experience counts for a lot more than a piece of paper."

"You must know Admiral Bush quite well."

"Oh, yes, and when he's on board he still calls me to his quarters, to get my opinion on how things are going. He was captain here for a long time, and in his heart he still thinks of *Armstrong* as his ship."

Thomas nodded wearily. "Layers upon layers of politics, I see."

"Research has always been a tight community. Did you know that Captain Lincoln's life-partner is in command of one of our scout ships, even though he's not qualified?"

"Really?"

Helena nodded. "And just last year Admiral Bush used resources from *Armstrong,* including me, to provide data gathering for his daughter's PhD thesis."

"What? How can he do that?"

"Who's going to check? Nobody's ever cared what Research does." Her voice changed. "Down at our level, we just have to roll with the whims of our commanders."

Jack felt himself stiffen with indignation. No wonder things were so messed up around here. Thomas frowned, apparently sharing Jack's opinion.

"But what if I wanted to speak to the admiral about Captain Lincoln's priorities?" he asked. "Would he listen to me?"

"Bush hand-picked Lincoln to succeed him, so you'd have a tough audience."

"Does the admiral not appreciate honest reporting?"

"Of course, but he's happiest when you agree with him."

Thomas's sigh turned into a laugh. "I obviously have a lot to learn."

"And I know everything about everyone," she said. "We'll make a good team, Thomas."

He nodded. "Thanks, Helena. I appreciate having you here with me."

She rose. "I'm going to get some writing done before I check on Amanda again. That girl really needs constant kicks in her big butt."

"Have fun."

Jack watched Helena depart the wardroom. Thomas sat for a few moments longer, examining the reports on the table before him. When he looked up, his eyes met Jack's, and the pilot suddenly realized that he'd drifted into view through the servery window.

"Hi, Jack," Thomas said as he rose to his feet.

Jack quickly grabbed at his snacks.

"Oh, hi, sir," he said. "Didn't see you there. I was just grabbing some fuel for Amanda, to keep her going."

Thomas wandered over and peered into the galley. "Good idea. Thanks for supporting her."

"Subbies have to look out for each other."

Thomas nodded, his expression one of easy confidence. Although Jack wasn't sure if Helena meant her words, he certainly agreed that he was glad to see Thomas again. Although from what he'd just overheard, it sounded like their acting-XO had some bigger problems to worry about.

"The probes are mostly recoverable," he said, suddenly feeling the need to defend his peer, "and Amanda is making great progress. She's really smart."

"She is," Thomas agreed. "I like her."

"I just know she gets ridden pretty hard sometimes, and I wanted you to know that any problems with the final reports and papers are because we're so rushed, not because she's messing up."

Thomas's smile returned, with a mysterious edge.

"I know, Jack. She's the target this week, but last week *you* apparently couldn't do anything right. The week before that it was Wong. You all get your turns being demonized by Helena. Don't worry, I make my own judgements—but it's nice to hear you defending Amanda."

"Well, sure." Jack didn't quite understand the glint in his superior's eye.

"We're getting back to Earth at the end of the week," Thomas said. "You two should get planetside for a couple of days and relax. Blow off some steam."

"Yes, sir."

Thomas laughed. "I'm not ordering you to, you twit. I'm suggesting it. I think you and Amanda would enjoy some quality time on your own."

Jack finally clued in. "Oh, it's nothing like that. We're just buddies."

"Good—that's a great place to start."

Jack shook his head. "Come on…"

"She's totally into you, Jack. It's that pilot charm I can never understand."

"She's *not* totally into me," Jack protested. *Who would be, with a plastic face like this?*

"I think she might surprise you."

"Well, I wouldn't want to lead her on." Jack leaned in, glancing past Thomas to make certain the wardroom beyond was empty. "She's not really my type."

"Why not?"

He gave Thomas an expectant look, then finally voiced the obvious. "She's a little chubby."

Thomas raised his eyebrows in surprise. "Yeah, a little: so? She's got pretty eyes, she's smart, sassy, and she's totally into you."

"Well, maybe I'm not into her."

"Okay, whatever." Somehow Thomas looked… disappointed. "I just know that guys your age are usually clueless to the subtle hints women throw their way. I know I was."

"I'll keep it in mind, sir."

Thomas shook his head, becoming exasperated. "While you're at it, keep this in mind, too—a good relationship is based on way more than just looks. Think of our good friend Breeze. Don't get suckered in by a pretty face."

Jack nodded and collected up his snacks. That was easy for Thomas to say, with his gorgeous wife. Remembering the amphetamines in his pocket, he decided that maybe he wouldn't take one after all. He'd stay with Amanda long enough to help her clean off the probes, but she and the drugs could do the rest of the analysis themselves.

The last thing he wanted was to give her the wrong impression.

16

Kete's heart skipped a beat as he processed Chuck's words over the Baryon. His cab descended swiftly toward his destination, but suddenly all his attention was focused on the reporter's grinning face on the screen.

"You got *what*?" Kete said.

Chuck was positively beaming. "I got access to the Astral Force science ship that's doing Dark Bomb research. I'm heading there tomorrow, when she gets back into orbit."

"How the hell did you get that?"

"It's about who you know, baby."

"And who do you know?"

"The husband of one of my friends is Astral Force. He's recently been posted to the ship as their XO, or something. Thomas Kane—that guy who had the garden party."

And Emmes's former CO, Kete recalled. Even more reason to get on board. He kept his face neutral, fighting down the excitement churning in his gut. "And I suppose you want a cameraman to come with you?"

Chuck shrugged. "I wish I could, but Thomas tells me it was hard enough just to get clearance for one person. I doubt he could pull off another miracle that quickly."

The cab glided to a halt on a beautiful, tree-lined street. Kete stepped out onto the shade-dappled sidewalk, Baryon in hand.

"Sorry to hear that," he said, "but let me see what I can do."

"You just going to charm your way through the airlock?"

"Something like that." Facing the front door of the luxury apartment building, Kete glanced up at the third floor. "What time are you cleared to board?"

"As soon as she docks—one o'clock."

"I'll get back to you." Signing off, Kete strolled up to the front door, allowing the security system to read his Terran ID. As an authorized guest he was allowed to enter, and an automatic message was sent up to the third floor to announce his arrival. Very quickly he was up the elevator, and walking down the increasingly familiar, bright hallway to the second door on the left. He knocked.

Breeze stood across the entrance as it slid open, one hand resting against the doorframe and allowing her loose-fitting dress to slip all the way past her shoulder. The garment draped casually to just above her knees, revealing enough of her shapely legs to titillate any other man. Kete noted her appearance coolly, focusing mostly on the genuinely happy smile that lit up her face as she leaned in to plant a full, sensual kiss on his lips. He pulled her closer and returned the kiss, judging his timing to indicate interest, but not to invite an escalation of passion.

"Hey, beautiful."

"Hey, gorgeous."

She released him only enough to take his arm and walk him into her apartment. It was impeccably decorated, with a pseudo-Centauri style that he actually quite liked. It amazed him how the Terrans could profess to love Centauri fashions and philosophy, and yet so utterly defy both in their daily lives.

The rock fountain built into the corner of her dining room would have been well-suited to the cool highlands north of Kete's home on Abeona, but it was a shocking waste of resources here in northern Australia. The amount of water pumped through its dappling descent each hour was probably equal to the annual natural rainfall for the entire Longreach region.

But he wasn't here to philosophize. He was here to play a role and accomplish a mission. He patted Breeze's buttock as he flopped down on the couch.

"How was your day, Breezy?" he asked. "Did you get any smarter?"

She sat down beside him, curling her legs up and leaning against her hand to gaze at him. "I can't get any smarter—I *am* Intelligence, but I think I might be even more beautiful." She batted her eyes playfully.

He grinned. "I don't think that's possible either. We have to get you on the network one of these days."

"I'd love to." Real interest flashed behind her sparkling blues. "But it would have to be something good."

"Yeah, it's a shame you're a spook, and not a weapons engineer—I might have had something."

She leaned in, doing well to hide her curiosity behind tracing a playful finger across his chest.

"Really? What was that?"

"You remember my friend Chuck Merriman? He has a gig on one of your ships tomorrow. Apparently it's been doing work on that Dark Bomb everyone's been talking about."

"Oh?" The finger stopped cold. Breeze shifted slightly on the cushion. "How did he arrange that?"

"The husband of one of his friends is on the ship, and got approval. I think the husband—what's his name? That guy who had the garden party… something Kane—is going to be leading the tour. I'd have loved to have gone along."

Breeze stared at him intently, all playfulness gone.

"Thomas Kane is being interviewed by Chuck Merriman aboard *Neil Armstrong* tomorrow?"

"Thomas Kane, yeah, that's it. Who's Neil?"

Breeze looked away, oblivious to his joke. He watched her carefully, wondering how quickly she'd take the bait. He didn't know all the details, but he'd deduced that something had happened between her and Kane. Infantile emotions, maybe, but anything could be useful when he was manipulating people of influence. Large egos were often the easiest targets.

She rose from the couch and crossed the room to access a discreet terminal. He pretended to gaze out the window while he tuned in to her terminal interface. He couldn't always access the military system, but he could always monitor what she was doing.

Breeze quickly checked her calendar, then she sent a few rapid-fire messages to the security commander of Astral Base One and the captain of *Armstrong*. He had to admire her decisiveness, and, he allowed himself a moment of contentment.

He wasn't bad at quick thinking himself.

"What are you doing tomorrow after lunch?" she asked.

Kete glanced at his watch, noting that it was precisely twelve-fifty when the dim, charcoal form of the Astral explorer ship *Neil Armstrong* emerged from behind the bulk of the giant Astral Base, on final approach to her exterior dock.

She was more elegant than a typical Terran warship, much like a fattened arrowhead with clusters of sensors protruding from her top and bottom tips, and a cylindrical spine reaching back to a bulb of engines. Even so, her shadowy color and clunky components gave her a brutish beauty at best, with none of the smooth lines and silvery grace of a Centauri vessel.

Already filming, Kete didn't move his gaze, but he did reach out to place a subtle hand on the small of Breeze's back.

"Beautiful ship."

Breeze was at her charming best, looking every bit the confident Astral officer in her undress blues, single campaign ribbon and silver qualification badge popping from the dark tunic beneath three silver bars on each shoulder. She'd chatted and flirted with Chuck during the entire ride up the space elevator, maneuvering aggressively to ensure that she was the focus of the story, and not Thomas.

Chuck, to his credit, wasn't so easily swayed by a pretty face, but Kete was pretty sure Breeze had won herself at least a cameo. He didn't care one bit, to be honest. His focus was entirely on the prize before him.

Armstrong approached the dock with the usual grace of a powerful starship, drifting to rest fifty meters or more off her berth, then gliding sideways into the waiting arms of the various docking clamps that took hold of her hull and bound her fast to Astral Base One. Airlock extensions immediately began reaching out from the dock to mate with their counterparts in the hull, and within minutes the airlock doors lit green and opened.

Chuck smiled and indicated for Breeze to lead the way. As

she passed, he let his eyes roam her figure once, then he tossed Kete an admiring nod. Kete patted him in the shoulder and leaned in quietly.

"Like you said, it's all about who you know."

He dropped back into Chuck's wake, playing his usual role as the invisible cameraman. Up ahead, the charcoal-colored hatch of the ship hissed open and the brightly lit airlock beckoned. Kete kept all his senses on standby, just in case there was some sort of security screen, then stepped over the lip into his first Terran warship.

They were met in the wide passageway by a small welcoming party in the same undress blues as Breeze. Kete recognized them from the Kane garden party, but it was interesting to see them all in their natural, military setting. The four silver bars immediately identified the captain of *Armstrong*, Lincoln's nervous smile lighting up his features. Beside him was a taller man with two bars and a star, Thomas Kane. It was interesting to note the easy confidence of the junior officer, compared to his captain. Kane had twice as many ribbons and qualification badges as Captain Lincoln, as well.

This was a mismatched pair.

Beside Kane stood the science officer, Helena Grey, with a white lab coat over her dark-blue coveralls.

Chuck attempted to explain his intentions, but Kete watched in idle amusement as Breeze, Lincoln, Kane, and Grey all vied for his ear with their specific ideas of how the feature should be conducted. The reporter listened diplomatically, subtly but firmly favoring Kane's vision while conceding small victories to each of the other officers.

Eventually it was decided that they would first film Captain Lincoln in his quarters, then head to the main laboratory. By the time Chuck had negotiated a consensus, Kete had hacked into the ship's integrated engineering network and downloaded a goldmine of data about the Terran propulsion system. The concept of accretion drives was taught in Centauri high schools, but to see the inner workings of an actual Terran system—in operation—was a once-in-a-career score.

He duly followed Lincoln, Chuck, and Breeze to the captain's cabin. There Lincoln chose to be filmed standing in front of his desk, the Science Institute of the Year award from his previous ship displayed behind him. Lincoln's words tumbled out of his mouth as they set up the shot, but as soon as Kete started filming the man went as wooden as a tree trunk, stumbling over his words and staring blankly at the bulkhead instead of engaging Chuck's eyes.

It was a ridiculous ten minutes, but thankfully it was entirely Chuck's problem to sort out. Kete spent the time interrogating Lincoln's private, secure terminal. He wasn't able to break the encryption, but he still garnered good data to help him understand the Terran methods of security.

Establishing a cyber-position at the network gateway, he identified the number of individual accounts to which it granted access. The crew numbered more than fifty, but right away he noticed that two accounts were much more sophisticated than the rest. One of them was the captain's, and the other... Thomas Kane, as XO. Hardly surprising, really.

The only surprise Kete felt was in discovering that *only* the two most senior personnel on board had full access and authority over all ship systems. Even as a sergeant in the militia back home, he'd been trusted with more than most of this full-time crew.

Walking through the passageways between the CO's cabin and the main lab, Kete isolated the sentry signals at critical junctions, and begin to assess how Terran security algorithms worked. They were different here from what he'd seen in routine civilian establishments, but not especially sophisticated. That made sense, actually—security aboard a warship was contained by the hull, and there was a very low volume of traffic.

By contrast, sentries in civilian locations had to daily assess thousands of people in a weather-driven, dynamic environment. It was sad, really, that Terra seemed to spend more time and energy watching its own people, than it did protecting its military secrets.

The lab was a large, well-lit space with more than a dozen workstations scattered around a variety of advanced scientific devices.

Perhaps a dozen crew members were present, all staring at

Breeze and Chuck as they swept into the room. Nary a glance came Kete's way, and he scanned the room quickly as he filmed Breeze saying a few words of gratitude and encouragement to the team.

As Chuck set up the next interview, this one with Thomas, Kete felt a brush against his arm. He looked over and saw a very junior officer glance up from where he'd positioned himself at the terminal to Kete's left.

"Oh, excuse me," the officer said. Kete wondered if the kid was still in training, but the silver pilot's wings on his dark-blue tunic said otherwise—as did the two ribbons beneath the badge. There was something vaguely odd about his face, but he couldn't say what.

"Am I in the way?" Kete asked.

"No, no," the young pilot said with a smile. "I just need to make sure there's nothing on the screen you shouldn't be looking at."

Kete returned the smile and made a show of looking away. Internally, however, he thrust his perception into the workstation's network access. Some gravimetric readings in a 4-D graph, a comparative cosmographic chart... A top-secret cosmographic chart. He probed further. Kete could access the entire library of Astral Force astrospatial data. Not of particular interest, but did that mean... Yes!

He felt a giddy rush through his mind as the entire Terran military network stretched out before him. It was vast, and deep, and completely exposed. He didn't even know where to begin.

Discipline, he chastised himself inwardly. *Use the methods.*

As quickly as he could, he began building an inventory of what was before him, prioritizing for search. It took many seconds to even list the largest of groupings, and even more to break down the most promising into sub-groups of data. Remembering his mission, he zeroed in quickly on the security and communications systems for Longreach.

He jerked as a hand tapped him on the shoulder.

"Hey, you ready?"

He blinked and focused his real eyes on Chuck.

"Sorry?"

"We're ready for the next interview."

Kete pulled his conscious mind back into the laboratory,

knowing that his subconscious now had a method to follow in a simple download and a solid link to the secure network.

"Yeah, yeah."

"You okay?"

"Yeah." He glanced at Breeze who was holding court nearby, then back at Chuck. "Late night." Chuck smirked and nodded.

He turned and rejoined *Armstrong*'s officers, isolating Thomas Kane from the others. Kete followed silently, giving Breeze a wink before setting up beside Chuck to film Kane.

The tall, handsome officer certainly was telegenic, Kete had to admit, and as the interview started he noted idly that Kane obviously knew how to act in front of the media. After the introductory questions and a description of Kane's current role aboard *Armstrong*, Kete listened as Chuck began to draw out this officer's recent combat experience.

"Now, I understand you were involved in the recent troubles in the colonies, Commander?" the reporter asked.

"Yes," Kane responded. "I had the privilege to command the fast-attack craft *Rapier* in both Sirius and Centauria."

Kete started a separate search for any references to *Rapier* in the past twelve months. Chuck queried *Rapier*'s role during the conflict, to which Kane presented the noble front of commending his crew for their actions under extreme combat circumstances. False humility if Kete had ever seen it.

He listened without surprise as Chuck expertly pulled out the fact that *Rapier* had rescued the hostages on Cerberus, had played a pivotal role in the Battle of Laika—in which Kane himself had ordered his crew to abandon ship due to battle damage, but then single-handedly saved his vessel from burning up in the atmosphere. And then, of course, how *Rapier* and a skeleton crew, led by Kane, had conducted the suicide mission to launch the prototype Dark Bomb, thus enabling the remnant Terran forces to escape back to Terra.

Yes, yes, truly heroic. Kete swallowed his disdain and launched a separate search for *Rapier*'s Dark Bomb mission.

Next up in front of the camera was Breeze, and Kete listened idly as she gave her version of how the Dark Bomb mission was entirely her idea, how her Intelligence efforts had located the hostages, and that she'd been aboard *Rapier* for the rescue. She detailed how her Intelligence efforts had also saved the Terran troopers, who were captured by the Sirians, several weeks later. Kete launched a search for anything associated with Commander Brisebois and the Dark Bomb mission.

Breeze yielded the camera, reluctantly, to *Armstrong*'s science officer, Helena Grey. She came across as rather sullen, explaining as best she could the importance of *Armstrong*'s research, but even she knew her words sounded hollow after the combat adventures of Kane and Breeze. Chuck threw some softball questions at her, but Kete sensed that her answers about the research were rather forced, and rather vague.

That final interview mercifully came to a quick end, and Kete rubbed his eyes as he deactivated his camera. He wasn't even close to finishing his download of the Terran database, though, and he had to stall the proceedings.

"Chuck," he said, "it might be good to have a few more faces to mix in." He glanced around the room, noticing the young pilot from before. "Maybe some of the youngsters on the team, to appeal to the key recruiting demographic."

"Good thinking." Chuck nodded in agreement. "Thomas, any recommendations?"

"How about two junior officers working on the Dark Bomb project?" Kane immediately motioned for the pilot and another young, female officer to approach. As he did, Grey looked as if she'd tasted something foul.

Chuck quickly introduced himself and had the pair stand side by side under Kete's renewed gaze. He addressed the pilot first.

"What's your name, sir?"

"Uhh, Jack Mallory." The young man glanced uncertainly at Kete, then back at Chuck. "I'm a pilot."

"How is it that a pilot gets dragged into research into theoretical, warped geometry physics?"

"Yeah, good question." Mallory rolled his eyes slightly. "Uhh, I guess it was because I came up with the idea for the Dark Bomb we dropped on the Centauris."

"Did you?" The surprise in Chuck's voice mirrored that in Kete's mind.

This kid? He immediately began a search for Jack Mallory and the Dark Bomb, while Mallory told—with increasing confidence—his own tale of heroism from the conflict, and how his role as an anti-stealth pilot had given him both the training and experience to develop the theory that led to the creation of the prototype weapon.

The only time he really stumbled was when Chuck asked him what role he'd played in rescuing the hostages from Cerberus. Mallory paled slightly, and he quickly covered one half of his face with his hand in what looked to Kete like a well-worn gesture. After he mumbled an answer, Chuck concluded the interview and moved on to the other youngster, Sublieutenant Amanda Smith.

That interview proceeded without incident or heroism, and Chuck quickly wrapped things up. Kete was still trying to wrench as much as possible from the exposed Terran network, but even he could only come up with so many reasons to keep filming in the lab.

A few establishing shots, and some posed footage of researchers hard at work, and Chuck began to get antsy. So Kete let himself merge into the background again as the reporter said his farewells to the *Neil Armstrong* research team, continuing the download of raw data even out into the passageway, until his distance from the terminals finally became too great.

Breeze was at his side as they exited the ship and strolled back through Astral Base One. She was pensive, he could tell, but she kept up the mildly flirtatious chatter with Chuck all the way to the space elevator. Kete was content to remain out of the conversation, churning over the goldmine of data he'd uncovered. Without question, he had to make direct contact with Centauri Intelligence, even if it meant putting his own mission on hold.

Based on what he'd already uncovered from the Terran network, the pace of this mission had suddenly accelerated. Soon it would be time to bring in the big hardware.

17

Thomas watched idly as Soma flitted around the great room, methodically locating the various items essential for her day out. It wouldn't be such a chore, he knew, if she just put everything down in the same spot when she entered the house, but to do so would apparently go against a lifetime of habit.

It was irritating as hell, especially when they were rushing out to a function, but he supposed it was just one of those things to which he had to resign himself—all part of getting to know his spouse and life partner.

"When are we going to get a maid?" Soma muttered. "This place is a mess."

"The maid was here two days ago," Thomas said. "She'll be back today."

The last essential item—her Baryon—was discovered under a pile of yesterday's shopping on the couch, and her mood immediately brightened.

"Ah, there we are." She crossed the rug toward him, the light material of her deep-red dress flowing around her calves. In a single, sweeping motion she bent over, kissed him, and started toward the front hall. "Jade and I will be at the spa, then we're meeting some friends for drinks around six. Will you join us?"

"Absolutely." Thomas knew that "six" more likely meant "eight-thirty" and he wondered idly what he'd do for dinner. "Just call me when you meet up with your friends."

"Love you, darling." Her voice faded out the door.

He sat back in his chair, savoring the peace. After two weeks aboard *Armstrong* he found he quite appreciated a Saturday at home. That ship was truly a mess, and it was going to take some time to get it moving in the right direction. It was probably a good thing his appointment hadn't been official, because then he'd be officially responsible for the success or failure of the project. As a temporary supervisor, he could take credit for success, but could just shrug and walk away from a failure.

The political games were getting easier.

The problem, as always, remained Breeze. By aligning his fate so closely to hers, he was probably safe from her Fleet Marshall Investigation, but Parliament wanted a scapegoat, and Breeze would provide them one with gusto.

A chill rippled through him at the thought. If he wasn't going to be the sacrificial lamb, then he knew who was.

Grabbing his Baryon, he started a search for addresses in the local metropolitan area. Katja had been based in Longreach fairly recently, but things could happen quickly with military postings...

No—she was still here.

He hesitated for a moment, knowing deep down that there was another motive behind his impulse, then typed her a quick message. She needed to know what kind of danger she was in.

The shade of the broad table umbrella eased the heat of the day, but he could still feel the glistening moisture on his arms as the hot desert wind gusted along the boardwalk. The worst of the storms had passed, but the air was still like a furnace, even here by the water. Heat rippled the view of the tall towers that lined the shore, and the space elevator cables further away.

He'd already sipped away half of his beer, but he wasn't sure if that was due to dehydration or nerves. He was surprised by the butterflies that churned in his stomach, feeling almost as if he was waiting for a blind date to start. In a sense, he realized, he almost was.

He glanced at his watch. Their agreed meeting time had come and gone fifteen minutes ago, and he was a little surprised at her tardiness. It certainly didn't match his memories of the straight-laced, ever-professional trooper he'd come to admire during the troubles. Then again, this was Earth, and peace time. He took another sip of his beer, scanning the pedestrians for a short, swift blonde.

He spotted her as she cut across the avenue from the bus stop, her lithe movements unmistakable as she navigated through the crowd without touching anyone. He leaned forward, feeling his stomach tighten again. She was dressed casually in a sleeveless top, knee-length walking shorts and sandals, her eyes hidden behind dark sunglasses. She still had her long hair, but it was tied back in a ponytail and gave her face almost the same appearance as the close-cropped blonde halo he knew so well.

Katja stepped into the dappled shade of the patio, slowly scanning from left to right. Her gaze went right past him, and he wondered why she didn't take her sunglasses off in the shade. He stood up, drawing her attention with his movement. She approached.

She was beautiful, he suddenly realized. Not stunning like Soma, nor sensual like Breeze, but intelligent and unbreakable. He could feel a rush in his chest as she came near. His profound respect for her, he quickly told himself.

"Hello, Katja."

He held out his hand, but she didn't slow her pace, sliding her hand right under his and wrapping her arms around him, pressing her cheek into his chest. With a new rush he closed his arms around her small form, holding her tightly against him. Her hair smelled of gentle soaps mixed with the faint scent of her natural musk that he remembered well, and just a hint of... tequila?

"Hello, Thomas." She turned her face to look at him through her dark sunglasses.

"Hello," he repeated, unable to think of anything else to say.

Slowly, reluctantly, she pulled back and sat down across from him. He followed suit, automatically taking a sip from his beer. He signaled for the waiter.

"Can I get you a drink?" he asked. "The beer's good on a hot day."

She shook her head. "No. Just soda water." She glanced up briefly at the waiter. "And a bowl of nacho chips, no salsa or anything."

Thomas couldn't help but smile. "A hard night, my dear?"

"Bite me."

He laughed out loud. Civilian Katja was apparently quite a different person from military Katja.

"Sorry I got you out of bed so early."

She tried to smile. "It's okay. I need the fresh air. I've been cooped up in my apartment for too long."

"Have you been posted to the base here in Longreach?"

"In a manner of speaking." Her order arrived and she busied herself in gulping back some water and chewing on some dry chips. He realized his beer was nearly done and he ordered another.

"Oh?" he said.

She took another long sip of her water.

He finished his beer. "Katja?"

She removed her sunglasses to rub her eyes, and dropped them on the table. When she finally looked up at him, her large, dark, almond eyes were bloodshot, and had deep bags beneath them. It was startling, but her gaze went right through him, and he couldn't look away.

"Thomas," she said, "how did you survive, the first time you came home from combat?" There was a subtle sense of urgency in her voice.

He nodded, trying to think back nearly fifteen years to young Sublieutenant Kane's return to Earth after the war in Sirius.

"I partied a lot, and played up being a local hero," he replied, "but after a few weeks of debauchery I realized it was all a sham, and I got back out into space as quickly as I could."

"I don't feel much like a hero."

He glanced around at their fellow patrons, at the blissfully ignorant civilians. "No, the State hasn't portrayed it as a triumph this time. Probably because we got thumped pretty hard."

"But I feel like I'm being punished by the Astral Force itself," she said. "By our own people, and not the enemy."

"How so?"

"I'm not allowed to return to my regiment," she continued. "I got sent to a backwater posting for a month, and then got sent home from that. When I say something's wrong, I just get given more drugs."

An unpleasant thought struck him. "Have you been allowed to speak to your troop commander?"

"No. I'm on medical leave, so I have to report to a doctor. I probably shouldn't even be speaking to you—they'll say I'm trying to circumvent my rehab by appealing to a fellow combat veteran."

If he'd been a poet, he might have said how he sensed a foul wind blowing... or at least a mean Breeze.

"Katja, that's complete crap," he growled. "No medical program should restrict who you can talk to. Forward me your doctor's details, and I'll look into this."

She nodded, reaching out to give his hand a squeeze. "Thanks."

His second beer arrived. She replaced her sunglasses and devoted herself for a minute to consuming dry chips and soda water.

"Doctors aside," he asked, "how are you feeling?"

She shrugged, still munching. "Tired. Paranoid. Did you have nightmares when you first came home?"

"Sometimes," he replied. "What are you feeling paranoid about?"

She tried to laugh, but it came out harshly. "Everything. People looking at me funny. People judging me. People deciding that I'm not worth anything."

"Katja..." He took her hand with both of his.

She waved him to silence. "You don't have to say anything."

The words he really wanted to say he swallowed down. He clasped her hand in his and watched her suck back the last of her water. She tried to smile, but it faded with a slight movement of her head to the right.

"Thomas, I feel like I'm being followed. Look slowly over my shoulder—do you see anyone watching us?"

He lifted his gaze slowly, casually scanning the other patrons and the pedestrians in the street. Nothing caught his eye as unusual. Certainly there was no one in uniform, or of obvious military bearing.

"I don't see anyone suspicious," he said, "but I think I might know why you feel that way."

"Why?"

"Our dear friend Commander Brisebois has been making trouble for me, and I'm guessing she's doing the same for you.

In her position she has fairly significant powers that enable her to meddle, and she's been tasked with finding a scapegoat for the war."

Her fingers tightened around his. "I will beat her to death with her own, severed arm."

He shrugged. "I've been drawing her fire as best I can. I was hoping to keep her focused on me, but apparently she's still had time to make your life difficult."

She pulled her hand back. "You don't need to look after me."

"I know, but I've been hoping to try and force her to let the whole thing drop." He briefly outlined his position directing the Dark Bomb research, and his efforts to improve his public profile. "It's forcing her to back off, because she knows her success is tied in with mine. It doesn't hurt that Captain Lincoln absolutely loves me, and holds me responsible for getting him on the news."

She nodded. "But how does all that stop Breeze?"

"It makes it harder for her to blame me for anything questionable, and it also gives me power to influence her success. If she does anything to hurt you, I can retaliate."

She leaned back in disgust. "I thought we'd just finished fighting a war."

His own enthusiasm for the battle faded. This woman had a remarkable ability to make him feel like an honest soldier—how he'd felt when he was Jack Mallory's age. He envied her black-and-white view of things, even though he knew it would only limit her in the real world.

"I don't like it either, Katja, but unfortunately not all our enemies carry guns."

"Still, that doesn't mean we have to fight alone." She motioned for the bill. "I know someone who has experience in this sort of thing, and she happens to be in town."

"Who?" He grabbed the bill before she could reach for it.

"My sister, Merje," Katja replied, throwing him a brief scowl. "It was her law firm that got that last Corps officer acquitted for his fuck-ups. I'm sure she'll know a thing or two about keeping a fuck-up like you safe."

"Thanks." He crossed his arms. "Nice to know I'm cared for."

"Astonishingly," she said as she rose from her chair, "you are."

He stood and followed her off the patio and toward the street. At the end of the block she quickly flagged down a cab and climbed in. He didn't know if it was the food and water or the new sense of purpose, but all of a sudden he was seeing a glimpse of the old Katja. It was good to see her again.

He followed her into the cab.

"So does it get any easier?" she asked as the cab pulled quietly out into traffic.

"What, fighting with Breeze?"

"No." She removed her sunglasses and turned toward him in her seat. "Coming home." She still looked rough, but there was life in her eyes again. He considered his return from his tour as a platoon commander, and now this most recent return.

"Yeah, but it's never easy."

She took his hand again and smiled. "I think having someone who understands can make it easier."

He smiled back, wondering if he'd ever understand her mercurial changes in mood. From "fuck-up" to "someone who understands" in the space of a city block.

It suddenly occurred to him that mistresses were an accepted fact in Terran high society. They weren't to be flaunted, of course, but an occasional, discreet dalliance when the wife was off-planet... Her shapely calves were hard not to notice, nor the physical reaction to the sudden, air-conditioned chill of the cab.

He looked away, letting her hand drop.

No, no, no, he told himself. He was married to Soma, and in a fight for his professional future. The last thing he needed now was another mistake. His eyes flicked over her form one more time. A mistake, he reminded himself, no matter how much he wanted her.

Thomas couldn't help but feel underdressed as he and Katja strode into the round, polished marble outer offices of the law firm Ryan, Ridley, and Day. High-collared private security guards watched them as they passed a steady stream of legal professionals in designer suits, moving through the rotunda between the various private corridors.

Katja, by contrast, strode right up to the nearest receptionist, military ID displayed.

"Lieutenant Emmes to see Merje Emmes, with a package."

The receptionist took a single look at the ID and activated her earpiece. She repeated the message, word for word, responded after a moment, then invited Katja and Thomas to proceed down the second corridor on the left and look for the third door.

If the lavish workplace was any indication, Ryan, Ridley, and Day had done very well for themselves. Katja's sister had only recently transferred here from the main office in North America. Although lawyers were hardly a "respected" trade in the modern sense of the word, they certainly managed to provide for their families better than most.

Katja gave a firm knock, then opened the door, and Thomas followed her through into the sunny, tidy space. Or at least, the floor was tidy. The desk that formed the centerpiece of the office was almost invisible under messy piles of hand-held readers, a personal smart board, and what looked like the remains of lunch. Behind the desk, rising with a big grin across her delicate face, was Merje.

She was slimmer than Thomas remembered from the military gala, dressed in a stylish blouse and dark skirt, her long, straight, blonde hair pushed back behind her shoulders. In her high heels she absolutely towered over her older sibling, but that didn't stop her from reaching down to offer a big hug.

"Hey, Katty."

Thomas raised an eyebrow at the nickname, and wondered if he'd ever have permission, or the courage, to use it himself. Katja, on the other hand, seemed unfazed.

"Hey Merry. I hope you weren't busy."

Merje waved dismissively at her desk, eyes already taking in Thomas from top to bottom.

"Never too busy for my favorite sis," she said. "What brings you and your... friend by?"

Katja stepped back and, Thomas noted, put a hand on his elbow. "This is Lieutenant Commander Thomas Kane. He was my skipper in *Rapier*, and we both think that there's a situation brewing in Astral internal politics. We could use your professional advice."

Merje glided forward, extending her hand to Thomas. "Merje Emmes, master of law. Weren't you at that gala a few months back?"

Thomas was intrigued at the subtle differences between the sisters. Their faces were a similar shape, although in place of Katja's large, dark eyes Merje had fine, blue ones that held his gaze fearlessly.

"I was," he acknowledged. "I saw your whole family being interviewed by Chuck Merriman."

Merje rolled her eyes and turned away. "State propaganda at its best." She sat down on the only clear spot on her desk, and motioned them toward the two chairs facing her. "At least that news hound hasn't chased me for a follow-up interview. One of the benefits of being the black sheep in the family."

Thomas liked her style. If Katja could display half this sass, she'd be unstoppable. He glanced at the seat next to him, where she sat with her knees together, leaning forward with earnestness.

"So, what kind of Astral trouble would bring you into my office?" Merje looked between them, crossed one long leg over the other, and gave him a piercing stare.

He briefly summarized the various twists and turns of the feud between him and Breeze, and the Fleet Marshall Investigation Breeze had been assigned to conduct. He left out a few rather intimate details, but painted what he felt was a realistic picture. Katja added in her own grievances, some of which Thomas had never known about before, but for the most part she let him describe the situation.

Merje asked few questions, mostly listening and taking notes on her smart board. It probably took an hour to lay out the gory details of the situation. At no time did Merje look either shocked or judgemental. Thomas guessed that she dealt with many cases involving far more devious characters. Finally she jotted some last notes and looked up from her desk.

"So, to summarize, we have an ambitious Astral officer, the delightful Thomas, locking horns with another officer, the villainous Breeze. My sweet sister wants nothing to do with any of this, but has been drawn in nonetheless because she's so damn awesome and she keeps making Breeze look bad. At present it seems like Brisebois has the advantage, and you think she's going to try to destroy one or both of you by damning you in the Fleet Marshall Investigation."

Thomas looked at Katja. She was staring at the floor.

He nodded to Merje. "Pretty much."

The lawyer tapped her pen against her chin. "I can probably help," she said cautiously, "but with a Fleet Marshall Investigation in play, we're going to have to tread carefully."

"Why?"

"Brisebois has unusual powers because she's been assigned to this inquiry, even more than what she'd already wield as a senior Intelligence officer," she explained. "And Parliament doesn't like to wait, so she's going to be under pressure to deliver quickly. We have to move carefully, and fast."

"What do you suggest we do?"

Merje fixed him with her gaze. "I'm going to do some serious digging first, to try to find some dirt on this woman." She gestured toward her screen, indicating that she meant to begin immediately. "If you want to stay and help, it might go faster."

Katja sighed, dropping her head into her hands.

"Please not today," she said. "I have a splitting headache. I'm supposed to be meeting up with some people later, and I need to have a nap first."

Merje gave Thomas a conspiratorial smile, and slipped off the desk. She knelt down beside Katja and put her arm around her.

"Okay, not today," she said. "And you better get some good sleep tonight, because our favorite family member's arriving tomorrow."

Katja muttered a string of words in what Thomas assumed was her native Finnish. They had to be expletives.

Merje kissed her on the head.

"It'll be okay, honey," she said. "I promise I'll even stay with you for the entire meal. How long can lunch last, anyway?"

Suddenly Thomas felt like he was intruding. He made to rise, but Merje motioned for him to stay.

"Thomas can help me get started today," she continued, "and then maybe tomorrow or the next day, I'll have some lines of enquiry you can help me with."

Katja nodded. She gave Merje's arm a squeeze then pushed herself up from the chair. She turned to Thomas.

"Thanks for calling," she said. "I needed to get out, and it was really nice to see you again."

"Likewise." He wanted to hug her, to tell her everything was going to be okay, but he refrained. This was a warrior, he reminded himself, and she didn't need protecting. "I'll call you soon." He watched her disappear into the corridor, then turned back to Merje.

She was watching him intently.

"So, my lovely," she said, "are you going to tell me the whole truth?"

Uh-oh. Suddenly he realized just how good she was at her job. He motioned for her to retake her seat, and pulled his chair over.

"I assume it's your father who's coming to visit?"

She rolled her eyes, then reached into one of the drawers. To his surprise, she pulled out a bottle of whiskey and two tumblers.

"I hope Katja doesn't have anything to drink tonight," she said, "because she gets stupid when she drinks. Me, I intend to stay buzzed from now until that bastard leaves town."

He watched as she made two generous pours. "How long is he in town for?"

"A couple of weeks." She looked up through long eyelashes as she sipped the amber liquid. "Apparently the Army is doing some ceremonial thing, in conjunction with the Astral Force. All part of the propaganda to make everyone feel good about Terra again."

That explains it, he mused. A call had come in for volunteers from the non-active ships. Since the *Armstrong* was engaged in a mission, he hadn't concerned himself with it.

"I wonder if we could get Katja assigned to that?" he suggested. "It might keep her busy."

Merje barked a laugh. "I'd just love to see my father's face when he stood at attention on a parade square, and had to take orders from Katty." She took another sip. "Honestly, I'd pay money for that."

Thomas smiled. "Does anyone else besides family call her Katty?" he asked. "It's endearing."

That look again. Merje shrugged.

"I doubt it—maybe her old artsy friends. You know, she was a lot more fun ten years ago."

"A military life can harden a person, especially after what she's been through."

"When was the last time she had a nice, stiff one in her?"

Thomas nearly choked on his drink. "I don't know." Coughing, he cleared his throat. "You two are cut from a different cloth, I see."

"You might say that." She smiled slightly. "She was always the good one."

Time to change the subject.

"Okay, so back to the case at hand," he said quickly. "What kind of things should we look for?"

"We can start with the whole truth," Merje said, glancing at her smart board. "Are you going to give it, or not?"

"Absolutely," he said. "What would you like to know?"

"Did you sleep with her?"

Thomas dipped his head to rub his eyes. He should have known this would happen. He sighed, realizing that Merje needed to be fully armed with the facts.

"Yes."

Merje nodded, and drew a line on her board between Thomas and Breeze. "Okay, that may be our greatest weakness, seeing as how you're married and all." She tapped his wedding ring with her pen. "But it might hurt Breeze, too. She isn't married, is she?"

He suddenly realized who Merje was talking about. He'd narrowly dodged a bullet.

"No," he said, "but I think she's dating Chuck Merriman's cameraman."

"Really. What's his name?"

Thomas thought back to the interview session in *Armstrong*. There had been a few subtle exchanges between the fellow and Breeze, but mostly he'd stayed in the background.

"I don't know, actually. He's African."

"Well, *that* certainly helps." Merje gave him a withering glance. "There's only half a billion of them—narrows it down considerably."

He felt his cheeks burn. "I'll call Chuck and find out."

"Good idea."

As the afternoon wore on, Thomas came to truly admire Merje's ability. She had quite a knack for uncovering dirt. For the moment everything they had was based on rumor, yet he began to feel more confident.

He also began to notice more and more similarities between the sisters. Their hair was the same color, and with Merje's behind her shoulders it didn't look much longer than Katja's new, civilian style. Her hands were tiny as she scribbled notes on her smart board, and her expressions were like those Katja made when she relaxed.

Her voice had the same hint of an accent that gave Katja a certain allure, and while she didn't drop as many f-bombs as her trooper sibling, Merje was anything but a prude. She was, Thomas decided, what Katja could be if she wanted to be. Fun, smart, beautiful and confident.

As he reached for his tumbler again—it never seemed to empty, no matter how hard he tried—he made a note to get Katja drunk as soon as he could. He wanted to see more of this sort of Emmes.

Finally, Merje tossed down her pen and sat back.

"I have to take a break. Want something to eat?"

Thomas nodded. He wasn't sure how much whiskey he'd consumed, but he agreed that a little food would be a good idea. It was still a few hours until Soma would be finished at the spa. At this rate, he'd fit right in with her and her friends at the club.

Merje called someone and ordered a refreshments tray for two. Then she put the bottle and the tumblers back in her drawer.

"Look sober," she said with a wink.

A few minutes later the food was delivered by a handsome young man in a suit. He cleared away Merje's lunch tray and set down the offering of fruits, cheese, and crackers. Merje stood with more confidence than Thomas would have expected, and walked him to the door. She made some flattering comment about his delivery technique, and that made him laugh. Then she shut the door with a flourish, turned, and walked back toward him.

Right at him, in fact. She reached his chair and leaned her hands on his armrests.

"These heels are killing me."

As her long, blonde hair fell forward past her face, she crouched down to pull her shoes off. In so doing, she brushed against his bare knees. When she looked up again, a few inches from his face, hair falling straight past her fine features, she gave him a very small smile.

He could feel his heart thumping in his chest. For just a moment he pretended it was Katja leaning over him, so sensual and seductive. In that moment his drunken hand reached out to caress the warm, smooth body in front of him.

She leaned in and kissed him, her warm lips firm against his. He felt a tiny hand slide up his chest and neck to caress his head. He felt the blouse loosen as his own hands pulled the silk free, felt the smooth, soft skin underneath.

"I figured you were that kind of man." She nibbled at his ear and whispered as she began to unbutton his shorts. "I'm glad you didn't disappoint."

He pushed up to his feet, tracing her high cheeks with his lips, down to the slender neck and shoulders. Clothes began to come off. Her body was thin and willowy, not as muscular as he remembered Katja's, but she was hot and willing, and close enough.

As she drifted down to her knees he closed his eyes, remembering back to that dark cabin, somewhere in the Sirian blackness. He gasped in pleasure, fantasizing about this new, experienced Katja. He ran his hands through her blonde hair, thinking of her dark, luminous eyes as she'd looked up at him in the dark cabin with such admiration.

When they went down to the floor he explored her white skin, tasted her small, round breasts. She moaned freely, digging her nails into his back. Then she pushed him onto his back, straddling him with a long, smoldering stare of anticipation. Her hair fell across his face, but he could still picture her features as she enveloped him and began to rock.

For a moment she lowered her face down to his, and he stared into Merje's fierce, blue eyes, but as he pulled her into a passionate kiss he held her hot body against him, grabbed her small, tight butt and thrust upward.

As the moment approached, he knew just enough not to shout her name, and as he bore down and gritted his teeth with pleasure, a single thought consumed him.

Katja.

18

The evening winds were warm and dry, and Breeze enjoyed their caress over her silk clothes. She'd been enjoying the sunset over Lake Sapphire, idly watching the pedestrians on the boardwalk, and suddenly she realized just how happy she was. Not content, not merely satisfied, but truly happy. She couldn't remember the last time she'd felt this way.

Everything in her professional life was coming together nicely. She'd secured a powerful patron in Admiral Chandler, and she was confident she understood his ego well enough now to know how to properly manipulate him. She had that letch Admiral Bush on a short enough leash that he could ensure that her Dark Bomb project got the proper support. She had to admit, as well, that having Thomas Kane aboard the *Armstrong* was proving to be advantageous. He brought some much-needed competence to the science team.

Unfortunately her deadline set by the Fleet Marshall was getting closer. She might have to take Thomas down before the Dark Bomb research was complete. Even so, it was all in a day's work.

She took a last deep breath of the warm air and turned away from the twilight vista. Heading back into her apartment, she began to set the mood for the evening. Lights were dimmed, fireplace ignited, table set. It wasn't often she prepared a complete meal from scratch, but her childhood in France hadn't been completely wasted, and this evening's meal was *coq au vin*—one of her specialties.

Breeze decanted the wine and briefly considered the choice of music. He liked jazz, she knew, and she selected the works of a newish band that specialized in the old school, with none of the fusion elements so common in the modern music scene. He'd like her choice, she was sure.

The chime sounded, announcing his arrival in the lobby downstairs. Breeze actually felt a bit of thrill ripple through her—when was the last time that had happened?—and activated the music. One last check in the mirror and she took her position near the dining table. Easily visible when he entered, but distant enough so as not to appear eager.

He didn't even knock. The door slid open and there he was, athletic frame filling the doorway, draped in Jovian-style clothes that seemed as if they'd been made just for him. His dark face was lit up by a sparkle in his eyes that overshone his usual expression of cool nonchalance. He was happy to be here, she could tell, and that made her heart flutter anew. He stepped into the condo, door sliding shut behind him.

"My dear, you've outdone yourself again."

"I'm glad you're so easily impressed." She fought to keep her grin reduced to a smirk as she walked slowly over to wrap her arms around his shoulders. "Maybe I'll hold back on what else I had planned for this evening."

A smile spread across his features. "Don't hold back because of me. I'll try to keep up."

"If you say so." She pulled herself against him, planting a passionate kiss on his soft lips. She loved the feel of his muscled body, of his powerful arms holding her in an embrace. His physical presence was intoxicating: it took a considerable force of will not to jump straight to the evening's finale. Reluctantly she pulled back, still resting her hands on his shoulders.

"Have a seat, Kit. I have a new wine I think you might like."

His hands lingered hungrily, but he kept his mask of easy confidence in place as he slipped away from her and headed for the couch.

"I'm intrigued," he said. "I thought we'd already tried all the good wines there were. You haven't gone off-world for this one, have you?"

She scoffed. "Like any grape could grow well in recycled air. No, my dear, I think you'll be amazed at just how many good wines come out of France."

He sat down, looking her over with a wry expression.

"No doubt a significant part of your education was devoted to learning them all."

"My unofficial education, for sure," she admitted, handing him a glass and holding up her own. "A girl needs a break from studying architecture and art. Surely you experimented a bit as well?"

He took a long sniff of the wine, swirling it expertly and taking the most delicate of sips. He nodded his appreciation, although his expression hardened slightly.

"Much better than the homemade beer we traded our food coupons for."

A witty retort died in her throat. Kit spoke so rarely of his youth as an orphan. He was so unlike what she would have expected, coming from West Africa thirty some years ago. The fact that he'd survived at all, let alone escaped and turned himself into such a success, made him that much more remarkable.

"Thank goodness those days are behind us all," she said seriously.

He poked her playfully. "Maybe one day you and I could set up a fine wine bar in Freetown—enlighten the masses."

She laughed, caught off-guard by his sudden return to good humor, and thrilled at his hint of a future together. In her mind, she would have pictured them embarking on a project to improve water coverage for the region—her as a senator, and him the devoted expert. But a wine bar sounded a great deal more fun. Maybe they could do it before she went into politics.

"I would absolutely love that."

He took another sip, glancing past her toward the dining table.

"Perhaps with some real French cooking to match?"

"I might be able to whip up a few dishes from time to time." She curled her legs up underneath her, enjoying the cozy feeling of just being with her man. "But don't be hasty. You haven't tried it yet."

He rubbed her arm. "Breeze, I haven't yet discovered anything that you don't do perfectly. So many people we meet are all talk, but you have such substance behind you."

Again she had to wrestle the threatening grin down to a smirk. She was thankful for the dim lighting, as it would hide the flush in her cheeks. Normally she'd respond with some self-deprecating remark, but his words were so sincere, and she so wanted to revel in his praise.

"Thank you," she said simply.

Over these past few months, she'd come to the same conclusion about Kit. He was so perfect. Blessed with excellent genes, he hadn't wasted them on gluttony and sloth, or on artificial augmentations. His vigor was refreshingly natural. His confidence and strength of character, likewise, were born of overcoming hardship, as opposed to prep-school training and privilege. Other men were mere caricatures next to him.

He was everything an ambitious Terran woman could want.

More than that, she really *felt* something for this man. He wasn't just a tool for her to use. She genuinely wanted to be with him. Breeze sipped her wine and let her eyes drift over his beautiful form, looking forward anew to how she intended to conclude the evening.

Six more months in the Astral Force before retiring as a senior officer and decorated veteran. It would be the perfect time to take a break and create a new life. With his media connections, she could probably skip her foray into business and go straight into journalism, building a public image for herself before making the dive into politics.

The wine bar might need to wait.

She took another sip, feeling her heart flutter again. She couldn't tell by his easy expression if Kit knew it, but this evening was the start of something amazing.

19

It was amazing how just getting off a ship gave him new energy. Jack used to hate the long elevator descent from Astral Base One to Longreach, but lately it had become one of his favorite things. It meant time away from the Terran Research Vessel *Neil Armstrong*.

It meant freedom.

"You want a beer?" he asked on a whim.

Amanda looked over at him. "Seriously?"

He shrugged. "Sure. They have a bar on this thing, you know."

"Really, where?" Looking around at the mostly full passenger deck, she pursed her lips in confusion. "And why haven't you told me about it before?"

He pulled her out of her seat. "It's on the bottom deck, where the best view is—but you have to pay to get in and the drinks aren't cheap. Just now I'm just feeling really pumped about escaping Helena's Hell Hole, and I want to celebrate."

"Bring it on, flyboy." She kept hold of his hand and strode for the stairs.

Three flights down and an extortionate entry fee later, Jack led Amanda into the dimly lit chamber with downward-curving polyglass walls and transparent furniture. A circular bar ran around the central pillar, behind which the space elevator whisked along the seemingly endless cable. Earth was looming large in all the windows, but Jack figured they had time for one celebratory drink before landing. He ordered a beer for himself, and a cider for Amanda. She accepted it with an expression of surprised delight.

"You know my drink."

It wasn't rocket science, but if it made her happy, it made the trip go quicker. She was fun when she was happy, and he'd decided to keep hanging out with her, no matter what Lieutenant Commander Kane said about her supposed feelings for him.

Maybe it was just the uniforms that were unflattering to her figure, he decided. In civvies she didn't look quite so tubby, and with her hair done she was actually kind of cute. Not that she was Jack's style, of course—and anyway he had someone he was looking forward to seeing in Longreach.

She seemed to notice that he'd taken some care with his wardrobe too. She touched his chest lightly and gasped in her best imitation of Helena.

"Oh, Admiral, I love your new shirt."

He stuck out his belly and chuckled. "Oh, why thank you, Helena. Perhaps I should give you a medal."

She pulled back her cheeks and gave her best coy expression. "They say a man is like fine wine, and gets better with age."

He chortled again, sounding more like Santa Claus than Admiral Bush. "Have another medal, and I'll promote you again, as soon as you finish polishing my sword."

Amanda looked startled for a second. "Okay, Admiral," she said. "You know how much I like it..." She began to make the universal hand gesture, pushing her tongue against one cheek.

It was Jack's turn to be surprised, and he leaned back. She laughed, punching him in the knee before reaching for her drink.

"I thought you were a pilot, Jack," she said, giggling. "Don't you know how to handle a lady?"

He laughed at that, and felt himself relax. She really *was* a firecracker, and she'd make some guy happy, for sure. He took another swig of beer and looked down at the rugged coastline of Australia, stretching off to the east.

The land at the north end was dark green and forbidding, but the red plains of the interior stretched away in every other direction. As he leaned forward to look down along the impossibly straight elevator cable, he saw the sparkling oasis of

Longreach. Green forests, blue lakes, and silver towers, it was really starting to become a home away from home.

Though that wasn't going to stop him from visiting his real home, and soon. Nothing could match the beauty of the land where the mountains touched the sea. On an impulse he tapped Amanda's arm.

"Hey, what're you doing after Longreach?"

"I didn't know there was an 'after Longreach,'" she replied. "Are you going somewhere else?"

"Yeah, I'm only in town for a few days," he explained. "I wanted to go see my folks in Vancouver. You want to come?"

"Really?" She stared at him for a moment, surprise turning quickly to a smile. "Uhh, sure. I'd love to meet your folks."

"Cool. Have you ever been skating?"

This evoked a stranger expression. "No..."

He laughed. "Then maybe I'll finally be able to teach you something you don't know." He raised his glass. "Excellent."

They chatted with new animation as the sky slowly turned blue around them. For some reason she really seemed excited at the idea of going to Vancouver. It probably wasn't any more exciting than her home town on Mars, but maybe he'd arrange for a boat ride or something. Every Martian he'd ever met seemed to love the ocean.

They arrived in Longreach uneventfully, found their individual quarters at the officers' residence, and quickly regrouped out on the street. A line of cabs stood waiting to take military personnel into the city. As they climbed into one, Jack thought he noticed a hint of perfume. It was nice.

"So who are we meeting tonight?" she asked.

"An old friend of mine, who I served with on the last deployment. We had a few adventures."

She smiled. "I can't wait to hear about them. For all your blathering on, you don't talk about the war much."

He shrugged. "Maybe I don't want to brag."

She gave him a long look. "From you, I don't think it would be bragging."

Was she looking at his face? He rubbed a hand across it and stared out at the evening sky. She'd wanted to come along—he just hoped she wouldn't be a third wheel.

They quickly arrived at their destination, a long boardwalk next to the largest artificial lake in the center of the city, the fabled Lake Sapphire. It was a beautiful warm night, and he breathed in the mixed scents of desert air, purified water, and deep-fried food. Amanda pressed her arm against his.

"Great choice, Jack," she said. "This is such an awesome place. Now, where's this buddy of yours?"

Jack scanned the crowd of pedestrians. The sun had just disappeared below the horizon, but the ambient glow made searching easy. The last of the families were leaving, and he noticed the first of the bums shuffling out of their make-shift shelters. Some youngsters were starting to mingle in small groups, not yet making trouble.

He still didn't see who he was looking for. He did notice, however, a stunning blonde strolling near the water. A tight, black party dress hugged her lean figure, shapely legs shown off from mid-thigh right down to the pointed toes of her high heels. Her blonde hair bobbed at her shoulder as she walked, one hand on her purse and the other manipulating what looked like one of those new Baryons.

Jack's own device suddenly buzzed. He pulled it out and read the message.

"Holy crap."

"What is it?"

Jack started walking toward the blonde bombshell. As he approached he got a better sense of scale, and realized that she was actually quite short, even with the heels. She noticed his approach and turned to look at him, revealing her face for the first time. His heart skipped a beat.

She smiled and waved, turning to approach him.

"Hey, you're Jack. And you're a pilot."

He had thought Katja looked pretty at Thomas's party, but to see her this evening, wearing such an elegant dress and—could it be?—make-up. He was speechless. He jogged up to her and wrapped his arms around her. Her body was firm against his, and as her muscular arms wrapped around him he felt the power within them.

She released him a little sooner than he'd have liked, but she was smiling broadly as she looked him up and down.

"You look good," she commented. "Did a girl pick your clothes for you?"

He glanced down at his outfit. In fact, his sister had picked it out for him on his last visit home, but no one needed to know that.

"The clothes picked me. I am a pilot, after all."

She shook her head. "Oh, subbie…"

"Okay," he held up a finger, "point of protocol. I don't think we have to use ranks when you have long hair."

"Fair enough, Jack." She looked past him and nodded. "Are you going to introduce me to your friend?"

He turned in surprise, suddenly realizing that Amanda had walked up behind him. She was standing with her arms folded, scowling at him.

"Oh, sorry," he said quickly. "This is my friend Amanda, from my new ship." He put a hand on Katja's bare shoulder. "Amanda, this is my buddy Katja. You didn't get to meet her at the XO's party."

"Nice to meet you." Katja stepped out of his grasp to offer her hand to Amanda. "Has Jack told you he's a pilot yet?"

Amanda took her hand. "He's said a lot of things, actually," she replied. "What exactly did you two do together?"

Katja stepped sideways slightly to face both of them. She gave Jack a long, pondering look.

"Well, I saved his life. And then he saved mine, and then we worked to piece together a mystery. Then he crashed another Hawk, I wound up in hospital, we had a few laughs, we nearly got killed again…" She shrugged. "You know, ordinary stuff."

Jack couldn't help but grin at her summary. She was so nonchalant about the whole thing. She wasn't bragging, but she made it sound pretty cool. He'd have to get her to teach him how to deal with non-veterans so well.

"Wow," Amanda said. "Sounds like you two went through hell together."

Jack put on his best, casual stroll. He moved behind Katja

to stand between the two ladies, draping an arm across each of their shoulders. Katja's were taut, smooth, and bare, while Amanda's were soft and round under her top.

"Well, we try not to make a big deal about it," he said. "Tonight it's all just about enjoying the freedom we protected."

Amanda gave him her most scornful gaze. Katja looked a little puzzled. Both girls stepped out of his gentle embrace.

That hadn't played out quite as he'd hoped.

He turned his attention to one of the nearby food carts. "Right now, what I'm most looking forward to is a deep-fried corn dog. Who's with me?"

Katja put a hand to her flat stomach. "I don't think I could handle one, Jack. Maybe I'll just have an ice cream."

"That sounds good to me," Amanda agreed.

He shrugged. "Okay, two ice creams and one stick of greasy goodness."

Suddenly shouts erupted down the boardwalk. He looked over and saw a scuffle in the dim light. Other pedestrians veered wide to avoid the conflict.

"We'd better keep moving," he said. "We don't want to be here when the police show up."

"*If* they show up," Amanda muttered as she pressed him forward into a walk.

Jack's corn dog was too hot to eat when he finally got it, but he savored the greasy aroma with anticipation. The ladies were quickly kitted out with ice creams, and he looked down the boardwalk anew.

"I think that fight's over. It should be okay now."

"Why do you want to stay out here?" Katja asked. She nodded down the lakeshore to where the paid section of the boardwalk started. It was well-lit and mostly empty, quite unlike the dim crowds where they stood. It did look inviting, but until that moment it had never occurred to him to even consider it. Not that money was really an object, so soon after returning from deployment.

"I guess we could splash out for one night," he said.

She looked at him strangely. "Jack, we're veterans," she said. "It's free."

That had never occurred to him. It was shocking to think that he was now a veteran, with all the rights and privileges that came with the status.

"Free for some of us," Amanda said.

Jack glanced at her. Amanda was still a serving member of the military, even if she wasn't a combat veteran. She'd pay a reduced fee, but looking again at the welcoming section of boardwalk he knew he didn't want to miss an opportunity.

"I'll pay for you," he offered.

"No thanks." She frowned. "I make more than you do, junior."

So much for gallantry. He shrugged. "Okay, then let's ditch this mob."

They started down the boardwalk, strolling at a leisurely pace until they reached the paid section. Jack let his memory linger on the sudden smiles and looks of respect as he and Katja presented their veteran cards. He wondered if the gatekeepers had assumed they were a couple—he certainly hadn't done anything to dissuade the notion.

He'd kind of hoped to see Katja's technique at licking an ice-cream cone, but she'd opted for a cup and spoon instead. On his other side Amanda, he noted, had gone for a double scoop.

"So, Jack," Katja said, "have you broken any more Hawks lately?"

"No way," he responded. "You should have seen how I put that bird in the nest on our last trip. Amanda was with me." He looked over to her for comment. She nodded sarcastically with a mouth full of ice cream.

After that there was a moment of silence, broken only by their steps on the wooden planks, and Jack tried to think of some suitably witty barb to throw at Katja. Disappointingly, he came up blank.

"Did you help Jack on the prototype Dark Bomb?" Amanda asked, mouth finally free of ice cream. Katja didn't answer right away, her dark eyes casting out over the lake.

"I was there for the launch," she admitted, "but I didn't understand the science."

"See," he said, gently poking Amanda. "I was doing science."

"Whatever, Jack."

"So are you a scientist, Amanda?" Katja asked.

"Trying to be. I did my masters thesis on prion incursions into the Bulk, but these days everyone's focused on the gravitons. My doctoral thesis will describe the effect on vacuum energy by Bulk gravitons excited by ripples from the Chtholian Deep. Our current research has quite a bit of relevance to my area of study, so I'm able to gather a lot of thesis data while still doing the State's work."

Amanda got really animated when she talked about her research, but Jack didn't want to bore Katja.

"What that means is that I have to fly the Hawk really slow and silent," he noted. "Kind of like our recce of Abeona."

Katja nodded, but didn't comment. They strolled along for a few more silent moments, and it began to feel uncomfortable.

"Have you seen your folks yet?" he asked Katja.

"Oh, yeah. More than enough," she said, her voice strange. "My father's coming into town tomorrow, actually."

"That's cool. Why's he coming?"

"Some Army thing." She shrugged. "I think they're doing some exercises for the Astral College students—something about improving cross-service cohesion."

He laughed. "I think the Astral Force should focus on getting the Fleet and Corps to work together, before we mix it up with the Army."

She smiled and shrugged again.

Try as he might, Jack couldn't really get the conversation going. He and Katja talked a bit about their time in space, but not as much as he'd expected. She didn't really seem to think their experiences were worth reminiscing about. It was a shame, because he really wanted to talk.

He wondered if Amanda's presence was making it awkward, and almost regretted bringing her along. She wasn't contributing to the conversation at all, anyway. By the time they reached the far end of the paid section, corn dog and ice creams were long since done. Jack stopped where the wooden walkway morphed into the start of a garden path, and looked at the ladies.

"So, thoughts for the evening?" he asked. "Maybe some drinks?"

Amanda stretched grandly. "I'm actually pretty tired," she said. "I think I'm going to head back, have an early night."

Good, she's taking the hint, he thought. "How about you, Katja? You didn't get all dressed up for nothing."

"Yeah, I thought I might be up for something this evening." She looked back along the boardwalk, her gaze turning distant. "But now that we're out, I'm not sure..." Her voice trailed off.

"Oh, come on," he said. "Just one?"

She frowned, but then gave him a wry smile. "Sure. Who can say 'no' to a pilot?"

Amanda started to back away.

"Okay then, you kids have fun."

Jack waved at her. "You still want to go to the matinee tomorrow?"

"I'm going," she said as she turned away. "Join me if you want."

"Good night," Katja called after her. Jack waved a dismissive hand at Amanda's retreating form.

"She's a nice girl, but she's moody sometimes." He took Katja's arm in his and started walking toward one of the nearby pubs.

"She's cute," Katja said. "When I first saw you, I figured that you two were—"

"Oh, no, no," he said. "We're just friends." He suddenly recalled that women usually became more interested if they thought there was competition. "I don't want to encourage her."

Katja laughed. "Oh, my little pilot."

She hadn't pulled her arm away, he noticed. Things had changed as soon as Amanda was gone. As they approached the bustling, open-air pub he noticed that there was an hourly special.

"What's your choice of shooter?" he asked as they sat down at one of the patio tables.

She looked at him strangely. "That's an odd conversation starter." She shrugged. "It depends—for close-in, or long-range?"

He was speechless for a moment, wondering if this was some witty retort. Then he was struck with understanding and he laughed, pointing at the menu board on the wall.

"Drink shooters, ma'am. Not bullet shooters."

She glanced at the board, eyes widening as she realized her mistake. Her lips curled in a smile. "Oh. In that case I'm not picky. Whatever you want."

The server appeared, and Jack ordered six of the first shooter listed on the board. He didn't know one from the other, so why not just go with the flow? The patio began filling up quickly, now that the sun was gone, most of the clientele well into their evening drinking activities.

"We'll have to drink up if we want to stay with this crowd," he observed.

"I wouldn't even try." Katja glanced around in disinterest. "These rich kids probably started boozing at lunchtime."

Her casual observation was spot on, he thought. Most of the other guests were about his age, all well-dressed and bejeweled. They called out to each other with the easy confidence that came from commanding their personal environments. He doubted whether any of them had ever worked a day in their lives.

"Yeah, you're probably right," he agreed. "I bet their wardrobes alone are worth more than my annual salary." The shooters arrived and Katja hefted her first with a wry smile.

"Welcome to the life of a veteran, Jack," she said. "It's yours forever now." He clinked his shot glass against hers, and downed the sweet, burning liquid without thought. Then he coughed as the burn flashed up his throat to his cheeks.

Katja laughed at him.

He forced a smile to his lips. "That was good," he said, choking a little. "I could get used to this veteran life."

She hefted her second shooter. "Well, in my experience there's a lot of this." She downed it and looked around at the crowd.

He followed suit, noting that his vision actually blurred as he set down the second empty. Whatever this stuff was, it was powerful. Kind of like Katja, he thought suddenly.

"You been okay since we got home?" he asked on an impulse.

She looked back at him. "Fine, why?"

"I dunno." He frowned. He'd wanted to talk about this with someone for a long time, but when the moment arrived, it was hard to find the right words. "It's kind of a shock, coming home after a deployment like that." He looked around at the festive crowd. "We go from dodging death to pounding back drinks."

She nodded, her dark eyes fixing on him.

"Yeah, but just like out there…" She waved vaguely at the stars. "We have to stay strong."

Sometimes that was the last thing Jack wanted to do.

"But it's hard, you know, to deal with all the stupid shit."

A sharp laugh escaped her lips. She reached for her last shooter, then changed her mind and gripped his hand across the table.

"We're always fighting battles, Jack," she said, sounding fierce. "Sometimes they just look different. We've got to stay strong." Her fingers were small but powerful around his. He squeezed them tightly, wishing he was as strong as her. He grabbed the last shooter with his free hand.

"To strength."

She hefted her own glass, and returned his toast before downing the drink.

A guy bumped into Katja from behind, knocking her in her chair. She tensed and her hand slipped away from Jack's as she straightened herself. The young man turned to face her and apologized, crouching down beside her to make sure she was all right.

Jack took the moment to signal for another half-dozen shooters. They weren't so bad once you got a few down range.

His pleasant buzz was interrupted by a loud arrival. She was tall and pretty, he noticed, and through all her make-up and jewelry was probably younger than him. Her smooth features twisted angrily, however, at the sight of the guy crouched next to Katja.

Feeling almost detached from the scene—like it was playing out on a screen in front of him—Jack watched as the new girl started berating the guy. He protested his innocence, but as she rebuffed his words with growing scorn, he started to get angry. Katja was still seated, trying to inch her chair away from the rising storm.

Then the newcomer turned her venom on Katja.

"Keep your slutty little hands off him!" the girl said as she pushed Katja's bare shoulder.

Katja was on her feet in a single, swift motion, chair tumbling backward into the next table. Even in her heels Katja barely reached the shoulders of the other girl, but there was no fear in her eyes. She took a single, slow step back. Jack wondered if he should get up, too.

"Back off," the guy said, trying to pull his girlfriend away. "I'm not interested in this little tart."

Katja didn't flinch at the reference, but Jack felt the heat rising in his own cheeks. Nobody talked about his friend like that. He stood up, and had already taken two steps around the table when Katja motioned him to stay still.

The tall girl looked at him with new scorn.

"And who's this?" she spat. "Your kid?" Her eyes narrowed menacingly. "Or your client?"

Jack saw the muscles tense under Katja's bare skin, saw the dark eyes narrow dangerously.

"Let's go, Jack," he heard her say with icy calmness. "Nothing good going on here."

"Yeah, that's right," the tall girl said mockingly. "You can go back to his place and play mommy. Maybe get him to—"

Her words were cut off by a single stab of Katja's hand to her throat. She gasped for air, eyes wide in fear.

Katja let her drop, then rounded the table. Jack stumbled as she took his arm. His own feet nearly tripped him up as she yanked him into motion, exiting the patio before anyone around them really knew what had happened. He got his legs working properly and struggled to keep up with her swift strides. They crossed the boardwalk and reached a taxi stand.

She signaled one over, and the next thing he knew he was being guided through an opening door into the plush rear seat. He expected her to climb in after him, and when she didn't he looked up at her questioningly.

Katja glanced back toward the pub patio, then shifted her gaze onto him. A smile broke under those dark eyes, and he was intoxicated by the intensity of her expression.

"We didn't pay for our drinks, Jack," she said. "I'll just go sort things out."

"I'm coming with you." He tried to climb back out of the cab.

"There's no need." She pushed him down against the seat with intimidating strength. "I'm heading home right afterward." Before he could speak again she pressed a finger hard against his lips. "That's an order, subbie. I don't want you getting all heroic on me."

She didn't need a gun, he realized, to be able to scare the shit out of him. He nodded, trying to turn his alcohol-fogged mind to the question of what directions to give the cab.

"Thanks for a fun night," he said. "Maybe we could get together tomorrow?"

"Sure." She smiled and kissed him on the cheek. It was just a brush of lips, so fast he had to convince himself it had happened. "You're a great kid, Jack. See you again." The cab door closed as she retreated. He watched her stride back down toward the patio, pausing only to remove her high heels and place one in each hand.

20

She lifted her head off the cold, sticky surface, but vertigo swept over her again like a wave. Her right hand gripped cold metal, while her left hand pressed frantically for purchase against the hard surface spread out before her.

The muffled sounds of the battle mixed with flashes of weapons fire as her troopers died all around her. She shut her eyes tight, but she could still see the silvery glint of Centauri war machines. Rockets and heavy slugs crashed overhead, almost drowning out the screams.

Katja gasped and heaved herself off the floor of the cell, shaking the hallucination. She fought to keep her stomach down as her vision slowly stopped spinning. Shivers ran up and down her exposed skin. She wrapped her arms around her knees and carefully lifted her eyes.

The cell was tiny, bars on one side, cot, sink, and toilet. The floor all around her was sticky with vomit. She peeled a few long strands of blonde hair off her face and looked down at her tattered black dress. She released a long, deep breath, trying to grab hold of reality.

She couldn't help but glance over her shoulder one more time. The walls were solid. No one was trying to kill her.

She shivered again, debating if she had the ability to climb onto the cot and drape the blanket over herself. Her body screamed for sleep, but the terror of the nightmare made her resist. Eventually she unfolded her limbs and crawled on hands and knees to the cot. As her head hit the built-in pillow she vaguely remembered that she wanted to get the blanket.

The cold touch of metal against her shoulder jerked her from sleep. She gasped and rolled, reaching for her assault rifle. Then she was flying through the air, slammed up against a hard surface. It was the floor, she realized, and as she rolled onto her back she saw a dark form looming over her.

A boot pressed against her chest. Something warm tapped against her throat and she recognized the awful tingling of a charged stun gun. She forced herself to go limp and look up with lucid eyes at the police officer who glared down at her through his visor.

"Don't make this difficult again," he said.

"I won't." The memory of the previous night was still very clear.

The officer studied her. "What's your name, and where are you?"

"My name is Lieutenant Katja Andreia Emmes, and I am in a jail cell in the city of Longreach on the planet Earth."

The stun gun retreated from her neck and the pressure eased on her chest. The police officer stepped back.

"You're free to go," he said. "Somebody vouched for you."

She looked over to the open cell door, wondering which of her superior officers had seen her like this. The police officer signaled back down the corridor, and she recognized the hand gesture as an "advance" order.

Katja tried to tidy herself up, but it was a lost cause. The black dress was torn in three places, scuffed in many others. Her shoes were nowhere to be found. Her hair was a matted mess, and as she tried to pull her fingers through it to straighten it she noticed that all of her knuckles were scraped and stained with dried blood.

She didn't know what could be more humiliating, until her mystery savior stepped into view.

Storm Banner Leader Günther Freidrich Emmes did not look impressed. He was dressed in his summer tans duty uniform, the crisp shirt and trousers framed by razor-sharp creases and mirror-like black shoes. Three rows of ribbons on his left chest gave subtle recognition to his decades of service, but obvious above them was the miniature clasp of the Cross of Valor. Even if his rank hadn't been enough to earn the respect of the police, that black-and-silver cross would certainly have earned him an audience.

He stared at her with open contempt. She forced herself to meet his gaze, but her own self-loathing robbed her of any will to fight. Why did it have to be today, of all days, that he arrived?

"I'm sorry," she heard herself say in Finnish.

"I hope so," he replied. "I don't like being met at the skyport by Longreach police, in front of my soldiers."

"I understand."

"I doubt you do," he said. "If you did, you'd never have put yourself in this position. When they told me that my daughter was in jail for drunkenness and assault, I figured it was Merje—but not you, Katja, not you."

It was about the closest she'd ever heard him come to complimenting her character. She forced her eyes up again to meet his.

"I... I'm having trouble, Father," she said. "I need help."

His gaze was stern, but somehow not entirely unsympathetic. "You know where you can get help. What you need to decide first is whether you really are a soldier or not." He turned to the guard and spoke in English. "This is my daughter, Katja. I will vouch for her good behavior."

"Come to the front desk." The officer left the cell and strode down the hallway. Her father turned and followed him. Katja had to move quickly to keep up. The quick, faint slap of her bare feet against the tile made her feel like a naughty child.

In the main lobby, the administration was quick and within ten minutes she was officially released from custody under a bond of guardianship. According to the special rules for veterans, she would not be formally charged for the previous night's misconduct if she could keep out of trouble for a day. As a highly decorated veteran, Father had officially taken responsibility for her actions.

They descended the broad steps of the police station in silence, entering the hot morning sun as a warm breeze funneled along the street. When they reached the sidewalk her father turned to face her.

"I assume you're in no condition for lunch."

She shook her head. The idea of food made her want to retch, and the blazing sun was already making her head pound.

"I'll endure your sister's company on my own, then," he said, "assuming I don't get another call from the police."

"You won't. I'm going home to sleep."

"I was actually thinking about Merje."

She felt too sick to even smile, but it was small comfort that no matter what decisions she'd made in her life, she would always rate higher than her sister in their father's estimation.

"I'm sure she's behaving well."

A long moment of silence passed between them. Katja was only too aware of how terrible she looked, barefoot and tattered clothing, next to the upright splendor of her father. She had no doubt he was aware of this contrast too.

"Katja," he said, "look at me."

Once again she forced her eyes upward—and once again she was surprised at the lack of disgust in his fierce stare. There was certainly no sympathy, but was there a touch of... understanding?

"I got a call from one of my colleagues, Storm Banner Leader Ciotti."

Her heart sank.

"He was impressed by you."

"What?"

Father nodded. "Few officers your age and rank would have had the guts to stand up to him—he's been terrorizing his own soldiers for years. He didn't appreciate having your gun in his face, but he respected your resolve."

"But I was removed from my post because of that incident."

"And rightly so. We can't have Astral Force members threatening to kill Army members over routine operations. But your spirit was strong, and in a shooting war that matters far more than regulations." He gave her an overall, appraising look. "I asked around, and I saw a few reports that were written about you, from the recent troubles. There's a clear pattern of carelessness, but your courage and ability show potential."

She stared at him, not sure what to think.

"If you'd gone Army, like you should have, we'd have trained you to think critically before you were forced to lead soldiers into combat. But because you went officer, you're running like a child into battle and getting too many troopers killed, even though you achieve your goals."

It always came back to that, didn't it? If only she'd followed in his footsteps. If only she'd done what he thought was right. If only, if only...

"Well, Father, I am what I am."

He nodded, the steel hardening behind his eyes. "Yes, and what you are right now is half-naked outside a police station, looking like a whore. You recognize that you need help, and that's the first step. But before you seek it, Katja Andreia, you have to decide first *who* you are. Are you a servant of the State, or are you really just that silly singer who's been playing at soldier for ten years?" He paused while that sank in. "Think hard on that, because I don't want more troopers to die if you make the wrong decision."

They were only words, but she wanted to lie down on the street and die. She knew she needed to stand up to him, but she couldn't muster the strength.

Damn him, damn him, *damn him!*

"I'll be here in Longreach for at least a month," he continued. "I hope you've answered that question for yourself before I go."

"Yes, Father."

"Go home and clean up."

With that he turned and walked away. Stray, annoying wisps of her matted hair caught the odd gust, and her bare feet were cold against the ground. Cars and buses rushed past on the street with little sound but the whisk of air in their wake. People on the sidewalk went about their business. A typical weekday on Earth. The war hadn't touched this place.

All of her experiences, the terror, the pain, the death, were nothing more than a dream here, a tale hinted at on the news channels and already forgotten as domestic concerns took center stage again.

A minor rebellion in the colonies. A week or two of exciting footage and media speculation, but nothing the military couldn't handle. Oh, there were still political and economic issues to resolve, but qualified people were looking into such matters, and they were nothing for peace-loving citizens of the Terran Union to worry about.

Katja gazed at the stream of self-absorbed faces hurrying past her, listened to the snippets of conversations about utterly mundane issues, and wanted to scream. She wanted to grab the nearest smug civilian and pound him or her into a pulp, make them understand what had really happened out there. She wanted to destroy something, to hurt someone.

It terrified her.

She rummaged through her little purse for the injector in the sealed side pouch. It was too much for her shaking hands, and dropping to her knees she upended the purse onto the sidewalk. She got her fingers around the injector and carefully pressed it into her thigh. A cool wave rushed up through her lymphatic system and the tension eased out of her body. After a few long breaths her fingers stopped shaking enough that she could gather up the spilled contents of her purse.

A public transit station was visible less than a block away, but she knew there'd be trouble if she tried to board with no shoes. Sighing, she flagged down a private cab.

Katja didn't know how long she slept, but the sun was low in the sky when she finally lifted her head off the pillow. Her head felt woozy, but the clanging pain was gone and, mercifully, there had been no more nightmares.

She blinked several times and looked around her bedroom. The tattered black dress was on the floor, her earrings not far away. The faint sound of the news wall from the living room momentarily suggested a visitor, but then she remembered turning it on. She'd intended to get changed into pajamas and regroup in front of the screen with a hot tea. Apparently she'd gotten as far as getting undressed before her plan had fallen apart.

She sat up gingerly and, assured of no nausea, put her feet down on the soft floor. She vaguely remembered agreeing to meet with Merje tonight, and she was pretty sure she'd promised to see Jack again too. As she stumbled into the bathroom she smiled: those two in combination might make for an interesting evening.

As always, the shower made her feel better. In clean pajamas she finally made herself some tea and sprawled out on her comfy chair, popping the pills she should have had that morning. They did their usual magic, and one cup of tea later she was actually looking forward to getting out. Dancing sounded like a good idea. It would be a better release for her energy than pounding the shit out of spoiled little rich girls who called her a prostitute.

For this evening, she figured, looking through her minimal wardrobe, maybe she should wear something a little less daring. Young Jack had struggled to keep his eyes up, and as she'd helped him to the cab she was pretty sure his hands hadn't really "slipped" onto her butt. She didn't expect anything less from a drunken kid, and in its own way it was kind of flattering.

She just hoped Amanda wasn't too pissed with him.

Katja chose a top with a high collar and slight sleeves, form-fitting enough but not revealing, and capri pants with sensible dancing shoes. Some fast-acting steroid cream on her knuckles helped to diminish the final evidence of last night's conclusion. A few minutes on her hair and face, and she inspected herself from all angles in the mirror. Not the least bit slutty, but maybe alluring enough to turn a few heads.

The downtown core was already thinning out by the time she made her way to Merje's office. The workweek was officially over, and most businesses shut down a little early for the long weekend, but many office lights were still on as she approached the edifice of Ryan, Ridley, and Day. The same receptionist was still at her desk, but she waved Katja through with a smile.

She jumped a little as she reached the hallway, nearly bumping into someone coming the other way. It was Thomas. He looked slightly disheveled, eyes widening as he saw her.

"Oh, hi, Katja," he said. "I didn't know you were coming by today."

Her heart clenched. Not even the drugs could completely

remove the ache she felt every time she saw him. Maybe getting him involved with Merje's firm was a mistake—she didn't know how much she could take seeing him on a regular basis.

"Hi," she answered. "You guys working late again?"

Thomas glanced back down the corridor. "Yeah, yeah. I think we're making some progress, though."

"Good. If you need me there, too, just let me know."

He looked at her strangely, then pulled her out of the rotunda and into the dimness of the corridor.

"Katja…"

He seemed at a loss for words, both his hands grasping her shoulders. The look in his eyes was something she'd never seen before, not even on that one dark night. Her heart beat faster, but she braced her emotional defenses.

"What do you want to say, Thomas?"

"I want to spend more time with you," he replied. "A lot more. I've missed you."

Her insides churned. Elation that she hadn't been fooling herself all this time, coupled with anger at everything that had happened since. When she spoke, it was slowly and carefully, to not reveal anything.

"What would your wife think?"

He hesitated. It looked as if he was fighting his own internal battle.

"She doesn't need to know. And—and it's okay in her circles. People have affairs all the time."

Her insides churned anew, but this time with revulsion. She knocked his hands off her.

"Listen to me, Kane," she gritted. "I am *not* going to be your squeeze toy. For once in your life, show a woman some fucking respect."

He stared wordlessly, eyes wide. Her words clearly stung him. He dropped his gaze and took a deep breath.

"I do, Katja, I do respect you," he muttered. "But I'm trapped in a situation that I don't know how to get out of."

She wasn't impressed by this new, fumbling Thomas. She stared him down.

"Tell me this—do you love your wife?"

He stared back, mouth opening slightly.

She waited as long as she could, letting the anger fuel her. When no answer came, she pushed him roughly aside and strode down the corridor, not once looking back.

Merje's office door opened at her knock. She marched in to see her sister picking up random bits of food off the floor. Strawberries, mostly, but some other fruit mixed in. Merje looked up suddenly, eyes widening under her mussed hair.

Katja stopped and studied her. "You look like shit," she said. Her sister dropped the last of the fruit on the half-empty tray on her desk.

"Long day—lots of hair-pulling." She crossed her arms and glared. "Where were you for lunch today, bitch? And thanks for putting the old man in such a shitty mood."

She sighed, suddenly remembering the family lunch date.

"Sorry. Father and I had breakfast of sorts. At least, I ate a lot of crow. I slept most of the day."

A glimmer of respect lit up Merje's face. "So he wasn't lying when he said you were passed out in a jail cell."

"Nope."

She nodded. "Cool. How many people did you actually beat up? Father said you were charged with seven counts of assault."

"I guess it was seven, then, but some jealous bitch started the whole thing."

"Ain't that always the way."

"I want to go dancing tonight."

"Sure." Merje slipped on her suit jacket and grabbed her bag. "I want to go home and shower first, though."

Katja nodded, wonderingly idly what had possessed Merje to wear her shirt with the top three buttons undone.

21

The warm evening air was dry and calm as Kete walked down the outside stairs to the waiting cab.

His target was already in motion. The flurry of Baryon messages between herself, her sister, and some friends had given him ample information to make his plan. The clear dagger was hidden inside one of his fashionable riding-style boots, and under his loose-fitting silk shirt was a skin-tight polyweave armor that would defend against hand-held weapons.

The pair of fops who lived two doors down from him were ascending the stairs, and both gave him less than subtle glances as they approached. Kete knew he was dressed to draw the eye, but his high fashion masked the true intent of his evening's activities.

The date of the final phase of the mission had just been set for two weeks tomorrow, assuming the final jump gate tests were successful. That was good news, but it meant he was running out of time on Earth, and he doubted he would ever be coming back. If he didn't kill Katja Emmes tonight, there might not be another chance. He knew, as well, that he would never be able to forgive himself if he failed.

As he settled back in the cab and let it carry him toward his destination, he calmed his mind and did what he had never done before. He reached for the nightmare. Closing his eyes, he forced himself to relive that terrible night on Abeona.

* * *

The dark buildings of the southern suburbs fell swiftly astern as Kete piloted the car at a suicidal speed up the long hill. The sky still flashed with weapons fire, and the ominous, orange glow of flames lit up the clouds moving in from the south.

He led a column of perhaps thirty private vehicles, the remnants of his militia unit. Valeria, Major Mullaly, even the cadets who'd been loading bullets into magazines—all crushed and splattered by the Terran shock trooper attack. Kete was in charge now, and he was determined to get his family out of danger.

As he approached the ridge, the silhouettes of the houses began to stand out against the glow, and he felt a moment of optimism. There would be anti-personnel robots there, as well, keeping the area secure—at least for the moment.

Then he saw three more shapes—the squat, deadly outlines of Terran drop ships setting down on the road barely a kilometer ahead of him. Instantly his blood ran cold. Two of the drop ships disgorged objects almost as large as they were.

Hover tanks.

Kete hauled his car hard to the right even before he saw the first flash of guns opening fire on his phalanx of cars. He heard the rush of shells whistling past, felt the explosions as cars behind him were obliterated by the strikes.

His car began slipping out of control, and he gasped as its right side skidded across the soft dirt of the hillside. He killed the thrust and fought to keep the vehicle upright as it sailed slowly to a crawl before finally losing its hover control and digging into the ground.

As Kete climbed out into the night air once again he scanned the area. Not all of the shells had struck home, and he still had about twenty-five soldiers under his command. Most were staring up at the vicious firefight underway between the Terrans and the APRs, but Kete had only one thing on his mind. He linked into the Cloud once more, sending a direct message to the artillery spotters.

<Do you have civilians in the house?> he demanded.

A harried reply came quickly.

<Yes. Three—including two small children.>

It was his worst fear made real.

<We're coming to evacuate them. Ensure they are ready by the front door. Keep them low and protected until we arrive,> he responded.

<Understood.>

The militia had gravitated around him, realizing that he had a Cloud conduit. He motioned for them to crouch down on one knee, and spoke with intense vigor.

"Our mission is to evacuate three civilians from the house being used by our artillery spotters," he said, speaking rapidly. "We will head straight up this hill, avoiding contact with the enemy. While you provide cover, I will personally retrieve the civilians, and then we will retreat back down the hill." He scanned the group. "Any questions?"

Some militiamen exchanged glances, but no questions were asked. Kete doubted any of them even knew what sort of thing should be asked. He hefted his rifle, flicked off the safety, and started up the hill.

The ground was very soft. Designed for hobby gardening, it had never been intended as the main line for a military advance, and Kete could hear his people struggling to make headway in the loose dirt.

Up ahead, the street lamps had been shot out, but in the distance Centauria B was rising, and its red glow provided some light. There was plenty of illumination from flame and cannon fire, as well, enabling them to see the pitched battle between Terran tanks and Centauri APRs.

As far as he could tell, the shooting was still a block away from his house, and the way in was clear. He quickened his pace, desperate to cover the last stretch and reach his family.

Then, just as he emerged from the loose embankment onto solid turf, he saw a long line of dark forms moving low and quick through the nearby row of backyards. Using the houses as cover, the Terran troopers were trying to flank the APRs occupied on the main street. Kete bent as low as he could and sprinted across the open turf toward the cover of trees that marked the edge of the nearest private property.

The jostle of boots and weapons assured him that his militiamen were still behind him.

At the trees he lowered to a crouch, breathing heavily as the other soldiers ran up and took positions around him. The corporal who had ridden shotgun up from the depot appeared at his side, waiting expectantly for orders.

"Those troopers are moving to make a side attack on the APRs," Kete whispered. "We'll wait here for them to move up that side street, then slip up to that house there." He pointed at his house. It was close now, the home where he and Rupa had settled to raise a family.

The dark, grotesque figures of the armored Terran troopers moved with frightening efficiency, gathering together as they assessed their next move. Then, as Kete gasped, they darted across the street, one by one, to continue their stealthy advance. Coming nearer by the moment. The corporal beside him muttered something. Kete watched the troopers, then looked back at his home.

It sat across the street from the last house in the line that was currently being transited by the Terrans. They were close enough now that he could see the lead trooper, referring to a forearm display.

He gripped his rifle.

"Change of plan," he gritted, keeping his voice low. "Those troopers are headed straight for the spotters' location. We need to draw them away. Corporal, take the troops, reposition by those sheds, and open fire. I'll go in alone and get the civilians out."

The corporal nodded. He was a young man barely of university age whom Kete had never met before tonight. With pale, shaking lips he ordered the two dozen remaining militiamen to follow him away from the trees, across the open turf, and toward the partial cover of the garden sheds perched on the hillside.

Kete raised his rifle, watching in sick fascination as the lead Terran trooper darted past the opening between the last two houses, and crept closer to both him and his home. Another reference to the forearm display. Another few steps forward.

He gritted his teeth.

The invader was armored and carried explosive rounds for a fully automatic electro-magnetic rail gun. He was in a t-shirt, and carried a semi-automatic rifle with impact-only rounds. If that trooper spotted him, he didn't stand a chance.

Kete aimed, and fired.

The crack of the bullet shattered the tranquility. He didn't wait to see if he'd hit his target, just squeezed the trigger as fast as he could, sending rounds hurtling outward. The Terran trooper staggered back, then swung that awful Terran assault rifle in a blind, fully automatic arc toward the hillside. The rounds were aimed high, and gone so fast they probably hit the sea before coming down.

The corporal and his men returned fire en masse, battering the Terrans with gunfire.

The response was swift and savage, but Kete was already on his feet, sprinting toward the darkened porch of his home. He fired off a shout into the Cloud, praying that the artillery spotters understood his meaning and had Rupa and the girls ready to move. He reached out with his full suite of detection sensors, but realized immediately that a stealth field had been erected—no doubt by the spotters.

He was almost there. The APRs were still holding the main line against the Terran tanks, although fire and debris littered what had been his neighborhood.

Then the Terran trooper rounded the last house, eyes on his home. Kete slid to the ground, cursing himself for being so exposed, but the trooper didn't seem to notice him. Another check of the forearm display. One hand to the helmet's ear. Kete lay frozen, wondering why the trooper didn't advance. Then he knew.

Terrans didn't endanger themselves personally. Not when a battleship in orbit could accomplish what was needed.

"No!"

He struggled to his feet just as the massive, orange fireball burst down from the gray heavens. The morning star that heralded a terrible new dawn, and ended Kete Obadele's life.

The blast struck his home with deadly accuracy, obliterating it in one blinding second. A few shards of the exterior survived to be flung outward, but it was the burning sledgehammer of the shock wave that knocked Kete off his feet. He vaguely felt his body thudding down on the firm grass of the road, felt the friction of the hard dirt underneath as he slid across it.

He felt nothing as he pulled himself to his feet. Heard nothing but an endless ringing in his ears—the explosions had stopped. Sensed nothing from the Cloud. Saw only two things—the glowing, scattered embers of what had once been his house, and the Terran trooper who lay unconscious nearby.

He didn't know that he'd dropped his rifle, or that his webbing had been ripped clear off his body by the blast. He didn't know what the relative silence meant—for the APRs, for his men. All he knew was that the Terran who had killed his family was lying on the ground, a scant distance away.

Smaller than he'd expected, the trooper was spread-eagled on the grass, rifle and helmet both broken free of their tethers and scattered. Kete dropped to one knee, wanting to see the face of the man—

No. Woman.

The woman who had killed his family was young and fresh-faced despite the dirt and blood, her cropped blonde hair matted with sweat. He lifted her forearm display—that essential tool of any Terran trooper—and was amazed at how small the hands were that had typed in the coordinates to summon the orbital bombardment. He looked again at her face, trying to activate his visual recorder, so that he would always remember it.

To know the face of the angel of death.

She was breathing. That gave him the power of life and death. His hand unconsciously drifted forward, closing on her throat, but as much as he wanted to, he couldn't tighten his grip. Killing this Terran wouldn't bring back his family.

His grip lessened, but he could still feel the weak pulse, sense the life draining from her young body.

Killing her wouldn't bring back Rupa, Olivia, or Jess.

Even so, his grip tightened again.

Movement in the peripheral snapped him back to the greater reality. He staggered back and threw up his hands in a desperate attempt to protect himself against the pair of troopers who were charging toward him.

They stopped next to their fallen comrade, one of them crouching over her while the other raised an assault rifle toward Kete.

"Get back," he shouted.

Kete continued to step backward, hands raised. Both troopers wore medical insignia, and Kete still wore civilian clothes. Rifle and webbing lost in the explosion, he probably looked to them like a stunned local, and nothing more. As he backed away further, the medics lost interest in him.

Kete retreated as quickly as he could to the shadows.

The cab pulled to a stop against a sidewalk bathed in light.

Kete shook off the last images of the nightmare, then stepped out into the heat and noise of one of Longreach's main entertainment districts. The crowds of merrymakers mingled with great good humor, the calm air promising a night of good weather and no curfews.

Through the revelry, Kete spotted his target. She was approaching the biggest nightclub on the street, escorted by a taller woman—her sister, Merje. Although it was his intention to be surgical, Kete had no qualms about killing any of Katja's family. Not tonight.

Tonight, Katja Andreia Emmes would pay for her crimes, and perhaps Merje Emmes would endure her own nightmare. That would be justice.

Feeling the slight weight of the dagger in his boot, Kete approached the nightclub.

22

Merje, of course, knew the best dance club. She'd only moved to Longreach a month ago, but she already had a better sense of the nightlife than Katja had gathered in four years at the Astral College.

The scene was just starting to get moving when they arrived, and they found Jack and Amanda inside, leading the efforts on the dance floor. The deep, pounding throb of the music allowed for very little conversation, but Jack seemed to have no trouble getting introduced to Merje. Amanda, to her credit, kept dancing with energy, but Katja sensed the possessiveness as clearly as if the younger woman had put a leash around Jack's neck.

The young pilot, for his part, seemed to love the fact that he had three women dancing around him, and he joyously took turns facing off with each one. Amanda got closest, pulling him almost against her as they bobbed and turned. After one particularly daring coupling, she wouldn't let him turn back toward Merje, but Katja could tell Jack still wasn't getting it. She decided to help things along.

She stepped between Jack and Merje, engaging her sister in a close coupling of their own. Merje grinned and played along, draping her arms over Katja's shoulders as they moved seductively around each other. Slowly they moved away from their two companions, opening up the floor.

More people joined in with the music, and soon the dance floor was a throbbing mass. Katja liked the crowded heat of the bodies, feeling the primal pulse of the beat flow through her muscles. It was pure energy, stripping away the trappings of this hollow society and letting the raw power of the soul come forth. She let her body go with the music, gyrating back and forth, up and down.

At some point Merje must have moved away, because when she opened her eyes she was alone in the crowd. She didn't care, and danced for herself.

Eventually, inevitably, a slow song came on. She figured it was a good time to get some water, but she'd barely taken two steps when Jack bounded up and took her hands. She blinked in surprise, but his big grin was just too disarming. She laughed as he tucked a hand into the small of her back.

"Do you know this song?" she asked him.

He shook his head. "It must have been released while we were away."

While we were away. Such a casual phrase to describe hell, and the worst part of that hell, she knew, was that she'd fallen in love with a man she could never have. At least, not the way she wanted. He'd made his choice, and that was that.

Then she realized, as Jack pulled her a little closer, that she shared just as strong a bond with the kid who held her now. She'd saved his life, and he had saved hers. What was more, while she'd just been doing her job, he'd gone out of his way to rescue her. He had real character—not like that wannabe-adulterer.

She rested her head against Jack's shoulder, feeling truly content for the first time since coming home. Here was a true friend who understood her, with whom she could feel safe. She hugged him a little closer.

Although, she realized suddenly, it would be better if he'd learn to keep his hand off her ass. Was he drunk already? What a lightweight.

The song lilted to an end. She lifted her head to tell him to get right back to Amanda if he knew what was good for him.

He kissed her. Square on the lips. With a little bit of tongue.

She pushed him away. He staggered back and nearly fell into some other dancers. He stared at her, his eyes wide. She shook her head, trying not to cry as yet another illusion of security was ripped away from her.

He approached her. "What's wrong?" The music was already blasting away again and she was forced to shout in his ear.

"Go find Amanda, you dumb shit!"

She left him behind to figure it out for himself, pushing through the dancing bodies and fighting down the anger. Amanda and Merje were both seated at a booth sipping drinks.

"Jack's looking for you," she said. "He wouldn't shut up about how good your moves are."

Amanda looked at her doubtfully, but with a touch of hope mixed in. She peered out across the dance floor, and scooted out of the booth, enabling Katja to sit down next to her sister.

The volume was considerably less inside the booth, and they could actually speak. She leaned her head against Merje's shoulder.

"I love you, Merry."

Merje wrapped an arm around her. "I love you, too, Katty."

"And I hate the rest of the world."

"Me, too."

Merje slid a fruity cocktail in front of her.

She reached for a water. "No thanks, not tonight. I've used up my free pass with the local law enforcement."

"Shame. It seems like a long time since I had a stun gun pointed at me."

They sat in companionable silence for a few minutes, occasionally able to glimpse Jack and Amanda tearing it up. She looked happy to have Jack to herself again, and he seemed to be enjoying himself.

"It's sweet, isn't it?" she said. "Too bad Jack's such a dumb-ass."

"She's trying hard, you have to hand it to her." Merje sipped at her cocktail. "I'd have moved on to the next sucker long before now. Of course, it never takes me that long to get a man's attention."

Katja smiled at her. "Merje, you haven't been bad again, have you?"

Merje wrapped her lips around the straw of the cocktail and gave her best wide-eyed look.

Katja laughed, looking out at the crowd again.

Someone in the shadows was looking back at her.

She didn't stare, but kept her eyes moving until they'd finished their casual sweep. Her tail was here—the person who'd been following her. Facing down toward her drink, she looked up through her lashes toward the spot. It was difficult to make out features, but she could feel his eyes on her. It was the same feeling she'd had before, of being watched.

Katja considered her options.

She couldn't get up now—that would confirm that she'd been looking his way. In a few minutes she could, but for the moment she had to stay put. Still, it would look strange to sit here in silence. She needed to show that she was carefree, and having a good time.

Merje finished her drink and started on Katja's abandoned one. Katja took a long, easy breath. If there was one place left in the worlds she could feel safe, it was here, with little Merry.

"So tell me about your latest naughtiness," she said with a grin. "Which partner was it?"

"Oh please," Merje said, and she made a face. "I have more style than that. Only whores sleep with their bosses." That stung a little bit, but Merje couldn't possibly know it.

"Then why was it so bad?"

"Well... he's married."

"Oh, for shame."

"And he's a client."

"And you with a father in the Army." She shook her head in mock disbelief.

Merje laughed. "Well, at least this guy wears a uniform too."

The witty retort died in Katja's throat. What did she mean by that?

"In fact," Merje continued, "I really should thank you for bringing him in. He's a treat."

Katja's heart went ice cold. The music faded from her ears, the dancing figures disappeared from her peripheral. All she saw was her sister's face. Then all she heard was her own voice.

"Are you talking about Thomas?"

Merje shrugged with her hands turned up, face all cutesie.

"Guilty! And I'm surprised you didn't have a go at him— man, he's got some passion in him that needs to be ridden hard."

In that moment the last place of safety disappeared from Katja's life. Her last connection to this foreign world was severed. There was nothing for her here. This woman before her, these people, this city. All were dead to her.

Merje had stopped talking, her face registering surprise.

"Katty... Hey, you asked."

She knew that the tail was still watching her. In fact, he'd moved closer since she'd spotted him.

"Katty, please..." Merje's face showed an expression Katja had never seen in her before. Fear.

Katja rose from the booth. "When things start to happen, get down and stay down."

She turned, coolly surveying the scene. The dance floor was full and pulsing. The bar to her left was busy with patrons and staff. The tables and booths to her right were mostly occupied with drunken revelers. The bouncers were positioned strategically around the dance floor, gazing around the entire space with bored expressions.

Her target had stopped moving, and was seated alone at a table on the far side of the floor. She assessed the elements in play, felt a plan form in her mind, and moved into action.

She strolled along in front of the tables, just off the dance floor. She passed the first bouncer. The second was ideally located, giving her a clear line of fire. A quick scan revealed two emergency exits on nearby walls—those would need to be covered, but not before the main threat was neutralized.

The second bouncer was more fat than muscle, but he was a mountain of a man. His stun gun was snapped in place low on his chest, ready to grab and pull free in the case of an incident. His expression was dull, and he was more interested in watching the girls dance than in the security of the club.

Perfect.

"Hey, big boy," she said in her best drunken voice, running her hand up his meaty arm. He looked down at her in vague surprise.

She opened her eyes wide.

"My friend is way taller than me, and she said that she could kiss every bouncer on her tip-toes. But I said I could kiss the biggest bouncer with my feet flat on the ground." She looked him up and down. "Are you the biggest bouncer?"

He gave her a cool smile and little laugh, but his beady eyes were already scanning her figure. She stepped in front of him and ran both her hands up his arms. Her face was even with the stun gun on his chest. It was fully charged but with the safety on.

"Can't you give me even a little kiss?"

He glanced around then leaned forward with an indulgent smile and closing eyes.

"Sure, little lady."

She head-butted him and pulled the stun gun free. Safety off. Trigger pulled and his fat, lumbering body collapsed backward in the sonic boom. Pivot to right. Take bouncer one. He staggered backward and collapsed before he could even pull his weapon free. Scan for other bouncers.

Fire.

Fire.

Fire.

Screaming crowds. Threat neutralized. Take target.

She spun around in time to see the dark form of her target sprinting for one of the emergency exits. She fired. Other patrons collapsed under the blast. Target was moving behind non-combatants. She fired into the crowd to clear a shot. Too many people in the way. She fired again and leapt onto the nearest table for a better angle. Waves of stunning blasts ripped through the panicked crowd.

Her target was at the exit.

Fire. Fire. Fire.

She jumped down and began climbing over the collapsed patrons. He wouldn't get far once she made it to the street. More screaming. People diving out of her way. Almost to the exit.

The door slammed shut. She spun around, hearing the click of another emergency exit lock. The main entrance was still open, and she hurtled onto the now deserted dance floor to start her sprint. She noted idly that the music had stopped.

Suddenly the main entrance was blocked with the massive figure of a policeman in full armor. He marched through the mayhem, followed quickly by another. Katja dropped into a slide and skidded to a halt on the slick floor, looking for a retreat. The police raised their forearm weapons.

"Drop the weapon," the mechanized command grated. "Put your hands on your head."

The stun gun was useless against armored troops. She let it slide from her grasp even as she scrabbled to regain her footing.

"Halt and put your hands on your head."

She considered leaping behind the bar. Maybe there was another door out behind.

"Lieutenant Katja Emmes, halt and put your hands on your head."

She froze. There was no escape now, and if she continued to resist they'd shoot her without question. For a split second she toyed with running, just to end it all, but that wasn't how she wanted to go. Not with Terran bullets in her back.

She remained on her knees, feeling the stickiness of the dance floor clinging to her, and in the strange silence slowly placed her hands on her head.

23

The regular drip of condensation off the roof of the concrete tunnel was the only sound to interrupt Kete's thoughts. He moved silently in the dim light, soft shoes making neither sound nor mark against the well-worn access tunnel path.

It had taken him nearly fifteen minutes to get this far into the City of Longreach aquifer system, but his next move might be the most dangerous one to date, and he didn't want to risk being observed.

A study of the municipal workers' work routine suggested that no one would be along this tunnel for hours, and he wore a stolen set of municipal coveralls, just in case. He understood well the omnipresence of chaos, however, in any human endeavor, and when he finally paused, halfway between the nearest two access doors, he stopped and listened.

As well he listened internally for the telltale EM emissions of an approaching machine or maintenance crew. Aside from the faint, consistent drip, the tunnel was like a tomb.

The setting matched his mood. He had very nearly wound up in an early grave, he knew, and he chastised himself again for risking Centauria's mission in order to pursue his personal agenda. Katja Emmes wasn't part of the plan, but his obsession with her had put everything at risk. Her speed and aggression two nights ago in the club had been formidable, and he had no illusions about how lucky he was to have escaped.

What he still couldn't understand, though, was how accurately she'd pinpointed him in that crowd of hundreds. In the last few moments before she'd seized the bouncer's weapon, Kete had almost felt connected to her as if through the Cloud, as if she herself had been implanted. The pain he'd sensed from her had been shocking—an almost animal rage, mixed with deep betrayal. It had washed over him with such power that he hadn't noticed her swift movements until the gun was pointed right at him.

He'd leapt through a bathroom window, and the rest of the night he'd focused entirely on disappearing, just in case she'd somehow managed to escape the armored police. Lying low for a day, he'd done a cautious scan of the Terran security network, but the only mention of Emmes had come from the report of her arrest. No record of incarceration, no formal charges, not even a transfer order.

Looking wider, he'd realized very quickly that her ID hadn't registered anywhere beyond the police station to which she was taken. It was as if she'd never left the station, but was no longer being held. Eventually Kete had drawn the grim, logical conclusion—Katja Emmes had been quietly executed.

Kete knew that summary executions happened on Terra, but he'd never heard of a decorated veteran meeting that fate. Perhaps something had gone terribly wrong, back in the night club. Or perhaps Emmes had become a liability to someone at a higher level, a trouble-making soldier who threatened the State-imposed harmony.

The thought chilled him even more than the damp, cool air of the tunnel. He shrugged it off.

Setting his backpack down, he carefully removed the cloaking device. Designed to create an interference zone that masked activities within, it contained technology that had already battle-proven against Terran forces. The projector itself looked like a simple wedge of concrete, and when he placed it against the wall it all but disappeared in the dim light. Even if a passing worker saw it they'd assume it was just another bit of minor repair work, done at some point over the years.

It was almost a shame, he realized, that he hadn't had more

time to investigate Emmes's apparent ability to tap in to the Cloud. No doubt her collapsing mental faculties had precluded her from responding beyond instinct, but it might mean that some Terrans were spontaneously developing an affinity for Cloud communications. In Centauria all citizens were trained to access the Cloud, but Kete had never heard of an individual acquiring the ability on their own. The thought was intriguing.

He checked the settings for the area the cloak would affect, ensuring that it was large enough to conceal both him and his activities. With a simple activation command, he felt the interference field wash over him and create an invisible, opaque bubble around him.

Safely ensconced, he removed another piece of equipment. It resembled a needle-fine horseshoe shape of polished brass, but it was heavier than lead. Kete felt his heart thumping as he placed the device carefully on the ground, truly hating the need to put his life in the hands of such an unknown. With another simple command he powered it up. A deep, almost sub-audible hum pulsed outward from the device. Kete watched as the air in front of him shimmered and danced, and he strained to detect the multi-dimensional signals that whispered on the quantum winds.

Then, in a sign almost comical in its banality, a tiny green light shone to life at the base of the horseshoe. The path was open.

Faced with the reality of what he was doing, Kete began to question what would come next. Pushing aside his trepidation, he lifted his backpack and, watching the air in front of him very carefully, threw the pack toward the concrete wall.

It shrank away and vanished from sight.

He exhaled, and raised slightly trembling hands.

The backpack reappeared, almost too tiny to see, then exploded to full size and flew into his grasp. He paused for only a moment, procrastinating by putting the backpack over his shoulders. Then, forcing his mind to go completely blank, he walked forward.

The dark, humid tunnel faded away, and he shielded his eyes from the brilliant light. Something pushed against the side of his body as a wave of dizziness washed over him. He staggered to his knees, feeling a soft, cool surface as his hands blocked his collapse. He blinked, looked down at the green, uneven surface.

Grass. It was grass.

He vomited, translucent bile splashing out over the well-groomed lawn. A hand gripped his shoulder firmly, and he felt a familiar presence looming in his mind.

"Kete, can you hear me?" The words, he realized, were external. Wiping his mouth, he sat back and looked up.

The brilliant light was Centauria A in the sky. The force pushing against him was the breeze off the sea. The grass was in a park at the top of a ridge, with a spectacular view down on his home city of Riverport. He was back on Abeona, and it was like stepping into heaven.

He looked up toward the voice, and the hand on his shoulder. It was Valeria Moretti. Beyond her, he saw, were other faces he knew well. Beyond them were three giant APR robots, weapon pods only now lowering away from him.

"Hi, Val," he said. "It's good to be home."

She smiled in relief, her eyes darting unconsciously to where he'd been sick.

"Do you feel okay?"

He nodded. "The jump gate didn't make me sick—I'm pretty sure that's just a release from the overwhelming fear I felt—at stepping through a trans-dimensional dark-energy gateway without any shielding." He took stock of all his limbs. "But here I am. I guess science works."

She helped him to his feet, mechanical frames whirring softly over spindly, regenerating limbs. He nodded politely to the waiting group of agents. Beyond them was what looked like a construction site, where some buildings appeared to be in the process of being demolished, while others were being built to take their place.

He cast his gaze out again toward Riverport below, breathed in the fresh air with its mix of flowers, herbs, and a faint hint of the sea, and suddenly realized that he knew this spot well.

This was where his home had stood.

Or, precisely, it was across the street from where his home had stood. His gaze snapped over to what he now recognized as the remains of the crater where his beloved Rupa and his precious

Olivia and Jess had been killed. Construction materials were piled next to the crater, and down the ruined street he could see those few houses of his neighbors that were still standing.

Valeria slipped her arm through his.

"It's going to be a beautiful monument," she said quietly. "The entire ridge is going to be dedicated to those who were lost. The main plinth is going to be placed where your house was, with a memorial wall naming everyone who died."

Ignoring the insistent mental calls by voices from the Cloud, he stared down the blasted, cratered road, at the half-collapsed houses still bearing the burn marks from the violence. This was where Katja Emmes had ordered the strike that had killed his family. Impotent rage burned within him, but a wave of overwhelming sorrow damped it down.

And then, for the first time, he even felt a moment of pity. Emmes was gone, perhaps even dead, cast aside by her own people. Her short life had been filled with pain and misery, and while Terra appeared to have wiped away her existence, Kete's family would be remembered forever.

Perhaps there was justice after all.

He turned to Valeria, giving her arm a squeeze. "Thanks for showing me this."

"We thought you'd want to see it."

Turning to the others who had waited patiently, he greeted the agents and various officials from within the department. There was much to discuss.

His return to Abeona was painfully brief, but Kete knew that if he'd stayed for even a night he would risk losing the will to return. After only a few hours—just long enough to download his complete report on the structure and weaknesses of the Terran military network and receive a briefing on the next stage of the plan—he stepped back through the person-sized jump gate and onto the concrete floor of the Longreach municipal aquifer.

His backpack was weighed down with two new jump gate anchors, and the entirety of the mission was buried deep beneath multiple protective layers in his mind. Now it was going to become truly dangerous, and he had to maintain the lowest possible profile.

Pausing within the cloaking bubble, he shivered off the unnerving aftereffects of passing through multi-dimensional spacetime, and looked left and right down the access tunnel. He listened carefully, but there was no sound of movement. Deactivating both the jump gate anchor and the cloaking projector, he stuffed them into his backpack, and moved silently back along the subterranean corridor.

When he emerged from the aquifer complex, he saw at least a dozen city workers in the courtyard, and not one of them glanced his way. No one challenged him, no one even noticed him. All it took to clear security was to wear the right uniform. It gave him greater confidence that the plan might actually work.

In a public washroom he stripped off the municipal uniform to reveal stylish hiking clothes underneath. The outfit matched his backpack, and no one looked twice at him as he strolled out to the street and hailed a cab. His next objective wasn't a precise location—it just had to be within a certain distance of the Astral Force Headquarters complex.

He'd been meticulous in his research, identifying locations that would serve his needs. The greatest difficulty had been that the target sector was so heavily populated, and the risk of being spotted was high. Nevertheless, as he climbed into the cab he reviewed the most likely candidates.

With a touch of irony, he realized that he knew the perfect spot.

Kete exited the cab outside a series of low-rise buildings on a pleasant street. The ground level was bustling with a wide range of shops, and he slipped easily into the throng of pedestrians. He strolled at an easy pace, casting unseeing eyes over the various shop windows as his mind sought the electronic code to one particular set of doors.

By the time he arrived he'd cracked the code and, with a show of swiping his own, irrelevant card past the sensor, he pulled the door open and walked into the lobby. His hiking boots thudded softly on the polished floor as he approached the elevator. A balding man in a suit was waiting, and Kete nodded politely to him as they entered the lift and selected their floors. Very soon Kete was walking along an upper floor corridor, senses focused intently on one particular door.

The lock was standard issue, but Kete wanted to make sure that the rest of the apartment hadn't been rigged with other surveillance gear or alarms. He didn't really know what the Terran State did with the assets of "disappeared" citizens. At the same time he established internal scans that would repeat at regular intervals, and alert him should certain keywords appear.

This was no time for surprises.

He opened the door and stepped through. The furniture, decor, and entertainment equipment were new and stylish, but it didn't take long to notice the subtle signs of a poor housekeeper. Tiny shoes littered the floor of the front hall. Throw pillows were bunched at one end of the couch in a way that suggested they'd actually been used for sleeping on. The empty beer bottle on the coffee table was matched by half a dozen more on the counter, and as he stepped into the kitchen Kete saw still more stacked in their cases on the floor. He wrinkled his nose at the smell from unwashed dishes, and guessed that the apartment had been unoccupied since the night of the incident.

He swiftly searched the bedroom and bathroom to confirm that the apartment was clear. The clothes strewn everywhere were surprising for their small size, and Kete wondered for a moment if a young girl hadn't lived here as well. He saw a framed picture of her entire family on the dresser, recalling each face from the interview at the gala. The proud Emmes family, and a proud legacy young Katja had clearly struggled to maintain.

He paused, a sudden surge of guilt sickening him at his blatant invasion of this woman's privacy. He closed his eyes and recalled the bulldozers pushing the soil back over the crater where his home had once stood, where his wife and children had died.

Where Katja Emmes had killed them.

He nodded to himself. This was the perfect spot for the next part of the plan. Terra would pay, and the fate of humanity would shift here in the home of the person he hated most in the universe.

Pushing the furniture against the walls, he created an open space in the living room where he set up the smaller of his new jump gate anchors, and with it the cloaking device. Then, settling himself into the available armchair, he closed his eyes and reached out carefully to locate the vast Astral security network.

It throbbed through the Terran proto-Cloud like an iron fortress, wrapping the space elevators, the Astral College, and the headquarters complex in a powerful web of detectors. He hadn't dared such an incursion before now—had he been detected, it would have meant an instant end to his mission.

Hidden throughout the city sector, defensive weaponry sat crouched in passive anticipation, but Kete wasn't concerned about the defenses against an external assault. His focus was on the available arcs of fire the weaponry could achieve once brought into play. Forcing his thoughts to remain disciplined, he slowly and carefully tracked each weapon system to its associated detection points, identifying the network strands that connected the entire system.

The electronic safeguards were robust, but thanks to the time he'd spent dissecting the data wrenched from the *Armstrong*, it was relatively easy to establish a series of false signal generators. In doing so he was able to isolate the network immediately around this apartment. As he set the last false relay to automatic, a timing alarm alerted him to an imminent arrival.

Rising from the armchair, he stepped through into the cloaking bubble and activated the jump gate anchor. The light signaled green and he stepped back. Moments later, Valeria warbled into view through the cloak, followed in short order by five other Centauris.

Each of them was dressed in unremarkable Terran civilian clothes, and each of them sported a backpack. They took in their surroundings with the calm professionalism of their trade. The last one knelt next to the anchor as both devices deactivated and the cloak vanished. The transit accomplished, Kete reached out to the Astral security network and removed his false signals and relays.

"Welcome to Earth," he said.

"Nice place." Valeria sat down in the armchair. "Yours?"

He shook his head. "Mine wasn't close enough for the test, but this one became available."

She glanced around. "Could use a maid."

He indicated her mechanized legs. "You don't actually think you'll be able to blend in with those?"

"No." She glanced around and sighed. "I just wanted to see Earth. I can't stick around to bail you out this time, though."

At least she'd finally seen sense. The mission was too important to risk it for the sake of her pride, or even for her anger. He addressed the other agents.

"The security blockers should have worked for your jump, but we'll want to wait a few days to be sure the Terrans don't pick up on it. We all need to lie low until then. Two of you can stay here, and two can come to my place."

24

It was hard to get a smile stretched across his face as he walked slowly down the familiar corridor. Breeze's apartment door loomed before him. As beautiful as she was, she had a thoroughly despicable personality and, despite his best efforts, he would never be attracted to her beyond the purely physical.

Breeze was used to taking whatever she wanted from men, and what he couldn't afford, as a Centauri agent, was for her to get suspicious of him in any way. Yet the images of his destroyed home, and the faces of his murdered family, were fresh again in his mind. The last thing he needed was to have this repulsive Terran woman touch him again tonight.

The door opened at his knock. Soft light cast a warm, evening glow around the apartment and he had to look hard to spot Breeze over by her secure terminal. The screen lit her face as a cold, pale mask and she barely glanced up as he entered. He forced himself to stroll in casually, but immediately his senses went into overdrive, seeking out any new security devices.

Breeze looked as preoccupied as he'd ever seen her. Keeping close attention on his peripheral, he moved toward her and forced an expression onto his face that was curiosity mixed with amusement.

"Working late?"

She tore her eyes from the screen and looked up at him. Her stare was intense, and behind it he knew her mind was grappling with something. She leaned back in her chair, eyes never leaving his.

"How do you know if you can trust someone?" she said finally.

He shrugged and glanced slowly around the room, as if pondering his reply. Another scan revealed no hidden weapons, and the window at the far end past the couch was the best escape route if the door became blocked. "Time and experience," he offered. "And by their actions."

"Do you trust me?"

"Not a bit," he said with a smile.

She folded her arms. "I'm serious."

"Of course I do, Breeze." He took another, testing step toward her. She didn't flinch. "Why are you asking this?"

The intensity of her gaze grew almost frightening. Kete forced himself not to take a step back. He shifted his weight to ready an escape run, if required.

"Do you trust me?" he asked. Then, despite all his implants, despite all his intelligence, despite all his insights into human nature, Kete was completely surprised.

Tears began to stream down Breeze's face. She quickly dropped her gaze and wiped her cheeks, but the shuddering of her body was impossible to suppress as the emotion flooded out.

Kete stood dumbstruck for a moment. His instinct was to move forward and comfort her, but his alert state was far too high to allow him to close the distance with an enemy. Still keeping his distance, he crouched enough to meet her eyes.

"Breeze, what's wrong?" he asked, trying for concern. "What's this all about?"

"I'm sorry." She was struggling admirably to regain her composure. She wiped her cheeks again and reached out to take his hand. "I'm just not used to this."

He let her grasp his fingers, eyes on her every movement.

"Used to what?"

She sniffed, laughing slightly. "Trusting someone." She looked up at him again, eyes shining with a new emotion. "I do trust you, Kit." She sounded as surprised as he was. "I really do. I think you might be the first ever."

Senses on full alert had revealed no traps, and the look in her eyes was like that of his beloved Rupa, once upon a time. He couldn't believe what he was seeing, but a cold part of him knew exactly what to do.

"I wasn't lying," he said. "I do trust you." He smiled and gripped her hand with new strength. The cruelty of what he was about to do was justifiable in war, he told himself. After a pause, he spoke again. "And more than that, Charity, I love you."

Breeze's expression melted anew into tears, and she threw her arms around him. He held her tightly. She was crying, but he sensed these were tears of release. He figured he should say something, but having just committed the ultimate act of deceit, he couldn't stomach more. Figuring that his Terran alter-ego was really more the strong, silent type anyway, he simply held her and let her slowly regain her composure.

When she pulled back she was grinning like a schoolgirl.

"I love you, Kit," she said. "And it's awesome."

He gave her a quizzical look. "Is that why you were acting so strange when I came in?"

She blinked. "What?" She glanced at her screen. "Oh, no. I was just realizing how few people we can trust in this world, and I'm so glad I found you. Everyone else is a bastard, and can go fuck themselves."

"I figured that was a given," he replied, "but what prompted your epiphany?"

She nodded toward her terminal. "Can I trust you to keep a secret?"

"Of course."

"That team of researchers Chuck interviewed has been trying to refine the science of the Dark Bomb, to build something we can actually control better," she said. "And I just got an order to report my progress to Parliament."

"Sounds pretty good so far."

She shook her head angrily. "I just got orders to report to Parliament on the progress of their work, and those eggheads are still months behind." She slammed her fist down on the console. "Honestly, how many times do I have to come down on them to get some damn progress? How hard can it be for scientists to do science?"

He sat down on the floor, coaxing her off her chair to sit facing him. She was too valuable an asset to be lost at this stage of the operation, so his concern for her career was suddenly genuine. He held one of her hands and stroked the stray wisps of hair from her face.

"If you're in charge of this team," he prodded, "can't you push the blame down to them?"

"If I'd known in time, sure," she answered, "but at this point I'll have been expected by Parliament to have already *dealt* with any problems. What they want to hear is that all's well. If it is, I'm golden. If it isn't, I'm dead."

His mind raced, knowing that her assessment was accurate, and literal. Terra didn't take kindly to senior officials wasting State resources. Yet surely, as a mere commander, she wasn't the highest-ranking officer involved. He thought back to their visit to the *Armstrong*.

"What about the ship CO?" he suggested. "He outranks you. The responsibility should be his."

She nodded impatiently. "But positionally I'm senior, since I'm at headquarters and overall in charge. It just so happens that the ship selected for this project has a full captain for a commanding officer."

Kete considered this, shifting absently to lean against the console as Breeze cuddled into him. Wrapping his arms around her warm body, he tried to think of an angle. In his short observation, Captain Lincoln had seemed like an idiot—a classic example of the old military adage, promoted a rank beyond his level of competency. It came as no surprise that Lincoln had missed his targets.

"Why was Lincoln talking so much about those awards he'd won?" he asked. "Do they count for much in the Research Squadron?"

"They shouldn't," Breeze scoffed. "But they certainly give Admiral Bush something to brag about at parties."

"Do you think Bush might have played a discreet role in knocking your research off the rails?"

Abruptly Breeze sat up. "He better not have." She turned to him with a new gleam in her eye. "But maybe... Let me check something." She climbed back into her chair and began navigating her console. Kete rose to join her, but she paused and glanced at him with a smirk. "Sorry, honey. I trust you, but the State doesn't quite yet." She jutted her chin toward the nearby couch.

He sat down without comment, resting back comfortably while his senses locked into her electronic activity. Using her top-secret access code—a gem he recorded and tucked away for future use—she accessed the personal message file of Admiral Bush. That she could even do this stunned Kete, but he'd always suspected she'd have unusual access rights. A few quick searches isolated the messages between the admiral and Captain Lincoln.

There were dozens in the last month alone, and Breeze wisely narrowed her search to focus on the conversations that referenced Dark Bomb research. It was a painfully slow process, and while she accessed data in a linear fashion, Kete turned his own attention to reviewing the entire Bush account.

Almost immediately he noticed an oddity. The admiral corresponded with hundreds of different people, and some addresses appeared regularly in both his send and receive folders, but one address in particular dominated the bandwidth. Whoever it was, this person sent multiple messages every day, mostly from a civilian account, but Bush hardly ever responded.

Who could it be?

Kete started reading the messages. It was Lieutenant Helena Grey, the plastic-faced officer from the *Armstrong*, a junior officer from one of twenty some vessels in the Research Squadron.

While Breeze still slogged visually through the messages between Captain Lincoln and Bush, Kete discovered that Grey was quite a little witch. Her frequent messages to Bush were hateful indictments of other members of *Armstrong*'s science team.

The vast majority were utterly trivial. Amanda Smith was clumsy with the equipment. Jack Mallory laughed too much in the lab. Enrique Vasquez had taken a longer break than normal. Thomas Kane gave confusing orders. The messages seemed endless, day after day and week after week. The sheer volume was astonishing, and that they were sent from her civilian account suggested she didn't want them to be monitored.

On an impulse, Kete cross-referenced the messages from Bush

to Lincoln. Sure enough, an uneven but blatant pattern began to emerge. Grey would spend a few days complaining about a certain member of the lab. Bush would send a demand to Lincoln to know why that person's performance was sub-standard.

Digging deeper, Kete used Breeze's access code to pry into the *Armstrong* personnel files. Negative comments from Lincoln were sparse, but they definitely correlated to the inquiries from Bush. Details were rarely provided, and few actions were taken.

When Thomas Kane had joined *Armstrong*, and shouldered direct supervision of the science team, the tone of the notes had changed. Kane filed regular comments on his team's performance, often praising and occasionally criticizing, and always providing specific details. Some of his reports came about as a result of Grey's complaints, but generally Kane dismissed them as having little basis in fact.

Kete sat forward on the couch, fighting disgust. Lieutenant Grey was a petty troublemaker intent on punishing anyone she felt had crossed her, and Bush took her word as gospel. Captain Lincoln didn't have the intelligence or the courage to put a stop to the bullshit. Lieutenant Commander Kane, at least, seemed to have an ounce of professionalism in him.

In fact, his most recent communiqué to Lincoln spoke gravely of Grey's negative impact on the team. As far as Kete could see, there was no response. All juicy gossip, to be sure, but it wouldn't be enough to get Breeze off the hook. What Kete needed was proof that Bush had ordered *Armstrong*'s team to focus their efforts on something other than the core mission, to the clear detriment of their research.

"Find anything?" he asked.

Breeze shook her head. "Nothing solid. Lincoln and Bush are idiots, but I'll be held accountable for that as well."

"How are they idiots?"

"All they ever talk about are the special experiments, and the awards they want the ship to win." She took a deep breath, then let it out. "I don't get it—it's not like either of them gets the award."

"What do you mean?"

Breeze turned to face him, rubbing her eyes. "Awards like that go either to the entire ship, or to an individual researcher. At best, Lincoln and Bush just ride on somebody else's coattails."

"Hmmm." Kete cast a query into the Terran network, seeking the winners of recent scientific awards. A common thread appeared. "If it's the leader of the research team who usually gets the award, who would that be aboard the *Armstrong*?"

Breeze frowned. "That old biddy, I think." She paused to think. "What was her name? You know, the haggard one."

"Lieutenant Grey, I think. Helena Grey."

Breeze turned back to her terminal. Kete waited patiently while she followed the line of thinking he'd so plainly laid out for her. Again she frowned.

"There are a lot of messages to Admiral Bush from this Grey woman," she noted. "Why is she talking to him?"

"Sounds a bit irregular to me."

Breeze started examining the long list of communications, unconsciously leaning closer to the screen as the minutes ticked by. Kete forced himself to be patient—it took Terrans so much longer to grasp the obvious.

Soon she left the message log and began a new search of the *Armstrong* security database. She started a facial recognition search of the ship's main passageways, identifying both Bush and Grey. Abruptly Kete found himself scrambling to keep up with her thinking as she conducted a lightning search of thousands of hours of camera feeds.

She pinpointed half a dozen instances of the admiral and the lieutenant, both entering the admiral's cabin within twenty minutes of each other. Then, several hours later, both departed— again within twenty minutes of each other. He looked over at Breeze with new respect.

She's sharper than I thought.

Breeze rose from her seat with an expression of vicious satisfaction, curling up next to him on the couch and draping her arms over his shoulders.

"Oh, my love, I've got that fat bastard over a barrel."

"Oh?" He found that the smile came easily to his lips.

She nodded. "I'm going to give him a choice," she said, "but either way I have my scapegoat."

25

Someone was in the room with her. She could tell before she opened her eyes. There was breathing nearby, and the faint smell of sweat.

Slowly, carefully, she commanded each of her little fingers to move slightly, then repeated the test with her big toes. Her limbs were intact and functioning. The breathing was to her right, so she lifted her left hand just enough to test for restraints.

None. A single flutter of her left eye gave her how much light there was in the room.

"Don't make any sudden moves, Lieutenant Emmes," a soft, male voice said. "I know that you're awake."

She considered her options. Surprise was out, so perhaps guile would work. Blinking her eyes open in the harsh light, she turned her head. A man of middle years sat in a chair facing her, one leg crossed over the other and hands in his lap. He was dressed in a plain, green jumpsuit of the Astral Corps, and her eyes were instinctively drawn to the rank on his shoulders.

A pair of stars gleamed on each epaulette. His face was lean and unremarkable, the kind of face she wouldn't have looked at twice in a crowd. Except that she *knew* this face.

"Congratulations, Brigadier Korolev." Her voice croaked through a dry throat.

He nodded slightly in acknowledgement.

"I gather your return home hasn't been as successful as some."

She felt her heart sink anew. Was the entire universe against her? A lover who rejected her, a sister who betrayed her, a father who reviled her—and now the commander of her former regiment knew of her failure at life. She doubted Korolev had even known her name during the deployment, and this was not the way to gain notoriety.

She averted her eyes and took in her surroundings.

The room was small and featureless, with nothing but the chair he sat on and the cot she lay on for furniture. A windowless door was closed in the wall behind him. It was unusually warm, and she realized that the sweat she'd noticed was her own. Her clothes from the club were mostly intact over her body, although her shoes were long gone. Wiggling her toes, she couldn't help but smile.

"Something funny, Emmes?"

She swung herself up into a sitting position, bringing her feet down to the smooth, warm floor.

"I just seem to have a habit of going to jail barefoot, sir." No point in trying to hide anything from him, she knew.

"You seem to have a habit of starting fights in public places as well," he noted, "and assaulting security officers. Or bouncers, anyway."

She glanced up at him, feeling her cheeks reddening.

"I'm sorry, sir."

His expression was neutral, but there was an intensity deep within his small eyes. She suddenly realized the odd nature of her situation. Why was she in a cell, with no one around except a very senior officer from the Astral Corps, who just *happened* to be the former commander of her former regiment?

She also realized that her head was clear. There were none of the after effects of alcohol or stun weapons, like last time. Nothing hurt, and her body responded easily to commands. Korolev continued to stare at her, his gaze momentarily going vacant before focusing on her once again.

"Sir, where am I?"

"You're in a world of shit, Emmes," he responded. "I'm here to figure out the best way to get you out of it."

She could only guess at what charges were being levied against her by the Longreach police, and she cringed when she realized that her father had vouched for her first release, risking his own reputation. If it suffered because of her, that was another bridge she'd burned.

And yet... Korolev.

She tried to switch into a trooper mindset.

"Can you tell me the situation, sir?"

He uncrossed his legs and leaned forward. "The situation has many levels, and they're all dependent on each other. I need you to speak with absolute honesty. Otherwise we'll make a mistake that will get people killed—including you, most likely." He let that sink in, then added, "Will you speak with honesty?"

Katja knew there were things in her past of which she wasn't proud. Things she'd hoped would never see the light of day, beyond her own tortured conscience.

"Yes, sir."

"Let's start simply."

"Yes, sir."

"Answer me this—what is the purpose of the State?"

She paused. She was in jail, her life was at stake, and he wanted to discuss high school philosophy? She started to think, but then went with her gut instinct.

"Uhh, to provide a safe environment for its citizens."

"Safe in what way?"

"In every way, sir. Safe from attack, from disease, from starvation and ignorance."

"And how does the State ensure that?"

She frowned, still not understanding the reasons behind his questioning. She dug into her memory for a nursery rhyme she and her classmates had often recited in primary school.

"Protectors, professors, providers, physicians... just like it's always been, sir."

He seemed to accept that. "But what makes up the State?" he pressed. "Who actually *provides* this safety?"

She wasn't sure she understood the question. She glanced at the stars on his shoulders again.

"We do, sir. As protectors, anyway."

"But who decides how we act?" His expression hadn't shifted

once during their exchange, but now his eyes narrowed slightly. "Who gives us our rules of engagement? Do the people give us those rules?"

The obvious answer was *yes*, since Terra was a democracy, but Korolev was after something else.

"Ultimately, sir, I'd say yes, but really the rules come from Parliament." Korolev's stare made her uncomfortable and she quickly added, "Which is elected by the people, of course."

"So Parliament makes the rules?"

She considered her answer carefully, fighting down the fear that was growing in her gut. She was a prisoner, apparently in a military installation. It mattered how she answered these questions.

Korolev continued to watch her closely.

"I want you to answer honestly, Katja."

She took a deep breath. "Yes, Parliament makes the rules, and they're held accountable every six years to the people."

"Do you believe that the people actually have a say?"

"Of course I do." Her fear suddenly shifted, and she wondered if she hadn't stumbled upon a mutinous branch of the military. How could Korolev ask a question like that?

If he noticed her reaction he didn't show it.

"And that's how Parliament maintains its moral authority?" he continued. "Through the people?"

She felt herself flush. "That's the only way, sir."

"So if Parliament derives its mandate from the people, does it have unlimited power to act? Does Parliament have to follow the same rules as the people?"

She opened her mouth to answer, but the words died in her throat. That was a question never asked in school. He sat there, awaiting her response.

"I don't know, sir."

He nodded, leaning back to cross one leg over the other again. She stared at him as a flurry of thoughts raced through her mind. Was he testing her? Was he trying to trip her up?

"What's the Astral Force rule on treatment of prisoners, Lieutenant?" His sudden change of tack caught her off guard. She mentally scrambled to recall the regulations.

"They're to be treated humanely, sir."

"Is shooting a prisoner in the genitals humane, Lieutenant?"

She went cold. She remembered pulling the trigger, at watching that Sirian rapist scream in agony. How could she think no one would ever find out?

"No, sir."

"Were you the commander of that mission, at that time, Lieutenant?"

"Yes, sir."

"So as commander, were you above the rules? Did they not apply to you?"

She hadn't thought about that moment for a long time. She'd been too preoccupied lately, thinking about that bastard Thomas Kane. Funny how remembering a bit of combat experience could put the rest of her existence into its petty perspective.

"As the commander, sir, the rules still applied to me."

"And yet you broke them nonetheless."

"Yes, sir." Sudden images flashed into her mind—of her on trial, yet another example of a military gone amok.

"Why, Lieutenant?"

She looked up at him. "Sir?"

"Answer me honestly." He leaned forward again. "Why did you break the rules, and shoot that prisoner?"

She thought back to the dirty cargo hold of the freighter. Her platoon had just been rescued by a pair of Astral Intelligence agents. Three Sirian soldiers lay dead behind her, one of them still with his trousers at his knees and penis erect. Before her, under guard of her troopers, knelt two Sirian civilians. One of them she knew nothing about, but the other, Thapa, she knew only too well.

He had murdered two innocent Terran sailors and beaten two others—including Jack Mallory—nearly to death. And when she was his prisoner, he'd planned on stringing her up in the center of town to be publicly gang raped.

"He was of no use to Astral Intelligence, sir," she replied. "And cut off in enemy territory, we had no resources to spare for a prisoner."

Korolev didn't blink. "That'd be enough to get you cleared in a court-martial." He opened a pouch on his belt and produced a standard-issue water bulb. He handed it to her.

She took it immediately and popped it open, suddenly realizing how thirsty she was. Instinct compelled her to sniff the contents, but otherwise she didn't hesitate in gulping down mouthfuls of the cool, sweet liquid.

"That medal for valor we presented you, Lieutenant, was well-deserved."

She lowered the water bulb, surprised at his latest shift.

"Thank you, sir."

"What made you do it?"

Again she considered her answer. "I wanted to help EF 15 win the battle, sir."

"You were in little more than an escape pod, your ship burning up beneath you, with the largest space battle in history raging above you. What in the worlds made you think you and eight other troopers could affect the outcome?"

She considered. "From what I could see, the Centauri battlecruiser was causing most of the damage to the EF. I had a trained and fully armed boarding party with me, and I didn't think they'd see us coming."

"Have you done a tour as a Line officer in one of the ships, Lieutenant?"

"No, sir. Just my time as officer of the watch in *Rapier*."

"And yet you felt your ability to assess the fleet tactical situation was adequate to break the rules and endanger your troops?"

She tried to remember what she'd thought at the time, crowded into the strike pod with half the surviving crew of *Rapier*, while the other half ascended in the sister pod next to her. All she could recall was the feeling of emptiness, thinking that Thomas was dead, and a desire to fulfill his wishes that *Rapier* would make a difference in the battle.

"There wasn't a lot of time to think," she replied. "It seemed the best option in the moment."

"You know you broke several major rules of engagement during that battle."

"I guess I figured that it was war, sir. Rules of engagement can change quickly."

"How many of your troopers died boarding that Centauri ship?"

She felt the chill of regret seep through her again.

"Four, sir."

"Out of how many?"

"Eight."

"And when the raid on Cerberus went to shit, why did you leave your position as advisor to Second Platoon and take command of Fifth?"

"Their commander was dead."

"But it was just a withdrawal—why risk yourself and your boarding party?"

She could smell the metallic air of that damned Sirian planet, see the red dirt on her boots as she tore off her helmet and slammed Wei's down in its place—switching helmets had been the fastest way to get onto Fifth Platoon's comm network. Wei's young body had already stopped leaking blood by the time she helped another trooper heave it aboard the drop ship, as Sirian aircraft strafed them again.

"It was the right thing to do," she said. "They needed a commander."

"And when you finally got them out—after I sacrificed two valuable assets to free you—how many were still alive?"

She didn't even have to think. "Twenty-six, sir."

"Out of how many?"

"Fifty-seven."

"And then, during the escape, you shot a prisoner in the genitals."

She dropped her head in her hands.

"Now tell me, Lieutenant Emmes, why you *really* did it."

"Did what, sir?"

"Why did you shoot that prisoner?"

She felt the warm grip of the pistol in her hand. She heard his curses as she stood before him, his unbroken fury even after she shot the other prisoner dead. She heard his name for her in her ears again.

Whore.

She who had broken another rule of the Astral Force, and slept with her superior officer. Fallen in love with him. And been cast aside by him.

She remembered the sweet ecstasy of pulling the trigger, of watching him double over in unimaginable pain. Of emasculating and humiliating him, just as he'd humiliated her.

Because the fucking bastard deserved to die.

"Because it was justice, sir."

Korolev leaned back again. "So in other words, you break the rules when it's the right thing to do."

A glimmer of hope sparked in the blackness of her mind. "Yes, sir."

"So as the commander of that mission, you were able to break the rules to do what was right."

"Yes, sir."

"Let me return to my earlier question. Does Parliament have to follow the same rules as the people?"

The glimmer of hope brightened into a dawn of understanding.

"Yes, unless breaking the rules accomplishes what's right."

"The Astral Corps trains its officers to know much more than just the rules. We're trained to know the difference between right and wrong, to think independently and keep our troops guarded against all threats. We're entrusted with information and perspective our troopers don't have, and we're expected to act accordingly.

"Parliament is made up of the best citizens of Terra, many of them former Corps officers themselves, and they have access to information we as citizens will never see. The people empower Parliament to act in the best interest of the State, and sometimes that means breaking the rules that rightly apply to the people."

Katja nodded. "I understand, sir." She could still feel the beating of her heart, and feared where this conversation was going, even as it fascinated her.

He stood in a smooth movement, rounding his chair and taking a few paces to the far wall of the cell.

"We've been reviewing your record, Lieutenant. You've shown a consistent pattern of breaking with doctrine in both exercises and combat operations, and while your unorthodox decisions have often baffled your superiors—and, as in the incidents we just discussed, caused half of your troopers to die—there's no question that your actions have been to the benefit of the State.

"Not necessarily to the benefit of those under your command, nor to the benefit of you personally, but always to the benefit of the greater mission. You've always done what's right—even when you couldn't articulate or explain it."

She recalled her father's words, spoken with scorn after her fight with Soren at the dinner table.

"Sometimes there's no time to think, so I act on instinct, sir."

His gaze went vacant, as if he was completely lost in thought. She waited for him to speak, growing uncomfortable in the lengthening silence. Looking down at her own ragged appearance, she brushed some damn hair out of her face and pulled the hem of her shirt straight.

"What do you know about the Astral Special Forces, Emmes?" His sudden words surprised her.

"Not much, sir. They do the most hard-core recce drops, and sometimes work with Astral Intelligence. I've never met any personally."

"Don't be so sure. Do you know how the members are selected?"

The fact that she didn't had always been a curiosity. There were no regulations published that spoke of standards or requirements that prospective candidates had to meet, or even who to contact if one was interested in applying. No one even knew where they were based. The ASF just seemed to exist.

"No, sir. I've never heard of anyone applying."

"No one applies," he said. "They're selected."

A sudden thought occurred to her: she was alone in a room with a senior Corps officer, wearing nothing but party clothes, and sitting on a cot—and she'd been unconscious and lying on it earlier. She pressed her knees together and gripped the cot's metal frame tightly.

"How, sir?"

He started a little, then gave her a withering gaze in the most expressive show of sentiment since this bizarre interview had begun.

"This isn't the Research Squadron, Emmes," he growled. "Promotions aren't based on blow jobs."

She relaxed slightly. "How are they selected, sir?"

"You have an uncanny ability to think laterally, to see all aspects of a complex scenario, to consider multiple solutions even with multiple variables in play. And you always—to date, at least—make the correct decision. This goes far beyond instinct, or even luck, and represents untapped power of the mind. While it would be very dangerous to reveal this fact to the People, we understand that certain individuals can be augmented, and trained to operate in secret. We feel that you're one of those people."

That came entirely out of left field.

"I'm interested to hear more, sir," she responded.

He crossed his arms. "Any trooper would be, so let me burst whatever bubble you might have. The work isn't glamorous. It's rarely pleasant, and it's always dangerous. No one outside the ASF will ever know what you do, so there will be no medals, no promotions." He gave her a raised eyebrow. "No network interviews with Chuck Merriman."

She considered how important any of that had ever been to her. Aside from trying to impress her father, did she even care about her medals?

"I understand, sir."

"You won't be part of a regular unit, and you'll have to sever all ties you currently have. You will, Katja Andreia Emmes, cease to exist in regular society."

She thought back over the past few months, and the personal hell that trying to live in society had become for her.

"I think I'd like that, sir."

He moved forward and took his seat across from her again. His gaze pinned her where she sat.

"You will have to inflict pain," he said. "You will have to terrorize. You will have to kill."

She couldn't tear her eyes from his, but her mind flooded with images of those she'd killed. Bodies disintegrating with the impact of her explosive rounds. Faces smashed by the butt of her rifle. Lives ruined with the destruction of homes, factories, and farms. Civilians burning alive in the fire of orbital bombardment that she'd ordered.

Charred flesh, metallic air, screams. Flowing smoke, her troopers dead, spinning stars. The blast of impact, honeysuckle, hands on her throat.

She dropped her face into her hands, trying in vain to stem the flood of tears. Moisture poured through her fingers and great, heaving sobs burst forth from her constricted chest. *Where were the drugs?*

Where were the goddamn drugs?

There was nothing to stop it. She grabbed her own hair and bore down as it came. The scream. The scream that had haunted her, mocked her, been barely held at bay by drugs, alcohol, and sheer will. A single, soul-emptying scream. All the grief, the horror, the shame, the fear.

She screamed with the full power of a trained opera singer. She screamed with the frustration of a little girl who was never good enough. She screamed with the agony of a human being who knew she'd made choices of her own free will, and caused others to suffer and die.

Katja screamed until there was nothing left inside her.

When she opened her eyes, she could see Korolev's boots. Wiping away tears she looked up. He sat before her, one leg crossed over the other, regarding her with a not unkind expression.

"Katja, you're too dangerous to send back to regular Astral duty," he said. "People like you are brilliant, but unorthodox, and to let that kind of behavior seep into the Astral Force would tear down our entire system of discipline. So you have a choice to make. You can either be discharged honorably and live a civilian life, or you can join the ASF and become an instrument of the State."

Her heart felt like it was in a vice. "If I was an instrument of the State, how would I be judged?"

"By how well you accomplished your mission."

"No matter what that mission was?"

He nodded. "You will live with the certainty that the will of Parliament—not the law—is supreme. Sometimes Parliament has to break the rules, and you will be the instrument with which they do so." He leaned in very close, almost whispering to her. "But that's all you have to be. Whatever rule Parliament needs to break is their responsibility. Not yours."

She pondered that for a very long moment. As she did, the dawn of understanding blossomed into the full, glorious light of revelation. No ties to society, no moral quandaries, just a cadre of like-minded ASF operatives who would support her always. This was what she'd been born to do. Relief washed over her like a flood. All the emotional baggage had been unlocked by the scream, and was washed away.

She rose easily to her feet. "Sir, I belong to the State."

Korolev rose as well. "This won't be easy. Your loyalty and resolve will be tested from the very start."

"I won't let you down, sir."

He held out a hand, and she grasped it. Then he gestured toward the door.

"Your training will start tomorrow, but first I need to introduce you to the ASF medical corps. They've developed some valuable devices that will help focus your natural, intuitive abilities in a new dimension."

Her curiosity was aroused. "Another dimension, like the Bulk?"

As he opened the door he shook his head.

"Let me tell you about the Cloud."

26

A person could go insane in the Cloud.

Eyes squeezed shut behind hands pressed against her face, Katja tried desperately to stem the waves of virtual noise that washed over her like a storm. There was so much information, so much raw data just swirling around out there, and nobody realized it. The first time she'd activated her implants in a public place, she'd nearly drowned in the noise. Then she'd learned to swim, at least in a rudimentary way.

In the physical world, she felt a gentle hand on her shoulder.

She retreated from the cacophony and straightened in her seat, then blinked her eyes clear and looked around the mostly empty deck of the space elevator. A few passengers sat within view, none appearing to be interested in her at all. The sky had turned black outside, and the shining curvature of the Earth was clear beneath her.

"You did better that time." The hand dropped away, back into Korolev's lap.

"I hope so. She scoffed. "There's hardly anybody here."

There were seven active devices among her fellow passengers, two live news feeds being transmitted from satellites above. Routine chatter between the elevator operators, the surface, and Astral Base One, and the incessant reporting of the elevator's engineering systems.

"That's why I suggested you activate in a relatively quiet place."

She nodded. "I feel like I'm starting to get it, but I can't explain how. I guess it's like learning to walk."

"Very much so. The Cloud uses a part of the brain dormant in most humans. The implants can help to stimulate it, but you as the user still have to bend it to your will."

"It's exhausting." She rubbed her temples, sitting back in her seat.

"Well, your mission today isn't going to require you to access the Cloud, but I still need you mentally alert," he noted. "So don't push yourself too much."

She looked out the windows again, at the black sky of low orbit. Their destination was Astral Base One, but from there they might travel to anywhere.

"What is the mission, sir?"

His eyes flicked around. "Don't call me sir."

"Sorry." She noted once again the standard dark-blue Fleet coveralls they both wore. He sported the unremarkable rank of ship's petty officer, and she was a squad leader. A tool bag sat on the seat next to her.

"So what's the mission?"

His expression was light, but the gravity of his gaze was unmistakable.

"Let's just say I need to see what you are really capable of accomplishing."

That sounded ominous, yet Katja was surprised by her own lack of concern. She'd killed before, and there wasn't a tactical situation she'd yet faced that had defeated her.

"You've had your implants for a few days now, and the surgery has all but healed," Korolev said quietly. "So there's something I want you to try."

She looked up at him. "Just tell me what you want me to do."

He peered back, his expression utterly calm.

<Can you hear me?>

She jumped. It was a voice in her head—but not her own.

<Lieutenant, can you hear me?>

It was his voice, inside her head. Even though she'd known this was going to be possible, it was still startling. She looked at him and nodded.

<Reply to me this way.>

Her own internal monologue was already in overdrive, and she was embarrassed that Korolev might detect all of her own uncertainties. She rapidly focused her thoughts into a consensus that yes, she could hear him.

<Can you reply to me this way?>

She frowned. "I did. Or maybe you just got hit with a jumble of thoughts."

<This isn't telepathy.> He smiled slightly. <I can't read your mind. You have to actively 'speak,' but without vocalizing. Try again.>

She focused on how she was hearing him, and tried to push back mentally in a way that somehow felt the same. It didn't make any sense, but it seemed the right thing to do.

<Yes, I can hear you.>

His smile became one of satisfaction. <Very good. Our implants allow us to communicate directly with one another, in the same way we access other communication devices. It's a very useful tool for our missions. You don't likely need to use it today, but I might speak to you during the mission and I want you to be ready for it.>

She nodded, feeling her head begin to hurt.

"I understand," she said, "but I think I'm going to stick with regular talking for the moment. It's a little soon for me to be good at it."

"Good idea," he replied. "Keep your mind sharp, and stay focused."

They arrived at Astral Base One without incident, and blended in with the hundreds of pedestrians moving through the base. Brigadier Korolev was a thoroughly unremarkable-looking man, but Katja knew that the blonde bob she'd been sporting for months was an easy attention-getter. She wanted to shave it all off.

Korolev had overruled her, saying that a woman with a close-crop would be just as quick to catch the eye here in the comfortable rear echelon of Earth orbit. In the end, she'd slicked her hair back into a practical and relatively unattractive style that still left collar-length hair. She'd happily discarded any make-up, and with a fresh face and regulation blue coveralls, she felt almost normal.

It was the first time in months.

They proceeded up several decks, eventually emerging onto one of the spars that extended outward from the Base's central body. This was where vessels tied up. Through the polyglass walls she saw several warships berthed in the distance, and immediately spotted the distinct hull form of one of the Research Squadron vessels, floating alongside the spar in the nearest berth.

"Is that where we're going?" she asked, indicating the arrowhead shape.

"It is," he answered. "The *Neil Armstrong*—the ship at the center of a particularly urgent Fleet Marshall Investigation. We're here today to ensure that investigation concludes successfully."

Katja frowned. A Fleet Marshall Investigation was a serious matter, and it didn't really surprise her that the Special Forces would be called in—but she hardly saw how a bunch of scientists would be able to challenge her newfound abilities.

Among the various people walking up and down the spar, one suddenly broke off and strode purposefully toward them. She wore undress blues instead of coveralls, the three silver bars on her epaulettes a beacon of her authority.

Katja felt her heart sink.

Korolev didn't turn.

<What is the most important quality in a servant of the State, Katja?>

She fought down the snarl that threatened to twist her face, and focused on keeping her walk steady. Every muscle in her body seemed to tense.

<Loyalty, sir.> *You bastard.*

<Loyalty.>

"Good afternoon, Commander Brisebois," he said aloud. "This is the operative who will be assisting you today."

As she reached the brigadier and his companion, Breeze stiffened, and every muscle in her body seemed to tense. She wasn't sure if it was from fear or revulsion. Korolev had promised her a Special Forces operative, a member of the most highly trained and dedicated servants of the State.

What he'd brought her was a maniac.

Katja stood before her in silence, expression neutral. Breeze had spent way too much time with her, however, to not see the glimmer of anger in her deep, dark eyes. Today was supposed to be a clean, decisive conclusion to the Fleet Marshall Investigation. With Emmes in the mix, who knew *what* would happen?

She glanced around quickly to ensure no one was in earshot. Then she turned to Korolev.

"Sir, this mission needs to be conducted with precision." She paused, choosing her words carefully. "Are you sure this operative is the best choice?"

Korolev's bland expression didn't change. "I realize you're in a position of authority now, Commander, and that those bars on your shoulders are still shiny and new," he said. "But please don't forget about the two shiny new stars that I normally wear on my shoulders, and the fact that I'm the commander of the Astral Special Forces. Do you want me to withdraw our support for your little witch-hunt?"

Breeze felt a chill ripple through her. Picking a fight with this man was not a good idea. Looking again at Katja, standing so still and quiet, she figured that some brainwashing just might have made a useful tool out of her. So she bowed her head in acquiescence.

"I meant no offense, sir," she answered. "Any operative would be more than qualified for what I require today."

Korolev took a step back. "I'll be observing remotely, but this mission is yours, Commander. My operative will take her direction solely from you. Fill her in as you go."

Well, that should be interesting, Breeze mused. "Thank you, sir."

She motioned for Katja to follow, and turned to enter the tunnel connecting the spar to *Armstrong*'s airlock. As they walked, she gave Katja the basics of what was about to transpire. It felt strange, yet satisfying, treating her as a subordinate.

There was a sailor standing at the entrance to the ship. His bored expression barely shifted as he glanced at the security readout of Breeze's ID chip and nodded. She'd expected that the arrival of a senior officer on board would spark at least a *bit* of interest from the ship's gatekeeper, but no one in the Research Squadron seemed to have figured out that there was war brewing.

Just another nail in the coffin. She walked down the passageway until they were out of sight of the airlock then turned to Katja.

"We need to enter the admiral's quarters at just the right moment, in order to maximize the impact." She studied Katja's face. "Can you assess from outside what's happening in there?"

Katja met her gaze, nodding.

"According to my records from the ship's security feed," Breeze added, "Grey frequently reports to Bush's cabin at about 14:00. Did she keep to the schedule today?"

"Just a moment." Katja's gaze went blank, eyes flicking slightly as she accessed the ship's data.

Breeze had seen it a couple of times before, during Intelligence briefings, but never in a live situation. She would need to learn more about it, especially now.

"Grey went into his cabin about twenty minutes ago." Breeze jumped a little when Katja spoke. "Recommend we recce the activities now."

Breeze searched her words for any note of mockery, but found none.

"Okay," she said. "I don't want to bump into the captain, Kane, or Mallory on our way. They'd just cause complications. Can you tell me where they are?"

The gaze went blank again, for longer this time. Katja even squinted at one point, but her unfocused stare didn't waver. She blinked heavily and looked up.

"The captain's in his cabin," she answered. "Thomas and Jack are both in the main lab."

"Good." She gestured. "The admiral's cabin is this way."

They ascended one deck and moved forward in the ship, passing occasional crew members who continued about their business with barely a nod of acknowledgement. Within minutes they were standing outside the door to Admiral Bush's quarters—or, more accurately, the guest quarters set aside for any visiting senior officer. Since Bush seemed to make *Armstrong* his home most of the time, she doubted anyone else ever got the chance to try them out.

Katja opened her tool bag and removed what looked like a maintenance helmet. Technicians wore such protection when they were servicing equipment, both to shield them from flashes, and allow them to access data inside the visor. She donned the helmet and moved slowly along the bulkhead, gaze pointed at the blank, composite surface.

Suddenly she paused, head sweeping from side to side. Then she moved back to Breeze.

"Targets are inside," she said, "and in a very compromising position."

Breeze suppressed a smile. This was kind of fun, actually. She had her very own pet operative.

"Go in quietly, and have your helmet-cam recording the entire time. I—*we* want to get as much evidence as possible."

Katja nodded. She reached into her tool bag again and pulled out a holstered pistol, which she attached to her belt. Breeze felt her stomach tighten.

"I don't want anyone killed in there."

"It's just to contain them, ma'am."

Katja Emmes had just called her *ma'am.*

The sense of fun began to return. True, Katja was armed, but she was a sworn servant of the State and she was working for Breeze. In effect, having her armed meant that Breeze had the power of life and death in her hands.

It didn't get much better.

"Open the door," she ordered.

Still wearing the helmet and with the visor down, Katja paused in front of the door. Moments later it slid open quietly. She disappeared through without a sound. Breeze stepped forward as softly as she could, passing the threshold to enter the dim room.

The quarters were divided into a sitting room, into which she entered, and a bedroom which was accessible through an open door to the left. The sitting room was dark, lit only by a pair of lamps next to the desk. A broad window looked out toward the upper edge of Earth's shining surface.

Unmistakable sounds left no doubt as to what was happening in the bedroom. Katja had already crossed the floor, and was crouched in the doorframe, helmet-cam pointed toward the source. Breeze rolled her eyes in distaste as she walked over.

They were coupled by the bedroom window. Helena Grey's bony body was bent over, her hands braced against the polyglass, Randall Bush's fat form thrusting from behind. Apparently the admiral liked to enjoy the view while he enjoyed his crew. The only light came through the window, and she didn't think that was quite enough to secure a positive ID.

So she flicked on the overhead lights.

The resultant flurry of flesh was quite amusing as Grey screamed and desperately sought cover. While Bush stood in shock, jerking in several directions without knowing what to do, she wound up cowering in the corner, barely hidden behind a table.

Breeze put a hand on Katja's shoulder.

"I think that's enough evidence."

Katja nodded, turning off the camera.

Bush finally found his voice. "What—what's the meaning of this?" A croak turned into a bellow. "How *dare* you!"

Breeze met his weasel gaze fearlessly. She didn't often get to use her authoritative tone, and now she let it belt out.

"I might say the same thing," she barked. "I come on board, to find out why my Dark Bomb project is so behind schedule, and this is what I find! The science team leader, whoring herself out to the man who promised me *personally* that this project would meet its deadlines."

To his credit, the admiral didn't surrender easily.

"Commander Brisebois," he pressed, "you are *way* out of line, and you are skirting dangerously close to a court-martial. Hand over that camera, and get *out* of my cabin."

Breeze squeezed Katja's shoulder. "Contain the admiral, please."

In a heartbeat Katja's pistol was out and pointed at the fat old man. Any sense of fight Bush might have possessed was suddenly whisked away. His eyes widened in shock.

"Sit down on the bed, please, Admiral," Breeze ordered, using a calmer voice. "Lieutenant Grey, please get dressed and report to the lab. I think you have some work to do."

Helena Grey, her face beet red to the roots of her dyed-blonde hair, gathered up her clothing and slipped through the door into the sitting room. Breeze was happy to have that withered old crone removed from her sight, and turned her attention to the bulbous, pasty old geezer plopped naked on the bed. His gaze shifted between her and the gun that was still pointed at him.

"Admiral, I'm very disappointed to discover the truth of why the Dark Bomb project is so far behind schedule," she said, as if talking to a child. "As you may know, I'm also the leader of the Fleet Marshall Investigation into the significant Terran losses during the recent conflict. As of now, I think I understand what's happened. Your Research Squadron has been squandering a golden opportunity to develop a weapon that could have stopped the rebellion as soon as it started."

She allowed herself a sneer. "If your Research Squadron had been doing its job, and not serving as your personal harem, thousands of brave men and women of the Astral Force would still be alive, instead of having their remains floating in pieces around the colonial worlds."

He was sweating openly. She let him stew for a moment, naked, frightened, and humiliated.

"What do you want?" he whispered.

She kept her face neutral, but inwardly she allowed herself a smile of satisfaction. This was certainly no brave, idealistic Thomas Kane before her. This old man was a survivor. She turned to Katja.

"Give me a moment with the admiral, please."

Katja retreated through the doorway, holstering her weapon. Breeze sat down on the bed next to Bush, and lowered her voice.

"I'm going to give you a choice, Admiral," she said. "Parliament must be handed its guilty party, but I have the power to decide exactly who that is. Clearly the blame for Terra's recent military troubles is going to fall on the Research Squadron, and its failure to provide the best weaponry to our fighting forces." She placed a hand on his cold, bare knee. "But who, exactly? Was it a failure at the very top, or was it a conspiracy at a lower level? I need you to make that choice."

Bush's eyes lit up with a glimmer of hope.

"I'll cooperate."

27

It was considered bad luck to whistle on a ship, but Thomas was in such a good mood that he was tempted to defy the ancient superstition and more than a thousand years of tradition.

As he flashed up the terminal at his personal workstation, his office door fixed open so he could hear the chatter from the lab, he contented himself with humming an old folk song.

The barrage of messages on his screen revealed the usual nuisances of a typical work day, and he doubted today would be any less frustrating than normal, but at least all his hard work was paying off. One message in particular caught his eye—forwarded from Admiral Chandler in confidence.

It was the sanitized version of Breeze's interim report of the Fleet Marshall Investigation, concluding the line of inquiry into the wartime conduct of Expeditionary Force 15. As he knew it would, it stated that the overall conduct of the officers in EF 15 had been exemplary, and any potential sources of embarrassment had been caused elsewhere in the Astral Fleet.

The investigation was ongoing, but no matter how much she might have wanted to fix the blame on him, Breeze knew that Thomas was the only thing holding the Dark Bomb research together, and that made him untouchable.

With that threat out of the way, Thomas was finally free to consider how best to deal with his own situation. Being the acting XO of a Research ship wasn't exactly the dream of the ambitious Line officer, but he could see the opportunities. Most importantly, his position was billeted for a commander, and if he could convince the necessary decision-makers to make his posting permanent, the necessary promotion would be granted immediately. None of his peers in the regular fleet had access to that kind of shortcut, and once his position was permanent he could *really* start to make some changes.

As if on cue, Helena Grey stormed into his office.

"Thomas, I think you should know that Amanda is not performing well."

He leaned back in his chair. "How so?"

"She's been burying herself in her equations for three days, with hardly any work on the latest batch of field results."

Thomas wasn't a scientist—and neither, he'd come to realize, was Helena—but he'd familiarized himself with the latest round of extra-dimensional experiments.

"My understanding is that the math needs to be sound before we can start applying experimental results."

"But not for three days!" Helena's plastic face began turning red. "I've never seen anyone need more than a full day to check over what hundreds of scientists have already proven, long before it comes to us." He could tell there was nothing to be gained by arguing, so he decided not to waste his time.

"Okay, Helena," he said neutrally. "Thanks. I'll look into it."

She stared at him, eyes beginning to bulge. "Why do I bother?" she snapped. "You don't even care."

"I said I'd look into it," he replied, a hint of irritation entering his voice. "What more do you want?"

She opened her mouth, then closed it again and stormed out, muttering something under her breath. Thomas shook his head, reining in his irritation. As soon as his position was made permanent, he'd begin the process to get rid of that old crone. After that, if he worked his connections well enough over the next year or two, he just might be able to prove Captain Lincoln's incompetence and assume command. That would put him firmly back on track.

There was a knock on his door. He glanced up to see Jack Mallory leaning in, concern etched across his features.

"Uhh, sir?" he said. "I think you better get out here."

His curiosity piqued, Thomas rose from his workstation and followed Jack out into the lab. There were half a dozen team members present, he noticed, but each one had stopped work and was staring toward the main entrance. Breeze was standing in the doorway. She stared at him with dangerous eyes, then cast her glance around the lab. It passed quickly over the various team members, finally coming to rest on Helena.

"What is this?" the older woman demanded. She didn't look as angry as he would have expected. If anything, Helena looked worried, perhaps even *afraid*.

Breeze didn't answer. She just stepped aside to allow Captain Lincoln to enter, his expression a mixture of confusion and irritation as he glanced back over his shoulder. Behind him stood a short, unfamiliar squad leader in standard blue coveralls. She wore a maintenance helmet covering her face and head. Thomas immediately spotted the pistol holstered on her belt.

Breeze produced a military grade info-pad and started to read in a steady, matter-of-fact tone.

"By order of the Fleet Marshall, the primary research project currently underway aboard the Terran Research Vessel *Neil A. Armstrong*—namely, the core research in support of a Dark Bomb weapon—is suspended," she stated. "All data and findings are to be collected immediately for Astral Force examination."

Lincoln finally found his voice.

"You can't do that, Commander," he protested. "This is my ship, and I'm responsible for that research."

Breeze and the helmeted squad leader exchanged a glance. The squad leader stepped forward and slipped her pistol free from its holster. Thomas recognized the easy movement of her hand on the weapon and, with growing fear, recognized the compact body beneath the coveralls.

He didn't need to see her face to know who held the gun.

"The Fleet Marshall agrees," Breeze said, "and as the senior officer responsible for this failure, Captain Andrew Charles Lincoln must bear the consequences."

Thomas watched as Katja Emmes walked up to Lincoln, raised her pistol to his face and pulled the trigger. The crack of the shot echoed off the lab walls as the back of Lincoln's head exploded outward. Blood and gray matter splattered across the deck as his body collapsed backward.

Thomas vaguely heard the screams around him.

He knew he should act to protect his crew, but he was paralyzed by the absolute obedience with which Katja had performed the execution. Her movements were fluid, her aim perfect, but it was as if, under that visor, she hadn't even been looking at her victim.

"By order of Admiral Bush," Breeze continued, "I have assumed command of this vessel, effective immediately."

Thomas felt sick.

"The Fleet Marshall is aware that no team succeeds or fails because of one individual," Breeze added, "and while Captain Lincoln paid the ultimate price, others have contributed significantly to this failure."

Katja had holstered her weapon and moved slowly toward Helena.

"Lieutenant Helena Jennifer Grey, you are convicted of conduct unbecoming an officer, of compromising the chain of command, and of engaging in improper relations with a superior officer. And you are charged with treason."

Katja grabbed Helena by the hair and pushed her face down against the nearest workstation. The old woman gasped loudly, then whimpered, then begged as Katja grabbed her wrist and began twisting her arm slowly backward. The begging turned to screaming as the arm twisted further, then snapped. Helena's body slumped over as she fainted. Katja wasn't even breathing hard.

"Lieutenant Grey," Breeze announced, "is under arrest and will be held until her trial."

Katja turned toward him. He tensed, shifting one leg back in preparation of defense against whatever onslaught might follow. Behind her, Breeze's expression was almost smug.

Thomas thought quickly. He called out to Breeze across the room.

"My thanks for arresting Lieutenant Grey, ma'am," he said loudly. "It's good to know that the Fleet Marshall is aware of the situation, and looks poorly on improper relations between personnel and their superiors." He paused, then added, "especially when that occurs shortly before a promotion."

Breeze's smug expression faded into a frown. She glanced at her info-pad.

"Be careful what you say, Lieutenant Commander Kane," she said, her words deliberate. "Be *very* careful." She locked onto him once again, frustration plain in her eyes, for those who knew to look. "While no specific charges are being brought against you at this time, this Fleet Marshall Investigation is still ongoing." He held her gaze, and frustration turned to anger. "You are relieved of your position, and placed under arrest until the investigation is complete."

Katja paused right in front of him, shifting her stance to allow her a line of sight back to Breeze. Breeze subtly shook her head. Katja turned her gaze back and the black visor fixed on him. Suddenly—and for the first time since she'd entered the lab—it seemed as if she was actually looking at something.

Looking at him.

A single, irresistible thought filled his mind.

Merje.

He never saw it coming. Her boot impacted his midsection with such force that his spine shuddered. Then he toppled backward, head slamming against the deck. Through ringing and stars he vaguely heard Breeze give some sort of warning to the remaining lab team. By the time he came to his senses, he felt the handcuffs locking behind him, and small but impossibly strong hands hauling him shakily to his feet.

28

After Thomas and Helena were led out of the lab—by a helmeted person Jack was pretty sure was Katja—the first sound Jack heard was Amanda throwing up.

He felt her hand gripping his arm, but he couldn't move to help her. He stared down at the body of his commanding officer, lying on the deck, wide eyes staring upward on either side of the single bullet hole to his skull. His brains were splattered beneath and beyond his body, and a gut-twisting odor was beginning to fill the room.

It was the smell that jerked him from his paralysis. Dead bodies were something he'd dealt with before—or rather, they were something he'd worked around to accomplish a mission. The five remaining members of the lab team were still frozen where they stood, except for Amanda who'd collapsed in a retching heap.

These were hardly battle-hardened warriors, and Jack could sense that military discipline was about to collapse. With the captain dead, and Thomas and Helena arrested, someone had to take charge—someone had to focus this team on a simple, important task. And the first thing that needed to happen, he realized, was to get that body out of sight.

"Tso, Sandhu," he said briskly to the two junior crewmen. When they didn't respond, he barked their names again. "*Tso! Sandhu!*" They turned stunned eyes toward him. "Go to sickbay and get a body bag. Bring it back here right away."

They nodded and fled.

Petty Officer Li was as white as a ghost. Jack stepped toward him.

"Li, go to the cleaning-gear locker," he said. "Get me general-purpose fluid and absorbents."

Li stared up at him. "What?"

"Cleaning fluid and absorbents... go!" He turned to the chief. "Lopez, go to the bridge and send a message to Squadron Command. Tell them that we've stopped our core research, by Fleet Marshall Order." The chief blinked several times, but seemed to understand. He hurried from the lab.

Amanda was still on the deck. Jack scanned the workstations and quickly spotted a translucent tub. Dumping its contents onto the counter he used the lid to sweep the bulk of Lincoln's brain chunks into it, then clicked the lid into place. A long burst-pattern of purplish blood still covered the central deck, but at least the smell decreased.

Grabbing a pair of emergency breathing devices from the bulkhead, he sealed one over his head and knelt down in front of Amanda.

She was visibly shaking, bile dripping from her bottom lip. She looked up at him with reddened eyes. Giving her a reassuring stroke across the cheek, he swept her hair out of her face and offered her the breathing device. She stared at him in confusion, then pulled it over her head.

Helping her to her feet, he wrapped her arm across his shoulders. She leaned heavily on him as he walked them to the door. The breathing device had eliminated the smell, but just as importantly it was feeding him pure oxygen, which gave him a rush of energy.

Through the door he sat Amanda down in the corridor, just as Petty Officer Li returned with the cleaning supplies. Jack grabbed them and re-entered the lab. He sprayed down the contaminated deck, as well as the workstation where Katja had snapped Helena's arm.

He dropped to one knee, the images of what had just happened there invading his conscious mind. Katja Emmes, the same girl he'd danced with just the other night, had shot dead *Armstrong*'s captain, right in front of the crew, then explicitly tortured the lab supervisor.

All at the order of Charity Brisebois.

He shuddered. What kind of person could...

His mind started to turn in a new direction, back toward another incident where brains and blood had been spilled. He blanked it out. Swallowing bile, he threw absorbent pads down on the blood and let them start to soak up the mess. Moving to the spot where Amanda had been sick, he sprayed down and padded that section, too.

Movement caught his eye.

Tso and Sandhu had returned with the body bag. Jack motioned them to lay it down next to the body. He took Lincoln's shoulders and helped them shift the body onto the bag, then sealed it. Noting their gray expressions, he sent them back into the hall while he mopped up the majority of what remained. It was several minutes of mindless work, and he forcibly kept his mind clear of any thoughts except cleaning. It was like preparing for an inspection, he told himself. The lab needed to look good for inspection.

Eventually he used up all his absorbents, and tossed the bloody rags down the disposal chutes. The worst of the horror was gone, and he decided it would have to do. He opened the doors and stepped out into the corridor, pulling the breathing device off over his sweat-soaked hair.

Amanda was still sitting on the deck. Those who had witnessed the incident were all there, standing or crouched by the opposite bulkhead. Everyone stared at him. Still flushed with pure oxygen, he tried to maintain his momentum.

"Chief, is the message to Squadron Command sent?"

"Yes, sir."

"We have to gather all the data from our core research and hand it over to the Fleet Marshall's team. Can you access the data from a workstation outside the main lab?"

"Yes, sir. We can download it to... to the captain's cabin."

"Good. Take Tso to Captain Brisebois' quarters and start to organize the data for download. Petty Officer Li, take Sandhu to stores and gather up enough crystals to store at least three copies of the data. Report to the chief with the crystals."

"Yes, sir."

The team moved off with purpose, just as Jack had intended. He then turned his attention to Amanda. She was watching him intently, although her entire body seemed ready to melt away into the deck. He crouched down in front of her.

"Hey, genius," he said gently. "I could use your brains right about now."

He instantly regretted his choice of words, as Amanda retched anew. She hung her head over shaking arms as she gasped for breath.

She was useless like this, he knew, yet he actually did need her. Thinking that sickbay might have something to help her, he tucked his arms under hers and tried to lift her. Her soft form was limp and unresponsive.

"Fuck off," she growled.

"Come on, Amanda, I need you to get up."

"I said fuck *off*." She shook loose. "I'm not doing anything." She curled herself more tightly into a ball.

A wave of such anger flooded through him that he nearly slapped her. Instead, he grabbed her jumpsuit with both hands and wrenched her to her feet.

"Get up and get useful," he gritted. She pushed him away again, stumbling backward into the bulkhead.

"What's wrong with you?" she demanded. "Didn't you see what happened? Watch while your little girlfriend Katja murdered our captain?" She glared at him, and hissed, "Don't tell me you didn't recognize her, you little skin-hound!"

The words were like a punch in the gut.

"She's not my girlfriend," he replied, "but she's strong as hell, and I'd take her over you any day, you weakling."

Amanda's mouth dropped open. Then she reared back and slapped him across the face. The blow was hard enough to jerk his head sideways, but the pain was distant and dull.

He took a step back, feeling what he suddenly recognized as combat adrenaline coursing through his veins.

"We've suffered casualties," he said, "but we have a mission to perform. Our team is working to achieve it, and I intend to see that they succeed. What are you going to do, Sublieutenant Smith?" He waited for her response.

She rolled her eyes. "Oh, spare me that combat fleet bullshit," she spat back. "We just witnessed murder and assault by our own organization. Are you telling me you're just going to follow their orders?"

Her question threatened his resolve, but he knew he couldn't entertain doubts. Not right now.

"I'm going to keep my team occupied and out of harm's way," he replied. "With a message sent to Squadron Command, I'll await further instructions from an authorized source."

"Are you kidding?" She stared at him with a mixture of anger and contempt. "You're just going to let them get away with murder? After what happened to you during the war?"

"What did you just say?" His mental walls buckled dangerously.

"Oh, come on, Jack!" She gestured angrily. "It was all over the news for days. I know what happened to you in Sirius. We all do! We saw the footage of your team being attacked, just like everyone else in Terra." She seemed to lose some of her rage. "I know what happened to you."

The images flooded his mind. The crazy speech by that Sirian terrorist leader. The gunfire past Jack's head, that killed the crewmen behind him. His friend Carmen being beaten to a pulp. And then the white-hot pain as his body was broken.

The darkness. And every night since then, the nightmares.

Every muscle tensed as he stepped forward again.

"You don't know anything about what happened to me," he said through clenched teeth. "You don't fucking know *anything*."

All of Terra had seen him being beaten by the Sirians. The full realization suddenly struck him. Billions had watched, over and over, the destruction of his body. No wonder so many people stared at him, he realized. It wasn't because his face was still broken. It was because they'd *watched* it being broken. He was entertainment, a minor distraction for people in their oh-so-busy little lives.

Amanda was glaring at him.

"I know you're just as crazy as the rest of the combat fleet," she growled. "Go follow your orders, soldier boy, but I'm getting off this tub and going for help."

Jack was in no mood to argue, and damned if he was going to carry Amanda through it. Let her learn for herself.

"Who do you think's going to help?"

That stopped her for a moment.

"The police."

"They have no jurisdiction."

"The military police."

"They're bound by the Fleet Marshall, just like the rest of us."

"Admiral Bush, then," she said, grasping. "When he finds out his precious Helena's been arrested…" Then Amanda's own quick thinking brought her to the only possible conclusion. He arrived there at the same time.

"Helena's been charged with improper relations," he hissed. "With a superior. Who do you think that is? And who put Breeze in command? Bush is saving his own skin."

She went silent. Wrapped her arms around herself and leaned back against the bulkhead. After a moment she spoke.

"Then he's the only smart person on board." She looked up at him, fear in her eyes. "This is insane."

It was his turn to be silent. He was still struggling to fight down the memories, still imagining all of Terra watching in their living rooms. He could feel the blood pumping in his temples. His fists clenched at his sides. He felt the rage well up within him—rage at all the worlds.

Those fucking people just sat and watched, as he was nearly beaten to death. Those fucking people were more interested in winning their fucking science awards than building a weapon that could protect soldiers like him. Those fucking people didn't care one bit about him. About *anything*.

But Katja cared.

And Thomas.

And even Breeze. All three of them had been on *Rapier* when the rescue came. All three of them had risked their lives for him, even though they'd barely known him. They mattered. Fucking assholes like Amanda Smith did not.

"Welcome to military life, Sublieutenant Smith," he said flatly. "Either you're with me, or you're against me—you decide. But I'm not waiting around."

He turned and marched off, headed for the CO's cabin.

Somebody had to make sure the download was successful.

It took hours to collect together everything that *Armstrong* had gathered and analyzed over the past few months. The process was made more difficult by the fact that most of the Dark Bomb research was scattered among the many special experiments that Lincoln had always been demanding.

It was a mess. Jack was glad he was only a subbie, and not responsible for the failure of the science team.

Breeze returned to the ship that afternoon and collected the data crystals. The new, fourth bar on her shoulders quelled any protests when she ordered the company confined to the ship, then went ashore. In Jack's experience, when officers reached the rank of captain, they could pretty much break whatever rule they wanted.

He wandered the decks for a while, recognizing the state of shock in which the *Armstrong*'s crew found themselves. These people weren't soldiers, he reminded himself. Even the crew members from engineering had mostly spent their careers in the Research Squadron. No one else on board had been deployed to the recent troubles.

Jack tried to join in a few passageway conversations that he happened upon, but no one seemed interested in hearing the opinion of a combat veteran. They were all convinced they knew best, and in this shocked state only like-minded opinions were welcome.

He didn't want to risk running into Amanda in the wardroom, and he just got cagey in his tiny cabin, so eventually he found himself back in the lab. It was deserted, workstations still active where people had abandoned them after the incident. The smell lingered despite the ship's ventilation system. Lacking any greater inspiration, he grabbed the cleaning gear and started working on what remained of the mess.

It was surprisingly soothing, so long as he didn't think about what he was cleaning up, and he felt his spirit lighten as the deck began to shine again. At the Astral College he'd always volunteered for the floors during pre-inspection work. It was simple work—just apply, rub, and repeat—and the sheer banality of it had often helped him work through problems his coursework presented.

Cleaning hadn't helped him master the math portion of his degree, but the philosophical insights he'd gained with a brush in hand had impressed many a professor. He sighed to himself. Maybe he should have been *Armstrong*'s janitor, not her pilot. The delays in the Dark Bomb research weren't just Lincoln's fault, he knew. If he hadn't overreacted when that ship had buzzed them during that first major field expedition...

He dropped his brush, straightening on his knees.

Where had that ship come from? In all the chaos and shouting that had followed his little maneuver, he'd spent all his energies trying to reschedule the experiments and he'd never followed up. But the question remained.

Rising to his feet, he crossed to a workstation.

All the official research had been locked down, but what he was looking for hadn't been included, since the experiment had been aborted. Even so, the instruments had been recording for the hours leading up to the close encounter, and that data had never been erased. So he started the playback right from the beginning.

The 4-D picture that came up in front of him was remarkably interesting in its mundanity. That particular region had been selected specifically because of its lack of spacetime anomalies, and the gentle curvature was virtually featureless. Yet the instruments they had employed were extremely sensitive, and as Jack watched he saw the readings blur from time to time as he maneuvered the Hawk.

The hunt controls to which he was accustomed were far more robust, and designed for high acceleration, but he had to admit that when the platform was stationary, these instruments provided an outstanding spacetime picture.

Tapping into the Hawk's flight logs, he quickly pinpointed the first moment when his brane sensors had detected the incoming ship. Because they'd been on their lowest power setting, the intruder had been inside of a thousand kilometers before being detected. With a bit of puzzling, he managed to cross-reference the Hawk's radar image with the spacetime instruments it had carried.

Sure enough, when he zoomed in he saw the tiny ripple in spacetime that revealed the gravimetric signature of the other ship. He was impressed, too—his hunt controls would never have picked up so small an object, moving at such slow speeds.

Having identified the ship in spacetime, Jack began to play the recording in reverse. The intruder maintained a steady course and speed for over an hour, and then it disappeared.

More accurately, he realized, it had been closing on his Hawk for more than an hour before the near miss. That made him frown. Where had it been before then? Had it been stationary? Velocity increased mass, so a stationary object would be harder to detect, but as slow as the ship had been moving, it really shouldn't have made a difference. He began to scan the data for any other evidence of where it might have been.

There was a sound. The lab door opened. He looked up.

Amanda peered in. Her cynical confidence was gone, replaced by a pale trepidation that only increased when her sweeping gaze landed on Jack. She stared at him silently.

He stared back, not knowing what to say.

She stood motionless for a long time, watching him. Then finally she stepped through into the lab. She looked around at the half-clean floor.

"Did you do this?"

He noticed where he'd dropped his brush. "I figured it had to be done, but then I got busy working on something else."

She moved toward him, studiously avoiding the center of the room.

"What are you working on?"

It was too hard to hold her gaze, and he dropped his eyes back to his screen. "Nothing important. Just pilot stuff."

He heard a scrape as she dragged a chair over to sit next to him, felt her warm hand on his shoulder. "Jack..."

He ran a hand across his face. He wanted to stay angry, but he just didn't have the will.

"You don't understand."

"I know." She pulled closer, her hand reaching to the back of his neck. "I am so sorry for what happened to you. And for what I said earlier."

He thought about Katja, and how she'd used her anger to stay strong. But he knew it just wasn't in him to be the same. Who was he kidding—he'd never be a real soldier, like her or Thomas. He turned toward Amanda, trying to put a reassuring hand on her waist.

She didn't drop her arm, and his movement turned into a hug as she pulled him closer. He found himself wrapping his arms around her soft, warm body, burying his face against her shoulder. She held him tight.

He hung on for dear life.

"I'm not the same guy who left Earth nine months ago," he said, his voice little more than a whisper.

"I never met that other guy," she said, "but I sure like you."

He laughed slightly. "Is that why you pull my hair and call me names?"

She turned her head, nuzzling her face next to his. "No. I do that because you're a jerk."

He snickered, the shudder rolling into a giggle that he struggled to stop. He pressed closer against her, trying to muffle the laughter that was bubbling up from within. It was crazy, but suddenly everything just seemed better.

"So," she said, "I need to think about something fresh. Do you want to tell me about this 'pilot stuff' you're working on?"

He pulled back from the embrace, but moved her arms to wrap over his shoulders as he sat up to the workstation again. She stood close behind him and listened as he outlined what he'd found so far in his search for that mystery ship.

"Why are you only using gravimetric sensors?" she asked when he reached his current dead end.

"What else would I use?"

She leaned against him as she reached forward to manipulate the controls. He'd never realized how good she felt up close. At her command, another set of readings appeared graphically on the screen.

"Well," she said, "for starters, here's what was happening to the dark-energy levels." Pausing, she looked closer. "Hmm, that's interesting."

"What?"

She pointed at a bright patch on the screen, quite close to where the ship had appeared. "That's an anomaly I noticed in the field data from the second run we did a few weeks later. But there were *two* anomalies in our official data. Here there's just one."

"What kind of anomaly is it?"

"Don't know. It's a concentration of dark energy on the brane. At the time I figured it was just a Kearns vortex, but it doesn't seem to be causing any unusual expansion of spacetime. The second one didn't either, even though its make-up was quite different. They were odd, but I never had time to look at them more closely."

"I suppose the other one is locked up with the rest of the official Dark Bomb data?" he suggested.

"Yeah." She looked around thoughtfully, and her face lit up. "But I never did get around to recycling those broken probes we cleaned up." She walked over to the far bulkhead and fished through the various pieces of blackened equipment, returning eventually with a handful of data drives. "It'll be on one of these."

A few minutes of searching revealed the readings from the second—and successful—experiment in the same region. Sure enough, a second dark-energy concentration appeared on the screen, sitting virtually on top of the older one. Both patches were bright, but the original one was diffuse and ragged, while the newcomer was very small and precise.

Jack did an analysis of the first one. The pattern was familiar.

"That looks like a jump gate, although not a stable one."

"There aren't any jump gates around there, Jack."

He turned to look up at her. "You'd be surprised where jump gates have shown up recently." Their faces were just inches apart.

She made to protest, but checked herself. "That would explain why the ship just came out of nowhere." She nodded.

"Yeah, but then why would a second object appear?" He pointed to the screen.

She leaned in again and opened a secondary display. "Let's do a search of known objects in the database."

Even as she started the search, he knew it would turn up empty. Whatever was going on here, it wasn't going to be recorded in the usual archives. He almost wanted to start cleaning the deck again, to find his thinking groove, but Amanda's presence around his shoulders was too nice to disturb.

Jump gates. There was something bad about jump gates going on here—and there was only one system beyond Terra that had the proven ability to create them.

"Do you think Centauria built a secret jump gate, in Terran space?"

"What?" She stopped dead, straightening slightly to shoot him a perplexed look. "Where did that come from? When did Centauria come into this discussion?"

He ignored her reaction—he was fairly used to it. "This area of space… It's way down south of the ecliptic, isn't it?"

"Yeah."

"And Centauria itself is south of Terra, by Sol reference."

"Yeah, but it's four light years away." She was trying to humor him, he could tell. "I don't think anything they did would… show up…"

She wasn't slow. He gave her full credit for practically reading his mind. "Come on, Jack," she said skeptically. "How could the Centauris make a new jump gate? The only way into Terra is via the regular gates, and we've been shooting at any Centauri ships that come through."

He looked back at the two dark-energy concentrations. One large and diffuse. The other small and very precise. *That's it*, he thought.

"I think there might be another way in," he said. "The original jump gate relay our grandparents built to reconnect with the colonies."

She shook her head. "Those were deactivated decades ago."

"Says who?"

"Says everybody!" She was back to chiding him. "Didn't they teach that at your school?"

"Yeah… but they also taught us that the colonies were grateful to be reunited with Terra, and to be brought back into the human family."

Her lips pursed in a frown. "If the old jump gates were still there, the database would have shown us. These terminals have access to that sort of info, remember?"

He looked back at the workstation. It was logged in as "Chief Lopez." Then his eyes darted around the room, remembering that every workstation had been abandoned after the incident, and the users were all still logged in. His eyes came to rest on the open door to Thomas's office.

He leapt from his chair and ran through into the office. Rounding the desk he grinned as he was greeted by an unlocked workstation. Sitting down, he began calling up the information displayed on Lopez's screen. Amanda followed him in, frowning again. Noticing her querying gaze, he spoke while he scanned through the unfamiliar menus of the command-level console.

"The regular database wouldn't show them," he postulated, "but if they exist, I'll bet the eyes-only database will tell a different tale."

Her mouth dropped open.

"What are you doing?" she whispered. "If Brisebois catches you, you're dead."

"This isn't the CO's account—it's the XO's. He's the only other person on board with the same level of clearance."

She shook her head. "How do you know this stuff?"

He couldn't help but wink at her. "Combat fleet bullshit, baby."

It took some time, but finally he found what he was looking for. He felt her hands squeeze his shoulders as a few of the most closely guarded secrets of the Astral Force appeared on the screen. Sure enough, the old jump gate still existed, and it was the larger of the two dark-energy concentrations. That could mean only one thing.

"Those bastards." He sat back, leaning against Amanda.

"What?"

"They used our old jump gate relay and plopped their own new gate right where we'd never look for it. Even if we did, we'd just think it was the old one." He pointed at the two concentrations. "My hunt controls would never have been able to distinguish between them, if they picked them up at all." He marveled at the cunning of the enemy.

This war wasn't yet over.

"Are you still talking about Centauria?" Amanda asked. "Even if they could build a jump gate—and I'm not sure any colony could—why would they want to build one there? It doesn't make any sense."

Jack swung the chair around, forcing her to take a step back.

"It makes *total* sense. They can sneak in and out at will." He felt his stomach tighten. "There might be an entire fleet of ships in our system already, and nobody would know about it."

"But Jack, jump gates are among the most difficult things ever built by humans," she protested. Scorn was starting to creep into her voice. "What are you trying to tell me? That one of the colonies can just whip one up?"

He smiled, confident for perhaps the first time since joining *Armstrong*.

"That's *exactly* what I'm telling you." He jerked his thumb back at Thomas's display, and the old jump gate it revealed. "What you learn in school isn't always everything there is to learn. Trust me," he said grimly, "they can build jump gates."

"Okay, fine." She raised her hands in concession. "So what the hell have we just found? And what are we going to do about it?"

A day ago, Jack would have gone straight to Thomas. His next choice would have been Katja. Who else could he trust? Who else would believe him?

Who else would even care?

"I think we have to tell Breeze."

29

Katja didn't have any particular problem with spying on the citizens of Terra. What bothered her was the fact that most people lived such boring lives. After only a couple of days peering into the unseen dimension of collective information, boredom was threatening her productivity.

Except, of course, when she tuned into what Breeze was up to. Connections between her various communications and movements revealed an ongoing plan that was stunning in its complexity and subtlety. Katja had never understood why the bitch did the things she did, but aided by her Special Forces implants and new Cloud-based perspective, she was beginning to appreciate the self-serving genius of her former cabin mate.

Having witnessed the pact made in Admiral Bush's cabin, she hadn't been surprised at his self-serving choice. What *had* surprised her was the agility with which Breeze had turned the situation to her complete advantage, finding a scapegoat for the inquiry, and getting herself inserted as the commanding officer of *Armstrong*.

On the surface it made no sense for an Intelligence officer to take command of a Terran warship, but as project director of the critical Dark Bomb research, Breeze had made her case, and won. Fortunately for her, with so much data already collected, there was no real need to go back into space. *Armstrong* had become a glorified orbiting lab under Breeze's control. In the process, that harpy had got herself promoted… again.

Helena Grey was going on trial and would hang, while Thomas Kane would likely be returned to duty when his hearing convened this afternoon. There was nothing they could pin on him, but Breeze's strong-arm tactics—or rather, Katja's—would ensure that he never again tried to cross swords with her.

Sheer, evil genius. Katja couldn't help but be impressed.

She had no official reason to spy on Breeze. Having successfully completed her test mission, she'd been formally accepted into the Special Forces and been given the task of mastering her use of the Cloud. To do so meant exploring the general data stream, and who better to spy on than the Demon Queen of Lies.

<Katja.> It was Korolev.

<Yes, sir.>

<I'm in the room with you.>

She looked up with a start. Sure enough, the brigadier was standing just inside the doorway, arms crossed and staring at her.

"Important lesson to learn," he said mildly. "Never lose focus on the real world."

Katja sat back in the chair, feeling her heart race. She was working in a small office at Astral Headquarters, standard desk and workstation set up to give the impression of a civilian employee, processing the endless flow of bureaucracy. Judging from the pattern of sunlight on the floor, she guessed she'd been in the Cloud for more than an hour.

Like Katja, Korolev wore civilian clothes. He sat down across from her.

"You seem to be getting more comfortable in the Cloud," he observed.

"Yes," she acknowledged, "although it's easier if I focus on a single subject or line of inquiry. When I try to cast too wide, it starts to get shaky."

He nodded. "Yet ultimately, that's where the power will lie—from the ability to access vast stores of information all at once. When you can observe it as a single concept, you can pick out the patterns very easily. Staying with a single individual won't give you the big picture."

"Still, I can figure out what that individual is up to pretty quickly."

"True, and sometimes that's our mission." He fixed his gaze on her. "Who have you been studying?"

She dropped her eyes, suddenly embarrassed.

"Breeze."

He smiled slightly. "Ah, yes. acting-Captain Brisebois. One of your favorite people."

"She's fascinating."

"I'm sure." Korolev leaned forward, his expression growing serious again. "But don't spend time on people you already know. You need to learn how to use the Cloud instinctively, and you need to learn fast. If you focus on friends or family, you'll be drawn back into concepts and patterns you formed in the real world, and you won't use your intuition to read the data properly. Relying on real-world impressions is a dangerous crutch."

"Yes, sir."

"Cast your mind wide." He sat back. "Try to look at this entire building and all the information floating around within its walls. Begin with the unclassified data—before long, you'll learn how to deal with encrypted assets as well."

Following his lead, she looked up at the bare walls and ceiling, imagining the invisible dimension around her. All these people were shouting into the Cloud, and only she and Korolev could hear it.

"Are there any other operatives in the building, sir?"

"I don't know." The man could have made a fortune at poker. "You tell me."

"How can I do that?"

He considered for a moment. "Sometimes a particularly sensitized operative can detect the presence of another. You have a gift, Katja—I think it's the same gift that's made your combat intuition so powerful. Given time, there's no telling *what* you can accomplish, but for now, just do as I say. Study the Cloud as a whole, rather than narrowing your perceptions unnecessarily."

"Yes, sir."

He stood. "One last reminder," he said. "Katja Andreia Emmes is off the grid now, and she can't keep popping up. I'll give you a few more days to close off any last personal matters. After that, for all intents and purposes, you no longer exist."

"Yes, sir." Katja nodded, wondering bitterly if anyone in her family had even noticed yet that she was gone. Without another word, the brigadier turned and left the room, shutting the door behind him.

Alone in the office again, she closed her eyes, and opened her mind to the Cloud. Despite Korolev's instructions, she cast her net along familiar lines. Family and friends were the easiest to spot. Without even trying she picked up a transmission from Merje to Thomas, confirming the timing of his hearing. She felt the anger boil up at her whore of a sister, and that wretched, wretched man.

She'd been so tempted by his offer—why hadn't she taken it? Clearly he'd made the same offer to Merje, and found a much more willing playmate. The thought made her stomach twist.

Her growing rage threatened to sever her link to the Cloud, and she channeled it into a single act of pique. Korolev wanted her to tie up loose ends? Slipping through the internal firewall of the law firm Ryan, Ridley, and Day, Katja hijacked the identity of Mr. Ryan himself and sent a one-line message to Merje Emmes.

Stop fucking your clients.

That would give the little slut a scare.

Forcing the rest of her emotions to disperse, Katja stilled her mind and tried to passively drift in the activity swirling in her vicinity. Terabytes of information flowed around her, mostly routine activity generated by the hundreds of personnel in her building. Breeze's office was almost directly above her, several floors up, and Katja instinctively started to focus there.

There were a number of communications between Breeze and *Armstrong*, as well as communications sent to Admiral Chandler and the Fleet Marshall's office. Nothing too surprising as Breeze consolidated her power base.

Suddenly Katja noticed another active node.

It was Breeze's personal Baryon. The device was active almost as often as the military account, and most of the messages were going to the same address. Katja knew she wasn't supposed to, but she drilled down to finer detail. Who was commanding so much of Breeze's attention?

It was someone named Kit, and judging from the choice

of words in the messages, Breeze seemed to be romantically involved with him. Expanding her horizons, Katja searched for information on "Kit Moro." Not much appeared in the regular databases. He was a freelance journalist, recently arrived at Longreach, with connections to Chuck Merriman...

She froze on the first image she saw of his face. She'd met Moro before—he was the cameraman who'd been with Merriman when they'd ambushed her for an interview at the skyport. She'd met him again at Thomas's party, where he'd been Breeze's date.

Who was Kit Moro?

Perhaps it was the memory of their strange encounter at the skyport, or perhaps it was just her natural tendency to be suspicious, but Katja decided to follow the thread. She traced his Baryon messages back over the past few days, using them to identify a residential address. She let her search flow outward from there, noting everywhere he'd sent communications. No obvious patterns emerged, other than the frequency of connections to Breeze, and Katja forced herself to stop hunting.

When she did, a more comprehensive picture emerged.

There were several encrypted messages even she couldn't read. For now all she could do was acknowledge their existence. Encrypted messages by themselves weren't necessarily suspicious—many wealthy citizens paid top price for personal privacy—but something about Kit Moro's encryptions proved unusual.

They were much stronger than the other civilian security codes she'd come across, yet they were much more subtle than the Astral Force secure comms through which she'd been wading. Moro's codes were tight, almost elegant, and several of his messages were received at an address that popped out like a flare.

Her own.

Someone was in her apartment, exchanging exquisitely secure messages with Breeze's lover. In the real world, Katja felt her fingers press against the hard surface of the desk.

Someone was inside her damned apartment.

Narrowing the focus again, she zeroed in on the most recent messages between Kit and Breeze. Nothing of note. He'd invited her to go for a boat ride on Lake Sapphire tomorrow afternoon. That was the full extent of it.

So Katja switched back to Breeze's military communications, scanning for any information about activities she had in her calendar. Nothing unusual emerged, and she started skimming through the messages individually.

One caught her eye. It was from Jack Mallory, and was entitled INTERESTING INFORMATION. There were files attached, and they were big. Breeze had read the message, but hadn't yet accessed the huge attachments. Katja mapped their source.

They came from the *Armstrong* database.

She pulled back to access them directly.

Then she saw it. "Centauria."

At the first mention, Katja stopped dead. First she read the report, and then its accompanying files. She did so at normal, analogue speed, unwilling to risk missing any detail. As she finished, she went cold.

Opening her eyes, she sat back in her chair and tried to slow her rapid breathing. Panic welled up in her, but she focused and fought it down. Her networked mind was already running in several directions, all of them leading toward disastrous conclusions.

She had to act, and quickly.

<Brigadier!>

<Katja.>

She didn't even know how to begin to explain what she'd uncovered. Then in a flash of insight, she realized that she didn't have to.

<Look at this.> She gathered together her sprawling network of connections, so that he could review them.

<Breeze. Kit Moro.>

<Sophisticated encryptions.>

<My apartment.>

<Jack's message.>

<Jump gates.>

Even as she held them she began to search for more connections in the Terran information networks, and added them to the list.

<Kit Moro's arrival on Earth, a day after Jack's close encounter.>

<Moro's purchase of a luxury vessel. Departure.>
<Jack's second set of readings.>
<The network story about the *Neil Armstrong*.>
<Chuck and Kit working together.>

She was still breathing hard, struggling to hold it together, when her door burst open. She leapt to her feet, hands up in a combat stance.

It was Korolev, eyes blazing.

"Pull back, Katja," he growled. "I've got this."

She released the information from her grasp, leaning against the desk in relief. The Cloud dissipated from her awareness, and she forced her senses to focus on the tactile. The dull beige of the walls, the hard surface of the desk, the gentle hum of the air conditioning. She shuddered, and it wasn't from the chill.

Korolev's eyes went blank, although she sensed he was still aware of her. She sat down, finally able to slow her breathing. Less than a minute later, he sat across from her, his eyes clear again.

"I've sent word to the Forces, and four other operatives are investigating this," he said quickly. "Nicely done. What do you think is happening here?" He was speaking aloud, but his rapid-fire delivery was more like their Cloud communication. She couldn't match his intensity, struggling to get her unplugged brain to keep up.

"I think there's some sort of Centauri activity taking place right here on Earth," she said, shaping her words carefully. "And I'm pretty worried about Jack's suggestion that they've snuck an entire fleet into Terran space."

"It's not inconceivable," he acknowledged, and he frowned. "But I think it's unlikely."

"Why?"

"They tried the full military assault last time, and it went against them. They know we'd prepare for a repeat performance." He shook his head. "More likely it's something new. Other colonies we can anticipate pretty well, but Centauria has often been a step ahead. The next war is going to be on their terms." Concern remained etched across Korolev's usually impassive face. She didn't like it.

"What does that mean?" she asked. "What terms?"

"I don't know." He rose to his feet. "But we need to focus every operative we can spare on this.

"Come with me."

There was a private car waiting for them outside the building. The human driver didn't speak to either of them, but steered the vehicle confidently through the morning traffic in Longreach. The vast complex of buildings in Astral HQ fell behind them, and Katja found herself scanning the landscape for enemies.

As their car skirted the shore of Lake Sapphire, she saw the College on the far side. In the distance the thread-like space elevator shafts stretched up seemingly to infinity. This was the military and economic center of Planet Earth.

"Sir, this is where Kit Moro plans to bring Breeze tomorrow."

He nodded. "We're already searching it."

The car descended into an underground parking lot in a mid-level, unsecured section of the city. It cruised to the back of the lot and slid into a maintenance parking spot that was obscured from the rest of the stalls. With a slight jerk, the floor of the spot began to lower swiftly, and they were swallowed up into a dark shaft.

Light began to seep up from below moments later and they emerged into another underground chamber. The walls were uniformly dark gray, and two other cars were parked neatly alongside several strange, military-looking vehicles and pieces of equipment. They exited the car, and Korolev led her toward a series of closed doors on the opposite wall. The central door opened as he approached, and she followed him through, hurrying in her silly civilian heels to keep up.

It was a locker room, empty but for one man who was in the process of zipping up his black jumpsuit. He glanced at Korolev, then nodded at Katja. She suspected that silent communications had passed between the two men.

They passed through another door into what appeared to be a command center. There were only two uniformed personnel visibly on duty, seated far across from each other with a vast, spherical network holographically projected between them. Other screens lined every wall, and multiple workstations sat ready for use.

"This is where I'll be running things," Korolev said without preamble. "The workstations are for non-implanted support operatives—like the two on duty now—who help feed us information. I expect this room to start filling up, once I've briefed the Fleet Marshall."

Katja took it all in. Then a thought struck her.

"Breeze is a support operative—has she been here?"

"No." Korolev shook his head. "All of her Intelligence work was done on Sirius, so she doesn't know of this location, and can't let this slip to her boyfriend."

That was something, Katja mused, yet his words didn't fill her with confidence, especially as she surveyed the power of information amassed in front of her. She'd seen with her own eyes what Centauria was capable of accomplishing. As with Earth's unrevealed assets, she worried that with the enemy, she'd only seen the tip of the iceberg.

"What's my role going to be, sir?" She gave up on the absurd heels, and yanked her shoes off.

"I need you to go to your old apartment and see what's happening there," he said. "It's remained untouched since you... disappeared, and you should be able to spot any changes, no matter how subtle."

"Yes, sir." Less than a day on the team and she was already on active duty. The Special Forces didn't waste time. "Can we scan the premises to see what to expect?"

"No there aren't direct sensors in a typical civilian apartment," he replied. "From everything we've able to observe remotely, nothing has changed. Yet those communications you discovered tell a different story. You'll have to see for yourself."

"Shall I take the car we came here in?"

"No. We have a better way to get you there." He turned to look past her. "And I'm sending you with someone you trust."

She almost laughed at that—as if she trusted anyone now. Nevertheless, she followed his gaze and turned around. A broad, muscular man emerged from another door and lumbered toward them. His olive skin blended with his dark, thick body suit, his moon face grim over close-cropped hair. He stared at her with the same inscrutable gaze she'd always known, small, dark eyes piercing but impenetrable.

She stepped forward, marveling again at Korolev's perception. There *was* one person she'd learned to trust with her life. It was her old platoon second-in-command, Sergeant Suleiman Chang. As they met, she was amazed to watch his expression soften into almost a smile.

"About time you got here."

She grasped his hand. "Have you been keeping tabs on me?"

"Just in combat," he replied. "It was a pleasure training you."

She laughed. "Fuck you, Sergeant."

He really did smile this time.

"It's Suleiman... or Sules," he replied. "Katja."

She laughed again. "Or Katty."

"I've been briefed on our mission." He nodded toward Korolev, who was speaking to the duty personnel. "You ready to go?"

She shrugged and looked down at her civilian clothes. "Can I change?"

"Good idea." He motioned her toward the locker room.

There was a locker with her name on it, and a bodysuit in the same dark greenish-brown as Chang's. Black boots fit perfectly, locking tightly against the suit legs. Skin-tight gloves were like paint over her hands, and a thick belt had enough pockets to wrap around her waist.

The pockets were empty, she noticed, as was the holster at her hip, but the lightweight pistol in the cage at the top of her locker filled the holster nicely, and the pockets proved ideally sized for the magazines of high-penetration, low-explosive rounds. She began to load them.

<Feeling good?>

She glanced up at Chang. Had he spoken aloud or not? He tapped the side of his head.

<Yes,> she responded.

"Good. Some weird things are about to happen." He cocked his own pistol and slid it home. "Best to make our Cloud connection now."

She understood, and resigned herself to whatever "weird things" he had planned next. The bodysuit was heavier than normal clothing, and was rigged like a spacesuit for basic life-support, but as she moved experimentally in it she found herself remarkably unrestricted. Armed and dressed, she looked to follow his lead.

He handed her a small helmet, then slipped his own carefully over his head. It locked into place with his suit's collar, visor sliding down tight over his face, like a sheen, leaving his features clear but slightly distorted.

She squeezed her own helmet on, feeling strange as it seemed to collect up her hair and flatten it out against her head. As soon as it clicked into place at the collar, the visor appeared directly in front of her eyes, then flowed down her face as it matched every feature. She felt a moment of fear as it covered her nose and mouth, but air continued to pass in and out of her lungs.

<Can you breathe okay?> Chang leaned down to look closely at her.

She focused on him. <Yes. I can see why we can't speak to each other, though. Not while wearing these things.>

He nodded. <These suits will get us to your apartment. This is nothing personal, but just humor me, okay?>

She wondered what the hell he meant by that.

<Sure.>

He came up right behind her and wrapped a strong arm across her chest to hold her close against him. She felt a moment of panic at being confined like that, but quickly made herself relax.

<Sorry. If you were taller I could have held your waist.>

<What now?>

<You know how Fleet stealth ships can move into the Bulk, and outside of our usual three-dimensional brane?>

<Yes.> *Oh no.*

<Well, these suits do the same thing. Each one can drive itself, but we've learned to not let a person go solo on their first entry into the Bulk.>

She suppressed a mental curse... at least she hoped she had.

<I've linked your suit to mine, Katja.> He didn't seem to notice her anxiousness, or didn't let on. <Just sit tight.>

* * *

Every single muscle in her body tensed. She reached back both hands to grab Chang's legs.

At first there was the sense of the floor beneath her, beginning to disappear. It wasn't like being weightless—she could still feel the belt hanging against her hips, and the suit on her shoulders— but more like being *disconnected*. Her vision began to gray, then darken. As the light faded out, everything she could still see suddenly began to shrink, vanishing into oblivion.

Breathe, she told herself, and hoped she wasn't transmitting.

She could still feel Chang's powerful grip around her, still feel her own iron grip against his legs, but there was nothing else around them. They were in the Bulk, in the fourth dimension of space where photons didn't penetrate and gravity ruled supreme. She kicked her feet down, feeling nothing—but still knowing it was *down*. Fighting the panic welling up inside, she scrambled to get her feet on top of his. The constriction tightened.

She began her heavy-gravity breathing drills, forcing deep, shaking breaths in and out.

<It's okay, Katja. I've got you.>

The constriction, she realized, was his arm holding her firm. She forced one of her hands to let go of his leg, sliding it up her own suit to wrap onto the arm he still had around her chest.

<Can you see?> he asked.

There was nothing but blackness. Then she realized that at some point she'd closed her eyes. Lifting her eyelids, she gasped as she saw a ghostly world of dim outlines drifting by her.

<What the fuck is this?>

His deep voice was very calm inside her head. <Our suits have tiny detectors that maintain a link with the brane. This gives an indication of where we are. Kind of like a periscope. It rides less than a thousandth of a peet into the Bulk, still able to pass through things in the normal world, but close enough to give us a glimpse of what's out there.>

They were moving quickly, objects wisping past. The objects started to fall away from her, until eventually she could make out the shapes of buildings and city blocks, and even cars moving beneath them.

<Are we in the air?>

<No,> he said, <we're in the Bulk, but it's easier to navigate in clear space.>

<How are we moving?> They appeared to be going at about the same speed as a car in the city.

<I don't know,> he admitted. <I'm just the ape who drives this thing. It's how I was trained. Here, I'll link you into my nav picture.>

Suddenly the phantom world around her lit up, with military standard labels overlaid across key landmarks. All at once she recognized where she was. That was the grocery, and over there was Merje's favorite purse and bag store. It was like flying thirty meters over the city on a foggy night—and ahead of them was a familiar shape

Her apartment building.

<Here we go,> he said. <Hand on your weapon.>

She almost made a smartass remark, then reached down through the blackness, and felt the pistol grip exactly where it was supposed to be.

<Ready.>

Their rate of approach slowed, but Chang didn't falter as they passed right through the outer wall. They came to rest in what she knew was her living room, although all she could see were dim shapes around her.

<I'm going to bring us back out to the brane,> he said. <Brace yourself. It's a bit disorienting, but the feeling will pass quickly. As soon as I let go of you draw your weapon and clear the apartment.>

<Roger.>

Ghostly images faded to black. For a moment she saw nothing, then a faint impression of her living room grew from nothing into full size around her. The gray light brightened, color appeared, she felt her feet touch the floor. There was a rush of air pressure against her and Chang's arm dropped away. Pulling out her weapon, she instinctively stepped forward into a crouch. Over the barrel of the pistol she scanned the entire room, darting forward to sweep into the bedroom and ensuite. When she emerged, Chang had searched the main bathroom and front hall.

He looked over at her. <Clear.>

<Clear.> She nodded as best she could in her form-fitting visor. <But somebody else is living here.> She indicated the tidy piles of clothes beside the couch. She hadn't been that neat a day in her life.

He moved into the kitchen, opening the fridge.

<How long since you left?>

She honestly wasn't sure. <Five or six days, I think.> Time hadn't been terribly important since she woke up in a Special Forces cell.

He checked the milk. <Fresh.>

Despite her decision to give up her previous life and live for the State, she felt a rush of personal outrage at the idea of someone squatting in her home. She started poking through the pile of clothes.

<Look for any identifying items,> she suggested.

He searched the kitchen while she nosed through the various personal items in the living room. At a glance she guessed there was more than one person staying here. Then she spotted a bronze, horseshoe-shaped object lying next to a clear patch of floor. Furniture had been moved to make space, she noticed, and nothing else lay near it.

<Look at this.>

Chang approached cautiously, studying the object, tapping his helmet on several occasions in what Katja assumed was activating some manual control, much as she'd used infra-red and quantum-flux to confirm Admiral Bush's lecherous activities.

<It's radiating energy,> he said finally. <But beyond its power source I can't tell what it is.>

She stepped closer, judging whether she should pick it up or not. The open end of the horseshoe was closest to her, and she glanced around for a long object to poke it with.

There was a sudden, tiny flash and Katja leapt back. The air above the object shimmered, and a man appeared in front of her. He was dressed in regular civilian clothes and his young, smooth face froze in shock as he stared at her.

Her weapon was up and firing before she even realized. The low-explosive bullets punctured his body and splattered his innards inside of his skin. Ugly bulges rippled his clothing as he toppled backward. She lunged and pulled him away from the horseshoe object.

Chang was in a combat stance, his weapon raised in readiness at the spot where the young man had appeared, Katja focused on hauling his body clear and rapidly searched his pockets. Nothing.

She looked up. <I'm checking the bedroom again.>

Entering what she had once hoped would become her inner sanctum, she began a detailed sweep, recognizing its desecration by the Centauri. Inside the closet there were suits of body armor, and the drawers opened to reveal small arms. No sources of identification, but she estimated at least half a dozen people were using her apartment as a staging ground.

She re-entered the living room. Chang was still guarding what could only be a tiny jump gate.

<We need to report back,> she said. <This is big.>

Chang nodded, holstered his weapon, and grabbed the Centauri body in one arm. Thanks to the low-explosive rounds, there was minimal blood—about as much as a minor puncture— so the carpet was clear.

He offered her his free hand. <Let's try it this way, this time,> he suggested. <I'll drive but you can float pretty much free.>

Not wanting to show any more weakness in front of her former sergeant, she took a firm grip of his hand and kept her distance. She nodded toward the body under his arm. <Are you bringing that back?>

<No. I'm dumping it in the Bulk. Let's keep them guessing where their buddy went.>

She suppressed a shudder, but the colder part of her brain agreed with the brutal simplicity of his plan.

As her apartment faded away into the ghostly shapes inherent to the Bulk, and she moved displaced through the regular three dimensions, her thinking began to coalesce around what they knew. She hoped Korolev and the team would have discovered even more by the time they returned, but a plan was forming in her mind, drawing on disparate elements that were all connected. It would involve people she knew well. Her father would be pleased. Jack Mallory would be willing.

Most of all, Thomas Kane would be destroyed.

30

"Lieutenant Commander Kane."

Thomas rose as the presiding officer addressed him. The hearing had been relatively short, with a generic military lawyer representing the charges against him, and Merje Emmes responding with what he thought was an excellent defense. Not that there was much to defend. He hadn't been the one sabotaging the research.

An expeditionary force commander was scheduled to preside over the proceedings, but she had been summoned to Astral Base One. In her place was the regimental commander from their last deployment. Though probably not as familiar with Fleet doctrine, Thomas remembered him as a common-sense commander who was highly regarded by his troops. It wouldn't hurt that Thomas had served a subbie tour in the Corps, as well.

Soma sat in the gallery, joined for the afternoon by her friend Quinton, and she held his hand for support as she waited for the verdict. Her large eyes were wide in anticipation, but she caught his gaze and flashed him a brilliant smile. He felt Merje's hand brush against him, and he looked back toward the presiding officer.

Brigadier Korolev stared down at him from the raised dais. He'd asked few questions during both lawyers' statements, and seemed quite comfortable with the responses.

"I've heard the arguments for and against your actions, and I've reviewed your service record," the brigadier said. "What I see does not impress."

Thomas felt like he'd been slapped. He heard a quick breath from Merje beside him. Korolev continued, his tone sharpening.

"What started as a promising career has, in my opinion, degraded into a self-centered mediocrity that is becoming a drain on the Astral Force." He looked down at an info-pad. "Your command tour in *Rapier* was checkered at best, and your service on the staff of EF 15 proved unequivocally that you lack the experience and maturity to rise higher in the ranks. The shameful mess that is the current state of research in the *Armstrong* only adds to your recent record of negligence. In this time of heightened military tensions, the Astral Force needs only the best and brightest in positions of leadership. You, Mr. Kane, have not demonstrated your worth to be counted among them.

"I see no alternative but to revert you to the last posting you held in which you displayed true excellence," the brigadier continued. "Perhaps there you will rediscover your dedication to the State. I hereby find you guilty of negligence leading to a strategic weakening of Terra. I sentence you to demotion of one rank and assign you to the command of a platoon in the Astral Corps, as the relevant commander sees fit.

"Bailiff, replace the defendant's rank insignia." He slammed his gavel down. "This hearing is closed."

Thomas leaned forward, resting his hands against the table. He vaguely heard shuffling as the few observers behind him started to move. A pair of highly polished boots came into view before him. He looked up.

"Sir, your rank insignia, please." The bailiff, a highly decorated chief petty officer, stared at him stonily. He held a pair of fresh epaulettes in his hand.

Thomas couldn't move. He couldn't even lift his hands to remove his own epaulettes.

"You do it, Chief."

The bailiff hesitated for a moment, frowning, but then moved efficiently to unhook and remove the epaulettes with two bars and a star, and replace them with the single bar of sublieutenant. Thomas glanced at them, fighting down the urge to throw up. Beside him, Merje began packing her devices into her leather bag.

She noticed his stare, her delicate features furrowing.

"That was strange," she muttered.

Strange? He straightened. "Strange? My career was destroyed on trumped up charges, and all you can say is 'strange?'"

Her expression hardened. "Well it was," she protested. "I had a solid case, outlining your exemplary service, and I presented it well." She turned to watch the retreating forms of the prosecution. "This was just a hearing too. Preliminary proceedings don't usually result in convictions." She fell silent.

"Usually?" he echoed. "What *should* have happened? You said this was just a formality."

She gestured impatiently, and his anger swelled.

"Well, it should have been," she replied. "Somehow we ended up with a flag officer who had an axe to grind." She gave him a withering stare. "God knows we've run into some crazy officers in the corps."

He just stared, knowing exactly what she meant. Katja had been missing for a week, and he wondered if her disappearance had compromised Merje's professionalism. He studied her in a different light, noted her sharp, pretty face, her smooth willowy figure, her stylish clothes and accessories. For so long he'd seen a willing Katja substitute. Now all he saw was the product of a sick society.

"You are nothing like your sister."

She scoffed slightly. "Amen." She nodded past him. "Now go comfort your wife before she figures out what a naughty boy you've been."

He turned away. The gallery was nearly empty, and Soma nestled against Quinton, her face buried in his shoulder. The Jovian dandy patted her shoulder comfortingly, then stared daggers at Thomas.

He strode over, letting his anger channel toward aggression.

"Get your hands off my wife, you little shit," he growled, his voice low, "or they'll need to hold another hearing, into the cause of your painful death." Quinton recoiled in shock, but in so doing did indeed release Soma.

Thomas crouched down next to her. She noticed him through teary eyes and gripped his hands. Her reaction seemed a little much, and he wondered idly what extra substances she might have enjoyed with lunch.

"Darling, it's okay," he said, calming his tone. "I'm not going to jail or anything, and I'm still in the service."

She stared at his new rank, and there was horror in her eyes.

"But-but... he only demoted you one rank," she said," her voice small. "You should be a *lieutenant*."

He looked again at the single bars on his shoulders, and sighed. "Lieutenant commander was just an appointment, not a rank," he explained, his heart sinking. "Officially I was still a lieutenant, so this is one rank down."

"But you'll have to start all over again!"

Her blunt observations weren't helping his mood.

"Let me worry about that," he said. "Let's just go home."

She sniffled and squeezed his hands again, but then rose. Quinton fired some scathing remark at Merje as she passed, but she was reading her Baryon and probably didn't hear. Thomas rested Soma's arm in his and led her out of the hearing room.

Out in the broad corridor, military and civilian personnel carried out their daily business with anonymous efficiency. Thomas was about to tell Quinton to get lost for the day when he noticed a large trooper approaching them. Thomas stopped suddenly.

"Sergeant Chang."

The former strike leader from *Rapier* nodded respectfully.

"Sublieutenant Kane," he said in a carefully controlled tone. "I have orders for you to join the basic strike leader course, in which I'm an assistant instructor." He handed over a pad, which had a posting message displayed on the screen.

"This course has already started," Thomas observed.

"Yes, sir," Chang replied. "You're to accompany me immediately to Astral Base One, to join your classmates there."

"What... now?" Thomas glanced at his wife, and at his own dress uniform.

"Yes, sir."

This was too much. "Sergeant, I'm having a challenging day. I think before I start a new training course, I should be allowed to pack and... and get my bearings."

Chang's expression didn't waver. "I sympathize, sir, but my orders are clear. And with respect, so are yours."

Soma squeezed his arm more tightly. "What's going on?" He

looked down at her. His mercurial wife was in no state to deal with Astral politics.

"Nothing, darling. Just a bit of confusion that I have to sort out. Sergeant Chang used to work for me on *Rapier*, and I have to go with him for a few hours. Why don't you go home and get some rest. I won't be long."

Her eyes moistened, but he recognized them immediately as stage tears. She wasn't stupid—though she apparently thought he was.

"Oh darling," she said, throwing herself against him. "Hurry home soon."

He kissed her head and gave her a gentle embrace. "I will, my love."

He handed her over to the waiting Quinton and followed Chang. The entrance to the space elevator complex was only a short walk away.

He didn't know how many times he'd taken the ride from Astral HQ up to the big orbiting base, but it seemed to Thomas that the elevator car was moving particularly slowly that day. He stood apart from his new course mates—a mix of junior officers and mid-level troopers—and stared out the window at the surface of the Earth as it fell away beneath him.

Chang had somehow produced a set of green Corps coveralls and black boots that fit Thomas well enough, and asked him politely but firmly to change into the standard course rig. The coveralls sported a Strike qualification pin, but Thomas hadn't bothered transferring his Line qualification pin or his command star from his dress uniform. He just couldn't summon the energy to explain to this group of students—who had greeted him with mild curiosity and basic courtesy—why, with two trade badges and a command on his record, he was a thirty-eight-year-old sublieutenant.

He'd called Admiral Chandler, and managed to get him on the line, but his mentor had been firm in his inaction. Although he was surprised by the verdict, and somewhat sympathetic to Thomas's situation, there was no way he could overrule a decision made within a Fleet Marshall Investigation. Yet the Chandler he knew had no fear of bureaucratic procedures. No, it was clear that the admiral, like everyone else, was keeping his head down and hoping this investigation had claimed its final victim.

With a sigh, Thomas lifted his gaze away from the Earth and toward the looming mass of Astral Base One. Out among the spars he could just make out the arrowhead shape of the *Armstrong*, tiny in her berth next to one of the massive Astral cruisers. He shook his head at the irony, thinking of how he'd planned to use the little science vessel as a stepping stone to get himself into command of a warship, just like that cruiser.

Now Breeze was in command of *Armstrong*, and he was a sublieutenant on his way back to the mud. At least he could recognize when he was beaten, though. Astral politics were far more devious than he'd thought, and apparently he didn't have what it took.

He glanced over at the scattered group of fellow students. They were all from the Corps, officers and troopers, ranging in age from a subbie who looked in her mid-twenties to a sergeant in his late forties. A few chatted among themselves, but most were quietly focused on their thoughts.

None of them were trying to chat up their instructors, or present themselves as the best and the brightest. They were just professional soldiers, looking to improve their skills. He remembered when the world had been that simple to him, when all that had mattered to him was being good at his job.

Maybe Korolev was right, after all.

The elevator docked without incident, and Thomas joined the rest of the students as they followed Chang and the other instructor into the depths of Astral Base One. Thomas had seen the inside of the station many times, but some of the younger troopers looked around with youthful interest. Some of these guys had probably been in the mud for the better part of the past decade—a tour of the Fleet would be quite a novelty.

The path they followed was surprisingly familiar to Thomas,

and it wasn't long before he realized that they were being led to the very spar at which the *Armstrong* was berthed. His heart sank when the head instructor paused at the Research ship's airlock tunnel, and briefly explained how they were going on board for a tour of the engineering spaces. Feeling sick, he tucked in behind the tallest trooper and hoped no one on board would notice him.

Was Breeze behind this cruel, final slap in the face?

They were met on board by the acting executive officer, Sublieutenant Smith. While she was speaking, the lead instructor and the *Armstrong* duty guard sorted out the security necessities of bringing the group on board. Amanda looked exhausted, but she put on a good show of welcoming the group.

She explained that the ship was in a bit of disarray, but that the engineering staff had prepared a thorough tour. He stuck close behind the big trooper, torn between a strong desire to hide and the urge to help his young colleague. She was a year senior to Jack, he knew, but that hardly made her qualified to run a warship.

She turned to depart, and he decided to stick anonymously with his class. Chang placed a strong hand on his shoulder, slowing him down.

"Sir, can you come with me, please?"

He turned in surprise. "Where now, Sergeant?"

"This way, sir."

He'd given up questioning, and followed along in silence as the rest of the students headed aft down the passageway toward engineering. Amanda was still visible up ahead and he watched as she disappeared into the main lab. That was no surprise, but curiosity turned to confusion when Chang activated the lab doors, and entered behind her.

The room was deserted except for Amanda. Thomas's eyes immediately went to the central deck area, and he was amazed at how little evidence remained of the violence. The usual clutter of equipment was piled against the bulkheads to his left, and except for the eerie lack of crew, everything appeared to be normal.

Amanda looked up, noted Chang and then spotted Thomas.

"XO!" she gasped. He stepped forward and squeezed her shoulder with a little smile.

"I think that's your title now, Amanda." He looked expectantly at Chang. "Would you like to explain what's going on, Sergeant?" Any response, however, was interrupted by the lab doors swishing open once again.

Jack burst in. "Okay, that torpedo's loaded but I still don't—" He stopped dead as he spotted Thomas. "Sir, you're back!"

Thomas nodded at his epaulettes. "You don't have to call me 'sir' anymore, Jack."

The pilot looked closer, his eyes widening. "Oh my God, what happened?" He realized the absurdity of his question as soon as it passed his lips, and he reddened slightly, mumbling an apology.

Thomas turned his eyes back to Chang.

"What's next, Sergeant?" he asked, emboldened by the sheer absurdity of the situation. "Will Helena Grey be joining us?"

Chang had removed a small device from one of his pockets and placed it on the nearest workstation. With a tap he activated it, and the power in the lab dimmed for a fraction of a second.

"This is a stealth field," he explained simply. "It will hide everything that happens in this room, starting with an overwrite of the last two minutes of the security cams. This meeting never happened—is that understood?"

Though it really wasn't, Thomas nodded. He heard affirmative sounds from the two subbies. Chang produced a holographic ID, and displayed it briefly.

"I'm with Special Forces, and we are in a state of emergency," he said, as if that explained anything. "We require your full and immediate cooperation."

Katja took a deep breath of the hot, dry air and enjoyed the feel of the light wind through her newly shorn halo of hair. She knew that it wasn't wise to keep her helmet off for long, but as the powerful drugs of the combat cocktail started to take effect, she felt the urge to experience reality in its full vitality, one last time.

Standing on the roof of what appeared to be nothing more than one of the many hotels in the central core, she had a perfect view of Lake Sapphire. Sunlight sparkled off the blue water from a cloudless sky, obscuring the dozens of boats plying their leisurely route across the man-made expanse. The boardwalk eight stories below her was busy with pedestrians enjoying the day, and on the far shore she could see the first of the Army units moving into position on the Astral College parade grounds, preparing for a scheduled demonstration.

The space elevator cables stretched upward as always, acting like a series of gigantic pointers that gave her a visual reference to Astral Base One and the assets poised high above.

She glanced back at a small, gray, capped pipe that poked only a few centimeters above the surface of the roof. Inside was a direct line to Korolev in the command center, eight stories and two basements below her. Unlike any communication device she'd ever used before, it was designed to amplify the Cloud-link between operatives.

<Brigadier. All quiet,> she said.

<Roger. Stay sharp.> It was strange enough to hear another person's voice in her head, but through the amplifier his tone was utterly flat. It was like speaking to a dead man, she thought.

A time check confirmed that Breeze's Baryon was blaring away as she made her way via cab to the public docks at the end of the boardwalk, off to the right. Katja looked again at the boats floating near the docks, and tried to guess which one held the Centauri agent. Breeze had agreed to meet Kit Moro at the docks at 17:00. That timing, Katja suspected, was no coincidence.

She closed her eyes, stilling her mind and sorting the links between the diverse aspects of what was likely to occur. The Centauris had figured out how to create jump gates on a planet's surface, much akin to the Special Forces jump suits. However, if they could send warships through, despite the presence of a gravity well, that could be catastrophic. And if the plan was to do so today, they had to be stopped.

Working with a number of special forces operatives, Koralev had sorted through a variety of scenarios, trying to cover as many eventualities as possible. The real trick, he'd explained, was to prepare defenses without alerting any Centauri agent who might be scanning Terran communications. They would cancel whatever they had planned, leaving the Astral Force once again utterly unprepared.

No one could be trusted. *Been there, done that*, Katja thought. A lake seemed an odd place to open a gate, she mused, but then she remembered that many of the Centauri war machines didn't require a solid surface on which to operate.

Her father's Army unit was scheduled to perform a demonstration to the Astral College student body. Special Forces had ensured that the ammunition supplied to the Army was real, although no one knew that yet.

Thanks to Jack Mallory, the one Astral platform capable of pinpointing a tiny Centauri jump gate was *Armstrong*. The CO, Breeze, wasn't on board, having come ashore. No one else had been granted the command-level authority to direct the ship's sensors, but they had snuck a Corps sublieutenant on board, thus ensuring that a competent commander would be in place.

In the process Thomas Kane's career had been destroyed. His demotion was a part of the public record, and given the secrecy with which this mission had to be conducted, under the auspices of the Special Forces, there would be no going back. But the security of Terra was at stake, and no single individual was too important to sacrifice. She was living proof of that ideal.

Chang reported that all orbital assets were in place.

She took one last breath of hot, dry air and donned her helmet. The visor slipped down and encased her in the extra-dimensional suit. Unrestricted movement would be essential. Her *official* role was to observe Centauri movements and provide on-scene direction, but she had another objective—one which came directly from Korolev.

She was going to find that bastard Kit Moro, and take him down.

There was a cool breeze coming off the lake, though Kete hardly noticed it as he maneuvered his rented boat alongside the public docks. The blue water sparkled in the brilliant sunlight, but all he saw was a reduction in visibility. Careful to keep his movements smooth and casual, he scanned the light crowds moving along the boardwalk.

As idyllic as the scene was, Kete was tense, his senses on high alert. Everything had been going according to plan. Agents were in place at various locations on Earth, equipment delivered and timings confirmed. His own crew had carried out their tasks efficiently and in complete anonymity.

Then Price had gone missing.

One of the support agents, he had departed Abeona through the personal jump gate, but had never returned to Longreach. His internal tracking beacon had gone silent, suggesting that his body, had he been killed, was nowhere to be found. If he wasn't on Earth, then he had to be back home. But he wasn't.

Absolutely nothing unusual had appeared in the Terran security network. No mention whatsoever in the Astral or Army networks. He found it difficult to believe that the Terrans could capture a Centauri agent without *something* making it into the official channels—the Terrans simply weren't that sophisticated that they could bury something without a trace.

That had left the disconcerting possibility that the jump gates didn't work as well as they had been told. The results could be catastrophic, considering the operation that was about to begin. Yet without a tangible reason to abort, they had to proceed. There were too many moving parts in place. Such an opportunity might never again become possible.

Thus his orders were unchanged, and they were clear.

Proceed.

The two-seat motor launch bumped up against the dock, losing the last of its momentum. Kete quickly tied off the bow and stern lines and stepped ashore. He forced himself not to look out toward the middle of the lake, to where a one-meter buoy floated just above the surface of the rippling waves. On it rested a larger version of the bronze horseshoe that he'd used for personal jumps. Within that, he knew, slumbered a gateway to hell.

He paused on the dock, closing his eyes in a show of appreciating the beautiful weather, but in fact casting his mind out one more time, searching the Terran security net for any sign of alert, any unusual activity. There was no change to the number of police on the nearby streets, nor any modification to their routine patrols. The Astral Force headquarters was on normal security alert, and the only Army unit anywhere near Longreach was the storm banner currently in the process of setting up a demonstration at the Astral College. That had been planned for months.

He'd eavesdropped on the Army circuit for a while as he sailed out to the center of the lake, but the chatter had consisted of the routine, almost bored exchanges of seasoned soldiers getting ready for an exercise. Kete had even gone so far as to stretch out to the orbital communication network, just in case there were any unplanned warship movements. All vessels were at stationary alongside Astral Base One, and no orders had been issued over the past few days.

The only ship that might have concerned him, the *Armstrong* with her specialized sensors, had been neutered thanks to a Terran purge. An unqualified sublieutenant was running the show in orbit, and the new captain was here on the surface and heading his way.

As he withdrew his mind from orbital movements, he picked up Breeze's Baryon radiating continuously as she arrived on the boardwalk. He looked up and spotted her easily in her duty uniform, walking among the civilian pedestrians. It was unusual for her to stay in uniform once out of the base, but he'd convinced her that for today's date it would be fun for her to show off her new rank and position.

His real target, though, was the standard-issue pistol on her belt.

Remembering that he was supposed to be in love with this woman, he waved to her and strode up the dock to greet her with a quick but intimate kiss. She restrained herself, as a uniformed servicewoman should in public, but the emotion in her luminous eyes was unmistakable.

"So," she said, starting to stroll along the dock back toward the boats, "I assume you've brought a vessel worthy of carrying me?" Her tone was light, but even so Kete had to fight down the disdain. Her face was so fresh and young—far too young to be flanked by the four silver bars of a captain in the military. She'd even pinned the star of command to her tunic, above her single medal.

Well, she could have her moment of fun.

"Oh, I think even you'll be impressed, madame," he replied with equal humor. They strolled along in the brilliant sunshine and gentle breeze. Overall visibility and weather were well within limits.

Stopping alongside his rented boat, he made a grand gesture. "Captain Brisebois, your command awaits."

She eyed the launch with her best haughty expression, then gave him a regal nod.

"You have done well, sir."

He gave her a quick kiss—which she returned a bit more passionately this time, holding him tight with one arm—and then invited her to board. Grasping his proffered hand she stepped aboard and settled comfortably into the far seat as he untied the lines and pushed off. Activating the engines, he steered them quietly away from the dock. The boat churned through the water as light wind and spray freshened the air around them.

He glanced at his watch.

Ten minutes to go.

He wanted to be on the far side of the lake when Judgement Day arrived. The thought caused him to smile. In the next thirty minutes, the core of Terra's infrastructure would be destroyed, and he was *personally* going to supervise the destruction of Astral Force Headquarters.

Pushing open the throttles, he grinned at Breeze.

31

Jack felt the old pit of excitement in his gut as he fastened the straps over his space suit. It seemed an age since he'd piloted a Hawk, but the mixture of fear and anticipation that churned within him suddenly seemed like an old friend. He glanced back over his right shoulder.

"You ready to go?"

Amanda was white in the seat. Staring at her console, helmet already fastened but faceplate up, she took a deep breath.

"How the *hell* do you stay so calm?"

He was tempted to make some wisecrack about combat experience, but then he remembered how, not that long ago, he would have been ready to soil himself in this sort of situation. He wondered if he'd been just as pale before his first real combat mission, and tried to recall the advice he'd been given.

"Just focus on your job," he said, damping down his enthusiasm. "Keep a close watch on the sensors, and find me that jump gate signature. We're just doing a routine surface delivery—down and back."

She turned her head to fix him with a penetrating gaze.

"If it was routine we'd be taking the elevator. We're going to be a man-made meteor over one of the biggest cities on Earth, with an atmospheric velocity greater than an emergency crash landing. With our beacon off, we'll be prime targets for paranoid aerial sentries who'll get all of a bunch of nanoseconds to visually identify us before they shoot."

He smiled. "Don't go all scientific on me. I just drive the bus."

She laughed slightly, the intensity of her gaze lessening.

"How many times have you done this?"

"What, a high-speed atmo entry?" He thought for a moment, counting down on several fingers, then smiled brightly. "Once."

"I'm really glad you're so confident."

"Hell, yeah," he replied. "When we get back this evening I'll even help you prep for your thesis defense."

She laughed again. "I look forward to that."

Lowering the faceplate of his suit helmet and locking down, Jack turned back to his checklist and scanned through the PLANETARY portion. He remembered that flying "in atmo" was akin to trying to walk underwater, and that the Hawk would be sluggish in its responses. Airspace over Longreach was likely to be crowded, too, but he figured by the time they launched he wouldn't have to worry much about civilian craft.

Besides, at the speed he'd be going, everything would draw left and right anyway. They'd be crazy not to.

He keyed the special, secure circuit Sergeant Chang had provided both him and Thomas.

"Apollo, this is Eagle-One. Radio-check, over."

"*This is Apollo, roger, over.*" Thomas's reply came from the lab. He glanced at his console to remind himself of the callsign of the cruiser *Admiral Bowen*, berthed aft of *Armstrong* on the spar. "This is Eagle-One, roger, break. Windmill, this is Eagle-One. Radio-check, over."

The response from *Bowen* was equally smart, and Jack wondered just how many people were closed up on the cruiser's massive bridge. Considering how few people aboard *Armstrong* even knew the bird was manned and ready, he imagined *Bowen*'s bridge being nearly deserted. That seemed like an awful lot of people, entirely in the dark, but then again, he'd never done a Special Forces operation before.

"All units this is Eagle-One." The excitement in his gut returned. "Entering airlock and standing by for launch."

* * *

Katja crouched on the rooftop, watching the swift motor launch blaze a white path across the calm blue surface. She'd tracked Breeze's Baryon down to the docks, and had zoomed her vision to maximum magnification to catch sight of her quarry. Sure enough, she'd just been able to make out the man who'd greeted Breeze with a kiss and taken her down to his waiting boat. They'd cast off quickly enough, and were moving at speed across the lake.

Scanning the far shoreline, she tried to guess their destination. That side of the water was lined with skyscrapers of the commercial district. Were the Centauris planning some kind of cyber-attack on Terra's financial infrastructure? She signaled her observation and hypothesis to Korolev at the command center below.

He acknowledged but didn't comment.

The temptation to enter the Bulk and chase after Kit Moro burned within her, but she forced herself to remain calm and stationary. Her orders were to observe and report. The Centauris were nothing if not devious—for all she knew Moro was purposefully trying to draw their attention away on a red herring.

Another glance at her watch.

Thirty seconds to 17:00.

She cast her gaze around the lakefront one more time, then closed her eyes and tuned in to the electronic noise—into the Cloud—all around her. Civilian traffic was normal. Security chatter was minimal. Astral circuits were—

An electronic scream exploded in her mind.

Piercing white light blinded her inner vision. She instinctively covered her ears and ripped her eyes open, vaguely aware that she was on her back on the hard rooftop. The pain faded as she rolled onto all fours. She tried to refocus, but her mind refused to reach out to the Cloud again. Staggering to her feet, she looked out toward the lake.

To her right, one of the 30-floor government buildings on the waterfront exploded outward from its middle stories. The blast wave rolled past her a moment later, followed quickly by the dull roar. The next building to the left shattered an instant later, and she recognized the explosion pattern caused by a projectile, rather than a static, planted bomb.

Someone was *shooting* at the buildings.

She stared out at the lake, looking for any telltale puffs of smoke from one of the many boats. Kit Moro's launch was barely visible as it dropped speed on the far side of the lake, white wake fading away to a ripple as he maneuvered. She zoomed in, watching for any sort of movement indicating a weapon.

The roar of another explosion tore her gaze back to the panorama, and she watched in horror as a third building erupted, then a fourth.

People ran pell-mell in all directions as burning pieces fell from shattered towers, flames leaping skyward through columns of thick, black smoke. The entire waterfront on that side of the lake was ablaze, debris scattered and burning across the boardwalk and docks. Two more explosions tore through buildings a block inland, the blasts smashing windows on the surrounding towers.

She looked back out at the lake. All movement had stopped, resulting in an eerie tableau of horrified onlookers on their tiny pleasure craft. Then, amidst the sudden stillness, she saw the ripple of air just above the water—caught sight of the puffs of vapor and spray of surface water that revealed supersonic movement.

She'd seen a ripple in the air like that before.

She forced her mind back into the Cloud. Blocking herself from the blinding light and deafening noise of the Astral network, she focused solely on feeling her way to Korolev.

<Brigadier!>

<Katja. What do you see?> His "voice" was very faint, nearly drowned out by the noise that pressed against her.

<Centauri jump gate, open over the lake. Heavy fire through the gate. Government buildings being destroyed. Can't access network.>

<Astral network is being jammed,> he said.

Katja pulled back for a moment, unable to bear the light and noise of the jamming. Focusing her eyes back on the lake, she saw the ripple again. Sunlight flashed off a silvery object, then another.

Then more. In the time it took her to draw a breath, the air over the lake was flooded with small, fast, silver flying machines. The swarm grew as more and more poured through the pulsing jump gate. The giant cloud of robots seemed to pause for a moment, swirling over the lake, before spontaneously darting outward as each machine cleared the water and swooped down on the city.

Each machine opened fire with short-range energy weapons. She threw herself down as bolts struck indiscriminately all around her. She heard the crash of crumbling facades, of screaming far below her. Crawling up to look again, she realized that the war she'd fought in Sirius and Centauria had followed her home.

Anger lit inside her, fueled her. As she quickly assessed the situation she embraced the anger, and felt a remarkable calm.

<Centauri swarm robots over the lake. Full attack underway.>

She had to strain to understand Korolev's response.

<Can you see the Army units at the college?>

Zooming her vision over the Astral College grounds, she saw lots of abandoned equipment, but no soldiers.

<Cowards have run away.>

<They think they're unarmed,> he countered <With military comms jammed, we can't explain.>

She cast her gaze over the grounds again, spotting slight movement among the weaponry and behind the buildings. So maybe the Army weren't such pussies after all. She could just imagine her father standing over the soldiers, daring any one of them to try to run from danger.

He might be a bastard, but he wasn't a coward.

<I'll try to contact them another way.>

<Be careful. Centauris will be watching other circuits.>

She reached tentatively into the Cloud again, focusing on civilian communication circuits and staying clear of military channels. Searching, searching, she found the network that carried Baryon signals, and drilled down into it to isolate the number of Storm Banner Leader Emmes.

Would he answer in a situation like this?

Only if he thought the caller could help him.

Discarding any thought that he'd pick up for his daughter, even if she had been missing for over a week, she scanned the database for a title that sounded official. Hoping he was as addicted to his device as every normal human seemed to be, she signaled under the identity of "Territorial Command."

The line rang. Then, amidst the din of background rumbling and urgent shouting, she heard the Voice.

"Hello?"

She stopped herself, remembering that the Centauris had probably bugged the entire network. She needed a simple code that he'd be sure to understand. Then she smiled slightly. What better code than a language like no other in history, spoken by less than two million humans and only on Earth itself?

"Storm Banner Leader," she said in rapid Finnish, "this is Astral Special Forces. Your entire storm banner is armed with live ammunition. Engage the Centauri swarm."

There was a pause, during which she could hear scuffling.

"Say again?" he said in English.

She repeated her message, staying in Finnish, then added, "Terra is under attack. All military comms are down. Your unit is the only one in a position to respond. Engage the Centauri swarm."

"Understood," he replied in their native tongue. "Wait one."

She opened her eyes and watched the silvery machines circling in chaotic patterns, covering the area around the jump gate as larger Centauri flying units began to appear. Lumbering in flight she recognized these silver beasts—AARs, or anti-armor robots. More than two dozen had appeared during her brief conversations. Already they were forming up and moving toward Astral Headquarters and the irreplaceable space elevators.

Then, from the quiet grounds of the Astral College, a single trail of smoke rocketed upward and exploded among the outer, smaller machines. The swarm scattered, but several machines dropped like charred stones toward the water far below.

The Voice came through her Baryon link, still in Finnish.

"You say we're fully loaded?"

"All the way down to emergency spares," she confirmed. "Stop those bastards."

"Roger that."

A hail of fire burst forth from one section of the College grounds, and explosions ripped through the cloud of invaders. Some tumbled downward, but others broke off and closed the source of the fire even as the massed AARs launched missiles at the revealed Army position. Katja watched in grim despair as the College grounds were chewed up by enemy fire.

The thunder of the Centauri barrage ceased. The AARs hovered, holding position over the lake and watching as the swarm moved around them. Thick smoke hung over the cratered remains of the College playing fields. Katja could just make out the dim walls marking the school boundary, and she saw glimpses of the tortured shapes of the nearest buildings beyond.

Half the city was obscured by the smoke and ash billowing up from the lakeside destruction, the only significant wind caused by the movement of the invading swarm, and the AARs as they began to sail toward Astral Headquarters.

Katja tried to send a signal to Korolev. The interference in the Cloud was too great even for her to focus a thought, forcing her to retreat. She watched as one of the burning towers to her right crumbled on its foundations, collapsing in a new wave of destruction across the waterfront. She could hear distant sirens from the streets, but she sensed no coordinated effort. In every direction below her, civilians ran past abandoned cars and burning buildings.

Longreach was ablaze. Suddenly a new thought occurred.

How many other Terran cities are under attack?

From the College, the smoke was pierced by dozens of projectiles lancing upward. Each lance was splintered as the swarm machines countered with energy weapons that picked off the Army attack. The AARs turned almost lazily and dropped another deadly salvo of rockets into the burning maelstrom.

Katja pursed her lips in frustration. The Army were fighting back, but randomly. They couldn't see their foes well enough, and they couldn't communicate with one another. She looked beyond the billowing wall of smoke toward the space elevators. Her father and his apes were all that stood between Astral Headquarters and destruction. This was no time for interservice rivalry.

She slipped into the Bulk, body turned toward the College. She pushed her suit to full speed in the twilight grayness of the fourth dimension, sighing with relief as her 3-D mapping program activated and gave her visual cues for the area. In her virtual view the College wall and buildings still stood proud, and no fire or smoke obscured her vision. She watched the flat image of the lake as it raced by beneath her, and sized up the best place to re-enter the brane once across.

<Katja.> The voice in her head was slow, almost robotic.

<Here. Who is that?>

After a pause, <Korolev. Only Bulk comms work.>

The simulated image of the lakeshore swept past beneath her feet, and she began to descend. She knew enough about graviton communication to know that it was slow. Her suit had to receive the stream of graviton waves in sequence, and then decode them. Extra words weren't appreciated.

<Helping Army,> she said. <Going in.>

<Space units striking.>

<Roger.>

At least the orbital part of her plan was working. If they could close the jump gate it would cut off reinforcement. Now she could focus on stopping the Centauris already here.

32

Thomas slammed his fist down on the console in the empty lab. All the magnificent sensors in the galaxy didn't help him if he couldn't speak to Astral Command.

Armstrong's finely tuned gravimetric instruments had quickly pinpointed the dark-energy concentration in the middle of Longreach, but a complete failure of the communications network left him deaf and mute, other than the Special Forces link directly to Jack's Hawk.

"Fucking comms are down, Sergeant," he spat. "What am I going to do—run next door to tell *Bowen* where to fire?"

His only response was silence. He looked over his shoulder to where Chang had stood, not seconds before, then scanned quickly around the room. He was alone.

The air in front of him shimmered slightly, and a crackling whisper broke the silence. Amidst the shimmer he saw a tiny, distant image of Chang. He tried to focus on it but it grew larger— or closer—even as he blinked and tried to clear his vision. When he could finally see clearly, Chang stood before him.

"Show me the jump gate location, sir," the man said through a transparent sheen over his face. Thomas pointed it out on his screen, highlighting the exact three-dimensional position.

"I've lost all comms, except with our Hawk."

"You'll lose that link soon, too." Chang didn't take his eyes off the screen. "Get the Hawk started on its run."

There was no time for questions. He keyed the Special Forces link.

"Eagle-One, Apollo: stand-by for final attack coordinates." He transmitted the last update from *Armstrong*'s passive sensors. "Confirm, go for strike?"

"*This is Eagle-One*," Jack's garbled voice responded. "*I am go for strike.*"

"Eagle-One, execute."

"*Wilco.*"

With no active sensors to track the Hawk, Thomas could only trust that his young pilot knew what he was doing from here. He turned back to Chang.

"How do I talk to *Bowen*?"

Chang was still studying the screen. "I will, sir. There's a Centauri invasion force near the Astral College—can you pinpoint them?"

Thomas stared at his display, which was set up for dark-energy detection over a standard map of Longreach. He thought quickly—what would the Centauri robots be emitting that was easy to track? He stabbed at his controls and overlaid infra-red on the screen. Red-hot plumes burst into view on three sides of the lake, massive regions of intense heat in stark contrast to the cool, dark water. He zoomed in on the south shore, noting the tiny dots of boats on the lake and a few swift cars fleeing along the streets.

There! A formation of white-hot pinpricks moving southward past the College. He zoomed in further, and the formation was surrounded by a haze of heat tracers. Swarm defense around the heavies. Their initial target appeared to be Headquarters. He motioned to Chang.

"Here, the main attack units are probably AARs, judging from their altitude, and they're guarded by swarm-bots."

Chang nodded. "Roger, sir. Stand by."

The sergeant stepped back. The same, weird, crackling whisper broke the air and he shrunk out of sight in a shimmer so subtle Thomas wouldn't have seen it, had he not been looking right at it. He stared at the empty air for a long moment, then forced his eyes back to the screen.

The resolution of the Research sensor info was extraordinary. He wished *Rapier* had been kitted out like this.

Seconds later, the crackling whisper indicated Chang's return—from wherever he'd gone.

"Sir, the Centauri are moving over a residential area. We're going to try and get them over the College before opening fire."

Thomas glanced back at the screen. The heat sources were already south of the College grounds. He turned back to Chang.

"And what if you can't?"

"Then a lot of people are going to die."

Katja paused in the silent grayness of the Bulk.

Korolev had said her life as an Operative wouldn't be glamorous, but she hadn't expected it to be so short. There was no time for thought, however. She had to act on instinct.

She exited the Bulk.

Her stomach churned as she fell to the ground, knees buckling on impact. She tumbled to the soft dirt and rolled, forcing her hands out to stop the movement. She slid several meters and came to rest on her back.

The sky was gray and close above her, and she realized she was in a freshly blown crater. She reached into the Cloud, straining against the chaos to find the Baryon network again. It took only seconds to see that it was useless—the jamming that had started in the military circuits had now spread to every network on Earth. She was going to have to find her father the old-fashioned way.

Scrambling to the lip of the crater, she looked out through the acrid clouds and just made out the dark-green shape of an Army troop carrier. She leapt to her feet and sprinted over the broken ground. Two soldiers watched from hunkered positions at the rear of the carrier, rifles trained on her. She ignored the weapons and crouched down to face them.

"Special Forces," she said. "Where's SBL Emmes?"

They stared at her in shock. Knowing that every second was crucial, she pushed the nearest rifle gently away from her and bypassed the young soldiers. The back of the carrier was open, more soldiers watching the skies and fields. Inside, a pair of medics worked efficiently on the wounded.

A woman stepped forward. "Who are you?"

Katja noticed her rank as storm leader—sort of like sergeant. "Special Forces. Where's SBL Emmes?"

The storm leader pointed to the west. "Next carrier. What the fuck's going on?"

"Centauri invasion. The ammo's my treat."

If the storm leader had anything else to say, Katja missed it as she sprinted once more over the broken ground, scanning through the clouds for the next troop carrier. She retracted her faceplate, and nearly gagged on the acrid stench of burning metal and plastic. Coughing heavily even as she ran, she made out the obvious shape of a carrier and clambered through another crater to reach it.

"Storm Banner Leader!"

There was a clatter of equipment as soldiers brought rifles to bear, but a moment later she saw the stocky, powerful form she knew too well emerge from behind the vehicle, tactical pad in hand. He looked out from under his helmet with stern, focused eyes, and if there was any surprise in his gaze it was hidden well.

She stopped, panting from her run, looking up at him.

He stared back at her, almost appraisingly. His eyes flicked up and down her extra-dimensional suit with some recognition.

"Operative," he said. "What's the situation?"

She closed into him and took the pad from his hand. To her slight surprise, he relinquished it. As expected, it had a digital map of the area, with friendly positions scattered along a line amidst the rubble and the estimated position of the enemy moving south. It tied in with what Korolev had relayed to her from Chang.

"The Centauri force is targeting Headquarters, then the elevators," she said. "We have bombardment assets in orbit, but they can't fire while the enemy is here." She indicated the general region of the city over which the Centauris were just now moving, between the College and Astral HQ. "Air assets are mobilizing to take down the AARs, but they'll never be able to penetrate the swarm defense in time. Our job is to draw the swarm back over our position, so that they can be taken out by orbital bombardment. Air assets will then take the AARs."

"So the Astral Force will bombard our position." Her father looked up from the map, locking on her eyes.

As she stared back, feeling the raw power of his will bearing down on her, she realized that this time, it didn't matter what he thought. There was a mission to accomplish for the survival of the State, and they were all expendable.

"Yes," she replied. "You have your orders, Storm Banner Leader. Inform your troops."

"Yes, ma'am." He nodded without hesitation. "Our comms are jammed. You and I will have to run down the line on foot and inform each position." He pointed at one of his soldiers. "Give the operative your pad." As Katja took the device and looked at the identical map on it, he ran his finger along the north-western half of the line. "You get to these positions, tell them to open fire with everything they have at—" He glanced at his watch. "—minute two-zero. Tell them to keep firing until they run out of ammunition."

He'd assigned himself the part of the line closer to the Centauris, she noticed.

"Yes," she replied, and she started to move, but he grabbed her elbow and leaned in.

"Katja Andreia," he said quietly in Finnish, "when you get to the end of the line, turn around and start back to this position. These kids are going to come under deadly fire and they're going to need your encouragement to keep going. Stop at every position on your way back, and make them proud to die for Terra." He tapped the front of his helmet gently against hers. "Go."

She broke free and started running for the next position on the line, barely hearing the Voice as it barked orders to the troops.

Kete held Breeze's hand as they ran across the main road. Four cars had smashed into each other when their auto-drivers had malfunctioned in the Cloud-burst. Mangled wreckage and body parts littered the asphalt from the terrible collisions. The distant roar of fires was accompanied by the faint wail of dozens of sirens, and the occasional shout or cry of injured and dying victims.

Those still on their feet did little but stand or stagger in shock. He steered clear to not draw attention, and Breeze—bless her—seemed equally uninterested in aiding the wounded. They leaned up against a giant oak tree on the edge of a beautiful city park. Kete glanced back at the devastation unleashed on the city, and for a moment felt a heaviness in his heart. But this carnage was nothing, he reminded himself firmly, compared to the unprovoked and useless slaughter brought down upon his home by these people.

This wasn't invasion. This was revenge.

"Where should we go?" Breeze asked between gasping breaths. He made a show of looking all around.

"The attack seems to be focused west of us," he said. "This area hasn't been hit—I think we're good for now."

She nodded, crouching down to sit on the thick roots at their feet. Her uniform was disheveled, hat and shoes long since abandoned, but she still carried herself with confidence. Breeze might enjoy the games, but at her core she was rock-solid and determined to survive. He may have been mistaken before. In other circumstances, he might actually have liked her.

He surveyed the park that lay before them. Broad fields of neatly trimmed grass were dissected by winding paths fringed with brilliant flower beds. A few tall trees stood in splendid isolation here and there to break up the sea of grass, but mostly the thirsty giants formed a towering, leafy rim around the "natural" space. Predominantly flat, largely empty, and barely five kilometers away from the space elevators, this park was the perfect staging ground for the real attack to begin.

He adjusted the backpack on his shoulders. The final horseshoe felt heavy after such an extended run from the boat, but he knew his job was nearly done. Scanning the copses of trees that lined the park's border, he spotted the particular grouping toward which he'd been heading.

Six trees stood close together, their smallish trunks weaving upward and dividing to create a tiny clearing that was, due to the rambling shrubs around it, well-hidden on three sides and wide open on the fourth. It was the ideal spot to activate the horseshoe and open the jump gate for the Second Centauri Army that waited on Abeona.

He crouched down next to Breeze, kissing her tenderly.

"Hey, Breezy. You okay?"

She smiled and rubbed her hand on his knee. "I've had better days. Next time don't feel like you have to do so much to impress a girl. A boat ride would have been enough."

He laughed in genuine surprise. Words actually failed him for a moment.

"How about you?" she asked. "I guess this is just a day at the office for an off-world journalist." She suddenly looked at him strangely. "Hey, why haven't you been filming all this? Isn't this the story of a lifetime?"

The sudden glint of suspicion in her eyes alarmed him, and he noted the location of the pistol still holstered at her waist. He forced a mysterious smile to his lips.

"Who says I haven't?"

Her expression turned to doubt, then turned to comprehension. "So you do have a proper implant, then?"

"You convinced me that I needed to take the plunge," he replied. "But this spot feels too exposed, and I'd like to protect the new equipment while it's still under warranty." He pointed to the copse of trees. "We should find better cover.

"Let me go first," he suggested, making an obvious show of examining the copse. "Although... I can't quite see what's waiting in there." He glanced down at her. "Can I borrow that pistol of yours for a minute?"

Her hand covered the holster, eyes suddenly steel.

"Not a chance."

He shrugged and adjusted his backpack. "Okay, but if you hear me screaming like a schoolgirl you better come running." With that, he started to move away, keeping low.

"Deal."

He tried to stick to a walk, but latent adrenaline and the sheer desire to complete his mission overcame him. He quickened to a light jog and covered the smooth ground in a matter of moments. Once behind the foliage he knelt down and tore open his pack.

The bronze-colored horseshoe was more than twice the size of the ones he'd used earlier, and it would open a much larger gate. Four light years away, a full division of anti-personnel robots stood ready to burst out across this grassy parkland, securing the area for the heavy units and—if the attack went well—occupying forces.

He dropped the horseshoe onto the grass with a thud and began the activation process. Because of its power, he'd been told, it would take nearly five minutes to marshal its energy and open the gate. He looked out between the leaves at the masses of smoke rising into the cloudless sky.

Five minutes, then he would take a single step and return home.

33

Jack's arm muscles burned as he fought to keep the stick under control. The visual was awash in orange as the Hawk slammed through the atmosphere, pushing a super-heated cone of air before it. The view was actually "backward" as the craft descended from orbit with main engines leading the drop on full burn against the orbital velocity, robbing the Hawk of speed and letting Isaac Newton take control.

Although he'd done it before, and he knew the science was sound, he wasn't about to lessen his iron grip on that stick for a moment. There was a reason, he knew, why humans used elevators to get between orbit and the surface—that method had a higher survival rate.

Eventually the pounding eased to a shudder, and the orange air faded from view. Jack checked his radar and found a reasonably clear picture, with most contacts sticking to the standard commercial air lanes. The Hawk dropped below three kilometers before finally slowing enough for him to take positive control.

With the Great Barrier Reef visible below, he hauled the stick to port and vectored his craft toward Longreach. Climbing to ten kilometers he noted the strange silence on all radio circuits. Astral circuits had taken heavy jamming, even before they left orbit, but now it seemed as if *everything* was down.

Radar revealed a pair of contacts that broke away from the lanes and increased speed to intercept him. He doubted even the

Special Forces had a way to tell these sentries what this little Hawk was doing, dropping out of nowhere.

He flicked on his beacon—the omnidirectional, encoded, agile-frequency identifier that would be immediately detected by the sensors on any State vehicle in range. Since it was designed for deep-space use, Jack was pretty sure it was burning through the detectors of every sentry aircraft from here to Vladivostok.

Better than getting shot at, though.

To his relief, the two approaching sentry aircraft veered off and continued their patrol. As the coast of Australia flashed past beneath him, he figured there would be more military units coming into play, so he decided the beacon was a good thing to keep on. Now that the engagement had begun, stealth dropped down his list of priorities.

"Amanda, you got that gate locked up?"

"Just a sec," he heard her say through the suit comms. He didn't glance back, but a moment later he caught her hand in his peripheral, reaching to adjust his hunt controls. "I've lost the feed from *Armstrong*, but I have the last recorded position, and I'm going to tweak your sensors."

The Outback was a ruddy expanse beneath them. On the horizon Jack thought he saw black storm clouds dead ahead. He checked his range and dipped the Hawk into a gentle descent.

"Not much time," he said. "I'm arming the weapon."

"Just wait," she snapped. "I haven't optimized the sensors."

He glanced at his 3-D display. "You have twenty-five seconds."

What he'd thought were storm clouds were actually huge columns of smoke rising vertically until they hit the stratosphere, then diffused across the sky. On the leftmost edge of the column Jack saw the distant, flashing lights of the space elevators.

"Holy shit," he muttered.

"What?" she asked.

"Nothing. Get me that target."

"It's not that easy!"

He pushed the Hawk lower, still aiming for the center of the smoke. He didn't dare turn off his beacon now as he lined up what could only be seen as an attack profile on downtown

Longreach. Fifteen seconds. The first white towers of the suburbs were visible ahead.

"Get me that target, Amanda."

"I'm refining it. Just wait."

"No time. Take your best fucking guess."

The suburbs were below him as the Hawk descended below two kilometers. He confirmed that the torpedo was armed and ready, and that all safeties were off.

"There are two of them," she said.

"What?"

"There are two jump gates!"

The last ridge fell astern, and ahead of them Jack saw the destruction at the core of Earth's gateway city. Black smoke filled the sky over a towering ring of fire. The lake where the jump gate was hidden was barely visible through the growing smog. He glanced at his 3-D display.

"Where's my target?"

Two red symbols appeared in his display. Two, perhaps three kilometers apart. Amanda overlaid the raw sensor feed. One dark-energy gate was steady but the other, smaller one burned with higher intensity, and was growing.

Two targets. One weapon.

"What do we do?" Amanda shouted.

Jack pulled back on the stick and pushed his throttles forward.

Katja reached the last position on the Army line, barely ten seconds before the coordinated start time. As she'd done twenty-one times before, she sprinted toward the soldiers, waving her arms at her sides to indicate the lack of hostility.

As so many other soldiers had done, they stared at her slack-jawed.

"Special Forces," she gasped, thrusting her tactical pad at them. "Train all your weaponry on the enemy position, and begin firing at minute two-zero exactly." She pointed at the mobile air-defense battery, looming to one side of the soldiers' dug-in position. "Start with those. Target the heavies, and then take the swarm-bots with everything you have. Right down to your pistols."

Behind her, the roar of missiles echoed off the College grounds. She glanced at her watch.

It was time.

She stabbed at the missile launcher. "Open fire!" she shouted as best she could. "And keep firing until you have absolutely nothing left. You are the only line of defense for all of Terra—we're all relying on you."

They leapt into action, and she turned to start running back. The thunder of weapons over her head indicated the final position's compliance with her orders. Within twenty seconds she was at the previous group. Their last missile soared up into the smoke even as she approached. The soldiers stood and watched it go.

She ran up and punched the nearest one in the arm. "Get your section weapon up, get your rifles ready. The next thing that's going to happen is the swarm will attack and try to finish us off. Keep firing until every last one of them is down, and then you'll start firing at the AARs."

One soldier looked up from his pad, his expression showing utter disbelief.

"The heavies are out of range."

She moved to stand where the entire section could see her, hands on her hips and feet apart.

"If we don't stop this invasion force, the space elevators are gone. If they're gone, this war is lost. You men are all that stand between us and total defeat. We need you to stand and fight. To the last survivor."

The soldier she'd punched climbed behind the heavy-barreled section weapon and pointed it southwest. He opened fire into the smog.

Katja made it to ten more positions before the swarm descended.

The steady chatter of weapons fire was overcome by a low, buzzing sound that was felt almost as much as it was heard. This particular group of soldiers was using a crater to dig in, and she paused at the lip, drawing her pistol. The constant fire from other positions broke into short, harried bursts. The awful hiss of energy weapons cut through the noise, followed by distant screams. Around her in the crater, the soldiers stopped firing.

She stood up, punching the men on either side of her.

"Whatever you see flying in that smoke, you kill it. Do *not* stop, no matter what." Without waiting for a reply she pulled herself out of the crater and sprinted forward through the smog.

The first swarm-bot was on her in seconds. A silver flash in the smoke above her. Burning heat against the left side of her head. She stumbled and fell, sliding along the rough ground. She lay on her side, gasping as the heat in her helmet faded. She forced her arms and legs to move slightly, to confirm they were still all there.

Reaching up to feel the charred outer surface of her helmet, she figured it was still mostly intact. Thank God the swarm-bot had taken a head-shot—her Bulk-suit wasn't armored, and would never have survived an energy strike like that.

Four more swarm-bots flashed by overhead, bolts of energy streaking from them as they assaulted the next position. Rattling thunder indicated the wall of explosive rounds they flew into, and she saw two robots stagger in flight and crash down in heaps. Screams in the smog indicated the corresponding Terran casualties.

Hauling herself up, she staggered to the next position. Soldiers were sprawled across the ground by their troop carrier. Some struggled to rise but others were immobile, faces burned beyond recognition. The gun on the carrier was warped and melted. One of the section weapons, however, still looked functional. She looked at her tactical pad. At best they'd been able to draw a third of the swarm-bots away from the AARs—not enough to make the heavies vulnerable.

Katja grabbed an abandoned rifle and pulled one of the soldiers to his feet. An ugly burn mark slashed across the breastplate of his armor, but he seemed otherwise unhurt.

"Get on that weapon," she barked. "Start firing at the heavies again."

He stared at her dumbly. She pulled out her tactical pad and shoved it in his face.

"If the swarm-bots aren't attacking you, then you're not enough of a threat. We need them to stay here, on us."

Still he didn't move, his stunned gaze wandering over the

casualties at his feet. She stepped back and pointed the rifle at him.

"Disobey me and you die," she growled. "Get on that gun, and you *might* live. Now move!"

Training appeared to finally kick in, and he climbed up behind the big weapon. He swiveled it back toward the southwest and targeted the distant AARs. A gun of this size, Katja knew, could still cause damage, and would definitely draw fire.

She looked around at the rest of the position. Three more soldiers were at least moving. She hauled them up, one by one, and thrust rifles into their hands. The section weapon began thudding away, heavy slugs punching through the sky.

"Defend this position," she barked. "Stand by for another swarm attack."

The next three positions were in a similar state, but with the initial swarm attack having passed them, they were enjoying a moment of reprieve. By the time she'd finished, though, each one was brazenly firing toward the southwestern horizon. She watched on her pad as more swarm-bots broke away to deal with this nagging threat.

Come on, you bastards.

The crumbling walls of the College boat shed were in sight when she heard the low buzzing return. Flashes of gunfire from the shed windows revealed the intact defenses of that position. Energy beams erupted from the high smog, and she tumbled for cover into a low crater, still ten strides from the building. Staying low, she saw one swarm-bot swoop over with a steady, cutting stream of energy that burned through the thin roof. Another bot lowered on the far side and cast sweeping fire horizontally at the structure. Then a third lowered to a hover, barely off the ground, directly between her and the building.

She stared in awe at its silver, ovoid body, tiny thrusters visible between multiple weapon points and sensors. It was no bigger than her, doubtless relying on speed to avoid being hit, but she'd already seen swarm-bots go down. Now it was hovering before her like a metallic watermelon. She raised her Army rifle and fired.

The burst of explosive rounds punched through the bot's outer hull and detonated among its innards. It crashed to the ground like a dead weight. Katja pushed up to run for the house.

Searing heat struck her from dead ahead, knocking her backward. She gasped as the ground fell away from her feet. Then it slammed up against her back, just as the darkness closed over her.

.

34

Thomas stared at the screen. "Sergeant, look at this."

Chang appeared again at his shoulder. Thomas pointed to the dark energy of the target jump gate, and then at a new reading several kilometers south.

"That looks like another jump gate forming," he said. I don't know where our Hawk is—it should have taken out the first gate by now. But we need to bombard that site."

"We don't think bombardment can destroy a jump gate, sir," Chang replied. "We'll just chew up the land around it."

"Then we need more Hawks. As many as we can muster."

"Astral comms are still down—all I have is *Bowen*."

Thomas turned angrily. "Then get *Bowen* to launch her three Hawks with as many modified torpedoes as they can carry. Secrecy doesn't matter anymore, Sergeant. Bring that fucking cruiser to action stations, and get her moving."

Chang's stoic expression didn't change, but he nodded.

"Yes, sir."

With a crackling shimmer he disappeared into the Bulk. Thomas looked back to his screen. The AARs had stopped their southern progress and were now hovering over a densely populated residential area. Nearly half of the swarm had broken off, and were buzzing angrily over the Astral College. Most likely the AARs didn't want to move too far from their full cover, especially as Terran air assets were even now launching from a base outside of Brisbane. Quick mental math told him that the Terran fighters wouldn't be in range for another five minutes, which gave him exactly that much time to take out the swarm.

He didn't know how the Astral College was drawing so much of the swarm into a targetable area for him, but he wasn't going to question it. But what the hell had happened to his Hawk?

Jack wasn't sure if it was him, Amanda, or the Hawk groaning against the g-forces of the turn, but it was clear the inertial dampeners were failing. With the number of energy shots they'd already taken from the swarm, he was thankful they were still airborne.

Straining his head back to look over his shoulder in the hard-right turn, he caught a glimpse of the blinking elevator lights as they passed through his line of sight. Using them as a visual cue, he eased back on the stick and fought the air currents to line up on a course.

The first gate—his original target—was weakening, and seemed to be collapsing. The second jump gate was still growing, and was already more than twice the size of the first. This had to be his new target, but it meant an attack run right over the Centauri invasion force. The torpedo would be safe a quarter peet in the Bulk, but his Hawk didn't have such stealth abilities. Up ahead, he could clearly see the sunlight flashing off the silver hulls of the enemy.

Amanda tapped his arm. "The new gate is steady in its position, but we can't get close enough to fire."

"Yes we can." He checked his range. "Ten seconds." As he flicked off the safety and assigned the weapon, he heard Amanda frantically tapping at her console.

"We'll fly right into the Centauris!"

He leaned forward against his straps, thumb poised on the release button.

"But the weapon goes first. Just hang on." He heard her gasp, but she shut up as he concentrated on lining up the shot. At this range, this deep into a gravity well, the torpedo wouldn't be able to adjust its course at all. The silver flashes were growing larger ahead. He wondered abstractly what the range was of the swarm's energy weapons.

In range.

Fire.

The Hawk's outer hull banged as the torpedo launched. He just caught a glimpse of it to the left as it shrank away into the Bulk.

Another flash—not silver—flickered in his vision. The Hawk shuddered again. Warning lights began blinking on his console. He punched the throttle forward, locking it as he released his hand to slam against the countermeasures button. Multiple bangs indicated the steady release of chaff and flares as he pulled back on the stick as far as he could before g-forces began to overwhelm him.

The Hawk shuddered again. He began to smell something burning below him. One engine failed. Then a second. He felt the Hawk lean to port and he fought to keep it level. The horizon ahead tilted, then began to spin.

As his vision faded to gray, and then black, he thought abstractly how nice it was to have had Amanda with him. At least now she'd understand.

Katja opened her eyes, saw low smoke wisping through a choked sky. Again checking her limbs, she looked around at where she lay on her back in the crater. She was intact, but the rifle she'd held was a red-hot pile of molten slag on the ground beside her. Listening, she could still hear bursts of automatic fire peppering amidst the constant buzz of the swarm.

Her tactical pad was partially melted and non-functional. Slowly she crawled up to the lip of the crater and looked toward the boat house. The swarm-bot she'd killed still lay in its heap, and she could make out two others crashed in the dirt around the Army position. Gunfire still streamed from the broken windows, and she heard the *ping-ping-crack* in the air behind her that suggested another swarm-bot going down.

The Army apes were tough, she admitted.

Useless here, she needed to get back to the command position to assess the situation and report back to Korolev. As much as she hated to run from a fight, she knew there was only one way to move across this killing ground. Quickly checking the integrity of her suit, she lowered her faceplate, activated her forearm controls, and entered the Bulk.

This time the formless gray looked little different from the smoke-filled grounds of the brane, but the silence was a relief. Until she probed the Cloud. Then the Centauri jamming was as deafening as before, and even fighting through it she couldn't make contact with Korolev or any other operative.

The virtual images of the once-intact Astral College formed around her, and she propelled her suit forward along the line she knew to be the Army defensive barrier. The eerie calm of these familiar shapes hinted at days long ago when she'd gone for runs alone around the College grounds, wanting to escape the competitive society and relentless pressure of the school, just for a few minutes.

Back then she'd retreated into her own private world, ignoring the chaos around her and wondering why she'd chosen such a life for herself. As she moved through the Bulk, sheltered from the slaughter just half a peet away, she felt the new calm descend on her once again, and she reflected on what her choices back then had led to now. She could never again, she knew, go back to that opera-singing girl who wanted nothing more than to be liked by her friends, and loved by her father.

Here in the Bulk, Katja let go of that dream, and felt that girl finally die.

A lot of Terrans were dying as well, and she had some Centauri machines to wipe out. She embraced the hot, comforting anger and closed in on her target position. Watching the horror of the brane grow ahead of her, she heard the sounds of violence. The Army command position was still fighting, but the dead were everywhere.

A gust of wind knocked her the moment she emerged fully from the Bulk. She staggered to her left, feet slipping on uneven ground.

A powerful hand steadied her. The Voice was in her ear.

"Good to see you. We've drawn nearly two thirds of the swarm, and the heavies have halted." She looked up into her father's face. Burns had mutilated his left ear and scorched away hair. Dirt, blood, and sweat covered most of the rest, but his eyes were the same—stern, penetrating, and calm.

"Your positions are fighting well," she said. "Do you have any comms with the outside?"

"No." He broke off to fire a sustained burst into the air. "You?"

"No."

He nodded grimly. "With this much of the swarm over us, that strike will be coming soon." He tapped her suit. "You have a way out of here. You better go while you can."

The anger swelled within.

"I'm not a coward. I'm not going to run."

He fired again, and shouted orders to his soldiers. They sprayed the air to the west with automatic fire. She heard several swarm-bots fall and just caught sight of others as they returned fire before veering off into the smoke. One soldier was hit, but his armor took the blast and he was quickly helped back to his feet. No further attacks came, but the buzz of the swarm was continuous... and loud.

The Voice pulled her attention back.

"There's nothing brave about dying, Katja Andreia, and there's nothing cowardly about living. You've done your job well, now get out of here."

Other emotions struggled within her, but the anger pushed them all down. She looked him straight in the eyes.

"I hate you," she said. "I hate you for controlling my life, and I hate you for what I've become."

He stared back at her. "Then hate me, if that's what makes you excel." He raised his voice to issue orders. Soldiers pulled more ammo out of the nearby troop carrier and began passing it around. He turned back to her, the voice lowering.

"It's a shame. You're the only child I have who's worth something."

Above her, the sky tore open. She spun around in time to see the first orange meteors of orbital bombardment strike down on the Astral College grounds. She gasped in terror, frozen at the nightmare sight. The thick smoke above her began to glow with a false, orange dawn, and the air began to sizzle and roar.

She barely felt the pressure of his hand on her forearm display.

"Goodbye, Katja."

The world became as bright and hot as the sun.

Everything disappeared into the gray silence of the Bulk. She screamed inside her faceplate. Screamed at an uncaring dimension where nothing lived, where things only died.

Then, suddenly, she was falling. Chang had said that couldn't happen. She scrambled with flailing limbs, reaching vainly for any purchase. Then her virtual map activated and she saw that she wasn't falling downward, toward the center of the Earth. She was falling sideways. Something massive was pulling her toward the edge of Lake Sapphire.

Kete looked vainly at the obscure feedback on the bronze horseshoe again. Three lights blinked in seemingly random patterns. Their progressive changes went from red through yellow and now, at least one of them, to green. While that suggested progress, he had no idea when the final jump gate would open.

The device was far too well shielded for his usual electronic queries to penetrate it, and he found himself in the unusual, frustrating position of not knowing. His watch told him he was only twenty seconds away. The dim roar of fires and chaos in Longreach still echoed around the waterfront, and he glanced around again to ensure no one was approaching.

Breeze had finally risen from her resting spot against the tree, and was moving toward the copse. The only other people he could see were civilians fleeing on foot along the main road. None of them paid attention to him.

He no longer needed Breeze for the plan, but he still wanted to get his hands on that pistol, just in case. But he couldn't allow her to see the jump gate activate—not while she still carried a weapon. Emerging from his shelter of trees, he jogged across the grass.

She smiled at him and stopped where she was. He kept his expression steady, even while he noted any movement of her hand toward the holster.

Sudden, rapid-fire bangs cracked through the air above them. In the vivid blue sky he saw brilliant flashes of white-hot flares, exploding outward in repeating patterns. The sound from their discharges rippled down seconds later. Defensive counter-measures, he recognized immediately, probably from a Terran craft on an attack run. Sure enough, he saw brilliant energy beams lance across the sky and puff against a dark gray flying machine at the center of the flares.

Traces of smoke seemed to bounce of it, until finally a steady stream of black started trailing from the hull. The craft—a Hawk—was moving fast but still descending as Centauri weapons stripped it to pieces.

He reached Breeze just as the doomed Hawk roared low overhead, spiraling madly with corkscrews of smoke wrapping behind it. The shock wave knocked them both to their knees, and Breeze clutched against him. From his crouch he saw the craft shatter the still water near the center of the lake, a huge wall of white blasted upward. Pleasure boats were flipped by the waves, their occupants sent flying through the air.

He ran his hand gently down Breeze's side, toward that holster. Abruptly he felt the air off to their left begin to burn. He looked over and saw, beyond the trees that lined the park, the same hellish sight that had haunted him since the day his family died. Orbital bombardment struck an unseen part of the city. Blast after fiery orange blast rained down with relentless precision. The very ground shook under the onslaught, knocking him down to all fours.

"You're shooting your own people," he said, unable to believe his eyes.

"Oh, sweet Mother of God," Breeze muttered, still clutching him. "We've got to get out of here." There was real fear in her voice, and he realized she felt more threatened by her own State than the attacking Centauri force. He stared at her, and suddenly considered something completely new.

Maybe he could bring her through the jump gate with him. She had no loyalty, and perhaps she could work for Centauri Intelligence. At the very least she had terabytes of valuable knowledge hiding in that pretty little head of hers. So he pulled her to her feet, his gaze turning toward the copse of trees. The jump gate should be open by now.

"Come on, let's get behind those trees."

They'd barely taken a step when they were pulled clear off the ground by a mighty, invisible force. Like a titanic wind, the force carried them forward. Trees at the edge of the park leaned inward, leaves tearing from their branches and flying like bullets toward the copse. As Kete watched, helplessly hurtling forward, the close-knit trees cracked apart, the trunks split open as bark and shards tumbled inward into a dazzling oblivion. The smallest trunks were sheared from their roots and toppled into what could only be a collapsing jump gate.

The force died away as quickly as it had arisen. Kete tumbled to the ground and slid against the flattened grass. He scrambled to his feet and ran toward the remains of the copse, climbing over the obscenely twisted wood. He looked for the bronze horseshoe amidst the earthen rubble, but found nothing.

Frantically he threw aside the piles of rubble, losing himself in sheer panic before his rational mind retook control, and forced him to stop.

The jump gate was gone.

Somehow it had failed, but there were five more attacks currently underway at other strategic locations on Earth. As he forced himself to climb out of the wrecked trees and survey the acres of burning waterfront, he consoled himself with the knowledge that the overarching mission still would succeed. Now all he needed to do was escape. The jump gate over the lake was probably collapsing, as well, but he could retreat to Katja Emmes's apartment.

Breeze was just picking herself up off the ground. Her uniform was in tatters, her face a mask of fear. She was no longer useful—indeed, she was now a liability. He walked over to her, opening his arms in an inviting hug. She gasped for air, her eyes shining as she stepped toward his embrace.

Just as her warm body pressed against his, he heard a faint crackling sound. The air shimmered nearby, and as he blinked to clear his vision a human form in a dark, helmeted suit seemed to grow out of nothing. The human was compact in form, and through a transparent sheen over her face she spotted him with large, dark eyes.

She isn't dead.

Strangely, he wasn't surprised.

His right hand was around Breeze's back and ripping out her pistol even as Emmes drew her own holstered weapon. Kete wrapped his left arm around Breeze's throat and spun her around to use her as a human shield. Emmes lowered into a combat stance, both hands steady on her weapon.

Kete moved as much as possible behind Breeze, and shifted the pistol to press it against her torso.

"Get back, Emmes," he said, "or I kill her."

Katja sized up the targets. Breeze was tall enough that the Centauri spy could shield himself behind her, but all she needed was a steady enough glimpse of one of his vitals to take him down. His threat almost made her laugh out loud.

"Please do, Centauri. Then I'll have a clear shot."

While still in the Bulk, she'd realized that the sense of falling was the gravitational pull of a massive object appearing nearby. Having been close to gravi-torpedoes and Jack's infamous Dark Bomb, she'd recognized what she was approaching. Now here on the brane, she saw the path of destruction pointing to the mass of broken trees behind her two targets.

Armstrong's torpedo run had worked.

A new, familiar roar began to grow in strength to the south, and in her peripheral she saw the brilliant exhausts of Terran missiles flashing by overhead. Explosions in the air far behind her indicated the destruction of the AAR invasion force. The threat to Terra was over.

There were still loose ends, though.

Breeze wore an expression of pure shock, and Katja wondered if that would eventually morph into betrayal. Or was she part of the Centauri plan, and just playing the role of victim? She searched Breeze's eyes for any of their usual cunning. For once, she saw none.

Her weapon remained trained to the side of Breeze's head,

just waiting for that kill shot. Looking hard for an opening, she became aware of something new—something in the Cloud. It might be dangerous to split her focus, but suddenly she had to know. She reached out with her mind.

<It's over, Centauri. Your forces are surrounded and cut off. You might as well surrender.>

For a moment he looked stunned, and she sensed surprise, but the response came from a disciplined mind.

<I don't think so.>

<Your gate in the lake is covered.> Her lips curled in new anger. <And the one in my apartment.>

Silence, both in the world and in the Cloud. Breeze's gaze flicked back and forth between Katja's weapon and the gun against her side. The Centauri didn't move. Finally she heard him in the Cloud.

<Then, Lieutenant, I ask for mercy,> he said. <Just as I once gave you.>

<I've never had mercy from a colonist.>

<Yes you have.> His voice was in her mind, calm but... sad? Despite her best intentions, she couldn't bring herself to interrupt him. She felt herself back on Abeona, creeping around the dark houses to find the exact location of the artillery spotters. Then she realized she was watching herself, from his point of view. She watched as she lifted her forearm, as she signaled the order for the orbital strike.

His family was inside that house.

His wife and children.

Rupa, Olivia, Jess.

She felt the shockwave of the blast that knocked her backward, watched as her body smacked down on the ground. Felt the agony of loss, the growing rage as his hand moved to close around her throat.

<I'd just watched you kill my family,> he said. <I had my hand around your neck, but I showed mercy and I let you live. The damage was already done, so I let you live.>

In her real vision, she saw the pistol pull back from Breeze's side. The Centauri—his real name was Kete, she now knew—pushed Breeze gently away and stepped clear. Katja followed him with her weapon, willing herself to shoot. He dropped his pistol and stood with his hands at his sides.

<The damage here is already done. I'm no further threat to you and I call upon your mercy, Katja, just as I once gave it to you.>

She stared into his dark features, barely remembering the hand at her throat and the shadowy form that had loomed over her as her life bled out on Abeona. Then she thought of another face, an Army face. A face sodden with dirt, sweat, and blood, half burned away by Centauri swarm-bots. A face that thought nothing of dying for Terra. A face she would never see again.

"Mercy is a founding principle of Centauria," she said aloud, pulling herself back from the Cloud, "and I'd have expected nothing less from you." She saw his expression soften momentarily, until he truly looked into her eyes.

"But this is Terra," she said.

She pulled the trigger without hesitation.

Then twice more just to be sure.

For a brief, dazzling moment, she sensed something from the Cloud.

Relief. And homecoming.

Breeze gasped as the body collapsed, then stifled a scream as she saw Katja point the weapon at her. She actually fell to her knees as Katja approached.

"Please," she said, "I didn't know anything. He took me as a hostage." Her hands came up to cover her face as Katja loomed over her. "Please don't kill me!"

Katja relished the feeling of raw power that coursed through her body, and stood in silence for a moment over her target. Then, efficiently, she reversed the pistol in her hand and swung it down in a swift strike. The metal thudded against Breeze's skull and knocked her flat onto the ground.

Katja kicked her onto her back and knelt down on top of her, pinning Breeze's legs with her own and leaning a forearm against Breeze's right arm. The gun she pressed up against Breeze's chin. Breeze's eyes rolled from the attack as blood trickled from her hair, but in a moment she regained her senses, and stared up at Katja.

Katja almost smiled.

"I'm not going to kill you, Breeze," she said. "I'm going to do something much better. I'm going to reveal you for the traitor you are. Then I'm going to watch you squirm in front of all the worlds.

"And then I'm going to watch you hang."

35

Thomas was already turning away as his sergeant gave the squads the final dismissal order. They were a competent bunch of troopers, the twenty men and women assigned as the security force aboard *Admiral Bowen*, and they didn't need him hovering over their every movement.

The day's boarding drills had gone well enough, especially considering he was still thinking with Corps tactics and signals he'd learned more than a decade ago. Enough had changed since he'd last worn a green jumpsuit that the next few weeks were going to be a self-taught firehose-in-mouth of information.

A few quick words to the sergeant about tomorrow's schedule, and Thomas left the training area. A modern cruiser, *Bowen* had the luxury of a dedicated space for the ship's security team to train and conduct meetings. As he made his way up the decks Thomas began to wish the designers had thought to add the luxury of an elevator. Six months planetside, living the life of a wealthy dilettante, had taken a shocking toll on his fitness, making him very grateful that his role as an officer could be largely supervisory if he wanted it to be.

Because that's all he was now: Sublieutenant Kane, the new kid dropped on board as a last-second replacement as *Bowen* deployed for war. He hadn't missed the surprised expressions when his new troopers had seen him for the first time—they'd no doubt been expecting a young snotter right out of training. The only logical explanation for so old a subbie was that he'd been commissioned from the ranks, and Thomas had done nothing to dissuade that notion.

With *Bowen* under radio silence due to the outbreak of hostilities, no one could uncover the truth for at least a few weeks.

The ship's other officers seemed equally ambivalent, too busy with their exhausting wartime watches to worry much about the new Corps guy. The lieutenants afforded him slightly less disrespect than they did the other subbies, and he'd learned quickly not to make a habit of hanging out in the wardroom. And so, inevitably, he found himself staring at the door to his new home—the four-person mess deck known as Club Sub.

Thomas closed his eyes as the door slid shut behind him, rubbing his temples wearily. At least he wasn't standing bridge watches. Those poor bastards were already suffering under strain of running at full combat readiness, while perpetually undermanned. The *Admiral Bowen* had been deployed with barely seventy percent of the crew embarked.

As he sat down on the single settee and slowly began to remove his boots, he glanced at two kids—two of the other subbies—chatting quietly between the sleeping berths.

No, he wasn't the captain. He wasn't the XO. He wasn't even a Line officer anymore. As soon as the battle over Longreach had concluded, he'd been ordered down the spar to the cruiser that'd supported him, been informed that the ship was departing, and that he would be filling one of the vacant positions.

So here he was, Sublieutenant Kane, security detachment commander. Under his charge were twenty Astral Corps troopers— less than half an actual platoon—with the responsibility for boarding enemy ships and repelling enemy boarders.

He sighed deeply, then immediately regretted it as his nose filled with the typical stench of Club Sub. No matter what the ship, subbies were never too bothered about regular hygiene or cabin cleanliness. Clothes were scattered around half-open lockers and the sink was barely visible under the dried toothpaste and shavings. As the senior sublieutenant, he figured he should probably instill some discipline.

"Guys," he said, "this place hums. Which one of you has the

slow leak out of his ass?" He was greeted by tired laughter as the subbies—Chen and Alex—sidled over.

"Can't you just get some troopers to do it?" Alex asked. "I thought you guys loved rolling in the shit."

Remembering that these kids were barely out of training, Thomas tried to recall the mindset.

"Sure, but even we know our Humane Convention rights." That elicited another laugh, although no one moved to actually clean anything up.

He tried another tack. "What are you guys working on?"

Chen showed him an info-pad. "We have to finish our reqs by the end of the week, so we can start full time on our bridge tickets."

"But everyone's so busy they don't have time to help us," Alex added. "We're just comparing notes."

Thomas remembered the endless slog of getting on-board training requirements, or "reqs," signed off between busy bridge watches. He and his friend Sean Duncan—who had apparently just been made a commander and given his own destroyer—had groaned for weeks under the strain of doing their training packages during the Dog Watch in Sirius while standing one-in-three bridge watches in the old *Victoria*. Their saving grace had been *Victoria*'s XO, Lieutenant Eric Chandler, who'd made it his personal mission to get Thomas and Sean trained up and useful for the captain.

Bowen's XO, apparently, wasn't stepping into the same role. Just because the whole ship thought of him as the new Corps subbie, though, didn't mean Thomas wasn't still command qualified.

He stretched. "What req are you working on?"

"Weapon safety firing ranges."

He took the info-pad and glanced at the list of Astral weapons for which the subbies needed to memorize ranges, safety corridors, and firing sequences. He picked the first one—long-range anti-ship missiles—and rattled off the required info.

Chen and Alex stared at him in shock.

"You want some help with this?" he asked.

They nodded.

He stood up. "Then first of all, help me clean up this shit-pit. I'll do the sink, if you guys get rid of all this gash." He gestured broadly at all the clothes and personal items strewn around. "And somebody find an air freshener."

"I have cologne spray," Chen offered.

"No, it just masks the smell, and then mixes with it. This place will stink like a whorehouse."

Laughter always lifted spirits, and as they cleaned Thomas kept up a wry banter with the kids, easily delving into his sordid subbie past whenever he felt a bit of gutter humor was required. By the time Club Sub was clean and he was sitting down to go through reqs, Thomas was smiling genuinely, and he saw matching expressions shining back at him from the subbies.

Eventually it was time for Chen to go on watch, and as Alex had the mid watch, he closed up in his sleeping berth shortly thereafter. Thomas leaned back on the settee, feet on the table, and clicked on the news feed at a volume low enough not to disturb anyone.

How in the worlds had it come to this? Terra was at war again, and he was buried as a Strike officer on a Fleet cruiser. Maybe it was karma, God's will, or the cyclical nature of being. Or maybe he'd just got what he deserved. He actually laughed to himself. At least he'd been here before. If his role in this war was to keep *Bowen* safe from pirates, and run the tidiest Club Sub in the Fleet, then so be it.

He could excel at that.

Reports were still coming in from the other cities that had been attacked by Centauri forces, and it was confirmed that the Army Headquarters, the Civil Defense Headquarters, and the Parliament buildings had all been destroyed. Only the Astral Headquarters had survived relatively intact, and the Longreach space elevators were the only ones still standing.

All military forces were on full alert, both because there might be another surface attack, and to contain the panicking civilian population. There were reports of rioting and looting in half a dozen cities, and security forces had been forced to employ "peaceful persuasion" to regain control. Suddenly he realized that he was probably in the best possible situation, considering the circumstances.

Safely in space, with no real responsibilities.

Longreach, as the least-destroyed major city, was the last to be covered in the network report. Chuck Merriman praised the Army's brave stand at the Astral College, and how an entire storm banner—commanded personally by Storm Banner Leader Günther Emmes—had sacrificed themselves to draw the Centauri swarm away from civilians. Emmes had been awarded his second Cross of Valor, and the screen showed the ceremony where the medal was presented to an ashen-faced, hoverchair-supported Miriam Emmes.

In a related report Merriman noted that Lieutenant Katja Emmes had also been killed in the Longreach fighting, reportedly serving alongside her father until the last minute. Thomas leaned forward on the settee, staring in shock at the old image of Katja in uniform. Her dark eyes stared outward at nothing, her pale, smooth skin contrasted against her black dress uniform.

Katja was dead?

Her posthumous Terran Cross was presented to her brother, Stormtrooper Soren Emmes, who stood at his mother's side wearing a stunned expression. Stormtrooper Emmes, apparently, was already deploying with his unit.

Thomas felt as if he was going to be sick. He looked around again at the close-in, metal bulkheads and sleeping berths of this spaceship mess deck. What was he doing here? What was he doing in this life?

His marriage was a sham, an elaborate production intended to further his own ambitions and, there was no point kidding himself, those of his bride. Now those ambitions were dead, his career in tatters, his connections lost, and his only allies a couple of subbies he was babysitting through their reqs.

Katja was dead.

He'd never allowed her to become the center of his world, but he realized that without her, his world meant nothing. If karma, God, or the cyclical nature of being had any mercy, *Admiral Bowen* would be singularized by a Centauri torpedo and his worthless life would come to an end.

The news moved on to another story from Longreach. Rescue personnel had managed to reach the Hawk that had crashed into

Lake Sapphire at the height of the battle. The two crew members had been recovered from the lake bottom, unconscious but still alive due to the fact that they'd been in full space suits. They were recovering in a Longreach hospital, and the unnamed pilot was being praised for his skill and quick-thinking in avoiding further casualties.

Thomas doubted whether Jack had been thinking at all—quick or otherwise—but it seemed as if the young pilot had more lives than a cat. His life was one worth sparing, for sure.

The news turned ominous again, however, with the next story. Although the reasons were still unclear as to how planetary defenses had been breached, the Astral Force had confirmed that they had a suspect in custody, and were conducting a Fleet Marshall Investigation. Due to the sensitivity of the case, no names were released, but unofficial sources had indicated that the chief suspect was a senior officer from Astral Intelligence. A quick clip showed the suspect's attorney, speaking to the media.

Thomas was riveted to the screen when he saw Merje Emmes standing in front of the crowd. She was dressed in a smart green suit and her long blonde hair shone in the sunlight. Her fine features were the perfect mix of concern, competence, and charm.

"Everyone in Terra is horrified by this unspeakable act of violence," she said, "but our system of justice does not allow the mob to choose a scapegoat. Our client is innocent and was, in fact, a victim of this aggression. We will stand firmly by her side and work untiringly to prove that she was not involved with the despicable actions of the renegade colony Centauria."

Thomas shook his head. Breeze and Merje. Now there was a combination to fear. If ever there was a good time to escape Terran politics, it was now.

His "beloved" Soma wouldn't want for company, he knew, and no doubt dear Quinton would soon be on hand to keep her warm at night. Such a joke. He yawned, and turned his mind to more mundane thoughts. There were updated Corps hand signals he had to learn, for non-verbal communications with his team. Quinton and the fops he could deal with another time.

* * *

An hour later Thomas was running through the signals in his head, recalling the old memory tricks he'd employed a decade ago. They came back to him quite easily, but he could feel his concentration waning as the long day finally caught up with him. He debated moving to his sleeping compartment but couldn't muster the energy to rise. He clicked off the light and the mess deck fell into darkness.

The air in the dark cabin crackled slightly. He froze as the cold, round pressure of a gun barrel pressed against his temple.

"Don't move." It was a quiet female voice.

She moved closer, and he smelled her fresh vitality. He couldn't see anything more than a shadow in the darkness, but he knew immediately who it was. Despite what the news had said, she was alive.

He wanted to grab hold of her, pull her down against him and never let her go, but the gun at his head tempered any enthusiasm.

"They say you're dead."

"I am."

"I'm glad you're here."

"The State doesn't like loose ends, and I'm here to tie one off."

His mind swept back to another Fleet Marshall Investigation— one that had just concluded. Admiral Bush had been shamed and silenced. Captain Lincoln was dead. Helena Grey had lost her commission and was in prison. Only Thomas was still free of the net.

"I think the State has already taken plenty from me."

"This isn't about the State," she said. "This is about you and me. Before I disappear I've been given the chance to tie off any loose ends in my life."

Thomas sat very still, feeling the gun pressing against his skull. Sleep with a girl's sister and you get what you deserve. At least Soma would be taken care of.

"I understand." He closed his eyes and braced for the shot.

He was surprised by the kiss. Her chapped lips pressed firmly against his, her face hovering in the darkness as he opened his eyes. Her suited body pressed against his chest as she straddled his lap and gripped his shoulder with her free hand, even as the gun remained firmly against his head.

Thomas kissed her back, focusing all his passion, all his love, into that one action. He didn't dare move another muscle. Then, finally, she retreated from his view. The pressure of the gun slipped away.

"Goodbye, Thomas."

"Goodbye, Katja."

The air crackled, and he sat alone in the darkness.

ACKNOWLEDGEMENTS

I'd like to thank everyone who contributed so importantly to the development and creation of this book. To my cadre of beta readers, your early input was invaluable. To my agent, Howard Morhaim, and the team at Titan Books, thank you for all your expertise. To the team at Promontory Press, thank you for giving me the time to work on this when I really should have been doing my day job.

And to my friends and colleagues from Syria and Lebanon, those days are burned into our hearts. Never forget.

ABOUT THE AUTHOR

Bennett R. Coles served fourteen years as an officer in the Royal Canadian Navy and earned his salt on all classes of ship, from command of a small training ship to warfare director of a powerful missile frigate to bridge officer of a lumbering supply ship. He toiled as a staff officer in the War on Terror, and served two tours with the United Nations in Syria and Lebanon.

He has maintained an interest in military affairs since his retirement from active service in 2005 and he makes his home in Victoria, Canada, with his wife and family.

VIRTUES OF WAR
Bennett R. Coles

The Terran military, the Astral Force, launches a mission to crush a colonial rebellion on the Centauri colony. Although Expeditionary Force 15 succeeds, the surviving veterans remain scarred—physically and emotionally, and the consequences of their actions follow them back to Earth when terrorists seek to exact catastrophic revenge.

Lieutenant Katja Emmes is a platoon commander, leader of the 10-trooper strike team aboard the fast-attack craft Rapier. Although fully trained, she has never led troops in real operations before, and lives in the shadow of her war-hero father. Sublieutenant Jack Mallory is fresh out of pilot school, daydreaming about a fighter pilot position in the space fleet. He is in for a rude awakening. Lieutenant Commander Thomas Kane uses a six-month deployment in command of Rapier to secure his rise to stardom within the Astral Force. He also plays the subtle politics of the military.

MARCH OF WAR

Bennett R. Coles

The Centauri terrorist was stopped, but not before he caused widespread death and destruction on Earth. This leads to an escalating war between Earth and Centauri.

Lieutenant Jack Mallory is on the front lines, leading a flight of Hawks into the battle zone. His mission is to rescue the demoted Sublieutenant Thomas Kane, whose Astral forces are under heavy fire and in danger of being overrun.

The Astral Force must establish a bridgehead in Centauri territory, where they will place a jump gate in anticipation of a new invasion. Lieutenant Katja Emmes works behind the scenes, to keep the Centauri from learning of the plan before it can be carried out successfully.

AVAILABLE JUNE 2017

TITANBOOKS.COM

For more fantastic fiction, author events, exclusive
excerpts, competitions, limited editions and more

VISIT OUR WEBSITE
titanbooks.com

LIKE US ON FACEBOOK
facebook.com/titanbooks

FOLLOW US ON TWITTER
@TitanBooks

EMAIL US
readerfeedback@titanemail.com